WE SURVIVORS

A Story from After the End

L.J. Thomas

First paperback edition October 2019

Cover design by Mallory Rock of Rock Solid Book Design
(rocksolidbookdesign.com)

Editing by Vicky Brewster
(vickybrewstereditor.com)

We Survivors
ISBN 978-1-7332610-0-5 (Paperback)
ISBN 978-1-7332610-1-2 (eBook)

www.ljthomasbooks.com

To all who have fought battles with their mental health

Be advised, this novel contains discussions of self-harm and suicide.

PART ONE

Friendship is unnecessary, like philosophy, like art...
It has no survival value; rather it is
one of those things which give value to survival.
— C.S. Lewis

1: Tomorrow
Nadia

Tomorrow.

Tomorrow I'll finally meet Jake.

The thought made my stomach twist and my heart pump faster. I laid my pen between the pages of my journal and leaned into the rough bark of my maple tree, too anxious to write. A thousand thoughts ran through my mind. What if we didn't get along? What if he hadn't told me the truth about who he was? What if something happened to him before we could meet?

Worst of all, what if my mind, lonely from the months of isolation and exhausted from constantly surviving on my own, had created Jake? What if tomorrow I found out that not only was I incredibly, truly alone, but that I'd gone insane too?

Moths fluttered toward the light of my camp lantern, casting shadows. My gaze was pulled out into the woods by a half dozen fireflies floating amidst the trees and my mind wandered back to that first night I heard Jake on the radio.

I still think it was the best day of my life. It saved my life, too. I'd followed my usual nighttime routine, flicking on my old HAM radio with the ever-shrinking spark of hope that there'd be someone on the other end. Then I'd gone to brush my teeth and stash my food in a tree. As I came back to my tent, I heard something—something more than the usual static—coming from my radio.

"If anyone is out there, please respond. It has been one hundred twelve days since the last person I knew died." A male voice. He spoke without emotion, as if reading from a script.

I fumbled with the zipper on my tent and scrambled inside, grabbing my radio's microphone.

"If anyone is out there, please respond," he repeated.

I paused for a moment, hands shaking and mind reeling with disbelief at my ended solitude. Then I pushed the button on the mic and spoke.

"I'm here," I said. "I'm… responding."

I'd had four months to think of something to say—four months of daydreaming someone else might be out there—and *that* was all I'd managed to come up with?

"Is someone really there?" A pause and a crackle of noise from the radio, then a beep as he released the mic.

"Yes, um. I'm here." I said, smacking my forehead. "My name is Nadia."

"Oh—hey, Nadia. This is Jake."

Over time, we developed such a keen ability to finish each other's thoughts and fill in any blanks that I smiled as I remembered the awkwardness of our first conversation.

I learned so many things about Jake. I knew he was dark-haired and, like me, would have been a high school senior. He used to enjoy movies and soccer, though now, he joked, he's all about fishing and backpacking. I even knew that, before the virus, he had a mother, father, and older brother. He didn't know about my family; I wasn't ready to face using past tense when I described them yet.

A few days ago, I agreed to meet. I couldn't bear the loneliness any longer, even if it turned out I'd imagined him. I'd been cautious before that. I didn't reveal my location, only telling him enough to make sure our radios stayed within range of each other. Tomorrow we'd both reach the rendezvous point.

I'd spent over a month talking to him before going to sleep every night, worrying he'd be gone the next day. Sighing with relief every time he picked up on the other end. I knew what his life had been like for the past thirty-four days. I knew so much about Jake, but at the same time, I didn't *know* him.

But that's all going to change, I thought as I traced over the word with my pen: *Tomorrow.*

2: Saving the Human Race
Nadia

The sun's rays shone through the translucent green nylon of my tent the next morning.

There had once been days when the sun was up for hours before I woke. I smiled at the bittersweet memories that followed but pushed them away before they hurt.

Now I lived and slept with the sun.

It didn't take long to pack up my campsite. Before leaving, I knelt beside a tree and pulled a framed photo and a few tealight candles from my pack. I held the frame against my chest and closed my eyes, trying to see their faces as they'd lived: smiling, laughing. Each day it was harder, and I felt hollow every time I wondered if I was remembering *them* or just the photo I looked at every morning. Their voices had vanished from my memory. Even my dad's, though I'd last heard it only a few months ago.

As I propped the frame against the tree, my face and those of my parents, sisters, and best friend smiled out at me from my sixteenth birthday, nearly two years ago. The five candles I arranged in a perfect row, then used the embers left from last night's fire to light a match-like twig. I sent a silent prayer to each of them as I lit their candle.

Not that I thought they could hear me. *It helps me mark each passing day,* I told myself as the flames flickered, reflecting on the glass. *That's all.*

I blew the candles out, letting the wax dry for a few moments before I shoved them in my bag, then put the frame carefully in the safest spot, against my back. After double-checking the coordinates I'd scribbled into a notebook and consulting my compass and maps, I set off for the day.

When I'd been following an old railroad bed for about an hour, a rustling in the grass behind me put me on edge.

I spun, nocking an arrow and drawing my bow in one well-practiced motion. I scanned the grass, knee-high in places, that had grown up between the railroad ties. An orange tabby cat jumped out, and I sighed in relief, re-quivering my arrow. Harmless.

This time.

The cat rubbed its body against my legs, circling as it purred. I used to like cats, until I saw one too many enjoying human remains for dinner. Well, *one* would be too many, but I'd seen dozens by now. Dogs, too.

Moved by this one's sweet face and the way I could feel her rib bones through my pant legs, I dug a pouch of beef jerky from my bag and fed her a scrap.

"You wouldn't eat me, would you?" I asked her as she gulped down the jerky and mewled for more.

But it wasn't a fair question. There was a time—in the darkest days of winter, when enough people were still alive that scavenging supplies was fraught with danger, and my dad and I were not yet skilled at snares or hunting—that I would've eaten her, too.

She followed me for a while after that, until she caught sight of a rodent in the grass and gave chase. I was sad to lose her company.

A few miles later, beads of sweat trailed down my forehead and my water bottle had run dry. I stopped at a nearby river and filled my bottle through the filter, then clicked on the UV light and waited, squatting by the river and splashing my face.

On the wavy surface of the water, I caught the reflection of something—like a small plane or a large bird—flying in the sky above me. But when I whipped my head up to look, there was nothing there. Just a cloudless blue sky.

Great. If I could imagine huge brown birds, was there any hope Jake was real?

I took a deep breath and let it out slowly, putting a stopper on my anxiety. I couldn't afford to think like that. Jake was real, and I'd be seeing him today. Cupping my hands again, I brought the cool water to my face. And caught my reflection in the river.

Yikes. My hair was matted and my skin more tanned than I'd ever seen it before. My torn tank top accentuated my now-wiry arms, and my eyes looked wild. No one who'd known the girl in my framed photo would recognize her in my face now.

Words my mother used to say came back to me then: *you never get a second chance to make a first impression.* I blushed at my unkempt appearance, threw on my plaid button-down, and raked my fingers through my hair. This could be the last first impression I ever made.

As if I hadn't made plenty of awkward impressions on Jake over the past few weeks. Like the time I inadvertently implied that the two of us might be the last hope for "saving the human race".

At first he'd snorted and said, "We're a bit late for that."

I was unsure what was safe to joke about after the end of the world—though what did it matter, with only us?—but Jake was always making jokes about dark topics. There weren't many other topics left.

I'd stumbled over my explanation, digging myself a deeper and deeper hole. In the radio silence that followed I grew increasingly uncomfortable, finally stammering, "I mean—I *don't* mean... *us.* Whoever is left, if there are others..." I was half-tempted to turn the radio off and pretend to have no recollection of this in the morning.

"Sorry," he said. "I was thinking. It's a big question. Does humanity deserve a shot at preservation? They did do... all of this."

I wondered if he, like me, was bundled in his sleeping bag, peering out his tent flap at the pointed silhouettes of evergreen trees against the stars. No other lights on the horizon. No one left.

After his usual goodbye, a quick "Sleep tight," I'd had to admit he was right. No one knew what caused the virus; with only two of us left and no sign of other people—alive ones, anyway—for months, no one would ever know. But before the world completely fell apart, everyone had suspected other humans were the cause. They just couldn't agree on which ones.

The UV light in my bottle clicked off, interrupting my thoughts, and I took a long, refreshing drink. Then I followed the river eastward, the sun high overhead.

As I hiked, I kept my doubts and fears about that night's meeting away by playing a game I'd come up with since The End. "Game" may have been the wrong word, as it wasn't very fun, and I always felt I lost.

The game was really a simple question: what would I give up to have things back the way they were? Eventually I had to limit myself, because the answer was always: *anything*. My hearing, my sight, any or all of my limbs. So I set the bar lower.

What would I give for a day?

One normal, before-the-end day. I'd hide my novel-reading from my trigonometry teacher and be grateful for the mushy cafeteria burgers—meat I didn't have to track, kill, and prepare myself. I'd pass notes to Anna between classes and laugh at her dirty jokes. I'd spend time with my sisters—push Nicole on the swing and help Natalie paint her nails. I'd hug my parents once more…

Anything.

The game had become more interesting since I'd heard Jake's voice. Would I give up knowing him, and live alone like this forever, for one normal day?

The answer was still "yes", of course. But I had to think about it.

3: Safety in Numbers
Jake

A few days before Ben died, he found us a HAM radio and insisted that I start the nightly broadcast seeking other survivors. It was past the most dangerous time; there were so few people left alive that there was no need to fight over resources. Still, I'd resisted. We had enough mouths to feed with the two of us.

"There's safety in numbers," he'd told me. "One day you'll learn that. If anything happens to me... I don't want you to be alone."

I think he'd already known then what he was going to do.

After he was gone, it was over a hundred days of traveling on my own—and over one hundred broadcasts—before I caught proof that I wasn't the last person alive.

Nadia. The name sounded easy, comfortable on my tongue after so many nights talking. I said it once or twice aloud to myself as I trekked along riverbank, the flowing water drowning out other forest sounds. The sun hung barely above the trees to the west, and I wondered if she'd have beaten me to the coordinates I'd given her.

She hadn't wanted to meet up for so long. She must not have shared my brother's beliefs about "safety in numbers". I'd been worried for her, to be honest. But it quickly became evident that she could take care of herself. There was no need to join up with me.

My heart pounded in anticipation as I came within view of the bend in the river where I'd asked to meet. Was there some reason she hadn't wanted to meet me?

We were the same age, assuming she was telling the truth about that. It was so easy to talk with her, unlike with most people, that I'd even wondered whether she was real and not just a coping mechanism my brain had invented to help the crippling loneliness.

I heard a female voice call, "Jake!" through the trees. Shit. *Is she hurt?* I broke into a run but was slowed by the sandy soil of the riverbank.

"Nadia!" I yelled in return.

I spotted a backpack, tent and sleeping roll strapped to the bottom. A bow and quiver lay next to it, at the base of an oak tree. I circled the tree, looking for movement.

"Up here!" she called.

I glimpsed wavy blonde hair and a flannel shirt through the branches. She scrambled down but fell toward the bottom. Nadia stood quickly, her cheeks turning pink with embarrassment as she brushed pine needles off her hands.

"Hey," I said, when other words failed. A better question would have been "Are you alright?", but I didn't want to embarrass her further.

"Hi," she said, flustered. "So you are real. Or, I mean, you're okay. I was worried you'd broken a leg or that bears or wolves…"

"Jake," I said, half-lifting my hand to shake hers but then dropping it back to my side.

"I'm Nadia." She attempted a smile.

I didn't know what to say next. It had been a long time since I'd needed to make small talk, and I'd never been good at it to begin with.

We sized each other up instead. Her tanned skin emphasized her light blue eyes. I had a few inches on her. She wore jeans, leather boots, and a blue plaid shirt that was as sun-faded as the forest green one I wore.

"So I'm not crazy," she said, laughing a breathlessly. "At least not creating-imaginary-people crazy."

I smiled. "I was thinking the same thing. Should we make camp?"

"Sure."

We dug out our supplies, checking out the ways we'd each been surviving. I admired her bow and quiver full of arrows, and she watched as I removed a fold-up fishing pole and a few boxes of ammo for my rifle from my bag. I'd been boiling my water and using purification tablets, but she had a UV bottle and a homemade particulate filter made from a cut up two-liter bottle layered with a bandana, sand, dirt, and rocks.

Pulling a hatchet from my bag, I wandered into the woods to collect wood, cutting fallen branches into one-foot pieces. When I returned, Nadia had set up her tent. She dug through her pack for her flint striker and a light green towel fell out.

I picked it up and gave her a quizzical look.

"A big fluffy towel is one of those little joys in life, you know?" she said, shrugging. "Plus, it's like they say in *Hitchhiker's Guide to the Galaxy*."

I laughed but didn't get the reference. "What *do* they say?"

"Something like, 'anyone who can hitch across the Galaxy and still know where their towel is must be a force to be reckoned with'."

"I see. Is all your survival wisdom from sci-fi novels?" I asked, my tone teasing as I cleared a space for a fire on the forest floor. Conversation was starting to feel easy again, the way it had over the airwaves each night.

"Before all of this,"—she tossed a hand out at the woods—"I wasn't exactly a doomsday prepper."

"No survival stories then?"

"Not unless you count reading *Hatchet* when I was twelve."

"Yeah, same here." I said, piling logs into a teepee shape as she lit the tinder beneath and added a few twigs of kindling at a time. "Maybe we're better hands-on learners anyway." I met her eyes and smirked.

I cooked a fish from the river over the fire in a cast-iron pan, and Nadia offered dried fruit, a can of tuna, and some almost-expired Oreos she'd been saving. She'd finished her last rabbit two days ago but hoped to snare another tomorrow.

We fell into a comfortable silence beneath the stars as we ate our smorgasbord dinner. I didn't know if Ben was right, and there really was safety in numbers, but there was something else. I couldn't put it into words, but I knew that, whatever it was, I'd found it again. And that it had been sorely missed.

◆ ◆ ◆

The next few days saw us settle into an easy routine. We'd wake in our tents and visit the river to splash our faces and collect water for the day. After a quick breakfast, Nadia would check her snares and gather herbs or berries. I spent the mornings fishing.

In the afternoons I'd set up my hammock and nap in it, or Nadia would curl up in it to read a book or write in her journal. I tied and painted new fishing lures or worked on the bowl I'd been carving out of an old stump.

When twilight began, we'd light a fire and I'd cook us a couple of fish or she'd make a stew. After dinner, I'd do my usual radio broadcast, though I no longer had to count the days since the last person I knew died.

Perhaps because it was already our habit from our HAM radio chats, the late evenings were spent around the campfire talking and laughing.

One night I'd finished our broadcast and set it to scan through the static of amateur radio stations like usual. Nadia had a solar charger that worked with the batteries for both our radios. We enjoyed the white noise while we slept and hoped it kept predators away.

A branch fell in the fire, sending up a spray of sparks, and the wind shifted so the smoke tickled my nose. Then there was another sound: a voice, faint and garbled through the static, coming from my radio.

Nadia's head whipped up.

"You hear it, too?" The radio sat between us and I adjusted the dial, my hand shaking, until we heard a distinctly human voice.

"Hey there world, if there's anybody left, why don't you call us up? It's Zara and Coby here and we'd be glad to, you know, meet some other civilized folks."

Nadia picked up the microphone to respond, her incredulous expression mirroring my own. Somehow, after months without either of us encountering another soul, we *weren't* the last people on Earth.

4: Empty Streets
Nadia

I used to love cities—the lights at night, the buzz of a million different people going about their day, the museums, the concerts. Now each one held nothing but death. I'd given up on them. I stayed in the wilderness for as long as I could, until I was forced to restock supplies.

Out there I could pretend my new lifestyle was a choice, just an extended backpacking trip or a Walden-esque stint in nature. Life went on as normal, like before, somewhere. In the cities there were too many reminders of The End and all I'd lost.

But I couldn't avoid them altogether. At first, I'd mainly collected food and water. Now that I was adapting to my primitive lifestyle, I stocked up on creature comforts like shampoo and deodorant, books and batteries, always searching for lighter, more portable cooking accessories and survival gear.

Soon, I thought, I could avoid them all but a few times a year. But that would change now. Jake insisted we head into a nearby city to gather supplies before we met Coby and Zara. As he pointed out, we'd become a group of four and there's no telling how well equipped the others were.

We didn't know much about our new companions. Zara had said she hated talking on the "phone" and insisted that we should meet. When we realized it was under a day's journey to do so, that became our plan. I felt steadier about this rendezvous than I had about the one with Jake. At least there was someone else to confirm my imagination hadn't run wild this time.

Jake usually stayed in the woods, too, but he didn't mind the cities as much as I did; he seemed immune to the desolation. As we walked through the empty streets together, I couldn't help imagining the ghosts of all the people who used to live there.

At times I didn't need to imagine. It had been long enough that most of the bodies remaining were down to bone. First picked clean by scavengers, then turned to dust by maggots and beetles. But a few people had locked themselves in their cars, windows up, so their decay took longer. I did my best to keep my eyes on the road and away from the bloated forms stuck in the seats of their cars.

Signs of the panic that had gripped the city were everywhere. Shells of weather-beaten cars were arranged haphazardly, blocking each other, doors left swung wide. Suitcases lay abandoned and water-damaged on sidewalks and a vulture flew overhead. I tried not to imagine what it had been feasting on. A girl's bike, still with training wheels attached and crumpled tassels streaming from the handlebars, lay in the road. It looked exactly like Nicole's.

I approached and tried to set the bike upright, but it was bent—as if run over by a fleeing car—and fell back over.

It broke me. I stumbled away from Jake, trying to hide my tears. As I sat against the empty hull of a building, I tucked my knees to my chest and sobbed. Jake must have realized I wasn't beside him, because after a few minutes he approached. I didn't want him to see me like this. I wanted him to think I was strong.

I buried my face in my hands and he knelt beside me on one knee. I peeked out and mumbled, "I'm sorry."

His face softened and he ran his fingers through his brown hair. I admired the way the stubble on his jawline accentuated his high cheekbones. "It's okay," he said, almost a whisper. "Let it out."

Then I saw him glance at my arm—well, at the one-inch, raised lines on my left arm. Some white, others still pink. He didn't say anything, but his lips tightened. I jerked my sleeve back down and shook my head, trying to stop the tears. "It's just—" I pleaded for him to understand. "I've been in survival mode for so long."

He nodded.

"And now—now we'll be with other people again. I have to get back to *living*."

Jake gripped my shoulder once, prompting me to continue.

"It's overwhelming. To be alive now, when no one else is. Not so long ago people were going about their lives. Now no one will ever be stuck in traffic, or have popcorn at the movies—or do any other of a thousand mundane things— again. All the things life is made of... they're gone now." I stared into the distance, wishing we'd stayed out in the woods and hoping Jake understood. If he didn't, no one would.

Finally, he spoke. "I know what you mean, Nadia. But you're wrong."

I looked up at him, my face stinging and prickly from the drying tears.

"As long as we're still alive, there's living to be done. We'll find Zara and Coby, and there could be others left in the world, too. Don't lose hope."

He squeezed my shoulder once more, then stood.

"And hey," he said, offering his hand. "Whatever these new people are like, I've got your back."

A smile tugged at my lips as I took his hand. "I've got yours, too."

He helped me to my feet, and we continued through the city. After we'd filled our packs with canned soup and vegetables, collected spare batteries for our radios and flashlights, and I'd traded my battered *Edible Plants of North America* for a similar book with more entries, we set off to meet our new companions.

5: The Stars Were Aligned
Nadia

"Jake?" I asked. We'd left the city still early in the day and had traversed several miles already. We hadn't spoken much, both used to solitude and conserving our energy as the sun beat down on us through the trees.

"Yeah?" He hoisted his pack and stepped over a log.

"You know how songs get stuck in your head?"

He smiled crookedly, holding back a branch for me. "Hasn't happened in a while, what with all the singers being dead, but sure."

"Do you ever have that happen, but it's not a song—it's a line from a movie or a book?"

Jake laughed. "What's stuck in your head right now?"

If it had been a year ago, and I'd been talking to someone who—well, who looked like Jake—I never would have admitted to thinking about poetry. But we were some of the last people on Earth, so he couldn't exactly judge me, right?

"It's from a poem. Robert Frost," I said. "My favorite."

He was following me along a deer path through the woods. We hoped it would be a shortcut to the highway where we'd meet the others. "What's the line?" he asked. "From the poem."

"The last stanza goes like this," I said, quickly running through the lines in my head. Then I recited,

"'The woods are lovely, dark and deep, / But I have promises to keep, / And miles to go before I sleep.' He repeats the last line: 'And miles to go before I sleep'."

"That seems appropriate," Jake said. "These woods are 'lovely', and we have miles to go yet. Plus we promised Zara and Coby we'd meet them this afternoon."

"That's true," I admitted, glad he'd liked the poem, and deciding not to mention any of its darker interpretations.

More light came through the trees ahead as we neared the highway. "How far are we now?"

"Not far at all," a laughing female voice called out from a branch above us. We both spun around, and Jake reflexively drew his rifle to his shoulder.

A girl hopped down from the branch of a tree above us. She landed gracefully on her boots and stood before us with her hands up. "Whoa there, cowboy. Don't shoot! It's us." She smiled and stuck out her hand to Jake, unfazed by the rifle barrel eyeing her.

Jake reluctantly shook her hand. "Hey there, Sarah."

A broad-shouldered guy in Converse—Coby, I assumed—stepped out from behind a wide elm tree.

"No, not Sarah. *Zara*. Like a Russian *czar* with an '*Ahh*'."

I smiled, and Jake asked, "Delusions of grandeur much?"

She laughed, the sound light and musical. "Now that everyone's gone, I can be czar of the world, Nadia can be queen, Coby can be emperor. Jake, do you want to be pharaoh or sultan?"

"I'll take supreme overlord, thanks." Jake said, his voice flat. He looked past them, as if trying to see whether they were alone.

"Hi Coby," I said, offering my hand. He shook it firmly. Freckles covered his nose and sharp jaw, and the faded red t-shirt he wore clashed with his short red hair.

I turned to shake Zara's hand, but she threw her arms around me instead. "I am *so* happy to meet you!"

"Um, you too." I patted her back awkwardly, unused to human contact.

She pulled away, and I got a better look at her. She had angular eyes, a small nose, and black curls. A few strands were dyed pink, contrasting with the bright blue jacket she wore over tight black jeans. Around her neck was a yin-yang pendant, and she sported deep red lipstick and perfect winged eyeliner.

"How did you find us here?" Jake checked his map, using the key and his fingers to measure the distance. "This is at least five miles from where we agreed to meet."

"We know," Coby said. "Zara wanted to surprise you."

"Yup," she agreed. "You told us where you were last night so we checked it out on the map and decided to wait for you to come by."

"I'm glad we were close," I said.

"*You're* glad?" Coby said. "If she'd had more time Zara would have devised an even crazier plan."

"You know me so well," she said warmly.

"Should we make camp for the night?" I asked. "We saw a good place a half mile back."

"Sounds great," Coby said.

Jake's hands were buried in his pockets and he scuffed at a tree root with his boot, then looked up. "Where are your supplies?"

"Oh!" Zara said, ducking behind the tree Coby had used to hide. She wrangled out a giant designer suitcase that had seen better days.

I laughed before I could help myself. "Do you really lug that thing through the woods?"

"No," she said. "We've got a pretty sweet ride."

"You have a car?" I asked, bewildered.

"Yep! Coby here is pretty handy. He keeps one going."

"That'll certainly make getting around easier." I caught Jake's eye and smiled.

"Yes," he said, smiling back. But it didn't reach his eyes.

◆◆◆

It was that time of night when birdsongs had faded and cicadas began to buzz in the trees overhead. Our tents surrounded us in a semicircle as we gathered around the warmth of the fire. Zara, who'd been lounging against her giant suitcase,

17

rummaged through it, then hid whatever she'd found behind her back.

"I'm so excited we found each other," she said, straightening. "Let's celebrate. *Voilà!*" Her red-painted nails shone in the light of the fire as she proudly displayed a bottle of champagne.

Coby smiled. They'd met up three months ago and become so comfortable together in that time. I glanced at Jake, but he had his eyes trained on the fire, half-scowling.

"I don't think we have any cups," I said.

"Don't you worry about that." She popped the cork and the liquid bubbled over. She took a swig directly from the bottle and offered it to me.

"Um," I said. "I've never had champagne before."

Zara shrugged. "No time like the present."

"Are you sure it's a good idea?"

She laughed. "It's just champagne. To surviving the end of the world!" she said, lifting the bottle in the air and taking another swig. Wiping her mouth on the back of her hand, she said, "I'll be eighteen in under a month. And we've all got to be adults now, whether we want to be or not."

"So soon?" I asked. "Mine's in September too."

"What month is it now? August?" Coby asked. "It's so hard to tell anymore. I guess mine's coming up too."

Jake perked up. "What date?"

"September 17," Coby said, fiddling with his car keys.

"What? No way," Zara said. "Mine too."

"And mine!" I turned to Jake. "Yours?"

He nodded, crossing his arms and leaning back. "That's a pretty big coincidence."

"Hold up," Zara said. "Are we all 17, about to turn 18?"

No one denied it. "How does that happen?" I asked.

"I guess the stars were aligned when we were born!" Zara's eyes sparkled in the firelight.

Jake shook his head. "That can't be it. The day you're born doesn't mean anything."

"Do you think there are others?" Coby asked. Zara's eyes opened wide at the possibility.

"I don't know," I said. "Neither Jake nor I have seen or heard from anyone else for nearly five months. The third strain of the virus seemed to kill everyone." Except, somehow, the four of us.

"Over four months for me," Zara said. "What about you, Coby?"

"Same," he said, gazing into the fire as it crackled. Then he looked up. "Could we be siblings? I mean, obviously not the same mothers, but maybe we were in-vitro kids or something?"

"No," I said. "Even if we were conceived at the same time, we wouldn't necessarily have been born on the same day."

"Not to mention none of us look at all alike." Zara pointed out.

"I don't look like my parents, either," Coby said. "I was adopted."

"Me too," Zara said.

"I looked like mine," Jake said quietly. "But I wasn't theirs. I found out when I donated blood. I'm type A and they were O and B."

I looked at him, surprised. He hadn't mentioned that detail in any of our late-night radio chats.

"I never told them I knew," Jake said so only I could hear him.

"Nadia?" Zara looked at me expectantly.

"No, I'm not adopted." I said. "Or at least, I don't think I was..."

"I'd be questioning that if I were you," Coby said, his eyes alight as a smile spread across his face. "I think we have a mystery to solve."

"The mysterious survival of the 17-year-old Virgos!" Zara shouted. She lifted the bottle in a toast again before passing it so we could all share. I laughed with the others, but my stomach was like a rock. What had my parents not told me?

6: Joyride
Nadia

"I know where the adoption agency my parents used is," Coby said the next morning while we ate a breakfast of dried fruit and granola bars.

We all stared at him. My mouth hung open, full of half-chewed banana chips, before I collected myself.

"Really?" Zara asked, taking the wrapper off another granola bar.

"Yeah, my dad took me there when he told me. We could check it out, see if there are any clues."

"Okay, Sherlock," Zara said. "Where are we headed?"

"It's a city called Newbury." Coby said.

Jake pulled out his road atlas. "That's at least 100 miles from here. But I guess that's not so bad when you have a car."

I laughed, realizing I'd been calculating the walking distance in my head. Five or six days, if the terrain was flat.

"It's parked up the highway, about a mile away," Coby said, taking a swig from his canteen.

"We do *some* hiking," Zara said as she zipped the granola bars back into her suitcase. "Shall we go?"

"I can't wait to see it," I said, looking at Jake, who only shrugged.

We quickly packed up camp. I was excited; I hadn't driven or ridden in a car in over a year, and having one again felt like we'd gained a huge technological advancement overnight. I longed for the feeling of the road beneath the tires, the scenery zipping by.

We trekked toward the car, chatting as we crunched our way through the forest. Birch trees and maples lined our path, and I viewed them with some regret. I wasn't ready to head back into an urban jungle, but the mystery was intriguing. Could there really be a reason the four of us survived?

"How do you get gas for your car?" I asked Coby as we hiked.

"We siphon it out of abandoned cars along the road."

"Oh," I said, feeling foolish. "That's obvious."

He laughed. "Each of us has been surviving so differently. I could ask you how you're able to hunt with that thing." Coby nodded toward the compound bow and quiver slung across my pack.

"I started when I was young," I said, shrugging. "I joined an archery club because I wanted to be like Robin Hood."

"Robin Hood, huh?" I liked his smile.

"Yeah," I said. "I didn't think I'd ever hunt with it."

"I never thought I'd be doing post-apocalyptic mechanic work." He laughed.

I tripped over a root and he grabbed my elbow, stabilizing me. "Thanks," I mumbled.

Behind me, Zara asked Jake, "Are you much for cars?"

"No," he said.

"How about archery?"

He didn't say anything, so he must have shaken his head.

"Not very talkative are ya?" Zara asked.

"He used to be," I said. I turned to look at Jake and he raised an eyebrow at me.

"Oh yeah?" Zara said. "What happened, Jake?"

He shrugged, looking uncomfortable. I tried to give him a look that said "we'll talk later" before I restarted my conversation with Coby.

"If you haven't been hunting, what have you been eating?" I asked him.

"Canned food, MRE's—you know, the military meals-ready-to-eat that you boil? But that's only when we can find them. We tried hunting. At one point I'd found a shotgun and shells, but I'm a horrible shot and I didn't have the patience for it. What have you taken out with that bow?"

"Not much, actually. A couple of turkeys and other birds. Rabbits and squirrels are easier to catch with snares."

"No venison?"

"I thought about it, but I didn't want to skin and clean a whole deer by myself and I wouldn't have been able to eat all the meat before it went bad."

"Not wasteful, huh?" He grinned again. "My dad's always saying, 'waste not want not'."

Zara interjected, "And those big brown eyes. It'd be tough to kill Bambi, right?"

I laughed. "I suppose so."

"I'm glad we found you two," Zara said. "It'll be nice to eat some real, fresh food again."

A few minutes more and we were at the old highway. Parked just off the road a few hundred yards down was a bright red Mustang. It was a classic version, sleek yet strong.

"*That's* your car?" I asked.

"Yup," Coby said proudly, spinning his keys around a finger and catching them in his palm. "There are so many options these days. And this is the one I always wanted, so I thought, why not?"

"Shotgun!" Zara called, swinging open the passenger door. Jake and I climbed into the back and Coby hopped in front. Zara pushed her seat back and shut the door.

"Thank God for these things," she said, popping a CD into the slot. "Otherwise we'd never hear anything good anymore. Now let's drive!"

I rolled down my window as we whizzed down the highway to a soundtrack of 1980s hair bands. The forest views made things seem almost normal again, and I enjoyed the breeze running through my hair. Right then I felt that anything was possible; that the world could be made whole again.

◆ ◆ ◆

I sensed someone near me when I woke and grabbed for the revolver hidden in my pack before I realized it was Jake. We were still on the road, and he was leaning across me to close the car window. I dropped my pack to the floor and relaxed.

"Sorry," Jake said, settling back into his side of the Mustang's rear seat.

"It's okay. I can't believe I slept." I rubbed my eyes and wondered how I'd been able to fall asleep in a car full of near-strangers. During The End it had been hard to sleep anywhere, never knowing if the next people you'd meet were diseased or dangerous.

"How could we all have the same birthday?" I asked, loud enough for Coby and Zara to hear. I was so thirsty for conversation after months on my own that silences among our group made me feel nervous, like we were squandering precious drops of companionship.

"I'm telling you, the stars were aligned *just* right," Zara said.

I rolled my eyes. "No, seriously. What could it be?"

"Maybe we were quadruplets," Coby said.

"But we look so different," Zara said. It was true. Coby, with his bright red hair and burly frame, couldn't have been more opposite to Zara's short stature and East Asian features.

"That happens sometimes." Coby glanced at me in the rearview mirror. "What do you think, Nadia?"

I glanced at the two of them and at Jake. *God that would be bad for the survival of the human race.* "I don't think so," I said. "Maybe the birthday is fake."

"Ooh, yeah!" Zara said. "We were *found* that day. In toxic waste that made us immune!"

"The hospitals could've given us medicine that day—a weird batch or something—that gave us all immunity to the virus," Coby suggested.

"We're immune to more than the virus," Zara said.

"What do you mean?" I asked.

"I survived one of the nuclear attacks, too," she said, without her usual carefree tone.

23

"Really? How?"

She looked out the window, her fingers playing with the hem of her shirt. "I'll tell you about it sometime." There was a note of pain in her voice.

Coby and I made wild speculations for a while longer, but then the CD hit Zara's "jam". She spun the volume knob and all conversation was drowned out by her loud, off-key singing.

I turned to Jake, who hadn't taken part in our guesses, and asked in a low voice, "What's the matter?"

He looked to be sure Coby and Zara weren't listening. Zara was still shout-singing along to the radio, adding air-guitar riffs where appropriate, and Coby was laughing and trying to join in, but he only knew parts of the chorus.

"It's nothing," Jake said.

I gave him my sternest glare and he, unexpectedly, broke into a grin. It faded before he spoke, though.

"We just met them."

"So?"

"It'll be a while before I trust them."

"Really?" I glanced at the front seat. Zara and Coby were still blissfully ignoring us.

"Yeah," he said. "Nothing against them, it's how I am."

"Do you trust me?" I whispered.

"Yes," he said immediately.

I had to stop myself from laughing. "Why? We just met too, you know."

He lifted his shoulders. "We got to know each other for a long time. Weeks. And, it's hard to explain—but I felt like I already knew you."

He lapsed into silence, so I sat back and looked out my window. We were entering the city of Newbury now, and I was happy to see how well-preserved it was. We passed a neighborhood of houses in pastel colors with cute front porches, an empty industrial park, a hospital, and several vacant stores. Only a few had smashed windows or other evidence of looting. Coby didn't stop, so I assumed we hadn't passed the agency yet.

Newbury must have been one of the cities evacuated after the virus was discovered. Those were the only cities I visited if I could help it. Those where the disease swept through quickly were veritable hellscapes, and those demolished by nuclear fallout were too risky to scavenge from.

"We're here," Coby announced as he pulled into the parking lot of a huge mall.

"Yes!" Zara said. "I haven't been shopping in ages." She turned and grinned at me.

"I thought we were going to the adoption agency?" I asked.

"We'll have plenty of time for that. First, see what you can find in there," Coby said, nodding his head at the mall's entrance. "Jake, I'd like you to come with me to the hospital we passed."

I sat up, alarmed. "Do we need medicine?"

"Something like that. You'll see." Coby said. The corners of his mouth turned up.

I glanced at Jake, not wanting to leave him. He looked calm, though. Zara pulled her seat forward and beckoned me to get out of the car.

"We'll be back in an hour or two," Coby said before taking off. "Meet you at this entrance."

"Sounds good," Zara said. "Let's go, Nadia!"

"See you in a bit," I said, looking at Jake. He nodded. My stomach was tight as they drove off. Now that we were all together, I didn't want to split up.

7: Electricity
Jake

After we joined the others it became clear to me that meeting Nadia—and whatever I had with her—had nothing to do with survival strategy. I should've been happy to Coby and Zara to our group. Safety in numbers, many hands make light work, the more the merrier, and every other cliché that tries to tell you it's wrong to be alone. But I couldn't make myself trust them.

And I wanted more time alone with Nadia.

Coby took me to a home improvement store first, where we loaded the Mustang with grill propane tanks. Several were stuffed into what little space there was left in the trunk with all our gear. The others were crammed into the backseat.

"What's the plan?" I asked as we pulled up to the hospital.

He grinned. "Electricity." When he saw my puzzled expression he added, "You'll see."

"Let's make sure we have the place to ourselves first."

He nodded as we got out of the car. "Zara and I call it 'checking the coasts'. You know, like 'the coast is clear'?"

Coby pulled a crowbar from the trunk and bashed a hole in the glass front doors of the hospital so we could reach through and unlock them. We scanned the lab side-by-side, lighting the way with flashlights, but like most of Newbury it was clean. Even after all this time the halls had a faint whiff of disinfectant.

On the second floor we found a small wing that had been cordoned off with caution tape, and a sign that read "Quarantine" and detailed the symptoms of the first strain of the virus. There were likely bodies beyond those doors, but I wasn't itching to find out.

"Do you think we could get the virus from…?" Coby asked.

I shook my head. I'd seen enough to know that I was immune to all three strains. And you couldn't contract the first or second strains from a dead host anyway.

"The coast is clear?" Coby asked.

"If we stay away from this part, yeah."

He led me down to the maintenance room in the basement and pulled a piece of metal piping from his bag. He knelt beside a gas line that led to the furnace and grinned. "All we need to do is switch out that nozzle for this one and we can run the generator on propane."

"I had no idea you could do that." I'd been living without electricity for nearly a year now and tried to think of what parts of it I'd missed. Mainly food preservation.

"Yeah, my dad showed me how. He's the best at all this stuff. Has a real mind for the mechanics of things. He says I do too, but—"

"Says?" I asked, raising an eyebrow.

Coby's face flushed pink and he stammered, "I mean—I meant 'said'." An awkward pause. "He's gone, of course."

"Sorry," I said, wishing I hadn't said anything. But hadn't we all got used to being alone, to them being gone, by now? "I'll grab us a tank."

He looked relieved as I left.

By the time I made it back down the stairs, hoisting the heavy propane cylinder in my arms, Coby was ready to hook it up. The light smell of natural gas hit my nose as he switched the supply line.

"Ready?"

"Fire it up," I said. He turned a switch and the generator shuddered to life. I crossed to the control panel on the wall and switched on the lights.

We went back upstairs, the atmosphere of the hospital completely changed now that it was lit. It wasn't long ago that I'd been living, hermit-style, in the woods. Now we had a car, electricity, and everything that comes with it. But I didn't know what to use it for, now that I had it. Then I remembered Nadia saying how no one would ever go to the movies again. There were large TVs in the waiting rooms, and I'd seen a microwave in at least one of them. If we could find some popcorn…

I explained my plan to Coby and he readily agreed. "Zara will love it, too," he said. "She's always up for this kind of stuff."

We chose the largest waiting room and arranged two couches in front of the TV. There was a DVD player, and in a cabinet full of puzzles and coffee accessories, I found a few DVDs.

"Check it out," I said, showing him *Breakfast at Tiffany's* one of my mom's favorites.

"What's that?" Coby asked.

My brows pulled together. "You know, Audrey Hepburn?"

"Who?"

I frowned. "How about these ones. *Babe? You've Got Mail? Die Hard?*"

"They don't ring a bell," he said. "But I've never been much for movies. Hey, do they have *Star Wars*? Zara and I watched them on a laptop a few weeks back. I loved them."

"No *Star Wars*," I said, trying to keep suspicion out of my voice. "We'll go with *Breakfast at Tiffany's,* I think. We can save the rest for future movie nights."

"Sounds like a plan," Coby said. "And hey—here's some popcorn." He'd been digging around in the cupboards beneath the microwave and pulled out a half-empty box.

"Great," I said. "We're all set."

"Think Nadia will like it?" Coby asked, looking up at me from where he was crouched next to the cupboard.

I swallowed. "Yes. I'm sure they both will."

He continued to dig through the cupboards, and I had to stop myself from peering at him as he did so. Something was off about Coby. I'd have to keep an eye on him.

8: Taken From Us
Nadia

After twenty minutes—enough time to pick up some fire starter and bugspray from a sporting goods store and ibuprofen from the pharmacy—I was ready to be done with the mall. Zara swiped some lipstick from a makeup store, then we wandered around, but I couldn't find anything else that I wanted. Just like old times.

It *was* like old times, except we had to use our flashlights to see anything in the darkened stores and there was nowhere to stop for a pretzel. Finally, Zara gave up on letting me lead the way and pulled me into shoe store.

After a few minutes spent pulling lids off boxes and rifling through tissue paper, she handed me a pair of thigh-high boots. "No thanks," I said. "I like these clothes."

Zara looked me up and down, as if seeing me for the first time, and laughed. "Quite the outfit for the end of the world," she said. "I think someone watched a few too many *Mad Max* movies."

I shrugged and shoved my hands into the pockets of my brown bomber jacket. I'd found it in a leather goods store a few months before. I'd left $300 on the counter for it, though it would never reach the long-dead owner, though my dollar bills were worthless by that point. My attitude towards "shopping" was very different from Zara's.

I watched as she threw boxes aside, stacking others neatly in her "to try on" pile. As she squealed over a designer pair with red soles I said quietly, "I don't like making a mess like this."

Zara looked at me, clutching a four-inch stiletto. She gently laid it back in the tissue-lined box.

"Oh Nod," she said, giving me a nickname and resting a hand on my shoulder. I'd never had a nickname before and found I didn't mind it. She sat on the mirrored bench across from mine and swiped on a new coat of lipstick.

"Look, I know what you're thinking."

My head shook "no", just a little.

"Part of you wants to believe that someday the owner of this shop, and all the employees, will come back. You want to believe that if we leave things the same it will all go back to normal."

I stared at her. We'd only just met; how could she know how I felt?

Her eyes were steely now. "But they're gone, Nadia. No one is coming back."

She blotted her freshly-red lips on a tissue, then folded it neatly and slid it into her bag.

"We've had a lot of things taken from us." She squeezed my hand once. "We can't do normal things people our age did—like concerts or prom or football games. Can't even raise hell with our parents."

Zara straightened, standing in front of me. "So," she said. "If we have a chance to do something fun that we couldn't have done before the end of the world—like an unlimited shopping spree—we should take it."

I considered this for a moment, then quoted, "'Though this be madness, yet there is method in it'."

"You're such a nut." She hugged me tightly, laughing.

"Does it have to be shoes?"

"You mean you'd rather have those,"—she pointed at my dingy combat boots—"than these gorgeous Jimmy Choos?" She offered me a pair of jeweled pumps from her pile.

I shrugged. "I guess I like practicality." And for things to stay the same. "I do like your necklace, though."

Zara's smile fell and her hand reached, first to cover the silver yin-yang pendant, then to hold it out to me. "Someone… special gave it to me."

Her voice was flat, and I felt sorry I'd brought it up, pressing into an old wound. "Sorry—I should've known. Most of our stuff now..." I trailed off, then forced a laugh. "That's why your 'shopping sprees' are fun, right? No emotional attachment."

"It doesn't have to be a shopping spree, but you should do *something* fun," Zara said, her eyes sparkling again. "We could rob a bank! Or a jewelry store. Get some fresh bling? Or I could give you a tattoo!"

"Have you done one before?" I asked, biting my lip.

"Nope!" She grinned.

"Definitely not *that* then..."

"What do you want to do? The world—what's left of it—is your pearl."

"I'm pretty sure it's 'the world is your oyster'."

Zara wrinkled her nose. "Oysters are nasty, slimy things. I'd rather have a pearl. What do you want your pearl to be?"

"There is one thing." A small, safe step toward Zara's way of thinking.

She rubbed her hands together. "What?"

"I'd let you dye my hair. I've never done it before."

I'd asked my parents once if I could dye my hair blue. They'd said no, and I'd never mustered the courage to bring it up again. Funny, all the stupid little things I used to fear.

"Really? Ah, you like my pink streaks, do you?" She tossed her curls and winked.

"Yes, but not pink." I said. "And only the tips. That way we can cut them off if I don't like it." Although I wasn't sure I wanted Zara cutting my hair either.

"You being blonde will make it easy. Let's find some dye." Zara slipped on the sparkly Jimmy Choos I'd rejected. "But I'm wearing these, and I don't care what you say about it!"

She hefted her shopping bag and slung her usual shoes of choice, deep red Doc Martens, over her back by their knotted laces. Together we walked off in search of a hair salon.

9: Creature Comforts
Nadia

We didn't have to wait long after my dye job was finished for Coby and Jake to pick us up. Jake was riding shotgun, so I slid into the seat behind Coby and Zara sat beside me.

"Don't you love Nod's hair?" Zara asked after Jake slammed the door shut.

I blushed and looked out the window for a moment, absently running a strand of still-damp hair between my fingers.

"Looks nice," Jake said.

"Think so?" I asked. Coby shot me a thumbs-up from the driver seat.

"Yeah," Jake said. "It works on you."

"Thanks," I said, unable to avoid smiling.

"I think I could've had an amazing career as a hairstylist." Zara said. "Good thing Nadia is still alive so I have someone to use my mad skills on."

We neared the hospital. Coby parked and we got out, entering through the glass doors.

Once inside, the first thing I noticed was the flickering lights. It had been half a year since I'd experienced electricity, and much longer since it had been reliable.

Jake was beside me and I stared at him, too amazed to form full sentences. "How?"

My stomach flipped when he grinned. "There's a generator here," he said.

"How'd you get it going?" I asked Jake.

"Magic," Coby answered, a gleam in his eyes.

Zara rolled her eyes. "It's easy. The generator runs on natural gas, so you just change out the nozzle to use propane. We've done it a bunch of times."

"That's awesome," I said.

"We got enough tanks from the home improvement store for a few days." Coby said.

"Hold up, does this mean we can have hot showers?" Zara asked with an intense look at Coby.

He laughed. "If the water heater's electric and the running water still works."

"It's worth a shot. Let's go," Zara said. She grabbed my hand and ran down the hallway.

After searching through half of the first floor we found a locker room with three shower stalls. We both held our breath as we turned the knob all the way to red, and we whooped for joy and hugged each other when steaming water flowed gloriously from the showerhead.

I pulled my trusty towel and shampoo bottle out of my bag and entered my stall as Zara shut the door of hers. We both showered until every drop of hot water was gone. Zara sang in the stall next to me, her voice echoing throughout the room. When I got out of the shower I examined my fingernails and smiled. They'd lost their usual crescents of dirt and had become clean and white again.

Afterwards, we found the least creepy room we could— one with wide windows overlooking a pond—and claimed hospital beds for ourselves. I tried to figure out how long it was since I'd last slept on a mattress, but I couldn't remember. Way too long.

"I feel like a real person again," Zara said, raking a comb through her hair while perched on her chosen bed. "So clean."

"I know exactly what you mean." I lay back onto my bed, tucking my hands behind my head and crossing my legs. I'd toweled my hair and a bit of the dye had come off, but now I took a strand between my fingers and examined it. Still turquoise on the ends.

"Do you want some music?" Zara asked, pulling something from her bag. It was a portable CD player, the kind I hadn't seen since I was a kid. She threw me her case of CDs. She had a good mix of 1980s rock, pop punk classics, and contemporary indie bands. I popped in a Green Day album, then put on headphones, turning the volume low enough so could still hear Zara.

"Thanks," I said. "I've missed this."

"I don't think I could live without it," Zara said.

I fanned out the piece of hair and brushed the aquamarine strands against my left palm. "This is perfect," I said after a song or two.

"Can we stay here forever?"

"Yes. Let's do that. I could get used to this." I stared at the white ceiling tiles and sighed. "It's been so hard for so long."

"I know, but it'll be easier now that we've found you and Jake."

"For us, too."

Zara smiled at me and examined her nails for any chips in the polish. A few bottles of nail polish sat on the bed beside her—red, black, and deep purple.

I remembered something I'd wanted to ask her. "So, you and Coby…" I blurted before I had time to chicken out.

Zara's lips pulled up into a coy smile. "You mean have we…?" She wiggled her eyebrows to complete her sentence.

"Yeah," I said, my face warm.

She laughed. "No, we haven't."

"Really?" I asked, looking up. "Nothing?"

"Nope," she said, swiping polish onto her thumbnail. "He's not really my type. I like shy. Nerdy. Not that we can be choosy these days. And you and Jake…?"

"No," I said, willing myself not to blush.

"But you want to," she said, shooting me a knowing look from beneath her thick lashes. I shrugged, failing a nonchalance, and she laughed. I dug through my bedside table finding a phone book and some pens.

"Hey this could be useful," I said, thumbing the phone book's pages. "Maybe the adoption agency is in here. What did Coby say it was called?"

"Yeah, sure, change the subject," Zara said, still grinning at my discomfort.

There was a knock on the door. "Come in!" Zara called. "We're decent!"

The door opened a crack. Oh God, it was Jake. *How much has he heard?* "Come quick," Jake said. "Both of you."

"What is it?" I asked. "Is Coby okay?"

"Yes, he's fine. Just come with me." He sailed down the corridor. My pulse quickened, and I exchanged an alarmed glance with Zara before we ran after him.

10: Get Like That
Nadia

We followed Jake into a waiting room. Coby was stretched out on a couch, two puffed-up bags of microwave popcorn beside him. The TV was on, playing music from a DVD title sequence.

"Are you telling me this wasn't an emergency?" I whirled toward Jake. "Nothing's wrong?"

He grinned in that way that made crinkles appear at the corners of his eyes. "No," he said. "Just a surprise."

Zara slapped Jake's shoulder lightly, laughing. "You scared us half to death!"

I glared at him while trying to catch my breath. "You're the worst. *Don't* do that again."

"Okay, okay," he said, hands up in surrender. "But hey, welcome to a night at the movies."

"This is awesome!" Zara said. She was quicker to forgive than I.

Coby smiled. "Jake was telling me how Nadia missed going to the theater, so we thought it would be fun to set up our own theater here."

"This is so sweet of you guys!" Zara said, throwing her arms first around Jake, then Coby, as she flopped onto the couch next to him.

"Thanks," I said, giving Jake a small smile. "This means a lot."

He half-smiled back at me and sat on another couch. I wavered for a moment, then sat beside him. Zara tossed us a bag of popcorn and I opened it, relishing the familiar waft of butter-scented air warming my nose.

Coby clicked the remote and the title sequence began. I offered Jake the bag and he scooped out a few kernels of popcorn. "I found some DVDs in here," he said. "I thought you'd like this one."

The melancholy tones of *Moon River* played as a taxi pulled up, dropping Audrey Hepburn off at Tiffany's.

"I do," I said softly. "I love this movie. We could find more back at the mall and do this every night if we wanted to."

Jake's eyes were transfixed by the pearl-bedecked Holly Golightly, who was now eating her breakfast. "It's weird to see other people. Even just on TV."

"I know," I said. "I miss people. It's so great to hear other voices, see other faces. Even when…" I let my voice trail off.

We quickly became enthralled by the movie, watching in silence, buried in a mix of the plot and our own thoughts. We had to be halfway through before I noticed my eyes welling with tears. I blinked them away, but Jake must have noticed because when the credits rolled he asked if I'd like to go for a walk.

I shook my head. "No, I'm too tired to go outside."

"Just around the hospital. I want to show you something."

I agreed with a shrug. After I said good night to Zara and Coby, Jake led me to the hospital gift shop.

"There are so many books," I said, trying to sound happy. He'd taken me straight to the back wall of the shop, which was lined with bookshelves and magazine racks. It was sweet of him, but even books couldn't make me feel better at a time like this.

Only one thing could, but I'd told myself I'd quit that. I hadn't been strong enough to throw out the blade, though; it was still hidden in its own pocket of my pack.

"I thought you'd like it," he said, noticing my slumped shoulders and failed attempt at a smile. "But then I thought you'd like the movie too." His hands were in his pockets, and he kicked at the frame of one of the shelves.

"I did like it, Jake. It was sweet of you. I didn't mean to get upset. I started thinking about how all of the actors in the movie are gone, how everyone's gone, and I got… depressed." I took a deep breath. "I know it's ridiculous to still be sad about it at this point, but I can't help it sometimes."

"It's okay to be upset. The virus swept the rug out from under us."

"I wish I could get over it like all of you."

"We're not over it," Jake said, finally looking at me. "We're just dealing with it in different ways."

I bit my lip. "I guess so."

We wandered out of the gift shop after I'd grabbed a couple of novels and found some comfy chairs in a waiting area.

"My older brother," Jake said after we sat down. He ran his fingers through his hair before continuing. "Before the virus hit, he fought in the war. But after it was over, it was like… he never came back. He bottled it up and tried to act normal, but I could tell he wasn't the same. And then all of this happened, and I guess he…" Jake looked away from me, but I could see that his eyes were rimmed with tears. "He couldn't take it anymore."

He'd told me his brother was the last person he knew to die, but I'd assumed it was from the virus.

"I'm sorry." I placed my hand on his arm.

He wouldn't look at me, and his voice was hoarse when he continued. "All he left was a note that said, 'I'm sorry, Jake. For everything'."

My heart broke. I wouldn't have recovered from a note like that from one of my sisters. "I don't know what to say. That's horrible."

Jake shook his head. "You don't have to say anything. But there's something you can do."

"What?" I asked.

"Look, it's none of my business, but when we were in the city the other day," he said, pausing to clear his throat. "I noticed the scars on your arm."

My throat went dry and I hugged my arms around myself.

"Just, if you ever get like that, Nadia, like Ben—swear you'll tell me."

I nodded. "I would."

"I can't handle another note."

"I know. But that won't happen. I won't get like that," I said, with more confidence than I felt. *At least, not again*, I added privately. "No notes."

"Good," he said, nodding once. My heart felt feather-light in my chest. Being believed makes all the difference. Especially when you can't believe in yourself.

11: Fish to Fry
Nadia

There was a knock on the door in the morning and when I opened it, still groggy, I wasn't surprised to see Jake. He held up the keys to the Mustang. "I got Coby to lend us the car," he said.

"For what?" I mumbled. Through my fog of sleep I noticed how short my pajamas were and blushed.

"To go hunting and fishing, out in the woods." Jake said. "Thought it might cheer you up."

As soon as he said it, I realized how much I *did* want to be in the woods again. "Yeah," I said. "That sounds great. Give me a minute to get dressed."

He nodded, and I shut the door. Zara was still lightly snoring, tangled in her blanket. I wrote a quick note for her and left it on my bed. We'd only known each other for a few days, but she would worry if I didn't tell her where I'd gone. The thought gave me a warm feeling.

I pulled on my jeans and a fresh shirt, then tied my hair into a loose braid. After I threw on my pack and grabbed my bow and quiver, I slipped out the door and closed it softly behind me.

Jake smiled when he saw me. "Let's go then," he said jingling the keys. I almost let out a sigh of relief. After our conversation the night before, I was afraid he'd look at me like I was fragile or broken. But he was treating me the same as before. I wanted to hug him for that.

Once on the road, we talked the way we used to every night on the radio, alternating jokes with philosophical questions. Slipping back into our usual routine made me relax, and laughter came easily again.

"So," Jake asked, glancing from the road to me with a smile. "Do you have a poem in mind for today?"

"No," I said as my face reddened. "Not yet, anyway."

"Disappointing," he said, teasing.

I laughed. "I don't know any poems about fishing or hunting. Or about investigating an adoption agency. Though if there were one it would be better for tomorrow."

"There's a project for you: Poem of the Day." His eyes crinkled into a smile behind his aviator sunglasses.

"I wish we were going today. Sometimes I'm so envious of my old life—not having to spend so much time just trying to feed myself. I took so much for granted."

"I don't know," Jake said. "I'd rather be out here in the woods than on a wild goose chase for answers."

"You think it's a wild goose chase?" I asked. "Aren't you curious?"

He shrugged. "What could we possibly find? And what would it change?"

I bit the inside of my cheek. At the very least I wanted to know if I was adopted. Though he was right; what would it change, now?

We came to a bridge over a wide stream, and Jake pulled off the road. We left the car and hiked into the woods, following the flowing water. A familiar sharp, clean scent tickled my nose as we passed through a cedar grove. Eventually we reached a pooled area beneath a waterfall. Jake sat on a boulder beside the stream and set up his fishing rod. I sat beside him on the rock, close enough that our arms almost touched.

There were ducks further downstream, and I had my bow in my left hand and an arrow nocked so I could shoot if one took off, but really I was enjoying the gurgling of the stream, the breeze stroking the leaves overhead, and the shafts of sunlight that fell over everything.

Jake had dug up some nightcrawlers before waking me. Now he pulled one from the old tin can he'd brought, put a hook through it, and cast his line.

I swung my legs over the edge of the rock, gazing at the rapids below my feet. The water was so clear I could see the stones lining the stream and tiny fish flitting by.

"You know how people love water?" I asked, my voice raised to be heard over the waterfall.

"What, because it's necessary for survival and cleanliness and everything?"

"No," I said. "Because it's beautiful. We all love waterfalls, the ocean, streams, things like that."

He watched the bobber floating on the surface of the pool. "Never thought about it before."

"A mountain scene is prettier if there's a river running through its valleys. And the snow on the mountain peaks— that's water too."

"You're right," Jake said, looking at the waterfall beside us. "It wouldn't be nearly so nice here without the waterfall. Or the stream. And fishing would be a *bit* harder."

"Do you think it's primal?" I asked. "Our love of water?"

"Could be," Jake said. His warm brown eyes met mine.

My heart pounded in my chest so loud I was afraid he would hear it. Hopefully the noisy spray of the waterfall was enough to cover it.

"Maybe since we need it for survival, over thousands of years we associated those places with safety, security. And now we instinctively find them beautiful."

"Or they're just beautiful," he replied. We'd been drawing subconsciously closer to each other. I could feel his breath on my skin and my heart wouldn't stop hammering and I imagined how his lips would feel against mine. Jake's smell, a pleasant mix of leather, pine, and something I couldn't quite place, filled my nose.

Our lips were so close that our breaths swirled together. My eyes were slowly closing when suddenly Jake said, "Shit!" and jerked away from me. My eyes flew open and my face warmed. *What did I do?*

But then I realized he was reeling in a fish, and by the arc of the pole, it was a big one. I didn't stay to see it. I hopped off the rock and headed downstream toward the ducks, my face still burning as I scampered away.

My approach spooked the mallards into taking wing and I tried to shoot one, but I was still flustered and the arrow overshot. I found a spot to cross the stream, teetering on a few stones peeking out from above the rippling water, then spent a good half hour digging around in the underbrush for my lost arrow. Served me right for trying to have a romantic moment when I was supposed to be hunting.

I walked downstream a bit further and managed to hit a duck. It was a fat one, and I considered not trying for another, but there were four to feed now and I wasn't sure when we would get out to hunt like this again. So I wandered back toward the pool where Jake was still fishing. The ducks were floating on the water again, and this time when they took wing I was able to take one down. I retrieved the duck and tied it to my pack along with the first one.

My stomach was in a knot when I walked up to Jake. I was afraid we'd ruined whatever was between us. I couldn't stand it if the comfort and familiarity I'd felt again in the car disappeared. When I got to him, though, he smiled crookedly and showed me his catch in the bucket—four fish.

I held up my pack with the ducks in response and said, "We'll be eating well for a week!"

Jake carefully descended from the boulder with his bucket of fish. We walked back downstream to the car together, trees filtering the afternoon sun.

When we parked the car I hoped and feared there might be another moment, between Jake shutting off the engine and getting out of the car, when we might kiss. But Jake just said, "Let's show Coby and Zara what we got," as he opened his door. I guess we were going with pretending it never happened.

Coby and Zara were impressed, and we cooked two of the fish for dinner, saving the ducks and other fish for later in a fridge Zara had cleaned out at the hospital. She heated some canned vegetables to go with the fish, and we had a satisfying meal. We were just missing dinner rolls.

After eating, I considered telling Zara about the almost-kiss, but held back. In fact, I tried not to think about it again. We had bigger fish to fry, figuratively *and* literally.

But as hard as I worked to push it out of my mind, my last thought in the moments before I fell asleep was how glad I was we'd eaten the fish that ruined my moment with Jake.

12: Clues
Nadia

A scream woke me in the dead of night.

I threw off my scratchy hospital blanket and blinked rapidly, peering into the dark and trying to make out silhouettes, or anything that made sense. Zara's strangled voice cried out, "No! No, please…"

I moved toward her bed, laying a hand on her shoulder to calm her thrashing. She stilled, so I said, "Zara, wake up. Come on. It's just a nightmare."

Now that my eyes had adjusted to the darkness, I could see the outline of her face by the dim moonlight coming through the window. Her forehead was wrinkled in distress. "Zara, it's me, Nadia. Wake up now."

Her eyes opened and she thrashed once more, wrenching her shoulder out of my hand. "It's me," I repeated.

"Nadia?" she said, sitting up slowly and wrapping her arms around her knees.

"You had a nightmare," I said, perching myself on the bed beside her. "It's not real."

"Not this time," she said, "but it *was* real." She began to cry and buried her face in my shoulder. I wrapped an arm around her, rocking her back and forth gently until she stopped shuddering.

"Are you okay now?" I asked in a calm whisper.

I felt her nod against my shoulder. "Yeah, I'm fine," she said, her voice still crackly. "Just a nightmare."

"Okay," I said, standing so she could lay back down. I wanted to ask her about the horrors she'd just relived in the arms of Morpheus—the ones she said had been real. But it was late and I didn't want to reopen any old wounds.

I lay in my bed but didn't fall back asleep. It had been weeks since I'd had a nightmare, and now I was terrified they'd come back to me if I drifted to sleep again.

◆◆◆

The next morning, Zara stirred, and I pretended to wake up too, shaking away my fears and painful memories.

I brushed my hair and threw on a new shirt and my favorite jeans. I grabbed my water bottle and a toothbrush and was about to head to the bathroom when I noticed Zara sitting on the edge of her bed. She was carefully brushing mascara onto her eyelashes, a compact mirror in her other hand.

"Zara, can I ask you something?"

"Of course," she said. Her voice came out funny because she had her mouth slightly open while she swiped on the mascara.

I had intended to ask her about the nightmare, but thought better of it and scrambled to come up with a different question. "Why do you bother to put on makeup these days?" The words came out too harsh. "Sorry, I mean—I was just wondering why."

Zara snapped her compact closed. "You're fine. Why do anything if you don't have a good reason for it?" She threaded the mascara brush back into the bottle.

"The simple answer is: I like makeup. It makes me feel like things are a little more normal. And my mom used to say 'always look your best because you never know when you'll meet your destiny'. I think she was paraphrasing Coco Chanel, but anyway I got used to putting time into my appearance. The end of the world didn't seem like a good enough reason to stop." Zara shrugged and pulled out her lipstick. "I guess it's my way of remembering her. Every time I put on lipstick,"—she swiped the rouge color across her lips for emphasis—"I think of her."

I nodded. "That makes sense."

"Besides, there are *tons* of practical uses. The SPF in foundation keeps my skin safe, polish helps keep my nails from breaking. And eyeliner. Did you know pirates and sailors used to wear it to reduce glare from the sea?"

I laughed. "No, I didn't. Maybe I should get some, too."

"I'll hook you up," Zara said, blotting her lips with a tissue. "It's like Nick used to say—"

Her voice cut off. She sat there for a few seconds, frozen in position with the tissue in her hands. I'd never seen her face so pale. Then she folded the tissue and looked away from me, as if she'd never begun to say anything.

I didn't ask about Nick. Zara could tell me about him, if and when she was ready. It wasn't like I'd told her all my deepest, darkest secrets yet either.

♦ ♦ ♦

The adoption agency was a brick building in the downtown area. Coby clicked the key off and we all stared at the four steps leading to the doors while the engine died.

"Are you sure this is it?" Jake asked.

Coby nodded. "That ice cream place over there?" He pointed down the block. "My dad took me there before we came here."

We walked up the concrete steps in silence, stopping before the faded wooden door. Coby tried the door, but it was locked. Without a word, Zara slipped a pair of bobby pins out of her hair and pulled one into a wide V. She bent the other and jiggled both pins inside the lock, the tip of her tongue out of the side of her mouth as she concentrated.

I turned and looked out at the neighborhood, imagining today was a sleepy morning in Newbury. It was early, so no one was out shopping yet, but soon Main Street would be filled with cars, bicycles, *people*. Someone might walk their dog along the sidewalk and wave to the people they pass. I realized they weren't anonymous figures I was imagining, but familiar: my best friend Anna and her bulldog. She'd named him Pilot, after Mr. Rochester's dog in *Jane Eyre*. And like everyone else, she was gone now.

Why should I live when she's dead?

I swallowed, pushing the guilt away, and turned my attention back to Zara and the locked door. I wouldn't let the tears fall. Not this time. Not in front of everyone, in broad daylight, and just before we might figure out everything.

Something clicked in the lock and Zara swung the door open, turning to grin at us. "Alright guys, let's find some clues!"

◆ ◆ ◆

An hour later, we loaded our "clues" into the trunk of the car. Unfortunately, the records were organized by case number, not birthdate, name, or something that would make it easy to find our files. The agency was three small rooms—a reception area, an office, and a back room full of filing cabinets. We'd taken all the drawers we could find that seemed to have dates in the year we were born. There were seven drawers in all, each containing a multitude of folders stuffed with files. Zara also grabbed the laptop from the office, hoping to get it working with the electricity back at the hospital.

"God, this is going to take forever to go through," Zara said as she heaved the last drawer into the trunk.

Coby shifted some of the drawers around, then closed the trunk.

"I can do it," I said. "Can you guys drop me off at the bookstore we passed? I can hang out there and read through them today."

"Are you sure?" Jake asked. "I can help if you want."

"No, it's cool. I'd like some alone time. And I have more experience with paperwork—I'll be less bored than most of you," I said, thinking back to my days helping my mom at the office. There was another reason, too. If I was going to find out

I was adopted, I wanted to read it myself, not hear it from Jake or one of the others.

Jake squinted at me for a moment, then nodded.

"I'll work on the laptop back at the hospital," Zara said. "Then we can meet up tonight and go over what we found."

I nodded, and we got into the car again. "Hey, what if there's a password?" I asked Zara.

"Not to worry," she grinned at me from the front seat and held up her hand. There was a sticky note attached to her finger with "New password: Password123" scribbled on it.

"Thank God for idiots," Jake said.

They helped me carry the drawers into the cozy used bookstore and left me, after a few more offers to stay and help. I stared at the mountain of drawers in front of me and bit my lip. I wondered, not for the first time, if something I didn't want to know lay hidden in those files.

13: Not From Around Here
Nadia

I heard the door open behind me and tossed the book I'd been reading aside guiltily. I didn't think that any of the others would be *mad*, exactly, that I'd taken a break from the records to read, but I still didn't want to own up to it.

"Zara insisted I bring you lunch," Jake said, holding up an open can of refried beans and a bag of likely-stale tortilla chips. He didn't seem to have noticed my book-toss.

"But I don't eat lunch. Not these days."

"I know that," Jake said, sitting across from me, a stack of manila folders between us. "I don't either, but apparently Coby and Zara do."

"You should've told them. No sense wasting food."

Jake laughed, pulling a jar of salsa from his bag. "I tried. Zara isn't one to take no for an answer."

I laughed too. "No, she really isn't."

"And so, here we are," Jake said. He opened the salsa and laid out the food on top of a stack of papers. Zara had heated the refried beans, and I was surprised by how good even stale chips tasted with them, and how much I was able to eat.

"What are you reading?" Jake asked, glancing at the book lying next to me.

"Oh, this?" I said, my cheeks warm. "I, uh, got distracted. Sorry."

He laughed. "It's fine. We're not exactly in a rush here. We've got the rest of our lives to figure this out."

"Yeah, we do." I dunked another chip in salsa and ate it. "I forgot how much I love spicy food."

"This?" Jake scoffed. "This isn't spicy. My grandma's salsa was much hotter than this. She'd be appalled to know any of her family ate jar salsa. Did I tell you she lived in Mexico City? I visited a few times as a kid."

"No, but she sounds amazing."

"She was," he said, nodding.

He looked around the bookstore, admiring the stained-glass windows, the overstuffed shelves, and the worn armchairs in the corner, as I had when I first arrived. The merchandise was primarily used books, so the whole place had that comforting, musty smell of old paper and book bindings. As far as places to sift through files go, I didn't think I'd find a better one in Newbury.

"So, what's up with you?" I asked when he looked back to me.

"What do you mean?" Jake looked down at his hands sheepishly, as if he already knew what I meant.

"Ever since we met Coby and Zara you've been acting weird. You're all quiet and snarky, and I'm pretty sure hunting yesterday was your way of avoiding them. We got along so well before. I know it was awkward when we first met, but—"

"No, it wasn't," he said.

"A little, anyways. But we were cool. You cracked jokes and made me laugh. Out in the woods yesterday you did, too. But last night at dinner—whenever they're around—you go all grumpy and reticent."

"I know," he said, rubbing a hand along the stubble on his jaw. "I'm sorry."

I wondered again about our almost-kiss the day before. It must have been a fluke. "Can we go back to where we all got along?"

"It's just—I had this vision of what it would be like once we met, you know?" I knew the "we" meant just me and him.

I nodded. "Me too."

"And it's different now, with them."

"Sure," I said, brushing my salty hands off on my jeans. "But not bad-different, right?"

"No," he said after a pause.

51

"The night before we met—"

"Yeah?" Jake looked up at me.

"I was afraid you weren't real. I thought I'd gone crazy and my imagination had created you so I wouldn't be alone anymore."

"Really?" Jake asked. He looked at me intently, the sun through the window lightening his brown eyes.

I felt self-conscious. "Uh, yeah."

"That's exactly what I thought too," Jake said. He made a half-laugh sound and ran a hand through his hair. "That you were too good to be true."

I blushed. "Yeah, right." I wished there wasn't a wall of documents piled between us.

"Things will turn out in the end, I think," Jake said. He was zoned out, staring at one of the bookshelves.

"Can you *try* to get along with Zara and Coby?" I asked. "It'll go a long way toward 'things turning out'."

He nodded slowly, as if he had to think about it. "Zara's a little crazy."

"In a good way, I think."

"Yeah, hopefully."

"I'm not sure if there even is crazy or weird anymore, Jake. There are four people left. Not enough of a sample to determine what 'normal' is."

I expected him to laugh but instead he looked at me and said, "Zara's fine. It's Coby that concerns me."

"Really? He seems cool."

Jake shook his head. "I don't think he's from around here." He swooped a chip through the salsa and into his mouth.

"He said he was."

"I know," Jake said, "that's why it's concerning."

"Why don't you believe him?"

"It's just… I don't know how much you've talked to him, but it reminds me of talking to someone from another country, or whose first language isn't English."

"I haven't been getting that," I said.

"I have, and it doesn't make sense. You, Zara and I all grew up a few states away from each other, and we talk the same way and understand the same references."

I nodded and munched on a chip pensively. "Go on."

"But when we set up for the movie the other night, Coby didn't know who Audrey Hepburn was. He'd never heard of the movie, of *any* of the movies in the waiting room."

"That's strange," I admitted, wrapping up the bag of leftover chips. "Maybe he grew up sheltered and didn't watch much TV. Or just didn't pay attention to stuff like that."

"Something's off about him."

I pursed my lips. "Maybe he isn't from around here. Who cares?"

"But then why not tell us that? Why lie?"

I shrugged. "I have no idea."

"Me neither," Jake said. "But it doesn't make me trust him. And…"

"And what?"

"When we were setting up at the hospital, he talked about his dad a lot. In present tense."

My face went hot with shame. If he looked down on Coby for that, what would he think of me, for being unable to speak of my family at all?

"Jake…" I said, my mouth twisting. "How can you count something like that against him? You're the one who told me that we're all dealing with things differently."

"I know. I'm just saying, in conjunction with the other things—something's odd."

When I didn't respond, instead handing him the empty jars and the leftover chips, he said, "Look, I didn't want to make you mad. Just be careful around him, okay?"

"Okay," I said shortly. "I'll see you tonight." I resented his warning. Hadn't I made it this far?

"Are you sure you don't want to come back with me now? Does it really matter what we find here?"

I frowned. "If there's a reason we survived, I want to know what it is."

"Seems like it doesn't matter now. What's done is done." He shrugged, then asked, "Do you want me to pick you up in the car later?"

"No, I'll walk. It's only a mile to the hospital and I miss walking."

Jake sighed. "I know what you mean," he said. "Can you do me one favor?"

"Maybe."

"Get to the hospital before dark, okay?"

"Yeah," I said. "I can do that."

Jake got up to leave, and I stood too. "Wait," I said. He turned, and I handed him the book I'd been reading. "Take this. I won't get anything done if it's here distracting me."

He ran his hand through his hair. A corner of his mouth perked up as he took the book. "Sure, I can do that. See you tonight."

"See you," I said as he left. I grabbed another folder off the pile and the whole stack fell over in a paperwork avalanche. I sighed, beginning to regret volunteering to go through them all by myself.

Not that I'd wanted Jake to stay and help. I gazed through the glass door he'd shut behind him as I sat back down. Is it *that* hard for him to get along with the last three other people on Earth?

14: Odd One Out
Nadia

A few hours later, I'd found records for Zara, Jake, and Coby. So far they had nothing in common except the birthdays.

I glanced at the papers again, which I had spread out to my left.

Child: Coby Frederick Fairfax
Sex: M
Adoptive parent 1: Dolores Fairfax
Adoptive parent 2: Timothy Fairfax
Birth mother: Mikayla Myrla O'Reilly
Agent: Piper Newt Roth

Child: Zara Brooke Nicollet
Sex: F
Adoptive parent 1: Lizbeth Anne Nicollet
Adoptive parent 2: N/A
Birth mother: [Redacted]
Agent: Trent W.I. Hopper

Child: Jacob Ray Atwater
Sex: M
Adoptive parent 1: Rick Jonas Atwater
Adoptive parent 2: Angela Marie Atwater
Birth mother: [Redacted]
Agent: Wipp Thorntree

There were a lot of agents for a three-room agency. I would have thought we would at least have the agent in common, but there was nothing to connect us.

I'd found eight other records with the same birthday. Nothing else on the records matched with ours, but I set them aside in a pile, just in case. I wanted to believe that a few of them had survived, too.

I took a deep breath before pulling the last drawer toward me. I wasn't sure if I wanted to find my record or not. Finding it would mean my parents had lied to me my whole life, but at least I'd have answers. If it wasn't there, I'd have no idea what made me survive when I wasn't like the others. With four people left, I'd *still* feel like the odd one out.

There were a dozen records left in the drawer when I got to the one with my name on it.

I stared at the document before me, my shoulders hunched in defeat. The evidence was right there:

Child: Nadia Elise Madison
Sex: F
Adoptive parent 1: Bradley Oliver Madison
Adoptive parent 2: Lucy Berit Madison
Birth mother: Deborah Jean Becher
Agent: Ron Trepp White

How could those insignificant ink marks on paper show the truth? I let my eyes unfocus, the letters blurring.

What about the other evidence—how my sisters and I all had the same shade of brass-colored hair, the same laugh? How everyone said I got my love of books from my dad, and my light blue eyes from my mom? I *had* to be related to them.

I scanned my record again and found an answer—the word "surrogate". I was related to my family, but my mom hadn't given birth to me. That made more sense, but how could something like that make me immune? Coby, Jake, and Zara's records didn't say that their mothers were surrogates.

And why hadn't they told me? Maybe they'd thought it didn't matter, but I remembered my sisters being born, my mom in the hospital. Why was I different?

I don't know how long I sat with the document, but eventually I noticed the fading light through the windows. I gathered the records—ours and those of the other children born on September 17—and put them in my pack. Then I hoisted it onto my shoulders and left the bookstore. The sun was setting, turning the wisps of clouds in the west pink as the rest of the sky was bathed in shades of tangerine and gold. I had to hurry if I was going to get back before dark.

I ducked into an alley, taking a shortcut to the hospital. In the old world, I'd avoid dark alleyways like this at night, but there was no one left to make it threatening.

Barking and howling echoed in the distance, and I quickened my pace. I'd encountered packs of wild dogs a few times before, back when it was just my dad and me. It had seemed terrible then—learning to hunt and live in the wild, grieving my mom and sisters. Looking back, though, we'd had some laughs and good times. We'd had each other.

Once, we encountered a pack of feral dogs in the woods. We'd climbed trees and stayed in them until the dogs got bored and left, sleeping up there overnight. In the morning, we both had that fresh glow that comes from surviving another harrowing adventure.

The barking grew louder. I turned off into a side street and quickened my pace. I walked along a chain link fence, holding onto the straps of my pack and calculating how many blocks I had left to the hospital. Five or six, I thought.

I heard a snarl behind me. Turning slowly, scared to look, I saw a huge mastiff about a block behind me. *Keep walking. Get back to the hospital, to safety.*

One foot in front of the other: step, step, step, step. The dog growled again. *Don't run, it will chase you.* I looked back over my shoulder. It was still following, gaining on me.

That was when I realized I'd entered a schoolyard. I was stuck in the corner of the chain-link fence. I turned around, wondering if this dog had ever had an owner. Maybe it wanted some human companionship?

No, I couldn't buy that shallow hope as I took in the size of the dog and its menacing fangs. It was large, his head level with my waist.

The hulking dog inched closer; I could see its wild and unfocused eyes now. Its fur was matted and there were globs of foam dripping from his mouth.

Shit. It had rabies, and I had nowhere to run, no trees to climb this time. The rabid animal continued its advance, one staggering step at a time.

15: Before Dark
Nadia

It wasn't the first time since this all started that I'd thought how useless my education was for the world we were in now. What did it matter if I knew what year Columbus sailed the ocean blue or the names of the planets in our solar system or my trigonometric identities if I didn't know the answer to the vital question: *can I outrun a dog?*

In the old world, if you had a question, you looked up the answer online. If you had a serious problem, you called someone else to fix it. Fire? Injured? Call 9-1-1. Rabid dog? Call animal control. Even the first aid class I'd taken was useless when the first step for everything was to call 9-1-1, and all they trained you to do was keep the person alive until people who knew what they were doing got there.

I gulped as the dog inched closer. I couldn't take the chance of running. With the fence behind me, too high to climb and blocking my retreat, I had no choice but to kill this dog.

Its eyes looked bloodshot and foam dripped from its massive jaws. I carefully slung my backpack around to my left arm so I could dig for my revolver. *Why did I bury it at the bottom of my pack?*

I tried to move slowly so I wouldn't startle the dog into charging, but I couldn't keep my breathing calm. Then I remembered reading somewhere that dogs can smell fear. *Oh God.*

Where is my revolver?

My hand swam frantically through the contents of my bag. The dog took three more staggering steps. I could smell his rancid breath. Finally, my hand grasped the smooth handle of my revolver and I pulled it out, spewing the contents of my bag across the ground in the process. The dog jumped back as it was almost hit by a flying book, then it snarled and continued its advance.

I pointed the gun at the dog's chest and cocked it. "Sit," I tried, my voice trembling. "Back! Down!"

The dog didn't listen. I squeezed the trigger and, without meaning to, fired with my eyes closed. The impact swung my arm into the air and pushed me a step back, rattling the fence. My ears rang and my eyes flipped open again and *oh God I missed*.

The rabid animal was angrier now and it lunged, jaws wrapping around my forearm. I tried to shake it off, but it was clamped down hard. Pain radiated through my arm and pulsed into my chest. I quickly cocked the gun again, aiming the barrel squarely between its eyes. I pulled the trigger, keeping my eyes open to aim this time, but looking away from the dog's face in the split second before I shot.

Blood and flesh spewed in front of me, splattering my face and clothing. I fell backward from the recoil and the dog, now lifeless, fell on top of me, its teeth still digging into my arm. I kicked its body, with the now-deformed face, off me and backed up against the fence, breathing heavily. I'd momentarily forgotten my pain during the struggle.

Now I cradled my arm in front of me and clenched my teeth against the tearing, burning sensation. My forearm was shredded from the dog's merciless teeth. Worse than that, I'd been infected. I grabbed my towel off the ground, shook it out, and wrapped it around my arm. I tucked it into my stomach and tried to put pressure on it, laying my right arm over it to staunch the bleeding.

I gritted my teeth against the pain and tried to remember if I knew anything about rabies, besides the fact that you didn't want to get it. There was a shot you could take after you were bitten, but I was pretty sure you had to take it within 24 or 48 hours. Now that I was facing death, whether I had that extra 24 hours or not was crucial. Yet another critical fact my before-the-end education had missed. Hopefully the hospital had the vaccine.

I pulled myself shakily to my feet, my right hand grasping the chain link fence behind me. I was careful not to look at the bloody dog carcass again as I grabbed my bag. I folded the adoption agency records and put them in my back pocket. Then I dropped my pack—it was too heavy, and we could always come back to get it later. If I lived.

The sun was sinking below the horizon, making it difficult to see. I prayed I'd find my way back to the hospital before it was completely dark.

I found myself limping. The dog had clawed up my right leg as well, tearing my jeans, and my calf was sore from when it had landed on top of me. Every step was an effort, and I mentally berated myself for not taking the car when Coby had offered to leave it at the bookstore that morning. Then I wouldn't be in this mess at all.

There was a noise behind me, and I tried to spin around to see what it was. The movement made me dizzy, and I had to stand still for several moments while my vision swam.

The first thing I noticed was the trail of blood I was leaving behind me. I attempted to readjust the towel and more spattered at my feet. It confirmed what I'd been thinking: I'd lost a lot if I was getting dizzy. The second thing I noticed were the hulking shapes of two animals a few city blocks behind me. The one on the left let out a bark, and they both sprinted toward me.

I pulled the gun from the back waistband of my jeans. The movement made me sway. I lifted the revolver, my right arm shaking while my body hunched to protect my left arm. Four rounds left. *Better make them count...*

The screech of tires on pavement filled the air as the Mustang ground to a halt between me and the dogs. Jake was driving. If I'd been able to form a clear thought at that point, I would have thanked my lucky stars.

"Christ, Nadia, get in!"

I managed to limp over and open the door, throwing my gun to the floor and flopping my body across the passenger seat. With great effort, I heaved forward and pulled the car door shut behind me. Immediately, Jake backed up and accelerated to the hospital.

"Rabies," I croaked out. "The dog... rabies."

The movement of the car made me dizzier, black spots and stars filling my vision as I pressed my forehead against the cool window. Jake was yelling something, but I couldn't make out the muffled words. He was mad at me, that was for sure. If I wasn't so tired, I'd be mad at myself too.

I attempted to sit up in the seat so I could hear him better, but when I did everything went black.

16: Everything She Needs
Jake

I burst through the hospital doors carrying Nadia and calling to Zara, my mind full of one repeated phrase: *don't die, don't die, don't die.*

Coby came running first. When he saw the blood covering Nadia his face drained of color and he put a hand against the wall to steady himself. "What happened?"

"Rabid dog," I said. "Where's Zara?"

"In her room."

I shoved past him, running along the hall and pushing into Nadia and Zara's room. Zara's CD player lay beside her on the bed. She ripped off her headphones when she saw Nadia.

"No," she said, freezing for a moment, then springing to action. "Lay her down, there. What happened?"

I gently lay Nadia on the hospital bed as Zara adjusted the pillow beneath her. "Attacked by a dog. She said it was rabid."

"Shit," Zara said. "We'll need a vaccine of some sort, won't we? Never mind, I'll look it up later. Let's get her cleaned up."

Coby came in then, carrying gauze, rubbing alcohol, and a small pair of scissors. "This is my fault," he said. "If she dies…"

"Don't talk like that," Zara ordered. "Thank you for the supplies, Coby, but you look like you're about to faint. Get out."

"Find us some medical textbooks if you can," I called over my shoulder as he left the room. "We need to know how to treat rabies."

Zara was already cutting off what was left of Nadia's sleeve to examine her arm. I turned my attention to the scratches on her legs, cleaning them with alcohol-soaked gauze. There was so much blood that I wasn't sure what was the dog's and what was hers.

"I'll need to stitch these up," Zara said as she cleaned Nadia's arm. Blood still flowed beneath the gauze she was using to place pressure on the wound.

I nodded and moved to leave the room in search of a needle and surgical thread, but Coby burst in.

"Here," he said, shoving a plastic case into Zara's hands. "This has what you need for stitches. And Jake, this book mentions treating rabies bites."

"Thank you. Zara, do you have the stitches under control?"

"Yes, just figure out the vaccine."

Coby opened the textbook on Zara's bed, and we flipped through the pages. "She needs four doses of the rabies vaccine," I said as I read. "One now, one in a few days, another in a week, and the last in two weeks."

"Let's find it," Coby said, his hand gripping the bedsheets. "It's a hospital. They should have it, right?"

"Hold on," I said, skimming the words. "We need one more. The rabies immunoglobulin injection. She'll need that too, since she's been exposed."

"Got it," Coby said, already out the door.

"Zara, can you handle this?" But I saw she could; she'd sewn up half the bite already.

"Yes. But while you're looking find something for infection—antibiotics, I guess—and something for her pain."

I nodded and ran down the hall, finding Coby in the hospital pharmacy. Torn boxes, ripped prescription bags, and toppled pill bottles littered the counter around him.

"I can't find anything," he said, his face ashen. "And this is all my fault."

"Christ, Coby. Calm down. This isn't your fault."

"I'm the one who wanted to go looking for clues, who brought us to the adoption agency. She got bit because she was going through the records."

I clenched my teeth. "She got bit because she's stubborn. This is not your fault. Just listen. We need the rabies vaccine, rabies immunoglobulin, antibiotics, and painkillers, okay? All those things are probably here in the pharmacy if we look. But we need to focus, be methodical."

He was breathing a little deeper now. "Yes, you're right."

"We'll find everything she needs," I said, my mouth going dry and my heart speeding up as I realized that might not be true. "Let's get to work."

◆ ◆ ◆

"You didn't find the vaccine?" Zara's voice was laced with anger, frustration, and worry.

"We searched the whole hospital. There's nowhere else to look. Someone could've taken it when they left. I don't know." My voice sounded strained.

"What are we going to do?" Zara ran her hands through her hair and turned away from me.

"The phone book says there's a family clinic across town. We'll look there. If we can't find any, we might have to go a couple towns over." I glanced at Nadia, unsure if she was really sleeping, and said in a whisper, "How long does she have?"

"I'm not sure. Most of these books just say 'as soon as possible'. One said the first 24-48 hours after a bite. All of them say once she shows symptoms it's almost always fatal." Zara whispered too. "At least I was able to give her the antibiotics and painkillers Coby found."

"How long has it been?"

"She was bitten around sunset yesterday, right?" Zara asked. I nodded and she continued. "It's been almost 20 hours. You guys need to find it before dark to be safest."

Nadia twitched in her bed and blinked her eyes open. "Zara?"

She rushed to Nadia's side, placing the back of her hand on her forehead. "How do you feel, Nod?"

"Good," she said. "I think the fever's gone."

"You're not as warm," Zara admitted, placing another pillow behind Nadia so she could sit up.

"Hi Jake," Nadia said, as if she'd just noticed I was there. "Thanks for saving me."

My blood simmered. Saving her was exactly what I was failing to do. I gave her a stern look. "Did you have to be so stubborn?"

"What?" she asked, incredulous.

"You insisted on going out on your own. You wouldn't take the car, you wouldn't let me come with you, and you didn't come home before dark like you *promised* me you would." My hands balled into fists and I looked away from her.

"Could you get me some water?" Nadia asked Zara, offering a chance to relieve herself from the argument.

"Gladly," she said as she left, clicking the door shut behind her.

I sighed and ran my hand through my hair. "I'm sorry," I said softly.

"I know," she said. "I'm sorry too. And… I want you to do something for me."

It was hard to see her so pale and weak in the hospital bed. So different than the girl I'd first met in the woods. I hoped she'd see the forest again, that we'd be out there again together.

She took a deep breath. "Jake, if I do get rabies…"

"You won't."

"Maybe I won't, maybe I will," she said, shrugging. "The symptoms sound pretty bad, and it's a slow way to go. So if I do, I want you to be the one to… you know."

I gave her a hard look. This was the last thing in the world I wanted to agree to. But I'd seen more than enough suffering in the last year, and if this was truly what she wanted, I didn't see Coby or Zara agreeing to do it.

"Are you sure that's what you want, Nadia?"

"Yes," she said, managing a nod.

My eyes pricked and I had to look away, clearing my throat. "Okay. But you don't need to think like that. It won't come to that. I'll find the vaccine." I put my hand against her forehead. "Zara was right. At least your fever's down a little."

"Yeah, see? I'll be fine." She smiled at me, but I couldn't return it.

"Feel better. I'll be back soon. With the vaccines."

"Okay," she said, squeezing my hand once before I left.

17: A Name
Nadia

I had restless, frenzied dreams, and I knew the fever had
come back. Hopefully it wasn't from the rabies this time. Either
way, I was stuck in a fever-induced, dream-like state along some
blurred line between sleep and wakefulness.

The names I'd uncovered yesterday were swimming
through my head. There was something about them—
something I'd noticed subconsciously. My mind tried to grasp
at what it was, but every time I got close it slipped away again.

The letters. I pictured the names in my mind. I rearranged
the letters in my head, sorting them in different patterns over
and over again, as if they were pieces from a Scrabble board,
until I got something that made sense. I felt myself, somewhere
off in the distance, smile when I got it. It was a clue, a hint to
our existence.

It was a name.

"Peter Winthrop," I said, as my eyes flicked open.

"What?" Zara asked. "Oh God, you're delusional."

Her expression was pained, and she rubbed her necklace
like it was a talisman. "No," I said. "The names. They're
anagrams."

"Anagrams?"

"Yeah," I said. "I thought there was something weird
about them, and that an agency that small wouldn't have that
many agents. They're like our birthdays. Fake. Give me a
notebook."

She obliged, and I wrote out the names of the adoption
agents: *Piper Newt Roth, Trent W.I. Hopper, Wipp Thorntree, Ron
Trepp White.* The letters were all the same, and when I rearranged
them they spelled the vaguely familiar name: *Peter Winthrop.*

"*This* is who we need to find," I said, handing the notebook back to Zara and grinning, unabashedly proud that I'd figured it out.

The worried look didn't leave her eyes. "Nod," she said, thumbing her pendant. "That's great and all, but we have more important things to worry about right now. We're trying to keep you alive, and we still haven't found any vaccine."

"I'm feeling better though! The antibiotics are working." I tried to sit up but the action made my head swirl and stars drift across my vision. I lay back down. "Okay, maybe I can't get up yet."

"You've lost a lot of blood." There was a crease between her eyebrows. "We don't have any way to do a transfusion, so you need to rest. And the rabies…"

"I'm not foaming at the mouth. And look," I said, reaching for the water bottle sitting on the bedside table. "No hydrophobia."

Zara pursed her lips and unscrewed the lid from the bottle for me. She handed me two pills, an antibiotic and a painkiller. After I swallowed them, I drank half the bottle and smiled at her.

"Maybe the dog didn't have rabies after all," I said. I didn't believe it, but I wanted to have my regular, smiling Zara back.

"Jake saw the other dogs. He was sure." She crossed her arms. By that point, smiling and talking had exhausted me. I yawned, and Zara tucked the hospital sheet around me. "I'll feel better if we can give you the shots," she said.

"Can you just talk to me, Zara? About anything that isn't rabies?" A dull ache pulsed through my arm with every beat of my heart. I hoped the new painkiller kicked in soon.

"Yes." She put her textbook aside and said, "You know what's funny?"

"Hmm?" I said, relieved to have my mind taken off my imminent demise.

"I actually like reading these medical books. The human body is amazing."

I laughed. "Yeah?" I pulled a book off the stack with my good arm and read a random sentence: "'The Golgi apparatus, part of the cellular endomembrane system, packages proteins into membrane-bound vesicles inside the cell.' Oh, I see what you mean now. That's... riveting."

"Fine, mock me for my new calling in life," Zara said, feigning offense.

"I thought you were going to be a hairstylist?"

"I always thought I'd do something like that, something creative. But this doctor stuff... it's pretty awesome."

"A real doctor would be fantastic right now," I said dryly. "I 100% support your career choice."

"What did you want to be?"

"A writer," I said, without hesitation. I'd never told anyone that before. But now that the world was over and I was about to die it didn't seem like a secret worth keeping.

"You would be good at that."

"How do you know?"

"I just know," she said, shrugging. "You read so many books, and I'm sure you have a lot to say."

"Yeah, maybe." I thought I'd be relieved to finally tell someone. But the possibility that I could hallucinate in the next few hours seemed to overshadow my confession.

"At least you can still be a writer, after everything."

"Yeah," I said. "And at least I get to die like Edgar Allan Poe. That's got to count for something." I let out an empty laugh.

Zara looked at me pitifully, and for the first time didn't object to the statement that I might die.

That's how I knew it was almost over.

"Is my bag here, Zara?" I tried to keep my chin from trembling.

"Yeah, Jake brought it in last time he came back to check on you. Why? Do you need something?" She quickly stood and grabbed my pack from the other side of the room.

Had it only been a day ago that I'd had to kill that dog? I was grateful Jake had taken the time to gather my things. If I didn't make it, there would at least be some comfort in having my few remaining belongings near at the end.

I ran my hands over the canvas and unzipped the bag, checking its contents. My candles were gone, but thankfully the framed picture of my family and Anna remained. My two rolls of aluminum foil and other cooking utensils, my hunting knife, and my flint striker had survived, too. Jake had collected all the books and clothing that had fallen out when I'd grabbed the revolver.

My hand wandered to the inner pocket where I'd hidden away the blade I'd promised myself not to use anymore. It was still there. I sighed, half in relief, half in disappointment that it wouldn't be so easy to rid myself of it. Finally, I reached the item I was after: my journal.

The leather spine cracked as I opened it to the first page and showed Zara my scribbled title: *A Story from After the End.* "You can read this after I'm gone," I said, giving her a weak smile. "And then it won't matter how shitty everything I wrote is."

I pulled the pen out of the middle of the journal and wrote:

Probably going to die of rabies.
Glad I got to meet Jake, Zara, and Coby before I'm toast.
Never fear, I got revenge on the dog that bit me.

I put the pen down and closed the book. One last case of writer's block; it seemed appropriate. I wanted to write an epic, thought-provoking poem about how many times I'd wished for death before, but, now that it was here, I didn't want it. I couldn't think of any words to say. How many poems were there about death over the years anyway? Hundreds? *And they all say it better than I ever could.*

I swallowed, trying to wash down the iron taste of fear, but it wouldn't leave me.

The door burst open, Jake and Coby tumbling in. Zara jumped to her feet. "You found something?" she asked, her voice edged with anxiety.

Jake was grinning ear-to-ear as he brandished a case of syringes. His usual stubble had turned to a two-day beard, and I wanted to kiss him right then and there, whether he'd brought the right meds or not.

"Where did you get those?" Zara asked.

"Jake had the brilliant idea of going to a veterinary office," Coby explained.

"Yeah," Jake said. "These are dog-sized single doses so you'll need like three shots each dose instead of one. Sorry." He glanced at me.

I snorted. "Don't be. You saved my life! For the second time in like, two days."

Zara fiddled with the box of syringes, wasting no time. "Anyone given a shot before?"

"No," Coby said, and Jake shook his head.

"Good thing I've been reading up on it all day." She turned toward me. "Which arm?" she asked.

"The left I guess? The bite's on that side if that makes a difference."

Coby and Jake watched as Zara wiped my arm with an alcohol wipe. She popped the lid off one of the syringes and squirted out a bit of vaccine, tapping it to clear any air bubbles. The professional way she did it soothed my fears. I watched her take a deep breath.

"Here goes," she said, pushing the needle into my arm. The other two were easy after the first one. I relished each sting of pain, because it meant I was still alive.

"Wait, don't forget the globu-whatever one," Jake said, handing Zara one more syringe. I groaned.

"Don't worry," Zara said. "I'm basically an expert now." She wiped my arm again and gave me the last injection. I winced, glad it was the last one for today.

"How many hours has it been?" I asked, looking out the window. The light was fading.

"Just under 24, I think," Jake said. "We barely made it."

"You'll be okay now," Zara said. She was smiling again.

"Thanks everyone. Sorry to be such a bother."

"Don't be ridiculous," Zara cooed. "You would have done the same for any of us."

I felt tired again, still weak from blood loss. The others looked exhausted. "You guys should get some sleep. Or some food. Or both," I said.

They all nodded, and Coby left the room. Zara quickly said, "I'll be back for bedtime," before she exited.

Jake stayed by my side.

"Thanks for saving my life," I said. "Twice." *More like three times, but who's counting?*

"I'm sorry I was a tool before," he said. "I was worried, and I had a shitty way of showing it."

I smiled and laid back on my pillow. "It's fine. You were right, anyway. I shouldn't have gone off on my own like that."

He shook his head. A smile tugged at his lips. "I'm so glad you're alive—that you're going to be okay."

"Me too," I said, laughing. "What a surprise, right? But you should get some sleep now."

"Yeah, I should." He ran a hand through his hair, then stooped and kissed me on the forehead. "Sleep tight," he said, and abruptly left the room.

I smiled to myself and pulled out my journal again.

Just kidding. Jake saved the day. Again. I scrawled. *Let me tell you, his face today—when he smiled at me because he knew I was going to live—was the goddamn sexiest thing I've ever seen.*

18: Stay in Bed
Nadia

I woke in the middle of the night, ravenous and desperately needing to pee. The bathroom was only a few doorways down from Zara's and my room, so I carefully swung my legs over the side of the bed and skimmed the floor with my dangling feet. I glanced over at Zara's bed. She was turned away from me and softly snoring. She'd want me to wake her to help me, but she'd sacrificed enough sleep for me.

Dropping my feet to the floor, I stood without getting dizzy, which seemed like a good sign. I took a few steps, holding onto the edge of my bed with my right arm. My bruised leg muscles ached as they stretched, but I was stable enough. I let go of the bed and inched my way over to my pack. My head swam when I knelt to dig my flashlight out, but after I held still for a few moments I was okay.

I limped my way to the bathroom without too much trouble and sighed in sweet relief when I made it onto the toilet.

Afterward, I washed my hands, treating my left arm delicately. I wanted to look under my bandage and see what damage the dog's teeth had left but figured I should wait until Zara could help me in the morning. There was a bit of bright red blood on the gauze, so the bleeding hadn't quite stopped yet.

Coby didn't run the electricity at night to save on propane, so to get a look at my appearance I had to awkwardly shine the flashlight over my face. I almost laughed out loud when I saw my reflection. It had me remembering late nights spent chanting into the mirror, trying to summon "Bloody Mary" with my sisters—Natalie always did love ghost stories. I had to look way worse than that old specter right now.

74

Zara must have washed most of the grime and guts off my face, but my clothing was soaked in hues of red and brown, and there were streaks of the dog's blood in my matted hair. The left sleeve of my shirt had been cut away so they could get to the bite and my jeans, already shredded from the dog's claws, had been cut in a few places so the scratches could be cleaned.

First order of business tomorrow: a shower and fresh clothes.

My bladder taken care of, I turned my attention to my vacant stomach. It was past the point of rumbling and onto that tight, unrelenting stage of hunger which is accompanied by a special kind of nausea. I realized I hadn't eaten anything in a good 36 hours and grimaced, remembering my last meager meal of tortilla chips with Jake. I should have eaten more. I hadn't been this hungry since my dad and I had first learned to hunt and live in the wilderness.

We kept the food in the nurse's lounge on this floor. Unfortunately, it was all the way at the other end of the hallway. I lifted each of my knees again, gauging the pain. I could still wake up Zara and have her grab me something. My sore muscles were tight and strained, but I was pretty sure I could do it.

This independent streak is going to get me in trouble some time. I frowned, remembering its role in my current predicament. *Again, that is.*

I hobbled down the hallway, my fingers tracing the railing, hoping my arms would have the strength to catch me if I fell. When I finally pushed open the door to our makeshift kitchen, I grabbed the first chair I saw and collapsed on it, panting. I swung my flashlight around, groaning when I saw that the cupboards were on the other side of the room.

With a gargantuan effort, I pushed myself up from the chair and clutched the table with both hands as I side-stepped my way to the cupboard. The neat rows of cans and boxes made me smile. Zara and Coby had scavenged while Jake and I hunted, but I had no idea they'd managed to get this much food.

I grabbed a can of peaches and the can opener from the counter and flopped into another chair.

The peach juice was too sweet after so long eating things like smoked rabbit and roasted pine nuts. I had to pull the slippery fruit slices out with my fingers to eat them, and when I was done I wiped my hands on my ruined jeans and leaned back in my chair.

I was alive and free of rabies, my stomach was full, and I had three great friends who'd proven they'd stay by me no matter what. Once my body healed, what more could I want?

Then I remembered the name. Peter Winthrop.

I wanted answers.

I shone the flashlight around again. The laptop was sitting across the table from me, still plugged into the wall socket. I leaned forward to grab it and was rewarded with a piercing pain down my left side. I lifted my shirt to inspect the damage and saw a mottled red-and-purple bruise, roughly the size of the dog's paw, on the left side of my stomach. I groaned and heaved myself across the table, barely grabbing the laptop with the tips of my fingers and pulling it toward me. My flashlight rolled off the table and across the floor, and the computer charger came unplugged and thudded onto the linoleum as I sat back in my seat. Stars dotted my vision and I wondered if I'd overexerted myself.

While they cleared, I pulled the folded records from my back pocket. They were only slightly crumpled and bloodstained. Then I flipped open the laptop and typed "Password123". The battery icon said I had two hours of charge, so I made the most of it by scanning through all the files on the computer.

Okay, maybe I played a couple games of solitaire, too.

When the laptop finally died, I'd only been able to find one reference to Peter Winthrop, and none to any of his pseudonyms. I rubbed my eyes. All I could find for Peter Winthrop was an address in a spreadsheet saved to the desktop, was in Newbury. It was a start.

I told my legs to stand then, but they wouldn't listen. I ended up sleeping on the table the rest of the night, using my elbow as a pillow.

◆ ◆ ◆

Zara was *not* happy with me in the morning. "Do you have any idea how terrifying it was to wake up this morning and find your bed empty?" she said. "That was not cool Nod, *not* cool."

"Sorry," I mumbled, lifting my head from my arm. Sleeping at the table had been a mistake. My whole body had stiffened, and I wasn't sure if I'd be able to get up on my own. I examined Zara's face; she was at least as scared as she was angry. "I was hungry," I offered as an excuse.

"You should have woken one of us up," she said, pacing back and forth in front of the table and thumbing her necklace. I finally noticed Coby and Jake in the room. "Do you know how we found you? There was a trail of blood leading from the bathroom to here."

I winced guiltily.

"Look what I found," I said, hoping to change the subject as I reached for the computer. But the laptop screen was black, of course, when I opened it. "I found an address for Peter Winthrop."

"Who's Peter Winthrop?" Jake asked. His arms were folded, and his mouth was set in a hard line.

"He's an anagram," I said. "For the names of all of our adoption agents. His address is 416 Ginkgo Avenue, here in Newbury. I found it last night on the computer."

"We should check it out," Coby said.

"Yeah," I said, smiling at the only person in the room who wasn't upset with me. Then I commanded my legs to stand. Nothing happened.

"Not you," Zara said fiercely. "You're resting today. The three of us will check it out and tell you what we find."

I wanted to protest, but when I finally did straighten my legs they crumpled under me immediately and deposited me back into the chair. "Okay," I said. "But I need help getting back to bed."

Without a word, Jake scooped me up and carried me down the hallway. His arms felt strong and firm as they supported me, and I leaned my head onto his warm chest. He lay me in my bed gently and then said, in a warning tone, "Don't get out of this bed until we come back. You'll be safe here, and we'll only be a few hours."

I nodded, still tingling from where his arm had wrapped around my back. Zara followed us into the room and set a water bottle and a box of granola bars on my nightstand. Then she efficiently checked my bandages and replaced a few of them. "Jake's right. Stay in bed, okay?"

"Only if you promise I can shower and change my clothes when you get back."

"Deal," Zara said.

Jake dug in my pack and I felt uncomfortable, remembering my last journal entry, but he was just pulling out one of my books and laying it on the nightstand by the water. "In case you get bored," he said.

"Thanks."

"Can we get you anything while we're out?" Zara asked. I remembered all the food last night. Zara and Coby had some serious scavenging skills.

"Yeah, actually," I said. "I need more rounds—.38 caliber. I wasted two on that dog, so I only have four left."

Coby had come into the room too and whistled. "That's gonna be tough," he said. "Ammo was one of the first things that sold out. everybody stockpiled it; we'll have to find someone's stash to get more."

"Well if you come across any… keep me in mind," I said, smiling.

Coby nodded. "Let's head out."

Jake looked at me one last time before he left as if he was worried about leaving me. I tried to smile reassuringly. When that didn't work I said, "I know, I know, stay in bed."

He smiled briefly and then said, in a mock-gruff tone, "You will if you value your life," and walked out the door.

I sighed into the empty room. Being alone was bad enough after what had happened the other day, and this big, vacant hospital creeped me out. But at least they might come back with answers.

Peter Winthrop, we're coming for you.

19: Unremarkable
Jake

Peter Winthrop's house was nothing special. It was a small one-story nearly identical to the others in its neighborhood, a development at the edge of Newbury.

"This is it," Zara said, checking the paper Nadia had written the address on as we pulled up to 416 Ginkgo Avenue.

Coby shut off the engine and we piled out of the car, working our way to the front door through the grass and weeds that had overrun the lawn.

Inside, Peter Winthrop continued to be unremarkable. Tennis shoes and loafers sat on a mat near the door and a khaki trench coat hung on a hook. We passed into the living room, which was overstuffed with a couch, a recliner, a desk, and a widescreen TV crammed in the small space.

"I'll check the bedroom," Coby said as Zara wandered into the kitchen and began opening cupboards.

I moved to the desk, shuffling through newspapers, magazines, and a few scientific journals to find letterhead stationery boasting his name. On the desk was a framed picture of two men in their twenties at a golf course. One had blond hair and a wide smile, his arm thrown around the other, who had dark hair and glasses. One of them had to be Peter. I didn't know what the others were looking for, exactly, on this wild goose chase, but I assumed Peter's golf hobby wasn't relevant. I set the picture aside.

Coby passed through the living room again. "Find anything?" I asked, my hands full of mail.

He shook his head.

"Me neither. Besides this from Australia," I said, holding the card out to him. It read "Happy birthday, Uncle Peter! Love, Julia", and was postmarked late August last year—around the time the world fell to pieces.

Coby took the card and glanced over it, then handed it back and said, "I'm going to try the other bedroom."

How does he know there are two bedrooms? Shot through my mind before I scolded myself. Coby had done everything he could to help save Nadia the other day, and even before that she'd encouraged me to give him a chance.

You could tell from the outside that there was room for two bedrooms in the house, anyway. He and Zara were more used to scoping out houses, searching them for useful finds, than I was.

I threw the card back onto the pile and scanned the rest of the room, but there was nothing of note. The sounds of cupboards and drawers opening and closing, the shake of a pasta box, and the stacking of cans still came from the kitchen, so I joined Zara.

She couldn't reach a jar of peanut butter at the back of the top shelf, so I grabbed it and handed it to her. "How's the scavenging?"

"Fine," she said, shrugging. "There are a few things we should take. But his cupboards are pretty cleared out."

"That bachelor lifestyle."

"Exactly," she said, pushing a curl behind her ear. "But I haven't found any clues, either. How about you?"

"No. This guy was boring. Seriously, a picture of him out golfing was the only thing I could find."

She sighed. "Coby seems upset that he hasn't found anything and I'm afraid Nadia will be, too."

"Where is he, by the way?" I asked, stepping into the dining room, then stopping. "Christ, have you seen this?"

Zara followed me, dropping a can that rolled across the hardwood floor until I stopped it with my foot.

"Whoa," she breathed. "That's crazy."

A four-person dining table sat over a shag rug and below a 1970s-era light fixture with its cord woven through a chain. But on the wall across from us, nearly as large as the tabletop, was an oil painting of two angels. Or a demon and an angel. They were engaged in a mid-air fight, each brandishing a sword. The one above had white, dove-like wings and colorful clothing, and the one below, fighting back, had wings like a bat and was nearly naked. Blood streamed from a gash across his arm.

Zara stepped forward, running a hand along the carved gilt frame.

"What do you think this means?" I asked. "Does this count as a 'clue'?"

She shook her head. "I don't know how this painting could have anything to do with how we survived."

Coby came in from the other end of the dining room, jingling his car keys and frowning. "I searched the other bedroom, bathroom, and basement. Nothing."

"Did you see this?" I asked, indicating the painting.

He stepped back to look, his brow furrowed. "No, I guess not."

Suspicion prickled again. He'd walked through here from the kitchen and not seen the wall-sized oil painting? Especially with its violent depiction, its rich colors.

"Think it means anything?" I asked him.

He shrugged. "There's nothing here."

"Yeah," Zara said, sighing. "Oh well. Let's gather up the food I found and get back to the hospital. Though I'll need to get Nadia a few things in town first."

Coby brushed past me into the kitchen, helping Zara bag up her finds. I glanced at the painting once more, a finger-like chill running down my spine, then turned and left the room.

20: Dead End
Nadia

Zara brought me fresh clothes from the mall when they returned and, true to her word, let me take a shower. She wrapped my arm in a plastic bag first to keep the stitches dry and stayed outside the shower in case I fell. I knew I wouldn't; I already felt stronger.

I let the warm water wash away the grime, pain, and fear of the past two days for a few minutes before I began interrogating Zara about what they found at Peter Winthrop's house.

"To be honest Nod, not much."

"What was his house like?" I asked, having to raise my voice to be heard over the shower.

"Small," Zara said. "He was definitely a bachelor. There were no decorations anywhere, except for this giant oil painting in the dining room."

"A painting?"

"It had these two like, angels on it."

"Angels? Really?"

"Yeah, but not nice ones with halos and stuff. They were warriors. It looked medieval."

"Do you think he was an art guy? Like a professor or a museum curator?"

There was a pause before Zara said, "I don't think so."

I finished working the shampoo out of my hair, one-handed, and shut off the water. I reached out and Zara handed me a towel. I fumbled for a second, trying to get it around me with my left hand in a plastic bag. Once I'd tucked it into place, I slid aside the shower curtain. Zara wouldn't make eye contact.

"Zara, what aren't you telling me?"

She sighed, then finally looked at me. "His house was like *all* the houses we scavenge from. Dusty and nothing had been moved for a long time. No one had been there in months. Whoever Peter Winthrop was, he's dead now, just like everyone else."

My mouth twisted, and I said, "That doesn't mean he isn't important. It's too much of a coincidence. The birthdays, the anagrams... they add up to *something*."

Zara shrugged. "I don't know, Nod. I think it's a dead end."

I wasn't ready to give up. I opened my mouth to continue, but Zara took the plastic bag off my arm and made me sit. "Time for a new bandage," she said.

I lost what I'd wanted to say, distracted by morbid curiosity over what my wounds looked like. Zara slipped off the bandage to reveal two teeth-marked crescents. The stitches all seemed to be in place, though a bit uneven, and the bleeding had finally stopped.

"It'll add some variety to the other scars," I said, trying to make a joke.

"That's not funny, Nod," Zara said, tightening her grasp on my wrist and looking into my eyes. "Have you stopped doing this to yourself?"

I swallowed the lump that appeared in my throat and nodded.

"Good," she said, wrapping fresh gauze around the wound. "When was the last time?"

I considered lying. "About two months ago," I said instead, struggling to keep my eyes dry and my voice steady.

"If you feel like doing it again, tell me. I'll stop you." Her hand gripped my wrist again. When I didn't respond, she added, "Agreed?"

I nodded, not able to look at her. All the emotions I'd felt, the fear over what Zara thought of me came back. She slipped out of the room, and I tried to compose myself. I pulled on my new shirt and yanked the sleeve down over my bandage, covering my scars. *Out of sight, out of mind.* Or at least, out of Zara's mind.

After I'd finished dressing myself in the new clothes we headed to our makeshift kitchen. Jake and Coby sat at the table.

"I'm sorry," Jake said. "We didn't find anything."

Coby sat back in his chair with his arms crossed. "We have to keep looking," he said, his voice rougher than usual.

"I agree," I said. "I want to go to his house. I might see something you missed."

"I told you," Zara said sadly, "we didn't miss anything. There was just nothing there."

Jake wore a defeated expression too, but Coby still looked determined to continue, like me.

"We should at least research the guy," I said.

"How?" Zara asked. "There's no one to ask, no more internet. We can't look him up and know everything about him."

"No," I said, sitting carefully in a chair. The shower had loosened my sore muscles, but I didn't want to push myself. "But we can go to the library."

"Do you really think we'll find anything about this guy there?" Jake asked.

"It's worth a try, isn't it?" I said.

"I'm in," Coby said. His nettled expression had softened. "We should try whatever we can."

"Fine," Jake said. "But not until tomorrow morning. It's getting late, and you need to eat something besides peaches."

I nodded. Lying in bed sounded appealing anyway.

"I'm going to cook one of the ducks outside. Do you want to help, Coby?" Jake asked, throwing a glance at me. I smiled, glad he was making an effort to get along with Coby.

Coby headed out with him and Zara helped me back to our room, insisting I eat dinner in bed.

I was surprised later when Coby was the one who brought me a plate loaded with roasted duck and green beans. Jake's words about Coby flashed through my head, setting me on edge. *It's Coby that concerns me.*

"Dinner is served," he announced, laying the plate on the bed tray and swinging it around to me. He looked nice when he smiled. His teeth were straight and white, and it made freckles vanish into the wrinkles next to his eyes. I wanted to trust him.

"Thanks, Coby," I said, laying the book I'd been reading beside me. He sat on the edge of my bed and handed me a cup.

"Look," he said. "Zara made lemonade out of the powdered stuff we found. It's sugar-free, but it tastes pretty good after nothing but water."

I gulped some down and smiled. "Yeah, for sure. The duck smells pretty good too." He hadn't brought his own plate, so I expected him to leave once I'd begun eating. I wondered where Zara and Jake were.

"We got you this," he said, placing a leather belt beside me on the bed. It wasn't just a belt, I realized; a holster for my revolver was threaded through it. "Jake said it would've helped you out with the dog."

"Yeah, it really would have." I said, touched by the gesture. "Thank you, Coby."

"You're welcome," he said, and looked toward the door, as if he was about to leave. After a pause, he turned back to me. "I wanted to talk to you."

My stomach tightened. "About what?" I asked, forcing a smile.

"It's about this whole Peter Winthrop business."

"Oh." This time my smile was genuine. "What about it?"

"We can't let the others give up on figuring it out." I'd just filled my mouth with a forkful of meat, so I nodded while I chewed. He continued, "It's the most important thing we can do right now. I mean, what if we found other survivors by figuring him out?"

My eyes widened. "You're right. There could be more." Something stopped me from mentioning the other files I'd found with our birthday.

"Sure," Coby said, standing. "But there's only one way to find out. We need to make sure Zara and Jake don't quit on us."

"I agree," I said. "We need to find out whatever we can."

"I'm glad we're on the same page," Coby said, flashing me another winning smile. "I'll let you finish your dinner now."

As he left the room, I wasn't sure what to make of our exchange. It was odd to be having conversations that didn't include the others.

But hey, I thought as I shoveled more green beans into my mouth. *I want to know the truth, and at least I have an ally in that.*

21: Manhunt
Nadia

The next morning at breakfast Jake tried to convince me not to go with them to the library. "You need to rest," he said, setting his empty fruit cup on the table.

"Come on!" I looked to Coby and Zara for support. "I rested *all day* yesterday. You can't leave me by myself at an abandoned hospital again. It was awful for those few hours."

"That would be hella creepy," Zara said.

"Like the beginning of a horror movie," I confirmed. "Besides, it was my idea to go, and you said I could yesterday. Libraries are my natural habitat. I can help you!"

Jake glowered at me with his arms crossed and said, "You're going to sit the whole time, and we'll bring stuff to you. No lifting anything, got it?"

Raising three fingers I said, solemnly, "Scout's honor." I grinned as a smile tugged at his lips.

We loaded into the car, me and Zara in the back. Coby drove, and Jake held the phone book, with its small map of Newbury, in the passenger seat. Zara had made me put on a sling that she found in the hospital, and I could already tell I would hate it. She was afraid that I'd rip open my stitches after my escapade the other night.

The library was larger than I expected. Serpentine shelves snaked across the wide main floor, and an airy balcony housed even more books. The tops of the shelves were decorated with busts of historical figures, globes, and faux houseplants.

"I'll sit there," I said, pointing to a table near the laurel-crowned bust of Caesar Augustus. My balance was still off from my limp and the sling wasn't helping. I had to grab the side of a table on my way to the chair.

Jake walked beside me, so he could be there if I fell, but he wouldn't help without being asked. I appreciated that. When I finally sat he said, "Stay put, Nadia."

"Yes, sir!" I said, saluting him. He smiled at that, and I felt my heart speed up.

◆ ◆ ◆

Eventually they sat with me at the table, all of us poring over the books and records we could find about Newbury. The card catalog had been digitized so we had no hope of finding any books Peter Winthrop might have checked out. Instead we searched Newbury's history for him. So far, we hadn't found anything.

I'd made it through a few years of newspapers but found no reference to a Peter Winthrop. I had to keep myself from reading any of the personal interest stories lest my eyes mist over for the dead.

"Look at this cover!" Zara came back from another book run, showing us one with an intricate design of icicles on the cover. "I miss winter," she said dreamily.

"Really? I don't," I said.

Jake looked up from his pile of newspapers. "Not a fan?"

"Who is?" I asked. "It's cold and sad, with so much less sun."

"Yeah, but there's snowboarding," Jake said. I could see how being out in the snow with Jake—and, well, warming up with him afterward—could be appealing.

"I guess," I said, trying not to blush at my renegade thoughts. "I've never been."

Zara gasped. "We'll change that this winter! It's so fun!"

A snort-like laugh escaped from me. "This winter we'll be struggling to stay warm and alive. I think you'll come over to my side on it."

"Never!" Zara said. "Winter's beautiful. Frost on windowpanes and pine needles. The way light sparkles on the snow, even at night."

"Everything looks fresh and new after it snows," Jake added.

"Yeah and then you go inside to regular lighting and everything looks all dull and yellow," I said. "What do you think, Coby?"

"Oh," he said, finally looking up from the regional history book he'd been flipping through. "I guess I like winter."

"Yes!" Zara said. "I knew he'd be on our side."

I crossed my arms, wincing at the pain the gesture caused. "You're not convincing me. The snow and cold this year will not be fun for us."

"But snow is fun! Just think of snowmen and snow angels, and the way you can see your breath. Right, Coby?"

"Sure," he said, buried in his book again. "You can see your breath—that's right—and it looks like... clouds. Or something."

"More like smoke," Zara said. "It's best when you blow it out your nose and pretend you're a fire-breathing dragon!"

Jake and I laughed, but Coby's eyebrows drew together in concentration as he stared at the page.

"We'll convince you that winter's great this year," Jake said.

"Yes, we can have an epic snowball fight!" Zara said. "You in, Coby?"

He ignored us. "Coby?" Zara asked again. She didn't seem to have noticed his mood.

He looked up when she repeated her question. Coby seemed agitated when he snapped, "What's a snowball fight?"

I exchanged a glance with Jake while Zara explained it to Coby. Maybe Jake had been right about Coby, and he was lying about where he was from. Everyone I'd known would understand this winter stuff.

"Can we get back on track?" Coby asked sharply, rubbing the back of his neck, his face red.

We didn't talk much after that, the atmosphere ruined by Coby's outburst. He didn't seem to notice, buried in his thick reference book.

How are we going to find anything here? Maybe Peter Winthrop wasn't interesting enough to make the town newspaper...

"Wait a minute!" I said suddenly. Jake and Zara looked at me. "Let's try a different approach. What if he *wrote* one of the books here?"

"Good idea," Coby said, suddenly brightening. What was *with* him? Jake and I exchanged another meaningful look.

It took a good hour for them to search the whole library for the last name Winthrop. The fiction section was easy, but it took a while to comb through all the nonfiction. *Curse the Dewey Decimal system for making this so complicated.* I impatiently drummed my fingers on the table. After a while, I took off the sling and picked at my stitches underneath the gauze.

Zara slapped my hand away when she came back to the table. "*Don't*," she said fiercely. "I'm not redoing those."

"But they *itch*," I said, and she gave me an exaggerated glare. I sighed. "Fine. Did you find anything, Z?"

Her body stiffened, and she narrowed her eyes at me. "*Don't* call me that. Ever."

My mouth went sideways. "I'm sorry." I said. "I won't. Did you find something?" I tried to make my voice upbeat again.

The shadow over her face evaporated and she grinned at me. "Yes, I did. Coby said he'd take 610—Medical Technology or something—and that I should take 570, Life Sciences, where I found this." She tapped the book she had clutched to her chest. "Where are they, anyway? Coby! Jake!"

They both came down from the balcony and stood beside her.

With a flourish, she plopped the book on the table and said, "Check it out. *Cellular Regeneration*, by Doctor Peter Winthrop."

"That's definitely something," Jake said.

Coby grinned, his mood suddenly lightening.

"It gets better than that," Zara said. She flipped to the author bio. There was no picture, but there was a full paragraph about him, and Zara pointed to one line in particular.

"*Doctor Peter Winthrop works at his independent laboratory, Winthrop Enterprises, in Marion*," I read aloud. "Jake, do you have your map?" I asked, but he was already pulling it out.

He searched the road atlas for a moment, and I peered over his shoulder. We found the city at the same time, and I felt a spark between us as we put our fingers on the same spot on the map. "There. That's about fifty miles away," Jake said. "He must have commuted to work from here."

"Then that's where we need to go!" Coby said, grabbing the book and stuffing it into his pack. At least he was happy again. For the moment.

22: Night of Secrets
Nadia

Shadows danced around us as twilight faded to darkness. Our faces flickered in the golden glow of the fire and the full moon was bright above us, competing with broad streaks of the Milky Way for dominance in the night sky. The air was crisp, carrying the first hints of autumn. It was a night for sharing secrets.

After leaving the library, we'd spent the rest of the day preparing for our journey tomorrow. Rather, the other three had prepared by scavenging and packing, forcing me to spend the day resting. In that time, I'd decided to tell them what happened to my family—not because they needed to know, but because I finally felt ready to tell someone. I'd read that in other cultures, the names of the dead aren't spoken. I didn't subscribe to that belief, but I did recognize it as a big step for me. Their stories deserved a voice.

Jake agreed to build a bonfire in the hospital courtyard where we'd been cooking our food. Coby cooked our dinner and Zara brought a bottle of rum she'd found while scavenging. It was like a party.

I told Coby and Zara about my confrontation with the rabid dog, since they still hadn't heard the full version.

"Wait," Zara asked, "what do you mean, you were trapped by the chain-link fence?"

I set my empty plate beside me and said, "I was trapped in the corner of it. There was no way out."

"Why didn't you climb it? How tall was it?"

I threw her a skeptical look. "It was taller than me—ten or twelve feet high. I never would've made it over without serious injury."

93

She scoffed. "Yes, you could have! Easy-peasy. I'll teach you sometime."

"If you say so," I replied. Zara's tantalizing past (full of lock-picking and fence-hopping, apparently) made me more determined than ever to share our stories tonight. I waited for my opening.

"I was thinking," I said, after both our conversation and the fire had died down. "I'd like to share how we all got here. What we were like before."

Zara took a drink from the rum bottle, then passed it to Coby. "Sure, Nod," she said. "Maybe it'll help us figure things out tomorrow, too."

Coby tilted the bottle into his mouth and grimaced at the taste. "I think you should go first," he said as he handed the rum to Jake.

"There's not much to say," Jake said, blinking in surprise. "My parents were gone after the first strain. My brother made it through the second, but not the third. After that I was on my own, until I contacted Nadia." He flashed a smile, laced with sadness, at me. My heart swelled; he'd told me much more detail about his past.

He handed the bottle to me. I hesitated, but they called it liquid courage for a reason, right? I took a deep pull, then coughed and cleared my throat before I began.

"Before The End, I had my parents and two younger sisters, Natalie and Nicole." I swallowed, vowing not cry.

"We lived in a medium-sized city like Newbury, and mostly, we were happy." I glanced at my left arm, imagining I could see my scars underneath the bandage. No, I couldn't tell them about that—about the self-hatred, the guilt, the numbness—without crying. I couldn't trust them with that secret yet. *Stick to what's important*, I thought as I took a steadying breath.

"Nicole, the youngest, got sick first. She was sick all the time. She had something wrong with her kidneys—so we didn't think much of it at the time. It was the first strain. You know how it was. People didn't worry. She'd had pneumonia the year before, so we thought maybe it was that again."

I kept my eyes trained on the campfire, and in my periphery, I could see the others doing the same. "But then Natalie got sick, and my mom stayed home from work to take care of them. After a week the first virus deaths were reported on the news. My mom made my dad and I stay in separate rooms from them after that. 'Just in case', she said.

"Because of that, the night Nicole died I couldn't hold her or tell her how much I loved her. All my mom let us do was send her notes or speak to her from outside the door of her room. Goodbyes are hard enough without sending them through a closed door."

Zara nodded. Now that I'd begun, I needed to finish the story. I took a deep breath. "Natalie was gone a few days later. It didn't come as a surprise, but it hurt just as much. At that point my mother was showing symptoms and my father insisted that she let him take care of her.

"She, um…" I tried to keep my voice from getting hoarse. "She wouldn't let him. She said that he wasn't sick yet, and she wouldn't let him get that way. 'You need to stay strong for Nadia,' she said. It was—" A small sob escaped from me, and I fought for control, clearing my throat. "It was the first time I'd seen my father cry. She locked us out and said she'd end it early if we tried to break down the door. She told us to leave and get out of the city, but we couldn't until she was actually… gone."

There was silence for a few moments while the others waited for me to continue. "It's funny," I said, my voice cracking. "It's funny how when shit hit the fan you realized who was really important. Beyond my family, the only person I found worth risking my life to check on before we left town was my best friend Anna. But," I swallowed. "Anna and her whole family were already gone."

I looked heavenward, trying to keep my tears from spilling over. Were Anna and my family, up there somewhere? Or still here on Earth in some other form? I couldn't pretend to know how the afterlife worked. All I knew was that they were gone, and I might never feel whole again.

"My dad and I got out of the city. We lived out in the woods, mostly. I think he was headed somewhere, but I don't know where. He wouldn't tell me. So when he—" I paused. "Anyway, I didn't know where to go, after. But when it was just the two of us... well, it was the happiest I've been since The End. We didn't notice the second strain, because we barely saw any people at the time.

"We didn't know about the third strain until we met three strangers on the road. They told us about the first nuclear attacks, the declarations of war after the second strain. 'Can you believe it?' I remember one man saying, 'Someone could weaponize a disease like this and get away with it, in this day and age?' I didn't think we *could* believe it. There was no news on TV, no newspapers anymore. Getting information from strangers on the road made the war seem distant, strange. Like it wasn't really happening. It couldn't be. People who'd managed to survive the disease couldn't be getting killed in some ridiculous world war, right?"

I plucked some grass from around me, then let it slide through my fingers and drift back to the ground. "We took all the precautions," I said. "We stayed ten yards away from the strangers. We wore our filter-masks. We gave the place they'd been standing a wide berth, hiking far into the woods before getting back on the road. But it didn't matter."

One tear threatened to spill, but I wiped it away with my knuckle. "As you know, the third strain kills quickly. Those strangers we met must have been dead an hour after we'd met them. My father was gone by nightfall.

"After that, I was on my own," I said, clearing my throat. "Until I met Jake."

I looked across the fire at my three companions, wondering if I'd told them too much. I'd never been big on sharing before. Jake was looking at me with something like

96

sympathy. Coby was staring at the hospital windows surrounding us.

Zara had been unusually quiet during my story. She stared vacantly into the flames. Then she grabbed the bottle of rum from my side, pressed it to her lips and took a deep drink. A drop escaped down her chin and she wiped it away with her sleeve. After screwing the cap back on, she tossed the half-empty bottle aside and finally looked up, away from the flames.

"It's about time you knew the truth about me," Zara said. She looked at each one of us, the fire reflecting in her dark eyes. "I'm a murderer."

23: Tell You My Sins
Jake

A tense quiet fell over us, broken only by a twig snapping in the fire. The shifting light over Zara's face and the way she looked vacantly into the fire had my mind alert and my body ready, in case she meant any harm to the rest of the group after her confession.

"I should start at the beginning," Zara said. Then she drew in a shaky breath and continued, her gaze back on the flames.

"When the first strain hit, my mom and I skipped town with my boyfriend, Nick. He and I were soulmates."

I rolled my eyes, and she must have seen because she held up a hand and said, "I know, everyone thinks that when they're in high school, and you can think it's stupid if you want, but to us it was real. We grew up in the same neighborhood. We played in the sandbox together, had our first kiss together when we were six. Even when it wasn't cool to like boys or girls we were inseparable. We knew we were in it for the long haul; it didn't matter what anyone else thought."

The fire crackled and I waited for her to continue. My hand twitched to reach for my rifle behind me. But she seemed more upset than dangerous.

Zara's voice came out in a whisper. "Then there's my mom. She had this way of charming everyone she met. She had friends all over the world, and at least three men were in love with her, totally smitten, for as long as I can remember. She always told me that she'd never marry. She did want a child, though, so she adopted me. 'You're all the family I need,' she'd tell me."

Zara smiled to herself at the memory, and the hairs on my neck stood up.

"Since my mom was always drawing people to her like a moth to flame, she had a lot of friends. We relied on them after the first strain swept through the city. Well, not all of them were friends, exactly.

"I don't want to say that my mom was a con artist, but not all of her transactions were above board. And there were guys that she led on when we needed their help. That anti-marriage speech was for my ears only. Anyway, one of the guys in love with my mom was Farmer Dan."

Zara laughed, and I jumped, still waiting to find out who she'd killed. This guy could be it. If so, that laugh was jarring.

"Obviously his name wasn't 'Farmer' Dan. But he was a farmer and in my head I always called him that. He was this handsome, burly guy who always wore plaid, and he was head-over-heels for my mother. He lived outside Philadelphia, which was virus-free. It was nice on the farm: Nick, my mom, and me with Farmer Dan.

"He also had a bunker full of supplies, so we felt safe there. If for some reason we couldn't get into the city or it became infected, we could hide out down there until it passed through. It seemed like everything would be okay. Like the worst was behind us."

She drew in another shaky breath and released it. "But it wasn't. Farmer Dan ran the city to stock up on supplies. It took all day because he had to pass the viral tests before he could get in to trade. Nick, my mom, and I were doing chores around the farm. I was in the barn with a couple of cows when this blaring noise came from the city.

"My mom came running and ordered us down to the underground bomb shelter. We didn't know what was happening yet, but I grabbed Nick from the pig shed and ran to the trapdoor of the bunker. He climbed down first, but when he was on only the top rungs of the ladder, the blast happened.

"I've never seen anything so bright as that blast. My mom made me look away, but even with my eyes shut I could see it. We turned back to the trapdoor, but it was closed. Nick must have slammed it shut. We pulled and pulled but it wouldn't open. 'Go!' my mom yelled, and she pushed me into a shed near the bunker. We made it in just before the heat wave hit; seconds later, the shock wave came and knocked us off our feet."

Fear shone in Zara's eyes. Time hadn't made the memory any less terrifying.

"When we got up we felt around in the dark to see what kind of supplies we might have. We were lucky it didn't have windows, or we'd have been burned alive in the heat wave, I'm sure, but the next two days there in the dark were hard. We found a tarp and hung it over the wall with the door to try to keep the radiation particles down. Then we huddled together and waited.

"We didn't know how long we had to wait before it would be safe to come out. We'd never learned anything about nuclear fallout or radiation—everyone was so worried about the virus and the bombings. All we knew about nuclear attacks was what we learned on the news after Washington, DC was hit. We didn't know much, but we formed a plan. We'd wait until the need for water was too great, then run as fast as we could to the bunker, hoping it would open.

"My mom would reassure me, 'There was something wrong with the lock. He'll have it fixed by the time we get there.' Our plan seemed perfect. In a few days, we would make our break for it, and hopefully the fallout would have died down enough for us to make it to the safety of the bunker. We thought we had a chance.

"But then Mom started getting sick. Really sick. The people who died right away in the blast were the lucky ones. She couldn't stop vomiting, even after there was nothing else in her stomach. She told me her skin felt like it was burning, and her mind became confused. There were a few times she passed out, and I'd shake her, panicking because I needed her to stay alive."

A tear glinted in the firelight as it ran down Zara's cheek. Nadia reached for her, then drew her hand back. The set of Zara's jaw said she needed to finish her story.

"Because we were in the dark, I didn't know how much time had passed. I would guess two days—not long. But then… she passed out again, and I couldn't wake her up this time. She was gone."

Zara's voice caught and she paused a moment, playing with a frayed hole in her jeans. Then she cleared her throat and continued.

"That's when I ran out of the shed, to the bunker, and pounded on the door as I cried for my mother. It opened. Nick stood on the ladder, his hand on the highest rung as he lifted the door open. He saw my tears and guessed that my mom was gone. 'I'm so sorry, Z,' he said. 'I just panicked and—'

"I've never thought as quickly as I did in that moment. Everything clicked into place. The door didn't jam. The lock wasn't broken. Nick, one of the two people in the world I loved, had locked us out. He'd killed the other person I loved, and left me to a slow, painful death.

"My vision flashed red, and I shoved him as hard as I could. He wasn't expecting it, and he fell backward into the bunker. His head hit the concrete floor with a sickening crack."

When she'd said "murderer", I thought she was exaggerating. I'd come close to needing to kill in self-defense a few times since the virus, but this was different.

"That scene has replayed over and over in my mind—and in my dreams," she continued. "I've tried to convince myself that I didn't know my own strength, that it was done in a moment of angered weakness, or that I didn't think he'd really fall. But the truth is, in that moment I wanted him dead. I watched the blood pool around his head on the floor, with this macabre, satisfied feeling that makes my skin crawl to this day. Then I realized what I'd done and I—I lost it.

"The whole city was dead. Farmer Dan was dead. My mom was dead. The pigs and chickens and cows were all dead. And I'd just killed Nick. I was totally alone, with no idea where to go. I went into the city, right in the middle where the bomb had hit. I told myself I was searching for other survivors, but really,

I was hoping the radiation from the fallout would kill me. It didn't. No matter what I did, I stayed alive. I felt cursed with survival."

Zara's gaze had been trained on the fire, but now she looked up at us. Well, not at us. Through us. "I don't know what else to say. I wandered for a long time. I drank a lot. I ate what I could find. By the time Coby found me, I was more stable.

"But I felt so guilty. Because I knew what I was, deep down. I'm a murderer. It wasn't self-defense. I didn't have to do it. Worse than that, I killed my *soulmate*. I relive it all the time in my nightmares. I'm always on the outside, watching myself do it, seeing Nick die. In the dreams, I scream at myself until no more sound will come out; I try to stop myself. But every time, it ends the same. I kill him.

"I told myself I wouldn't keep this secret from you forever. And now you know. I'm sorry I didn't tell you sooner, but—I wanted you to know the before-the-end me. I wasn't ready to face that she's gone."

None of us knew what to say as she stared off into the woods with a dead, ghostlike look, beyond tears now. I saw Coby's jaw hanging open before he shut it. Nadia looked at me, trying to see how I was reacting, like she didn't know what to think herself.

Coby stood and offered his hand to Zara. "It's late," he said. "We should get some sleep."

Without looking at him or taking his hand, she stood and walked back across the courtyard to the hospital. Coby followed. He opened the door and followed her inside with one last glance back at Nadia and me.

Just when it was his turn to tell us about his past.

24: Never Go Back
Nadia

Jake and I sat together for some time after Coby and Zara went inside. The silence was only broken by the wind rustling the trees overhead. What was there to say? I couldn't imagine what Zara had gone through this whole time, with that secret, the guilt weighing her down. At the same time, I had no idea what to say to her.

After the moon had risen in the sky, Jake said, "Coby didn't talk about his past," as he stirred the fire with an arm-sized stick. He added another log, and the fire was smothered for a moment before it burst back to life.

"Oh, come on, Jake. After Zara's story... it wouldn't have seemed right," I said, though I was suspicious too.

"If you say so."

"I do say so. Look, something weird is going on with Coby, but maybe it's not anything that should make us doubt him. He's only ever helped us."

"So far." Jake stopped poking the fire and we both gazed at the dancing flames. Eventually he asked, "Are we sure we want to go tomorrow?"

I shivered, but not from the chilly night air. "Don't you want to know the truth?"

"I'm not sure. Once we know we can never go back." His brown eyes shone in the firelight. "Like when I found out I was adopted—you know what that's like now, too."

I crossed my legs and ran my hands over the damp grass around me. "I'm still glad I know," I said. My parents using a surrogate still confused me, but... "The truth is better, even when it's painful."

"I keep thinking of that story about Pandora's box."

I nodded, smiling. One of the ways to my bookworm heart was Greek mythology. "That's a good one," I said.

"Right, and it had all the shitty things in the world in it, but she couldn't resist opening it," Jake said. I liked his summary. "What if that's us? We should leave well enough alone."

The wind shifted, and smoke from the fire filled my nose and made my eyes water. "What else would we do if we don't figure it out?" I remembered Coby urging me not to let the others give up. Wasn't Jake curious?

"We could find a place, a hobby farm or something, and settle down. Grow our own food, make a real plan for how we'll live the rest of our lives."

I couldn't help but smile when I imagined it. "Sure," I said. "We could have chickens and goats. A cow, even, and a big garden."

"We'd have bicycles to get around better, or maybe horses, and we could journey out sometimes to find other survivors. If there are any."

Shaking my head to clear the image away, I said, "There's plenty of time for that *after* we figure this out. Don't you need to know? What if it's our fault?"

Jake laughed. "There's no way it could be our fault. And I do want to know. I just don't know if we'll be happy that we found out afterward."

I nodded. The fire was dying again, and I watched the fading embers. "Do you know what I remember most about Pandora's box?"

"What?"

I shivered again, and Jake moved closer to me. "The last thing in the box—or the last thing to fly out, in some interpretations—was Hope. I think that was the biggest evil of all."

He studied me a moment. "Why?"

The warmth in my stomach from the rum was long gone now, and I felt tired. "It's the thing that keeps you holding on, long past the time to give up. It doesn't let you quit, even when that would make things better."

Jake put his arm around my shoulders and said, "Don't quit on me, Nadia."

I bit my lip and looked up at the stars to keep my eyes dry. His arm around me didn't radiate comfort as it should have. It just felt heavy.

"Hey," he said. "I got you something when I was out getting firewood today."

"You did?" I asked, surprised.

"Yeah," he said, pulling something from the bag at his side. "I—well, I noticed one of the trees had changed to its fall colors. It was a maple, and—here it is."

He dropped the broad leaf into my outstretched palm, and I admired its burgundy hue, laced with veins of gold. "Thank you," I whispered.

"So, uh, do you like it?" he asked, and I smiled to think Jake could feel self-conscious.

"Yes," I said. I longed to be living in the woods again. Fall had been my favorite time for hiking in the old world. "Thank you, Jake," I said again. "It's beautiful."

I spun the leaf stem between my fingers, transfixed by its colors. I couldn't have loved it more if he'd brought me a bouquet of a dozen red roses. This small gesture seemed to confirm Jake's interest in me. That should make me happy, right? I swallowed back the threatening tears.

Falling for him while he remained oblivious or indifferent was one thing; the chance that he could fall for me too was another matter entirely. The tragic end of Zara's romance, and her words, saying she couldn't pretend to be someone she wasn't anymore, came back to me. She was brave enough to reveal her whole story to us. I wasn't, not even to Jake.

I liked him—I couldn't help it. But he deserved better than me. If it wasn't the end of the world, a guy like Jake wouldn't look twice at me. He didn't know who I really was. He didn't know the whole story: the guilt, the need to punish myself, the shame.

"It's a little early for the leaves to turn," I said softly, still lost in my thoughts.

He didn't know I was a girl planning suicide when we first talked. Or that I'd rarely gone a single day without crying since my father died. How could he respect someone as weak as me? How could he love—no, I couldn't even imagine him loving me.

I didn't want to be the girl who had to lie about herself and pretend to be strong to deserve him. I could tell him the truth, but I also didn't want to be the girl who needed pity, who would make him feel heroic for saving me from myself. I just wanted to be me.

"I think the climate's changed, since the war," Jake said. I was only half-listening. "Fall is coming earlier."

There was no way to be who I was while also being with Jake. I couldn't let him fall for me. He wasn't falling for *me*, anyway. He was falling for the girl I was trying—but failing—to be.

I excused myself before things could get any more intimate. "Thanks again, Jake," I said softly. I let myself squeeze his hand, once. Then I stood, sliding my shoulders out from under his arm. "We might have a long day tomorrow. We should get some sleep. Sweet dreams."

He studied me for a moment, then said, "Sleep tight, Nadia." There was disappointment in his eyes, and I felt them trained on me as I walked back to the hospital's doors. When I slipped through, I glanced back and he waved to me. I returned the wave without smiling. The gesture had the somber feeling of a farewell, though I knew I'd see him tomorrow.

I kept the leaf, though. I pressed it between the pages of a book and set my pack on top, so it would hold its colors forever.

25: Dust of the Dead
Nadia

I woke the next morning with a throbbing headache and a swollen tongue. Since the virus, any unexplained symptoms set me on edge. I'd already taken my temperature (normal) and swallowed an aspirin (just in case) when Zara woke. She said it was time for my next series of shots, and I tried not to be jumpy about getting them from a newly confessed killer.

She was silent as she prepared the syringes. I watched her expressionless face as she pushed each dose into my arm, barely registering the pain. I wondered how things had gone so wrong in her life—in all our lives. How had the world made such a beautiful and carefree person into a killer, burdened her with guilt for the rest of her life? I felt a sudden flare of rage at humanity, for causing The End and making the lives of those left so tragic and precarious.

Next Zara examined my stitches, not touching my arm—a great contrast from before, when she'd gripped me and commanded that I share if I was tempted to cut again.

I wondered if she was really "guilty". What happened to her could've happened to any of us. Not that it mattered now. There were no more judges or courts, no one to figure out laws and justice. The line between right and wrong was as fuzzy as ever.

At least she'd been brave enough tell us what she'd done, her worst secret. I wasn't.

"These should be better healed by now," Zara said, without her usual lightheartedness. "Nothing looks wrong, it's just healing slowly. I can't take them out yet."

"We should find some vitamin C tablets," I said. "We're probably all deficient." I watched her carefully, and she seemed to be choosing each word cautiously.

"That's a good idea," she said. Then she pulled a towel the color of new leaves in spring out from the side of her bed. "I, uh, I got you this yesterday but forgot to give it to you."

I took the towel from her and smoothed it out on my lap, touched by the gesture.

When I didn't say anything, she continued, "I know we had that extra one you'd been using, but I felt bad because your nice one was ruined by the whole dog-thing."

Finally looking up at her, I said, "Thank you. It's even better than my old one."

"I tried to match the color," she said softly. "It's your favorite, isn't it?" She smiled, just a little.

I hugged her. "Yes, it is. Thanks."

Zara pulled out of the hug too soon, a shadow crossing her face.

I needed to tug the old Zara back to me. "Speaking of Vitamin C," I said. "I'm not feeling well this morning. I've got a terrible headache and I feel all groggy. Do you think something's wrong with me?"

She smiled, enough to dimple her cheek this time. That hint of normalcy—of the Zara I knew, and who was becoming like a sister to me—felt like a triumph. "You're hungover, Nod. That's all," she said.

"God, *this* is what hangovers feel like? Why would anyone drink?" I folded the towel smaller and crossed the room to stuff it into my pack.

Behind me, Zara said quietly, "Sometimes for fun. Sometimes to sleep, to forget…"

There was a knock on the door, and I heard Coby call, "Girls, are you ready? We should be hitting the road!"

I glanced at Zara and she nodded. "We'll be right out," I called back.

◆ ◆ ◆

If Newbury was an oasis in the desert, a place of safety (rabid dogs aside) and respite hidden among the desolate world, then Marion was Death Valley itself. The third strain of the virus had swept through the city quickly, leaving a trail of bodies and destruction.

The buildings here were beyond crumbling. Some were toppled, and others were scorched and charred from fires that had run rampant through its streets. I was used to seeing the haunting carcasses of cars arranged in a traffic jam; I wasn't used to seeing so many skeletons that still held human flesh sitting in them. Too many to look away from. A few trees and vines had dared to claim back some of the land, but for the most part the town was ghostly and grey.

The worst part, though, was the stench. It was at times like these that I remembered with vivid clarity that smells were not intangible things but actual particles of whatever you were smelling in the air. I pulled my shirt over my nose and mouth and tried not to hyperventilate; it would only cause more corpse particles to enter my lungs.

Eventually we got to a knot of cars that Coby couldn't weave his way through in the Mustang. I realized with dread that we had to leave the car and find the laboratory on foot.

Jake walked beside me as we continued, but the same eerie silence that had hung over the four of us in the car persisted. What was there to say in the face of so much devastation?

I struggled to keep my eyes strictly on the road in front of me, relying on the others to spot the lab, but a flap of crows' wings made me look to the right. They were feeding on two mostly fleshless human skeletons. One was seated on a bench and the other was lying on the ground, bones strewn about from the feasting scavengers.

I coughed, trying to rid my lungs of the dust of the dead. The cough turned into a retch and I ran behind a pickup, emptying the contents of my stomach onto the pavement.

When I came back to the group Jake handed me his water bottle in silence. I swished and spit, then gulped down more to soothe my burning throat.

"Disgusting, isn't it?" Coby said. His voice broke the silence and echoed as it carried through the defunct neighborhood.

"Yes," I said, my voice sharp, like ice. "But that's not what bothers me."

Zara pulled her shirt collar further up over her nose and Coby coughed. No one responded to me.

How was I the only one affected by what we were seeing?

"These were once people," I continued. "And they died in agony. The plague swept through so fast they had no time to bury the dead, no time to mourn. And before they knew it, there was no one left to miss them." My eyes grew wet and I knew I shouldn't have started. But I wanted to go on, to defend my tears. "No one but us. We can't grieve for them, because we never knew them."

My throat constricted, preventing me from saying more. Jake tried to put a hand on my shoulder, but I shrugged it away. I shoved his water bottle back into his hands and kept walking, now leading the way through the rubble. I didn't understand how the others could be so cold to the human lives lost here, and I was frustrated with all of them. A part of me missed being alone.

Nearly black clouds roiled overhead, choking out whatever sunlight attempted to break through. The air hung moist around us, intensifying the deathly odors and hinting at storms to come.

As the day wore on, my hope of ever finding the lab in this lifeless wasteland waned. Coming here had been futile. We'd never know why we'd survived when all the people in this city, and in the world, hadn't. I glanced over at Zara, who was ambling through the destruction with a vacant stare. A tear rolled down her cheek. Maybe she did feel the suffering that had happened here. Or she was still upset from the memories her confession had brought to the surface last night.

After a while my not-quite-healed muscles ached, and I asked the others if we should call it a day and return to the car.

"Not yet," Coby said.

"We should go back," Jake said. "We're far from the car now, and I don't think Nadia's up for this much walking yet."

"I'm fine," I lied with gritted teeth. I shouldn't be his concern.

"I want to keep going," Coby said. "I have a feeling we're close. Let's walk down that wider street up there. If we don't see anything by the end of it, we'll go back to the car."

I hoped that wider streets meant fewer jammed cars and rotted skeletons. "Okay," I agreed.

"If we don't find anything we can come back tomorrow and approach from a different highway," Jake said. "But I'd rather be back in Newbury where it's not as... you know."

We trudged down the street in silence, scanning the signs on the empty buildings we passed for the words "Winthrop Enterprises". I felt relieved, at least, that we had a plan to return to Newbury, and I was half-hoping we wouldn't find the lab. The air was thick with the smell of ozone and I knew it would rain soon. With all of the decaying bodies here, I imagined the after-rain smell wouldn't have its usual charm.

Coby stopped on the road ahead of us, and Zara, who wasn't looking, ran into him. He turned around to grin at Jake and me, then pointed down the street to our right. There was a large building of an architectural style that favored mirrored glass and sharp angles. It was relatively untouched compared to the other structures in the city. A few of the glass panels were broken, and it was clear that it was abandoned, but it was unburnt. The most important detail, however, was the sign. It was missing a few letters, but it read "Winth op Ente pr ses".

"We found it," Coby said. I could hear the smile in his voice.

26: Brewing Storm
Nadia

A flash of lightning, followed quickly by a peal of thunder, brightened the sky for a moment as we stood. We were still a few blocks from the building that was once Winthrop Enterprises.

Jake's words from the night before came back to me, and I wondered if he was right, and we should turn back now without any answers. The decaying state of Marion and the brewing storm both seemed like clear "turn back" omens to me, but Coby wouldn't let us leave now.

"It's going to rain," Jake said. "Let's get inside before it starts."

Coby and Jake led the way through the few cars that were abandoned on the street. Well, not all of them were abandoned. I felt my stomach turn over again as we passed more putrefying bodies. Some were strewn about the ground; others still sat in their cars. Death had caught them while they tried to escape their fate. I had to rip my gaze away from a skeleton with hollow eyes and bony hands, that had been pulled halfway from its car by scavengers, one of its hands still clutching the steering wheel.

Another rumble of thunder, then the floodgates opened. Rain fell in sheets and soaked through my clothes in moments. Since the war, you never knew if the rain stung your skin because it was cold or because it carried new dangers— radiation particles, the possibility of chemical burns.

"Get inside!" Coby yelled, running for the building's front doors.

Jake ran too, glancing over his shoulder to see me sprinting after them. "Zara!" he shouted, and I whirled around to see her still standing in the rain.

Raindrops pelted her face as they stung my own, but she didn't seem to notice. She stared vacantly at the ground, her hair drenched and plastered to her face.

I ran back and grabbed her hand, pulling her toward Coby and Jake. She wouldn't come; she was a dead weight against my arm. "Zara!" I shouted through the pounding rain. "Come on! It's not safe here. We need to get away and dry off."

She shook her head, droplets flying off the ends of her hair. "Leave me," she said. The drumming of the rain almost drowned out her voice.

"We need you Zara!" I shouted, yanking her arm harder. This time she stumbled after me. We reached the building after sprinting past the last few empty cars. We ran up the concrete steps and ducked under the awning with Jake and Coby, relieved to be out of the downpour.

"The doors are locked," Coby explained.

"Can Zara unlock them?" I asked. I wasn't hopeful as I saw the steel doors had no visible keyhole or lock, just two metal bars across each door that didn't budge when Coby pushed on them.

Zara shook her head to my question. Her teeth were already chattering.

"A lot of the windows are broken," Jake said. "We could try to crawl through one of them."

I was momentarily distracted by the rain glistening on his face and the way his shirt clung to his chest. "Uh, yeah, that's a good idea," I said, then leaned over the railing, peeking out from under the overhang and hiding my pink face. I refocused, examining the windows along the building to our left. The rain was still thick, but I could make out a shattered pane of glass on the ground floor.

"I see an opening," I said, turning back to the others. "It's close and might be big enough for us to squeeze through."

I kept my eyes trained carefully above Jake's muscled torso as he responded. "It's the best we've got. Ready?"

"Let's go," Coby said, and we all made a run for it.

As we reached the broken pane of glass, I realized bleakly that it was narrower than it had looked through the downpour. Zara, the smallest of us, wriggled through first. It likely wasn't her first time entering a building this way. Coby clambered through next, almost clipping his broad shoulder on a shard of glass.

I struggled to see Jake through the rain and the drops hanging from my eyelashes. He motioned for me to go next and I crouched, angling my shoulders to avoid the jagged window. I swung one leg through without a problem, but on the second leg my foot slipped. My knee would have been sliced open if Jake hadn't caught it and shoved me through. I rolled onto the tile floor and sat up, checking myself for any cuts. I was unscathed.

I turned to help Jake, but he was already through the window. He must have come through as he pushed me, and his hand was now dripping blood.

"Are you okay?" I asked, breathless. I pulled a bandana out of a side pocket of my pack. Taking his hand in both of mine, I covered the gash with the cloth and put pressure on the wound with my right hand.

"I'm fine," he said, grimacing. "It looks worse than it is."

I was as gentle as I could be while still applying the necessary pressure. I stole a glance at his face and my heart sped up, but not from fear. This wasn't good. "Zara?" I asked. "Do you have that first aid kit with you?"

"Yeah," she said, setting her bag on the ground and rummaging through it.

"Here," I said, placing Jake's left hand onto the bandana. "Keep pressure on it."

We'd climbed into some sort of conference room, with a long table and a dozen chairs. My skin wasn't tingling, so I didn't bother with my towel. Ready to explore, I turned toward Coby, but he'd already gone out the door.

I followed and found myself in a reception area with tall ceilings. Chairs and couches were arranged in huddles throughout the wide space and a large "Winthrop Enterprises" sign hung behind a broad front desk. Long-dead potted plants were scattered here and there. I crossed the room toward a darkened doorway, trying to get my flashlight out while still wearing my backpack.

Coby's face appeared, making me jump back and yelp. "Thank God," I said as I struggled to catch my breath. "It's just you."

He smiled and said, "We should see what we can find down this hallway, don't you think?"

"Sure Coby," I said as we walked back toward Jake and Zara. "Jake's hurt—"

The view stopped me in my tracks. The lab sat on a hill, and I hadn't looked behind me as we'd run up the sloping street to escape the rain. Now I couldn't look away.

Floor-to-ceiling windows offered a sweeping view of the city. At one time, it must have been beautiful. Now the panorama of cars scattered in random directions amidst disintegrating and scorched buildings, marred by the rain that flowed down the windows, made my heart ache.

"The bleeding's slowed," Jake said as he strode over to us, followed by Zara. "Let's get going."

She turned to see what I was staring at. "Oh," she breathed, touching my elbow briefly before pulling back her hand. "That's terrible."

We stood there for a few heartbeats, and my knees began to tremble. I didn't want to be here. We should head back to Newbury where we could pretend that everything was mostly okay—that things could go back to normal someday.

"We should see what we came to see," Coby said, breaking the spell.

I cleared my throat. "Yes, we should."

"I'm thinking we split up, two-and-two, and each take one side of the hallway," Coby said. "We'll look through the rooms and see if we can find anything."

Zara and Jake nodded, and my chest went tight with panic as I saw Zara move toward Coby.

I didn't trust myself alone with Jake. Not yet. My resolve not to let him fall for me was still new, soft. It would be some time before I could rely on it. "Coby and I will head down this hallway," I said, forcing a smile. "You guys head down there and check it out. We'll meet back here."

I was met by three surprised faces. The worst was the wounded look in Jake's eyes. I threw Zara a look.

The confusion didn't leave her face, but she said, "Let's go, Jake," and pulled him down the hallway to the right. "I need to finish bandaging your hand anyway," she said as they walked away from us. "Did I tell you I'm officially the team medic now?"

"After you," Coby said, sweeping an arm in front of him and smiling as he clicked on his flashlight. He, at least, didn't seem upset with the arrangement.

Water droplets from my soaked hair dripped down my back, chilling me, and fell onto the tiles as we walked.

"What are we looking for?" I asked, swinging my flashlight beam across the walls to either side of us. Up ahead were a few doors with windows in them.

"I think we'll know when we find it," Coby replied. Besides the beams of our two flashlights, the hallway was dim. I caught a light antiseptic smell that reminded me of the hospital.

We reached one of the doors and I peered through the wire mesh that went through the glass, one eye closed. It looked like my high school chemistry lab. Wooden cupboards topped by black counters lined the walls, some with sinks in them. "Do you think there's anything in here?"

"No," Coby said. "Let's try this one." He'd already moved on to the next door. As he swung it open, I wondered why it wasn't locked. Maybe looters just weren't into lab equipment.

I passed through the door and my light illuminated various large machines sitting throughout the room. I couldn't identify most of them, but they looked scientific and expensive. There was one with two eyepieces which I guessed was a microscope. My fingers moved to switch it on instinctively, but of course there was nothing to power it. A glass slide was clipped onto the platform beneath the lens. I reached in to pull it out, careful to touch only the edges of the slide.

"'*Hemidactylus frenatus*'," I read from the label. "Any idea what that means?"

Coby snorted. "You think I know Latin?"

I squinted at the slide, seeing only a speck, and sighed. For all I knew, Coby spoke Swahili. I was going to comment on that when I realized he'd already left the room. Slipping the slide back under the clips of the platform, I picked up two others from the counter: "*Aquila chrysaetos*" and "*Blattella germanica*". They seemed like scientific names for plants or animals, but I didn't know enough about biology to recognize them. I set them back down and followed Coby out of the room.

He turned a corner up ahead, out of sight. I jogged to catch up with him, irritated that he'd left me behind. He skipped another door to our left and I called to him, "Coby, wait—let's look at this one."

The doorknob jiggled open with a push and I walked inside. This room was full of old medical equipment. There were racks with hanging IV bags, wheeled stretchers, and carts full of devices topped by computer monitors. Boxes were stacked against the wall, but when I lifted the lid to look through one, Coby said, "There's nothing here. Let's keep going."

I jumped at his voice. He leaned against the doorway with his arms crossed. Lightning struck outside and flashed across his face in an unsettling way. I swallowed the words I was going to say: "How do you know?"

Instead I nodded as I followed him out the door. *You trust Coby. He's fine, it's just lightning,* I told myself as my heart pounded against my ribs and I mentally berated myself for not pairing up with Zara.

Coby skipped all the other doors as well. I glanced into the ones that had windows but otherwise followed him, not

117

wanting to push any buttons and anxious to get back to Jake and Zara. We rounded the next corner and almost ran into the two of them.

They were grinning, their eyes still full of laughter. One of them must have made a joke. I crossed my arms. If I hadn't paired us like this, I could be laughing with either of them instead of worrying about Coby.

"Did you find anything?" Coby asked, calm.

"Nothing interesting," Jake said. "There was a room like a doctor's office, one labelled 'operating room' that was locked, some storage, and another conference room."

Coby nodded. "Let's go upstairs."

We were next to a stairwell, the door marked with a red logo that showed a man running downstairs, away from a fire. Coby held the door open and Jake smiled at me as he passed through. *Wish I could run*, I thought to the man on the door. Though I wasn't sure what from.

I trudged up the stairs behind Zara and Jake. We reached a landing area with another door. I couldn't hear anything, but the air seemed less stale. This floor felt more 'alive' than the other.

"Shall we?" Coby asked as he grasped the door handle.

The door swung open and Zara gasped.

There, in the second-floor laboratory of his headquarters, we found Dr. Peter Winthrop himself.

PART TWO

That's the thing about human life—
there is no control group,
no way to ever know how any of us
would have turned out
if any variables had been changed.
— Daniel Keyes

1: 0.2%
Nadia

A figure clothed in a yellow hazmat suit stood in the room, faced away from us. My breath caught, waiting for a sound or movement to indicate life, proof that it wasn't a mannequin wearing the suit. When the right arm moved, placing something on the table, we all jumped.

My mind raced. I struggled to adjust to the fact that there was another living person besides the four of us. I wasn't sure if it made me hopeful or terrified.

Coby, apparently the bravest of us, stepped forward and said, "Hello?"

The figure turned, and the slowness of the movement did not agree with me. If I were them, I'd be startled to see four teenagers in my laboratory after the world had ended.

It was a man. The bottom half of his face was obscured by a respirator, but I could glimpse a bit of short grey hair and black-rimmed glasses through the clear plastic of the respirator's face-shield. Beyond him I could see that this floor was one giant laboratory, with more machines than I'd seen in any of the rooms downstairs. Fluorescent lights flickered down on us, so he must have had a working generator as well.

"What do we have here?" the man said, and I flinched. His voice was gravelly and machine-like through the respirator.

I tensed, barely stopping myself from grabbing Jake's hand, which dangled close to mine.

Coby spoke again. "Survivors. We're hoping you can tell us how we're still alive."

"Perhaps I can. What are your names?"

"We'd like to know yours first," Jake said.

I thought the man smiled, but it was hard to tell through the shiny plastic. "Of course," he said. "Doctor Peter Winthrop, at your service."

It wasn't unexpected, but my eyebrows raised in surprise anyway. The four of us stood in stunned silence, although Coby grinned.

"And your names are?" the Doctor prompted.

"Jake Atwater." He didn't move to shake the doctor's hand, so the rest of us didn't either.

Zara said, "Nice to meet you, Doctor. I'm Zara Nicollet." She bowed theatrically, and I was glad to see a spark of the old, happy Zara.

I shivered; my clothes were still soaked. "Nadia Madison."

"And you?" he turned to Coby, whose smile faltered.

"Coby. Coby... Fairfax," he said. His chin tilted down, and he frowned.

"Ah, yes. I'm delighted you all survived!" the doctor said, his expression indiscernible through the suit.

"You know who we are?" Zara asked.

"Yes. I *created* you," he said.

"Like... you're the father of all of us," Zara said. She didn't say it as a question; acknowledging that him "creating" us could have any other meaning would be insane.

The doctor laughed then. It came out as a deep, mechanical snigger through the mask. "No, not at all like that," he said. "I created you here, in this very laboratory."

My heart pounded in my ears, but I was too afraid to ask the next question.

"How... how did you do that?" Zara continued, her voice trembling.

"What's different about us?" Jake spoke this time, slowly, as if it took an effort to sound calm.

"I performed an experimental procedure on your DNA," the doctor said evenly, as if he was discussing the weather or a news article. A chill ran down my spine and my knees wavered.

"Wh-what sort of experiment?" Zara's chin trembled.

"I combined your DNA with that of *blattella germanica*."

"Hold up, you're telling us… we aren't completely *human*?" Zara asked.

There was a wrinkly noise as the doctor nodded in his suit. "Not entirely. About 99.8%."

I glanced at the others. "What else are we? What's this… blat-something?"

I caught the doctor's grin through his suit. "I'll give you three guesses. And a hint: I created you when I thought the world would end by nuclear war."

Jake had crossed his arms. He uncrossed them and said, "You don't mean…"

Zara inhaled. "Not… *cockroaches*?"

The doctor grinned wider, raising the hairs on my arms. I looked at my hands and wondered if they could truly be 0.2% insect. My skin crawled as I felt phantom cockroach legs run up and down my arms

"That can't be," Coby said tonelessly.

"That's what everyone told me," the doctor said. "But, here you are. *Survivors*."

I fought the urge to empty the contents of my stomach for the second time that day. "You really *created* us?"

"Yes."

He seemed to relish our stares, continuing, "First I isolated the protein that controls how often cells split and multiply in the cockroach. If I could add that to the right allele of *your* DNA, the rate at which your cells multiply would slow. This makes them less susceptible to radiation. The drawback is that any injuries take longer to heal in your bodies than in those of regular humans.

"Of course, that doesn't seem to have hurt you thus far. It also made you immune to the disease. A curious side effect of the recombinant DNA."

The more scientific he got the less I understood. One thing was perfectly clear, though: we'd survived because we were science experiments. *Freaks.*

That should have upset me, but I felt oddly serene. I didn't like being here with the doctor one bit, but I didn't feel surprised. Deep down I'd always known I was different, wrong. *Inhuman.*

I glimpsed his frown through the mask, but he blathered on again. "You see, with the slowed rate of regeneration, less cell death from the radiation will occur. My theory was that you could survive a dose as high as 2000 rem." The doctor ended his onslaught of scientific words. "You're dripping on my floor, and I'm in the middle of an experiment. Why don't you go upstairs? I'll be there in half an hour. Do you have dry clothing to change into?"

I glanced at the other three, but they all seemed stunned, trying to process what they'd just learned about themselves. I spoke up. "No, they're—" I started to say "still in the car", but caught myself. I wasn't sure if we should tell him we had a vehicle. "Not with us," I finished.

"Very well, I'll get you some dry clothing, too. But I really *must* finish this experiment. It's time-sensitive." He opened his arms wide and made a shooing motion with his yellow-gloved hands.

I pulled Jake with me and wrapped my other arm around Zara. Coby followed the three of us back into the stairwell.

2: Very Bad or Very Insane
Nadia

For the first time since we'd all met, I was the one keeping it together. Out in the stairwell, Coby slid down the wall into a seated position. His face was pale, accentuating his freckles. Jake ran upstairs to the third floor before I could say anything to him. Zara sat next to Coby, wrapped her arms around herself and shivered. She bit her lip and stared blankly at her knees.

At least we were all freaks together. *You can be strong for them.* I crouched beside Zara and she let me gently pull off her backpack. I took out her towel and wrapped it around her shoulders, squeezing her wet hair out onto the floor beside her. She took one side of the towel and threw it over Coby's shoulders.

"He has to be lying," she murmured, her eyes vacant as she stared at the ground.

"Maybe," I said as I patted her knee. "But I don't think so. I'm going to check on Jake, okay?"

She nodded. I stood and looked at the two of them, huddled together. Coby looked so stricken, crushed by what we'd learned, that I felt awful for being worried about him a few minutes ago.

How often in life does everything completely change in just a few minutes? Too many times in my life so far.

Zara looked almost as pitiful, but at least they were together and could dry off now. I dropped my pack next to them after I extracted my towel from it. Swinging the towel through the air and wrapping it around myself like a cloak, I followed Jake, my boot heels clicking on the steps.

I opened the door to a hallway like the one we'd explored on the first floor, except this one was well-lit. The first door on the right was ajar, light shining out from it, so I slipped inside.

The room was another lab, filled with cages and tanks of various animals. There were albino rabbits, birds in cages, lab rats running in exercise wheels, aquariums of fish and lizards, and even a pen with a small pig. I found Jake there, staring into a tank full of cockroaches.

I went to his side, peering into the tank and shuddering at the insects' jittery movements. The thought of having DNA in common with these filth-eating pests made bile rise in my throat. I swallowed it down and looked at Jake. "Hey," I said weakly.

"Hey," he said back.

"Are you okay?" I asked. "This is some weird shit we found out."

Jake laughed, one sharp *ha!* "That's an understatement." He turned to me. "How are you okay with this?"

I winced, remembering how often I *hadn't* been okay around Jake and the rest of them. "I don't know," I said, shrugging one shoulder. "I always felt something was messed up with me. Now I have confirmation."

"There's nothing wrong with you. Or at least, nothing wrong with you that isn't also wrong with the rest of us." He sighed and stared at the roaches again, unable to keep his eyes from them. My skin crawled and seeing them skitter around didn't help.

I wanted to say or do something to comfort Jake but was at a loss. We'd had too many reality shifts for one day. It was a bit much to ask that we adjust to the fact that not only was Peter Winthrop real, and alive, but that he'd *created* us, and in a completely sickening way.

"He must have made it up," Jake said, crossing his arms. "This is like something out of a bad sci-fi movie."

"Do you have a better explanation for why we're still alive?" I asked. "If any of us hadn't already contracted the third strain of the virus, walking through Marion today would have given it to us. We'd all be dead by now. And you heard Zara's story, about surviving the nuclear attack."

I circled the room, looking into tanks and cages. One of the rats had strange fur, almost like feathers. I was about to point it out to Jake when a turtle in the next aquarium caught my eye.

"Look at this." I peered into the tank, admiring the glowing blue stripes on the turtle's shell as it munched a piece of lettuce.

"Christ," Jake said. "That's not natural."

"Seems like proof that he really could have experimented on us. That it's true."

Jake looked up at the tank above the turtle's, which held a bright green snake. Sharp bumps, some up to two inches in length, protruded at random along its back. They looked painful, and the snake was lethargic, its forked tongue slipping out of its mouth and lolling to the side as it stared at us. I shuddered; snakes always did that to me.

"What kind of person *does* something like this?" Jake asked.

I straightened, speaking around the thumbnail I'd been chewing. "Either a very bad or a very insane one."

We glanced around the lab, looking for more of the doctor's creations, but besides a few more rats and hamsters with feather-like fur, the other animals appeared normal. We found ourselves returning to the tank of cockroaches.

"We would be perfectly normal people if he hadn't used us for his twisted experiment," Jake said. "Just like that snake."

"If we were normal people, we'd be dead now."

"What?"

"Whatever he did to us, it made us immune to the virus," I said. "Unfortunately, we owe him our lives."

"You know it's not enough to be thankful that we've survived. What about everyone we've lost. What about *living*?"

"I... I know. What he did was wrong—immoral and unethical on so many levels. But at the same time, we're *alive*."

Jake nodded slowly. "But for how much longer?"

"What do you mean?" I took a step back from the cockroaches, closer to Jake.

"We're experiments—he has no idea what could happen with us. We could have the lifespan of a cockroach now and all die in a couple of years. Or we get some horrible disease that *normal* humans can't get." He kicked at the aquarium stand and we both watched the wretched insects skitter around.

I shuddered and waited for another wave of nausea to pass. "But we've *already survived* the deadliest disease in human history. It's not all bad, being a—" I meant to say "cockroach hybrid", but found I couldn't push the distasteful words out of my mouth.

"Didn't you hear him?" Jake said. "He was *surprised* that we survived the virus. He had no idea we'd be immune."

"Okay, so it wasn't intentional, but he still saved us. We owe him *something*." I boosted myself onto the countertop behind us. Letting my legs dangle, I focused on them and tried to block out the quiet noises of the lab animals in the room.

Jake leaned on the counter next to me. "He couldn't have known what doing that to our DNA would do to us. He didn't even know we'd survive the virus."

"Lucky break for us. But how could he have known about the virus? No one knew. That's why everyone's dead and we're alive—by accident."

"He did *survive* it. Are we *sure* he didn't know about it?" Jake held my gaze for a moment before I had to look away. There was something fierce—wild—in his eyes.

"He does seem awfully prepared…" I admitted.

"It's hard to piece together what happened after the second strain, since everything fell apart then, but didn't they think the disease was developed as a biological weapon?"

My hands shook when I realized what he was implying. "Yes," I whispered.

"What if Winthrop had something to do with it? What if he *helped weaponize it?*"

I took a deep breath. "It's possible. But even if he didn't, I want to get the hell out of here."

"I agree. We have our answer, let's get out. This whole place gives me the creeps and I don't trust Winthrop at all. He might want to run tests on us. Expose us to radiation—who knows."

"We were his guinea pigs," I said, nodding. "But we can't leave tonight. It's late, still raining, and it would be hard to find the car in the dark. Plus, we haven't eaten anything all day."

"Agreed. Let's stay here tonight, but right before first light tomorrow we'll sneak out and leave. If we find any supplies that would be useful we'll take them, but we really just need Coby and Zara." Jake squeezed my hand then, impulsively.

I smiled at him. "We'll get through this. There's four of us and one of him."

Jake nodded, still unable to smile.

"Speaking of which, we should get back and let them know what's up."

"No," Jake said suddenly. "Don't tell them. Or at least not Coby."

I rolled my eyes. "Come *on*, Jake. He doesn't know anything. You saw him! He was devastated. He's one of us. *On our side.*"

Jake sighed as he slid his arm off the counter. He took both my hands in his to help me hop down. I was gentle with his left hand, which had been carefully bandaged by Zara. His right palm was warm and rough in mine. Our faces were close as he said, "Maybe you're right. But can you trust me on this? I'll tell him in the morning before we leave."

"Okay," I breathed. But I would have agreed to anything right then. His eyes, a warm dark brown, like coffee, and his woodsy scent were taking all my attention.

There was a loud *thunk* as one of the roaches in the tank flew up and hit the glass, and we pulled away from each other, remembering what we were. I hoped there were working showers in the building, though I knew I wouldn't ever be able to wash the roach out—it was embedded in every one of my cells.

Jake looked at the tank and said, his voice laced with bitterness, "I'm adopted. I probably have more DNA in common with those *things* than my own parents."

I put my arm around his shoulders, half to comfort him, and half to move us out of the room faster. "That's not true," I said halfheartedly. But what about my parents? If they'd used a surrogate, did that mean they knew? Did they give him permission to experiment on me?

We reached the top of the stairs and I withdrew my arm from his shoulders. As we descended, turning around the railing and toward the door to the second-floor lab, my stomach dropped. Coby, Zara, and my pack were gone. There was a puddle on the floor where they had been.

3: Accommodations
Nadia

I started to run, but Jake grabbed my elbow and pulled me back. I almost tumbled down the steps, but caught myself and turned to him, on the edge of tears. *They have to be okay.* Jake held one finger to his lips, and I took a deep breath. *Quiet.* I nodded my head, and he released my elbow.

We crept down the stairs and over to the laboratory door. I felt my hands shaking, so I clenched them into fists as Jake clasped the door handle and slowly pulled it open. The lab was dark. Jake stepped into the room, and I followed closely behind. He illuminated the room with his flashlight, making the humming lab equipment cast long shadows across the walls and floor, before he found the light switch and flipped it on.

"No one's here," Jake breathed.

"We should check the third floor," I said. "We don't know what's up there, and that's where he told us to wait, isn't it?"

"But we were just there."

"Wait—up there," I said, pointing.

On top of a set of cabinets sat a collection of specimen jars. We stepped forward to look, and I yelped when I saw what floated in the largest: a rat with wings like a crow's. Other experiments were suspended in each jar, but none looked quite as successful. A rat with claw-like hands, a lizard missing a few limbs, a hamster with a forked tongue.

"Yeah, we need to find the others and get out of here," Jake said. "*Now.*"

We exited the lab. I blinked, trying to adjust my vision in the hallway. The storm had calmed outside and there was no lightning to guide our way.

"The first floor looked abandoned. I don't think the doctor goes down there," I whispered. We started back up the stairs, placing our feet carefully, not making any noise.

A shaft of light split the hall ahead, and we heard voices wafting through the sliver of doorway. We reached the door as quickly and quietly as we could and swung it wide. I wished I had my bow or my gun, but we were totally defenseless.

The room was not another laboratory, as I had expected, but a bedroom. Zara was perched on the edge of a double bed, and Coby sat on a wooden chair turned outward from its matching desk. My pack leaned against one side of the desk. The doctor stood next to a half-open door, through which I could see a small bathroom. They all stared at Jake and me as we entered. Zara and Coby smiled, and I tried to relax.

"Ah, there you are," the doctor said. "I was showing Zara and Coby their accommodations."

I saw Jake swallow and try to relax out of the corner of my eye. His shoulders stayed stiff. *Jake's paranoia strikes again.* Hadn't the doctor told us to wait for him up here?

"Do you mind sharing with Zara?" the doctor asked me.

"Oh, um, no. Not at all."

"Excellent." His cheeks lifted, and I imagined a flash of white teeth through the respirator. "Let me show Coby and Jake to their rooms then."

The doctor left the room and Coby followed. Jake turned to me. "See you in the morning," he said.

"Okay," I said. "Stay safe."

He nodded and left, after one last glance at me. I deadbolted the door behind them. I was alone with Zara, who was still wearing her towel and didn't look half as anxious as I felt. "Is everything okay?"

"Yeah," she said. "Even more okay because there's a shower in here. I'm grossed out, but it'll help to get clean." She grabbed the shampoo bottle we shared from her pack and slipped through the door.

I dragged my pack next to the bed, then sat and stared at the locked door while Zara was in the shower, my determination to be strong starting to crumble. Tears didn't come, though, and I puzzled over why that was. Maybe my tear ducts had finally reached their lifetime limit. Perhaps I was just thankful that we'd found Coby and Zara. Or maybe the relief at having an explanation for the "otherness" I'd always felt was outweighing the creepy-crawlies that explanation had given me.

My hunger had come back, so I pulled a can of Spam from my bag and popped the top open, then used the fork from my mess kit to gulp down half the contents. I set the remainder on Zara's bed. It wasn't great cold, but I'd eaten much worse.

Flopping onto the bed, I exhaled slowly and stared at the fluorescent light bulbs on the ceiling. We'd be leaving at first light, and everything would be fine. Or as fine as it could be under the apocalyptic circumstances.

A doorknob jiggled and I bolted upright, my hand reaching instinctively for the revolver in my pack. It was just Zara though, coming out of the bathroom wrapped in a towel, her hair dripping. She didn't make eye contact with me as she crossed the room. Her skin was pink and raw, as if she'd scrubbed it too hard, trying to get the cockroach out. I tried to think of something to say but failed. I bit my lip, grabbing my towel and heading to the bathroom myself.

Sitting in the tub, I turned the shower as hot as it would go and let it pound my back and scalp. Between the ghastly trek through the city that morning and the horrifying revelation of the afternoon, a hot shower was exactly what I needed to clear my head.

But instead of relaxing, I panicked as my thoughts ran wild.

Sure, we could leave at dawn tomorrow—but what then? Would the doctor come after us? Could he, without his hazmat suit and stockpiled supplies? Had any other normal humans survived? If we found some, would we have to hide what we were from them? What if Jake was right, and we'd die sooner than other humans, or develop a disorder? What if we were infertile? The doctor might have doomed humanity while trying to save it. If we even counted as "the human race" anymore.

I tried to keep my breathing slow, to avoid panicking. The spray of the shower was cooling off, and I realized I still hadn't washed myself. I stood unsteadily, taking another deep breath. *In, out.*

That was when I saw Zara's razor, sitting on the edge of the tub. It looked just like the one I'd taken apart when I first started to cut. I tried to keep my eyes off it, shampooing and washing myself quickly, racing to finish before temptation could claw into me. I'd been doing so well since finding the others.

I slammed the knob off and jumped out of the shower, wrapping the towel around me and sitting on the toilet, my face in my hands. *You resisted. Be proud*, I told myself. But instead I felt guilty for thinking about cutting in the first place.

Zara was already sleeping—or at least pretending to sleep—once I'd dressed in my pajamas and reentered the bedroom. I curled up beneath the blanket, on the opposite side of the bed from her, and let my weariness pull me into sleep.

◆ ◆ ◆

I woke to knocking on the door. Zara woke too, but I mumbled, "I'll get it," and rolled out of bed. It was a few disoriented moments before I realized where we were, that yesterday hadn't been an insane dream. I stretched as I crossed the room and tried to look through the crack in the door, but I couldn't see anything.

"Who is it?" I asked.

"Jake. Open up."

I slid the deadbolt to the side and cracked open the door, yawning. "What?"

"Coby's gone."

That woke me up. "Seriously, *again*? How does that happen?"

136

"We had separate rooms. What was I supposed to do, sneak in there and watch him sleep all night?"

"At least we'd know where he was!" My heart pounded and I fought back panic.

Jake's lips were a tight line. "We've got to find him."

Zara had heard our exchange and was already throwing on her jacket. I shut the door and dressed quickly too, pulling my boots on without tying them. I didn't make the mistake of leaving my pack this time—I swung it over my shoulder as we met Jake outside the door.

All the labs on the third floor were empty, except for the one with its test animal occupants. "First floor?" Zara asked as we watched Jake's flashlight beam move around the empty second-floor lab.

"I guess," I said. "God, I hope he's okay."

We checked the unlocked rooms on the first floor, but there was no sign of him there either. A twinge of doubt pulled at my mind. Was this just Jake's paranoia? After all, we'd been looking for Coby and Zara like this yesterday and there had been a perfectly logical explanation.

"Should we re-check the third floor?" Jake asked.

"I don't know," I said. "We checked it pretty well the first time. Is there a base—"

"Shh!" Zara hissed, and we all stood at attention, listening. A murmur of human voices echoed down the hall. "They're in the lobby," she whispered, and took off running.

"Wait—Zara!" I whisper-shouted. Jake and I both ran, trying to stop her, but she was too fast for us. We both careened around the corner as she entered the lobby.

"Oh, hey guys," I heard her say, not out of breath at all. Jake and I jogged into the room behind her.

If I hadn't already been gasping from the exertion of the chase, I would have gasped at the heartbreaking view, before us once again. How could the doctor stand to be here? Didn't he feel the emptiness, the isolation of being one of the last people on Earth?

Maybe it was our presence. Maybe he hadn't been able to look at it when he'd believed he was the last man alive, but now we'd brought him hope.

Coby and the doctor, who was still in his yellow hazmat suit, sat at two of the chairs in the lobby. Zara had taken a seat near them, and Jake and I stood facing them and tried to catch our breath.

"There you are," the doctor said. "I was about to send Coby to wake you. We're having breakfast." He swept a yellow-gloved hand over the low table between them.

Four plates were laid out, and a scent I'd never expected to smell again—melted butter and maple syrup—hit my nose. On each plate was a stack of toaster waffles. The one nearest Coby was half-eaten.

"How did you manage to get these?" Zara asked conversationally, scooping up the plate closest to her and grabbing a fork from the middle of the table.

"I have several freezers full of food like this," he replied. "As long as the generators continue to run, you won't go hungry here."

I glanced at Jake. So much for our escape-at-dawn plan. "And," I said, biting my lip. "How long do you plan on us... being here?"

Jake shot me a glare that said I should have kept my mouth shut, and Zara looked at me as if I was crazy, but I didn't care. I wanted straight answers.

The doctor laughed in response, the sound as jarring through the respirator as it had been yesterday. "As long as you'd like to stay!" he said. "You're certainly free to leave if you feel unhappy here. Though I'm not sure how waffles could cause such offense."

"That's... not what I meant," I said meekly. Jake and I approached the table and took our plates. I hesitated before taking a bite, glancing first at the doctor, then at Coby. Coby was still alive and conscious, so they must be fine. The way the

138

doctor looked at me after I'd swallowed the first bite made me second-guess myself, though. I set them back on the table.

"Delicious," I said. "Thank you."

"Eat up," the doctor said. He stood, and the suit made a rippling noise. "I've got another long experiment today, but I'm hoping you'll all join me for a formal dinner tomorrow evening."

Coby nodded enthusiastically, and Zara said, "Sure," smiling at him.

The doctor left the room without waiting for a response from me or Jake. As he passed I noted that he was my height. Yesterday, in the laboratory, the situation and his suit had made him seem to tower over us. He turned before he left and said, "Oh, and Coby tells me that the rest of your things were left in his car out in the city. Perhaps you could retrieve them today?"

Jake and I turned synchronously to glare at him as the doctor swished out of the room. *Damnit, Coby. The one thing we had going for us—a secret escape vehicle.* I knew we should have told him about the plan.

4: Paranoid
Jake

"Coby, why *the hell* would you tell him about the car?" Nadia hissed, crossing her arms.

A crease appeared between his eyebrows. "What? Why wasn't I supposed to tell him?"

"Because we were going to escape this morning!" Nadia rolled her eyes and flopped onto the chair next to Zara's.

"Escape? Why do we need to escape?" Coby sounded utterly confused, with an undertone of hurt. Nadia glared at me. She had wanted to tell the others last night.

"Because we don't trust him," I said.

"Why? Did he do something?" Coby asked, and Zara gave us a puzzled look, too.

"It's a gut feeling," Nadia told him. "Even if we didn't leave this morning, like Jake and I wanted to, we at least could have kept the car a secret as a backup plan."

"Look, I'm sorry, but I don't see why you want to leave," Coby said.

"Me neither," Zara said, setting her empty plate back on the table. "Don't get me wrong. What the doctor did to us was hella creepy. But we're alive thanks to him, and it doesn't seem so bad here. It's safe, and there's electricity and plenty of food. Besides, I think the doc wants to get to know us. In a super twisted way, we're like his kids."

"*Or* he wants to run experiments on us," I said. "We saw all kinds of crazy stuff upstairs—feathered rats, a glowing turtle."

"Yeah, and don't you find it a bit suspicious *how* prepared he is for the end?" Nadia added.

Coby was starting to look angry. "The guy's a genius! Of course he's prepared. Why are you being paranoid?"

Nadia sighed. "We're trying to be careful, that's all."

"I get that," Zara said. "But he hasn't *done* anything to make us not trust him. Give the guy a chance. I'd like to see that turtle, by the way."

"Coby, you didn't tell him *what* we had in the car did you?" Nadia asked.

"I told him we had clothes, canned food, first aid supplies, and—" He paused, as if realizing he'd erred, and continued in a lower voice, "Jake's rifle and your bow."

I threw my hands in the air. "Our *weapons?* Coby... Winthrop doesn't need to know about those!"

"What was I supposed to do?" Coby asked, holding his hands out in a helpless gesture. "Lie to him?"

"Did he *ask* you what weapons we had?" I asked.

"What? No, of course not."

Nadia groaned. "Then why would you tell him?"

Coby stared at his sneakers. "I'm sorry," he said softly. "I just hate lying."

The anger melted from Nadia's face, and she knelt beside his chair. "I know, Coby. But this isn't the world we grew up in. Sometimes a lie could be the difference between life and death. Just try not to tell him any more than necessary, okay?"

His hazel eyes met hers and he nodded. I stood and said, "Alright then. We should go to the car."

"I'll change," Zara said. She was still wearing her pink fleece pajamas with polar bears on them under her jacket.

"And I need my pack," Coby said. He grabbed his plate and fork and the two of them headed upstairs. Nadia and I, who both had our packs with us already, were left alone.

"Stick together!" I called after them, too late.

Nadia sighed and sat back in her chair, pulling a plate of waffles onto her lap.

Clearly Zara and Coby were still alive and conscious, so I reluctantly crossed to a chair and grabbed the last plate. I sniffed them, and Nadia laughed.

"Jake, they're fine. You can't tell anything by smelling them anyway." I took a bite, and she stifled a laugh again. "I've never seen someone glower while eating waffles."

"These are cold," I said.

"Obviously. We spent forever talking to the doctor and yelling at Coby."

"No, I mean... they've been out for a while. Long enough for Coby to tell Winthrop everything about us." I forked more waffle into my mouth.

"Coby trusts him, I guess, though I have no clue why. You know, we could drive off when we get to the car, get out of here. I just... I don't know if we can convince Zara and Coby to go." Nadia stared at her hands in her lap.

I set my fork down and asked, carefully, "Would you be willing to leave without them?"

"No," she said, her voice suddenly rough. "I can't."

"I didn't think so," I said, setting my empty plate back on the table. "We need to convince them to leave. Or at least not to trust Winthrop so much."

Nadia stared at the city through the floor-to-ceiling windows and nodded. The shattered panels of glass broke up the view unnaturally.

Zara and Coby swept into the room, laughing. I felt a prickle of irritation. Why were they letting their guard down? Zara chucked something at me, and I caught it by instinct. I turned it over in my hands, examining it, then watched as Zara put on hers.

It was a respirator, like those everyone tried to wear during the second strain, before we knew they didn't work.

"No, I am your father," Zara said, doing a decent Darth Vader through the mask before devolving into a fit of rasping laughter.

"Where did you get these?" I asked, my voice tight.

"We ran into the doc while we were headed to our rooms," she said after removing the mask. "He said that if we made it through the city without getting the virus yesterday we're probably fine, but that we should take these as a precaution."

Nadia glanced at me as I held my mask by the strap, away from me. She clasped hers in one hand but didn't put it on. *Are we being too cautious?* I tried to think if there was any way the masks could be harmful. If there was knock-out gas in them, Zara would already be out cold.

"Let's get going," I said, interrupting Zara and Coby's reenactment of another scene from *Star Wars*.

"I find your lack of faith disturbing," Zara intoned through the respirator, then turned back to us, and said, "Sure, Jake."

I dropped my mask on the table in defiance as I stood.

The four of us set off, being sure to prop open the front doors this time so we wouldn't have to crawl through the broken window again. The sun was warm overhead, making the earthy, sickly sweet smell of rotting bodies worse. With that constant reminder of death all around us, we didn't talk much. As if we didn't want the dead to overhear. Despite the sunny day, I shivered.

I hadn't paid close attention to our route, and we found ourselves following Nadia. The trek felt shorter than yesterday. The way back, when the destination and distance are known, always does, and we reached the car as the sun reached its highest point overhead—solar or high noon.

Nadia and I reached the car first. After pulling my rifle from the unlocked trunk, I turned to watch Zara and Coby, who were a half-block behind, catch up. "We might never be able to leave if we don't go now," I said, shading my eyes to see Nadia through the sun reflected off the Mustang.

She nodded and sat on the hood of the car, her foot resting on the chrome bumper.

Squinting in the sunlight, I saw Zara take off her mask, and her solemn face—so unnatural for her—showed that she already knew what we had planned. Coby looked as confused as he had at breakfast. He removed his respirator so we could talk.

"Jake and I think we should leave," Nadia said.

Zara blinked a few times. "Leave?"

"Why?" Coby asked.

I stifled a groan.

"Because we don't trust that madman," I said, adjusting the rifle strap on my shoulder. "We're better off on our own."

"He doesn't seem bad to me. Crazy, sure, and I'm disturbed by what we are, but he seems like he wants to take care of us," Zara said.

"What if he's taking care of us the way he does his *lab rats*?" Nadia asked.

Coby opened his mouth to speak but stopped.

Zara shook her head, her black curls sweeping over her shoulders. "I don't think he'd do anything without our permission," she said. "And it's safe here; there's food. Not to mention, he's a doctor, and I want to learn from him. How else will I become a proper team medic?" She paused for a moment, looking between the two of us. "Don't you think he gets lonely? What happened to the whole 'we need to stick together' attitude we had going around here? Shouldn't it apply to him, too?"

"He's crazy," I said firmly.

"We're *all* crazy, Jake. That's what the end of the world does to you!" Zara pulled lipstick from her pocket and applied it.

"Okay," Nadia said, perhaps sensing the need for compromise. "What if we drive the car back and hide it near the lab? *We don't tell the doctor this,*"—she shot Coby a pointed look—"and keep it there in case, for some reason, we need to get the hell out. How does that sound?"

Zara nodded, and Coby exhaled, relief seeping into his confused expression.

"But," I said. "If Nadia and I agree that we need to leave, that something's wrong, you guys have to trust us and come with. Or we'll have to leave without you."

"I can agree to that," Zara said.

Coby nodded, but crossed his arms over his chest, frowning.

"Are you *sure* we can't drive away right now and forget we ever came here?" Nadia asked.

Coby's eyes widened, panicked for a moment, and Zara gave her a sad smile. "No, Nod, you know we can't."

"Okay," Nadia said. "It's a deal then."

We piled into the car, and I navigated while Coby drove a circuitous route outside of the city that allowed us to hide the car a block from the lab. It was right off the highway, so we could escape quickly if necessary. We ate a hearty lunch from our supply of soup, warmed with a tin of canned heat.

As we approached Winthrop Enterprises, the sun glinting off the glass panels covering the building, I told myself that the ominous feeling I'd had toward it yesterday was just a result of the thunderstorm and the uncertainty we'd all felt. That the doctor's experiments—including us—were nothing to be afraid of. But I didn't quite believe it.

5: Sutures
Nadia

Zara and I took a different set of stairs up to our room and found ourselves face-to-face with a giant sculpture of an angel. We stopped for a few minutes, surprised, and took in the muscular figure, the grey-veined marble, the sweeping wings.

"Didn't you say he had an angel painting at his house? What's his deal with them?" I asked Zara as we continued up the steps.

"And cockroaches... maybe he's got a thing for wings?"

"You really want to stay here with him?" I asked dryly.

"Let's see how dinner goes tomorrow night," she replied, examining her nails. "I should touch these up before then."

I suppressed a groan. What would it take for her and Coby to see the potential danger here?

The first thing we noticed once back in our room were two evening gowns laid out on the bed. Zara dropped her suitcase and picked up one of them, running her hands over the silky fabric. It was a long silver-and-black number. "It's gorgeous," she breathed.

My dress was a midnight blue velvet, also long and covered with rhinestones down one side of it. I barely glanced at it as I stashed my bow and quiver beneath the bed.

I strapped my hip holster on under my jeans. With my loose shirt pulled down, you'd have to be looking for it to tell I was wearing it. The revolver's weight against my hip gave me a cold comfort.

When I turned around, Zara had disappeared into the bathroom to don her dress. She came out and I helped her zip up the back, sighing. "Don't you find it weird—and by that, I mean super, disturbingly weird—that he has ballgowns lying around?"

Zara shrugged, and the shiny fabric of her sleeves crinkled. Though the dress was a little loose on her, she looked stunning. "I mean, he's a weirdo. But not *that* kind of weirdo. Put it this way—I think he's already done everything he wanted to do to us."

I bit my lip, hoping she was right, and looked at the other dress laid across the bed.

"Aren't you going to try it on?" Zara asked, watching me.

"I've never been much for dresses," I said, deciding against it. "But I'll put a clean shirt on now that I've got my stuff." I crossed the room to my bag and pulled out a shirt, smelling it. For having been stuffed in my bag for so long, it was pretty odorless. I pulled off my old shirt and slipped the new one on over my tank.

Zara had picked up my dress to look at it, but she laid it back down now. Hers had two long slits down the back, near her shoulder blades. "I've never seen a backless dress like that before," I said.

"Isn't it great?" Zara said, grinning at me. "It gives it some... *je ne sais quoi.*"

"I'm glad you like it," I said, not sounding glad at all.

"He's trying to be nice to us," Zara said. "Are you sure you won't wear yours? Maybe you'll change your mind before tomorrow."

"Positive," I said. *More like, he's trying to make it harder for us to run away.* "Do you think there's any way you and Coby would agree to leave before dinner?"

She had her nail polish out and was carefully touching up a thumbnail. She smiled and shook her head. "Don't think so, Nod."

"This place gives me the creeps. I don't feel like we're being watched, exactly... but there's something there."

"I know what you mean," Zara said. "And you and Jake have a point—it's good to be cautious. But it's not like he's keeping us prisoner. We'll be fine here." She reached out and touched my arm.

"I guess," I said.

"Don't you want answers?"

"We have our answer. We were created by a madman, and by some ridiculous stroke of luck we survived the end of the world."

"Yeah, sure, we know *that*," Zara said, flopping onto the bed and blowing on her nails. "But what about the *why* behind it all? I want to know more about Doctor Peter Winthrop."

◆ ◆ ◆

"Why didn't you tell me you're still bleeding?" Zara asked, pursing her lips.

"It's fine," Jake said as he pulled his hand out of her grip and rewrapped the gauze.

Jake, Zara, and I sat in the lobby. I had my journal open in my lap, Zara was sorting through the new first aid supplies the doctor had given her, and Jake had been trying—yet again—to convince us to leave. Coby was with the doctor in his lab.

She rolled her eyes. "This is no time for stoicism. You need stitches. The doctor said we don't heal as fast as normal humans."

"Might as well do the stitches if it's not healing," I said, closing my journal. "We don't want Zara to have to learn amputation."

He blew out a breath, then ran his good hand through his hair. "It's not bleeding much. I'm sure it'll stop soon."

"Hey," Zara said, jumping up. "I'll ask the doc if he can show me how."

"No. If you're going to force me, you do it. Nadia's turned out fine."

I put a hand on his shoulder. "Come on. He has to wear the suit so Zara will still be doing them, I'm sure. It can't hurt to get his professional opinion."

A few minutes later, we were dragging Jake up to the lab. Coby and the doctor looked in the middle of a tense conversation when we entered. Coby quickly excused himself, his eyebrows furrowed and his mouth sideways.

"Hey, Doc," Zara said. "Sorry to interrupt. Are you, by chance, a medical doctor?"

A grin through his face-shield. "Yes, I have my MD. And several PhDs. Why do you ask?"

"Jake hurt his hand yesterday," I said, nudging him to show his hand to the doctor. He obeyed, though his expression darkened as he unwrapped the gauze.

"We think he needs stitches."

"The medical term is sutures. Let's see," the doctor said as he reached out a gloved hand. He clasped Jake's hand and peered at the wound. "Fascinating. I always wanted to see how the healing process would work with your altered DNA."

I cleared my throat, not liking his tone. It somehow conveyed a sense of wonder while sounding clinical.

"I've done stitches—sorry, sutures—once before," Zara said. "Nadia had an incident. They aren't very even, and I'm not sure I did them right."

The doctor turned to me expectantly, though he didn't release Jake's hand. I stepped forward and swallowed nervously, feeling both exposed and a sudden prick of anger at Zara. There was no way to show her stitches without also showing him my scars.

Maybe she realized that too, because she went pale for a second and started to stammer, but I pulled my sleeve back quickly and showed the doctor.

He studied them for a moment, then my face. He addressed Zara, "Those look fine, especially for one with an unpracticed hand. Use the new supplies I gave you. I really must be getting back to this."

Zara said, "Thank you," as he turned back toward his lab bench, but he waved her thanks away.

I yanked my sleeve down and left the lab quickly, my face burning with shame.

6: Self-Preservation
Jake

You're doing this for survival. Self-preservation is a basic instinct that should be obeyed. They made it clear they won't leave.

None of the things I was telling myself were helping to slow my heart or calm my nerves while I packed up everything I'd just retrieved from the Mustang.

Winthrop had claimed to be working on an important experiment, so we'd ended up eating a quick meal in Nadia and Zara's room. I'd done my best to convince them we needed to leave, but they outvoted me. Even Nadia wanted to stay through the "formal dinner".

"I just want more answers," she'd said, biting her lip as her eyes met mine.

I shook my head, wiping away the memory. That image wasn't going to help me right now.

Flipping off the light in the room Winthrop had given me, I tested my flashlight beam. I'd put on the red filter—the best for preserving night vision. Then I hoisted my pack and grabbed my rifle. I peered down the hall after cracking the door open. No one there. The only sound was the light spinning noise of a rat in its exercise wheel.

I closed the door behind me, careful that it didn't make any noise. Tiptoeing down the hallway, I paused at Zara and Nadia's door. I pressed my palm to it, took a deep breath and released it. "Goodbye," I whispered.

Before I could change my mind, I hurried along the hall and down the two flights of stairs. This was the cowardly way. I knew that. I should've at least said goodbye to Nadia, but I was afraid if I had to look in her eyes again, hear her asking me to stay, that I wouldn't be able to leave.

Flexing my palm, I felt my skin pulling at the sutures. They were what sent me over the edge. The way Winthrop held my palm in his gloved hand, peering at my wound through his glasses and the face-shield of his suit. How fascinated he'd been by the defective body he'd given me, this body that healed too slowly. It had reminded me what we were to him: experiments.

I wasn't going to stick around for it. No one would be doing further experiments on me.

The steel front doors creaked when I opened them. I froze but heard nothing. Everyone was still asleep. A gust of cool night air carried the smell of decay to my nose, and I had to turn my head back indoors to catch my breath.

This will be the worst part, I told myself. Seeing the dead city again, avoiding bodies in the dark, the stench. But I'd mapped the shortest way out of Marion and into wilderness again. By morning, I'd be away from this nightmare.

Maybe I could start my broadcasts again. Nadia might decide to leave the lab eventually, might find me.

No, I couldn't think like that. I needed to be free of all of this. The lab, the doctor, the cockroach DNA. Even her.

I braced myself and swung the door wide, stepping out into the night. The stars were clouded over, but it wasn't raining.

When I turned to shut the door behind me—quietly, so the others wouldn't hear—I found myself frozen. If I shut the door, if I turned and left, I'd be free of this place. I could move on, forget about the last few days.

But what else would I lose?

Damn it.

I stepped back inside and closed the door gently, cursing myself. I'd stayed with the group too long, grown attached. If the doctor really *was* going to experiment on them, I couldn't leave them to that fate. Especially Nadia.

Creeping back to my room, I swung the door shut behind me quietly. After taking off my pack and setting my gun beside the bed, I flopped my head onto the pillow and groaned.

I'd just have to hope Winthrop said or did something bad enough at the dinner tomorrow that they'd agree to leave.

7: Underdressed
Nadia

We spent the morning and early afternoon touring the laboratory. The doctor's research must have been well-funded. The offices and conference rooms held modern furniture and the labs were full of state-of-the-art machines. However, nothing we saw was as interesting as the room of experimental creatures that Jake and I had seen a few nights before.

The bioluminescent turtle, when Zara met him, was quickly dubbed Humphrey Bogart. We sat surrounded by cages and the scents of hay and wood pulp, watching Humphrey happily munch on the pellets of food Zara fed him.

"You're a cutie, aren't you?" Zara said as she stroked a glowing stripe of his shell. "Even cuter than the pig, and I loved those the most when I lived on the farm."

The pig snorted, as if in defiance. "Aw, you're cute, too, Bacon," I said.

"We really need to workshop a better name for him."

I chuckled. Laughter had come easier as we explored the lab, and I felt less on edge. The doctor still seemed unbalanced, but he'd been through The End. It was understandable.

"Too bad he'll be too full to attend dinner with us," I said, nodding at Zara's new pet. "Bet he'd look cute in a bowtie."

"That's a great idea," Zara said. "A craft project for us."

She gave Humphrey the last pellet and brushed off her hands, then rolled back on her heels. "We should get ready. You still won't wear the dress?"

I shook my head.

"It seemed like you were warming up to the doc, though."

"I am, I think. To him and to this place. You and Coby are right. We have electricity, food, shelter... even basic medical knowledge. It seems silly to leave when we have all that."

"But Jake…"

"Yeah," I said. "Maybe he'll come around at dinner."

"They do say the way to the heart is through the stomach," Zara said, laughing.

Humphrey swallowed the last of his pellet and bobbed his head up at her, looking for more. She picked him up and carefully placed him back in his tank.

"Sorry, hon. We've got a dinner date."

◆◆◆

I immediately regretted not putting on the dress when we went downstairs to dinner, which was in a previously locked room on the first floor. Coby looked dashing in a grey vested suit and the doctor wore a tuxedo over his hazmat gear. It was a weird combination, but it still made me feel underdressed. The hazmat suit was seafoam green instead of the yellow one he had worn before, and somewhere he'd found a red rose to put in his jacket lapel.

I smiled with relief when Jake joined us, wearing jeans and the forest green shirt he'd worn when we met. At least I wasn't the only one in normal clothes.

The room was sparse, containing only a dining table with five chairs, a low corner table, and a door to another room. Four of the chairs matched, but the fifth had been added to make room for all of us. Candlesticks in the middle of the table lit the room, glinting off the crystal glasses and silverware that were set in front of the four matched chairs. On each plate was a small salad of lettuce, carrot slivers, and cherry tomatoes. A piano solo filled the space, emanating from a stereo set up in the corner.

With the dresses, the doctor's suit, the music, and the candle-lit ambiance, I was reminded of a masked, misunderstood character who liked to kidnap pretty sopranos.

While I stared at the table and contemplated where he'd found fresh produce, the doctor pulled out Zara's chair for her to sit, then held mine away from the table. He didn't comment on my outfit, instead smiling at me and pushing in my chair when I sat. I crossed my legs, then uncrossed them, glancing nervously at the three forks—surely an excessive number—next to my plate.

I poked at the salad with one of the forks, trying to tell if it had been frozen and thawed. Coby, Jake, and the doctor were all seated now, the doctor without a plate or table settings in front of him.

"Thank you for joining me," he said. "I hope you'll enjoy dinner."

I felt my holster shift against my hip as I leaned back in my chair, arms crossed. "Why aren't you eating?" Jake met my eyes; he'd been thinking the same.

"Because I'd have to take off the suit, of course." It was hard to tell, but I thought his face was plastered in a condescending smile, and it made me bristle.

"How do you *ever* eat, then?" Zara asked, her tone much friendlier than mine.

"I have a special clean room in the basement," the doctor said. "It filters out microbes, including the virus, and allows me to be without my suit for things like eating, showering, and the like."

"How did you know you'd need that?" Jake asked. He sat across from me. Coby was beside him and Zara was to my left. The doctor sat between Zara and Coby, at the head of the table.

"I didn't," the doctor said, unfazed. "The lab was for research, but now it allows me out of the suit without being infected."

Zara and Coby devoured their salads. I forked a small piece of lettuce into my mouth and chewed. Nothing seemed amiss, so I took a full bite.

"Where did the fresh vegetables come from?" Jake asked, failing to sound conversational.

How would one drug lettuce anyway? I wondered. You couldn't dissolve anything in it. I let myself polish off the rest of my salad, enjoying the juice of the cherry tomatoes and the flavorful crunch of the carrots. I'd missed these vegetables that couldn't be found in the woods.

The doctor replied, "I have a small greenhouse to the east of this building. I grow fruits, vegetables. Even some flowers."

"I'd love to see it," Zara replied.

"I can show you tomorrow." He stood and gathered our plates. "Waste not, want not," he said as he picked up Jake's untouched salad and set it carefully on the stack of empty plates.

"Do you guys feel okay?" I asked when the doctor was out of the room and, hopefully, out of earshot.

"Yeah," Zara said.

"Why wouldn't we?" Coby asked. The way his forehead never ceased to be wrinkled in confusion lately was getting on my nerves.

"Because he could have drugged or poisoned the salad," Jake said, a bit too loudly.

Coby's mouth fell open and he hissed, "He wouldn't do that!"

Jake shrugged and started to say something, but the door swung open and the doctor was back in the room with us. He carried four steaming plates on a tray with a bottle of wine. The heavenly aroma of warm butter and garlic filled the room, and my stomach growled impatiently.

The doctor passed out our plates, then held the wine bottle against his side and twisted the corkscrew.

"This looks and smells delicious, Doc," Zara said, then took a bite.

"How did you have it ready so quickly?" Jake asked, examining his plate as if it wasn't making his mouth water. I had to give him credit for how distrusting he could be in the face of steak and potatoes.

"The key to fine dining," the doctor said, grunting as he pulled the cork from the wine. "Is perfect timing." I thought his eyes crinkled into a smile through the mask and wished again that it wasn't so reflective.

"Wine?" the doctor asked Zara. I felt myself begin to panic. Was his plan to get us drunk?

Zara nodded, and the room filled with its rich, smoky scent as he poured her a serving of the red liquid. She picked it up and I kicked her under the table, making the wine slosh in her glass. She gave me a confused look. Then, seeming to understand, she took a tiny sip and put her glass back down. Coby's was filled too; I attempted to kick him, but he was too far away. Jake and I both refused the wine, which, comfortingly, did not upset the doctor.

"Do you know of any other people who've survived?" Jake asked as the doctor sat again.

"No," he said. "I have not come into contact with any others since the third virus came through here."

"What about,"—I swallowed, then pushed the words out—"anyone else like us? How many are there?"

"I like to think of your kind as superhuman," the doctor said. He laughed gently, but it still came out harsh through the mask. He looked into the distance, as if pulling up a fond memory, as he continued, "There were fifteen of you, at first. But only twelve of the embryos survived the process and were able to be implanted."

My hands went clammy and I wiped them on my jeans. I picked up my fork and cut a bite of steak. The doctor didn't seem to care whether we ate it or not—Jake was still refusing— so I chewed, enjoying the way it nearly melted on my tongue. I never allowed myself to cook anything rare over my campfires. It was too risky, I'd thought, but now I wondered if I should change my policy.

The doctor continued his tale. "It was remarkable that all twelve survived to term and were born without issue. Now that I know you four are immune to the virus, I'm curious about the other eight. Perhaps they survived too."

I dropped my fork and it clanged against my plate. With all the new information of the past day, I'd forgotten about the other eight records. I wondered if the doctor knew of their whereabouts, or if he'd suggest we try to find them.

"Really?" Zara asked him. "The others could be alive, too?"

Coby was staring at his plate as if reading something on it, and the doctor watched him as he said, "Yes, I believe there could be more."

My heart lifted. More survivors.

"That's fantastic!" Zara said. "I'd love to meet them. I bet we could track them down." The four of us exchanged excited glances at that, but I didn't want to discuss it further with the doctor present.

I took a bite of bread. It was still warm from the oven, and I lost all train of thought while I enjoyed the soft, airy texture and comforting flavor. We needed to figure out how to recreate this out in the woods. I scarfed down the rest and reached for another from the basket the doctor had placed on the table.

Soft piano music and the clink of silverware on china were the only sounds until Zara broke the silence. "What first interested you in science?" she asked, looking at the doctor as she took a bite of potato. "What started you on the path to becoming a doctor?"

"Oh," he said, waving a gloved hand in the air. "That silly little dream all young people have of making the world a better place." His voice held a bitter humor. "I didn't realize it was too late for that."

"Surely that's not a silly dream," I said, shifting in my seat. "Everyone tries to leave their mark."

"And look what you've built here," Zara said. "It's impressive."

"Ah yes. It took many years for Winthrop Enterprises to reach its potential. And many doubted me along the way. Of course, they're all gone now." He snickered to himself and leaned back in his chair. "I've made such strides in my research since the virus, now that I have unlimited time and resources and no red tape. The only one who needs to approve my experiments is me."

I exchanged a glance with Jake, my stomach turning. Could the doctor be so cold as to laugh at the deaths of his critics?

"Coby, are you alright?" Zara asked. "You look sick."

It was true; he'd gone pale and hadn't touched his food in a few minutes. "Fine," he muttered, picking up his knife and fork again.

"So, the adoption agency," I said, glancing up at the doctor from my plate. This was my chance to learn how it had worked—perhaps even why my parents had used a surrogate. "How did you set it up?"

The doctor leaned back in his chair. "The fertility research I did early in my career was quite profitable," he said, and I could hear the grin in his voice. "With some cash, it wasn't difficult to set up an 'adoption agency' that was really a front for my human hybrid research."

"But our parents—" Zara said, hand shaking a little as she set her wineglass down. "Did they know?"

"Your parents were easy. People looking for a child of their own are not hard to come by, and there was no reason to bother telling them about my little secret hidden in your DNA." He waved a hand dismissively, then dropped it to his lap. "The birth mothers were harder."

"Oh?" I asked, trying to sound only politely interested.

"Yes. But I found young women for the task soon enough. As I said, I had money then. Jake, your birth mother used the money to pay off her student loans."

Jake glanced up sharply but didn't say anything.

"And Zara's mother had medical bills. Her husband was sick with something. It's so hard to remember now… but yes, I did so much good for those women. And look what I got in exchange." He chuckled to himself again as he looked between the four of us.

I stared at my plate, my pulse racing. I still knew nothing about my parents and the surrogacy. One more question might

159

do it, but I found myself afraid to ask—afraid I might not like whatever response came from the doctor's mouth.

The last course, cheesecake topped with strawberries, passed in friendly conversation between Zara and the doctor, with some input from Coby, who was still a bit sullen. I gave up on interrogations and Jake remained quiet, though he did eat his dessert. His head was tilted toward the doctor, as if to catch every word he said. I tried to catch any slip-ups or out-of-place words, but it seemed he was telling the truth about everything.

Perhaps that was all the doctor wanted from us—to track down the other eight of our kind so he could experiment on us *together*. He couldn't get far with that suit of his, so it made sense to use us to find them. This made me feel better. It would be easy to agree to look for the others—we wouldn't even be lying because I *did* want to find them—and never return to the lab.

Zara's voice interrupted my thoughts. "Nod? Come on, the doc's going to walk us back to our room."

Jake and Coby had already left the table, and I stood, blushing at how vacant I'd been. Zara's arm was linked around the doctor's right elbow, and he offered me his left. I shook my head but walked beside him out of the room and up the stairs.

I felt calm in his presence for the first time. With the doctor stuck here, tied to his suit and clean room but wanting to find his other cockroach creations, it felt like we had the upper hand.

8: Not a Monster
Nadia

"What's with him?" I asked the doctor, indicating the angel sculpture as he so chivalrously walked us back to our room.

"Oh, that," he said, turning to look at it and smiling. "That's Cupid."

Zara gaped at the winged marble heartthrob before us. "I thought Cupid was supposed to be a fat baby."

"Not this one," he said, placing a hand on the marble sculpture's bicep.

"Are you into romance? Like, Valentine's Day stuff?" Zara asked.

The doctor let out two small laughs. "Not exactly."

The way he beheld the sculpture made the hairs on the back of my neck stand up. It was a look somewhere between worship and pride. "Did you make it yourself?" I thought out loud.

"Oh no, of course not," the doctor said, finally turning his attention back to us. "But I enjoy collecting fine art."

Zara and I exchanged a glance. Besides the giant angel painting, Zara had said there wasn't other art in his house, and I hadn't seen any besides the sculpture here.

"Good night, ladies," the doctor said when we reached our door. He inclined his head toward us, but it was barely noticeable in the suit.

"Night!" Zara said, smiling.

We slipped inside the door, and I clicked the deadbolt behind us. "God, he's creepy," I said.

"He likes muscular Greek sculptures," Zara said, shrugging. "Not the weirdest thing to like. I mean—*so do I.*"

I was too tired to have the is-the-doctor-okay-or-not argument again today, so I changed and got into bed after helping Zara unzip the back of her dress.

I fell asleep immediately, only to be jerked awake by Zara shouting Nick's name in a strangled voice and thrashing beside me in the bed. I grabbed her shoulder, shaking it to wake her. "It's a nightmare, Zara. Come on, wake up."

She sat up after a moment and said, "I'm sorry," before bursting into tears. "Why... why are they still happening?"

I didn't have an answer, but I put an arm around her and she rested her head against my shoulder.

Zara tried to speak through her sobs. "I thought if I told you and the others about Nick, the nightmares would go away."

Her voice sounded hopeless and helpless. I wrapped my arm tighter around her. "You have PTSD, Zara. Post-traumatic stress disorder. It doesn't go away."

"How do you know?" she asked, sniffling.

I sighed. The lateness of the hour seemed right for this conversation. "After my dad... passed, and I didn't think there was anyone left, I went to a dark place." I pulled more blanket onto my lap. "I'd cut a few times before The End, because I was stupid and thought things were bad then. I always did it on places I could hide—my thighs, my hips. All the ones on my arm," I swallowed, "They're from after."

"I'm sorry, Nod," Zara said. She was the one holding me now.

"I was so lonely and numb. It helped me to feel something, to feel better, for a while. I could focus on the pain and not worry about the rest of it. Other times I felt like I deserved it, because something was wrong with me, and I'd lived through the un-survivable while everyone around me died. I deserved to live far less than any of them.

"I started to lose hope," I said, my voice cracking. "And I thought about ending it—all the time. There was no one left. What was the point anymore? I needed to do something, to stop myself. Maybe if I could figure out *what* was wrong, I could fix it."

I was glad for the mantle of night around us. I couldn't tell her these things if I had to meet her eyes.

"I found books on psychology, mental disorders, stuff like that. I read as much as I could, and from what I could tell, I had PTSD, depression, and a bad case of survivor's guilt. I thought knowing what was wrong would help."

"Did it?" Her voice was small in the dark room.

"No," I said, feeling a tear slip down my cheek. "Because there's no cure. Before The End, they had psychiatrists and drugs and therapy, but they were just coping mechanisms, not cures. You have to learn to live with it."

Should I tell her the rest? I was so close to revealing everything. She was playing with my hair now, and as her fingers parted it and moved down my head in a French braid I felt calmer. I took a deep breath and tried to keep my voice steady.

"After that I made up my mind to end it. One night, I loaded a round into my revolver. I spun the cylinder, and pressed the barrel to my head..."

"Russian roulette," Zara whispered.

I nodded. "I pulled the trigger and *click*. Nothing happened. The gun spared me."

Zara let out a breath beside me as I fought back tears.

"I, uh... I thought I'd be happy, that I'd suddenly feel more alive, like I did when I cut. But I didn't. Mostly I was... disappointed. I knew I wouldn't have the courage to try again that night."

Zara finished my braid and tied it off. "Oh, Nod."

"I was planning to try again with more rounds loaded, working up to it—when I found Jake."

The tears spilled over, and I started to sob. Zara hugged me again. "Shh," she said. "It's alright."

"He saved my life, Zara."

"I know, I know," she soothed.

Now she knew. *I'm not strong, I'm not okay.* I sobbed into her shoulder, then sat up, wiping my eyes and steadying myself with a deep breath. "It feels good to tell someone."

"We'll get through it together. We can help each other, you know?"

I nodded, then realized that she couldn't see me. "Yeah, we will. Are you okay to go back to sleep?"

"Yeah," she said, and the bed shifted as she laid down, her back warm against mine.

"Sweet dreams."

"You too," she said, sounding half-asleep already.

◆◆◆

Later that night, a noise woke me from my dreamless sleep. I carefully raised myself onto my elbows and looked around, opening my eyes wide as if to help me see more in the darkness. All I could make out was Zara's silhouette beside me. I reached my arm over and shook her.

She mumbled, "What?" and sat up.

"I heard something," I whispered. There was a shuffling noise, like footsteps. Close, in the room with us. "There! Did you hear it?"

"Yeah," she said. She reached over to the lamp on her nightstand and flipped it on.

We both jumped out of bed, screaming at the creature crouched in the room with us.

The creature straightened and stood. It was shaped like a man, but its skin was tinged a greenish color and covered in an odd texture. Scales, I saw as I took a step closer, clutching my bow, which I'd instinctively pulled out from under the bed. There was no hair on his head either, just more scales.

I glanced at Zara, who was shielding her body with the lamp from the nightstand. The monster brushed his hands on his pants in a very human gesture.

My brain was still foggy from sleep, but it finally registered: *Pants? Why is the creature wearing clothes?* It wore black pants, a blue collared shirt, and shoes. My mind stuck on the shoes. They were shiny black Oxfords. It sure was a gentlemanly monster.

It cleared its throat, and we both flinched when it spoke. "Don't be afraid. Desspite my appearance, I'm not a monsster." He pronounced the S sounds in a strange way, between a hiss and a lisp.

Zara and I were understandably unconvinced, so he said, "I won't harm you."

"Then why are you in our room? *What* are you?" I asked, frozen in my defensive posture, arrow drawn.

"I'm a hybrid, like you."

"Not like us," I said, staring at his scales. Some weird, *Emily Post* part of my brain wondered if I was being rude.

He sighed, and I glimpsed his slightly forked tongue, the cause of the lingering S's. "Not quite like you. I'm of the lizard, rather than cockroach, variety."

"How do you know what we are?" Zara asked.

"Because I live here, with Doctor Winthrop."

"Why?" I asked, though it was hardly the most relevant question. My mind moved slowly. Its cogs creaked and groaned against each other, struggling to comprehend this reptilian man in front of me.

"To my knowledge the doctor keeps one of each subsspecies here at the lab. I'm the, well, the *Hemidactyluss frenatuss* hybrid he keepss here."

"How many subspecies does he *have*?" I asked.

"What kind of lizard is that?" Zara asked. Her voice had ceased trembling.

"It'ss a type of gecko," he said, with considerably less revulsion than I felt toward my cockroach DNA. He sounded resigned. "Doctor Winthrop created me when he thought the world would end by climate change. But he added a bit too much lizard DNA. I wasn't supposed to have scales." He smiled—sheepishly, I thought.

165

I paused for a moment, wondering what I could possibly say to that. Then I asked, "So he just kept you here? Your whole life?"

The lizard-man nodded.

"Do you have a name?" I asked.

"Yess," he said. "I'm Sloan."

How cruel to give him a name that he has to say with that hissing S of his. "I'm Nadia," I said, re-quivering my arrow and extending my hand for him to shake. His palm felt surprisingly normal in mine.

"Zara," she replied absently, chewing the inside of her cheek and not looking at him.

Sloan looked between us for a moment, seeming unsure what to say next. I was about to ask why he was in our room when Zara spoke.

"Wait," she said. "Then there's another one of *us* here too, right?"

Sloan's eyebrows drew together, making ripples through the scales on his forehead. "Oh," he said, "I thought you knew. There was one of your kind here. His name is Coby. Wasn't he with you?"

9: Find My Way Home
Nadia

My father had told me not to trust anyone, when it was just us after the virus. He'd warned me about my dangerous tendency to give people the benefit of the doubt.

"That was a good thing in the old world, Nadia. Second chances, compassion, seeing the best in people." We were out in the woods and he was cutting firewood while I sat on a mossy tree trunk, tying a new snare. "But you can't do that anymore."

"Is it so bad to give people a chance?" I'd said, thinking of all the shit people had been through since the world ended. No one's path had been easy.

My father had dropped the axe then and knelt in front of me. He startled me by looking straight into my eyes. "Nadia, dear, I'm sorry. I'm sorry that this is our world now. I wish you could be the caring, trusting person you've always been. But you can't."

I'd looked away, turning the snare wires in my hands. I wasn't used to this intensity in our conversations.

He sighed and looked into the woods for a moment. "I may not always be here to protect you. If you're ever on your own… you need to do whatever you can to survive. If you run into other people, be wary of them. Always second and third-guess their motives. Watch your back. Sleep with one eye open."

"Okay, Dad," I'd said, shifting on the stump. He studied me for a moment longer, then nodded and backed away, chopping wood once again.

Four days later, I'd buried him.

Now, I kicked myself for not heeding his advice. I'd been cautious with Jake; I hadn't revealed my location for two weeks, and hadn't agreed to meet until over three weeks, when I believed I could trust him. Why hadn't I been leery of Coby? I never should have let down my guard.

Zara, Sloan, and I headed down the hallway to Jake's room. I knocked on his door, and after a few moments, he opened it a crack. "Nadia?" he said, his eyes squinting in the light from the hallway. "What's wrong? Are you okay?"

I took a deep breath and tried not to be distracted by the fact that he wasn't wearing a shirt. "Nothing's wrong exactly, but... you'd better get dressed."

He nodded and shut the door. In a moment, he was out in the hallway with us. He stopped short when he saw Sloan.

"Jake," Zara said, "this is Sloan. He's a gecko hybrid, and he's lived here with the doctor his whole life. Sloan, meet our friend Jake."

"How do you do?" Sloan asked, extending his hand as if this wasn't the weirdest introduction he'd ever experienced. If he'd spent his whole life with the doctor, maybe it wasn't.

Jake reluctantly shook his hand. "This isn't a dream?" he asked, turning to me.

I shook my head.

"There's got to be a threshold, right?" Jake asked, still speaking to me.

"What?"

"Some threshold past which things can't get any weirder. We've got to be close. No offense," he said, turning to Sloan.

"None taken," Sloan said.

"Speaking of which," Zara started, then nodded to me.

"There's more," I said. "Coby was raised here, too, like Sloan."

I watched a few expressions play out over Jake's face—confusion, realization, then a wry grin.

"Do I need to say it?" he asked. "Do I need to say 'I told you so'?"

I rolled my eyes, and Zara asked, "What's he talking about?"

"Jake never trusted Coby," I said, seeing her brow furrow. Then I turned back to Jake. "Can we at least get his side of the story?"

"Yes," Jake said. "Let's wake him up."

We burst into Coby's room, then all stood in a half-circle around him as he woke and sat up in his bed. Confusion and fear spread across his face, then recognition when he saw Sloan.

"What's going on?" he asked.

"It's about time you tell us what you've been hiding. Everything." Jake said, scowling.

I moved over to Coby and lay my hand on his striped pajama-clad shoulder. "If you don't, Sloan can. But wouldn't you rather tell us the truth yourself?"

He nodded slowly, his eyes still on the ground. Then he sat on the edge of his bed as we all waited for answers. His shoulders moved up and down as he let out a long sigh.

"Before I start, you need to know that I never wanted to lie to you—any of you. But I didn't have a choice. I know what I've done is wrong, and that you may never be able to trust me, but I ask that, after learning the truth, you try to understand and—if you can—forgive me." He looked at us each, one at a time. Sloan was last, and when they made eye contact, Sloan inclined his head.

"I didn't grow up with parents and a family like the rest of you. I grew up here, with Doctor Winthrop and Sloan. I didn't want to lie to you—I just wanted to find my way home."

"What about the adoption record?" I asked. "You had parents on there."

"It was a fake," Coby said. "Doctor Winthrop gave it to me when he sent me away. I slipped it into a drawer when we loaded the car at the adoption agency." At that, he looked down at his hands.

I swallowed and tried to ignore the goosebumps appearing on my arms.

"Sloan doesn't know this part either," Coby said. "The doctor sent me to find the rest of us hybrids. He didn't prepare me, though, and it took me a month to figure out how to feed and shelter myself. After that I found Zara." He looked at her then, but her face stayed unreadable.

"A few months later, I heard Jake's broadcast over the radio. I lost the signal, but the next time I found it again it wasn't just Jake—Nadia was talking to him too."

"Oh my God, how long were you listening in on us?" I asked, raking my hands through my hair. The last thing I'd ever considered was Coby spying on us before we'd met him.

"I wasn't listening in! I just needed to know where you were so Zara and I could find you. I heard you mention the coordinates where you were meeting, so I had us move in that direction, too. I asked Zara to do a nightly broadcast on our radio, hoping you'd overhear it. Finally, after you'd met up, you did."

"You were manipulating me the whole time?" Zara said, tracing fast circles around her pendant with her thumb. "Why didn't you tell me you'd heard them?"

Coby hung his head. "I know, I'm so sorry. But I didn't know if they were the right people or not—they didn't say their names that night I first heard them, and I couldn't be sure he'd said Jake on the first transmission. There was a lot of static, and I had no way of telling you why we needed to find the 'right' people."

"Why not? Why not tell me what we are?" Zara's voice was cracking, her eyes shiny with tears. My heart went out to her. This was a more hurtful betrayal for her than for me or Jake. She'd spent three more months with Coby than we had, without suspecting anything. They'd become close friends, relied on each other for survival. And now to learn it had all been based on lies...

"Would you have stayed with me if I told you the truth? Would you have believed me if I told you that we both had

170

cockroach DNA, and that's why we survived?" His voice was ragged, and a part of me wanted to hug him.

"I would have thought you were crazy," Zara said in a strained voice. "But I wouldn't have abandoned you. We could have come here together, and then I would have believed it."

"I'm sorry, Zara."

"What about when we were all together?" I asked. "Why didn't you tell us then? You could have taken us to the lab and we all would have found out. Why bother with pretense—the adoption agency, Peter Winthrop, making us find our way here?"

"I did my best not to lie to you," Coby said. He seemed to have control over his voice again. "I mainly left out information. The one actual lie I told you was that my parents took me to the adoption agency, and that's how I knew where it was. And that was mostly true. The doctor was the closest thing I had to a parent, and he took me there. That's where he dropped me off when he sent me out to find you. He gave me the record that you saw, with my fake parents, and told me to use that as a cover."

"Why bring us to the agency at all? Why not lead us straight to the lab?" Jake asked. His arms were crossed, his legs planted firmly apart on the ground.

Coby shrank away from him. "Because I didn't know the way back. The doctor forgot to give me directions. You have to understand. I'd rarely been outside this building before he dropped me off at the agency, and never alone. I had no idea how to get here, or even in what city it was located. I spent a lot of that first month trying to retrace the route back to the lab, with no luck."

His chin trembled and his voice wavered. I tried to imagine being Coby. Surviving after The End was hard enough; it must have been worse if you were raised in a laboratory, then left alone in the outside world. He was lucky he'd made it through alive.

"I was supposed to find all twelve of us," Coby said. "But I thought that, if I brought you back here and you learned the truth, you'd help me find the other eight. I couldn't do it on my own," Coby said, taking a deep breath. "The doctor was disappointed that I'd only found you three, but he agreed that you could help me find the others."

Jake looked at me. He didn't seem surprised by that last part; I wondered if he'd had the same idea at dinner. *Find the others and never return.* Simple enough. I glanced at Sloan, wondering if he'd help us.

Coby spoke again. "I swear to you, that is the complete truth about everything—or at least, everything I know. I'm sorry I lied and manipulated you all, but I hope you understand that I had to."

Silence filled the room for a few moments, and I studied Coby. He was close to tears. His shoulders were slumped, and he stared at the floor, not able to make eye contact with any of us. I wasn't angry at what he'd done. Instead, I felt pity, as well as relief that I finally knew the truth about him.

Zara must have felt the same, because she sat on the bed beside Coby and wrapped her arms around him. He didn't hug her back, but she whispered, "I forgive you."

He looked up at her, his mouth open in surprise. "Really?"

"Yes," she said, pulling out of the hug to wipe tears from her eyes. "It's a rough world we're in now. I can't hold someone doing what they had to do against them."

"I forgive you too, Coby," I said, the words bypassing my brain and falling out of my mouth. But after I'd said it, I realized it was true. Though trusting him would take more time, I wanted to forgive.

"I do too," Jake said. "But from here on out you've got to be completely honest with us. No secret conversations with the doctor, no withholding information. Step out of line again and you'll regret it."

Coby nodded, but he was smiling now. "I swear," he said.

Zara hugged him again. I grabbed Jake's wrist and pulled him into a group hug around Coby. Jake pulled out right away and said, "Alright then. What do we do now?"

"Let's tell the doctor that we'll find the others. Then we find them and don't come back here," I said.

"He's not so bad," Coby said. "I know you guys don't trust him, but he won't hurt us. He's always been good to me."

"That may be," I said. "But I think he wants to experiment on us and I'm not okay with that."

Sloan cleared his throat; we'd forgotten he was in the room. "He doesn't want to experiment on you," Sloan said, training his green eyes on each of us. "He wantss to *exterminate* you."

10: Perfect
Nadia

"What the hell are you talking about?" Coby asked while the rest of us were trying to figure out if we'd heard Sloan right through his lizard accent.

"Coby," Sloan said. "I didn't want to tell you like thiss, but... the doctor wantss to wipe you out."

"That doesn't make any sense," Coby said, shaking his head. "You must have misunderstood. Why would he send me to find the others when he could easily have gotten rid of me?"

"Look, when I assked him when you were coming back he smiled and told me, 'Oh, he won't be'. He thought the third strain of the viruss would kill you and all the others. If it didn't, you would still round them up and he could take care of you when you were all back here. Or, more probably, have the Sirin take care of you."

Coby shook his head again and crossed his arms. "He wouldn't do that. And that doesn't explain why *you're* still alive."

"Hold up," Zara said. "What was that word you said? 'Sirin'?"

Sloan turned to us, and though it was hard to read his facial expressions with the scales, he seemed somber. "I think you should sit for thiss. We have much to explain."

We glanced around at each other, then Zara sat on the bed with Coby. I sat next to her and Jake next to me. Sloan stood in front of us, and I felt as if I was six years old with my sisters, being scolded by our parents. I fought the urge to grab Jake's hand.

"Let'ss start at the beginning," Sloan said. "Mine was the firsst type of hybrid. As I said, he created uss hoping we'd be able to survive in a broader range of temperatures than normal humans."

"Can you?" Zara asked.

"Yess. But it isn't pleasant." Sloan grimaced, and my heart wrenched when I thought of the experiments that must have been performed on him to determine that.

He continued, "My type was not a success. We weren't supposed to have scales or other lizard features, but he didn't issolate enough of the gecko DNA. I'm the only one still living."

He paused a moment, and I felt my throat constrict. How many had died because the doctor had played God?

"How old are you?" Zara asked.

"I'm twenty-two," Sloan said. "We lizard-hybrids were created four years before your kind. He told me once that after my kind were so unsuccessful, he'd almost given up on the idea. But the cockroach-hybrids, as you all know, worked out conssiderably better."

"Exactly," Coby said. "Why would he want to get rid of us?"

Sloan pursed his lips, and a chill ran down my spine at the way it made the scales around his mouth ripple. I wondered if I'd ever get used to his reptilian appearance.

"As Coby knows," Sloan said, straightening his collar and turning to us. "There is a third type of hybrid."

"No," Zara said, and I felt goosebumps rise on my arms. What other monster could there be?

"It's true," Coby said.

"What are they?" I asked. "How many are there?"

"The doctor calls them the Sirin. It's a new subsspecies of human he created. They look like regular humans, except they have wings. And he was more selective about this subsspecies' human DNA than with mine or yours. Mosst of them are exceptionally athletic and intelligent."

"We need to hurry with the explanations," Coby said. "It'll be morning soon."

I glanced at the high window and saw the first light of morning streaming through. Why was Coby worried about the doctor finding us together? I swallowed.

"Alright," Sloan said. "I can't be sure, but I believe he created fifty Sirin. It was two years after all of you, making them about sixteen years old now. The doctor raised them all in a special academy. When they were thirteen he started to train them himsself. I'm not sure how or why, but he was gone a lot over the past three years."

"Even if we buy that these Sirin angel-things exist, what's the point? Why would he want to, as you said, exterminate us?" Jake asked.

"Because he wantss the Sirin to replace uss. They're a better version of you, and he wantss to forget about your kind now that he's upgraded."

"Look, I don't know how we're supposed to believe you about anything," I said. "This story is crazy, and we haven't even got around to asking *what the hell* you were doing in Zara's and my room tonight."

"He was in your room?" Jake asked me. "You were in their room while they were *sleeping?*" he said, stepping protectively between Sloan and me.

"Yess," he said, backing a step away from Jake. "I was looking for evidence."

"Of?" I asked, my arms crossed. Zara and I were standing too now, facing off against Sloan, with Coby to the side and Jake between us.

Sloan looked sideways, then said, "I'd rather not say."

Zara snorted. "Right. And we're supposed to believe that you're not a creep? How did you get through the locked door?"

Coby said, "The doctor is going to be up any minute. He didn't want you guys to meet Sloan yet, so we all need to go back to our rooms."

"I have an idea," I said, surprising everyone, including myself. "The way I see it, we don't know who to believe right now," I said, and Jake nodded. "Sloan, I'm sorry, but we have no idea about you and it's super sketchy that you crept into our room tonight. Coby, I want to trust you, but we just learned that you've lied to us about everything until now."

Coby's eyes sank to the floor. Zara said, "And the doctor?"

"I don't trust him, personally, but Sloan and Coby, who have both known him their whole lives, disagree about his motives. We need more information," I said. "Zara, weren't you going to the greenhouse with him today?"

She nodded.

"Do you think you could go as planned, and see if you can get a better feel of what the doctor wants from us? He clearly doesn't want to kill us off *yet* or he would have already done so."

"Yeah, I can do that," Zara said, but her face was pale. "I want to believe he's okay."

"I'll go with you," Coby said. "You'll be totally safe."

I nodded. "You can take him, or you can take me or Jake if that would make you more comfortable."

Jake opened his mouth to protest, but Zara said, "I'm fine with Coby."

The corners of Coby's lips curled up. "I swear, you'll be completely fine," he told Zara, then crossed his arms. "Sloan doesn't know what he's talking about."

"Sloan, you need to go back to—well, wherever it is the doctor's been hiding you," I said, turning to him. "Jake and I will look for this 'evidence' you want, but you'll have to tell us what it is."

He shook his head. "No. I'll help you look for it, tonight. It has to be while the doctor is assleep in his clean room or there's too much rissk he'll catch us."

"Fine," I said. "Then Jake and I will prepare to make an escape in case we end up leaving tomorrow. Tonight, after dark, all four of us will meet Sloan here, and we'll find this 'evidence' he wants and discuss what Zara and Coby found out about the doctor. Does that plan work for everyone?"

"Yes," Coby said. "Now can we please get back to sleep before the doctor notices that something is wrong?"

We all assented and went our separate ways. Sloan slipped off without another word, and Zara, Jake and I continued to our rooms. Outside his door, Jake said, "Sleep tight. See you in a bit, Nadia."

Zara and I returned to our room and flopped onto the bed. "Pinch me," she said. I obliged her and she yelped. "Ow! Okay, just checking. How about dinner? Was it drugged? Were we hallucinating?"

"Did you see a greenish, scaled man who called himself Sloan?"

"Yes."

"Then no. Because that's what I saw, too."

"Okay then," she said, "this shit *is* real."

We stared at the ceiling for a while, trying to sleep, but before long there was a knock on the door, and Coby summoned Zara for their trip to the greenhouse.

◆◆◆

Preparing for a quick departure went faster than Jake and I expected. We were both already packed, so after a quick trip to check on the hidden Mustang and a scan of the laboratory to find all possible escape routes, we didn't have anything to do. We circled the lab again, trying to find something Sloan might call 'evidence' or prove to ourselves that the Sirin existed, but there was nothing beyond the angel sculpture in the stairwell and the winged rats in the specimen jars.

We ended up back in Zara's and my room. I sat on the bed and Jake sat beside me. He did it as if it was completely natural to be sitting next to each other like that, so I tried to be calm too and ignore the pounding in my chest. I gave him a book to read, trying not to inhale too much of his intoxicating scent, and pulled out my journal to write.

Things I've Learned in the Past 24 Hours:
1. Doctor Winthrop has access to women's evening gowns.
2. He has to wear the suit and do things in the clean room to avoid getting the virus.

3. He created another type of hybrid before us. Sloan is the only one left. He's part gecko.

4. When I write it out, I can see that my life has gone irrevocably batshit crazy.

5. Also, Coby lied to us about everything.

6. He's sorry about it. I don't know if that helps.

7. Oh, and Coby and Sloan say that the doctor has yet another hybrid.

8. It's a human with wings. That explains the angel sculpture. Apparently, they're supposed to replace us. Sloan says the doctor is going to 'exterminate' us because of them.

9. But how do we know if Sloan and Coby are to be believed? Sloan's a lizard-man who was sneaking around in Zara's and my room last night.

10. Coby apparently likes the doctor and we already know that he's lied to us before. See (5).

I doodled, scribbling a dark smudge on the page. Then I wrote:

11. At least I can trust Jake. And Zara.
12. I can trust them both, right?

"Am I in there?" Jake asked, making me jump and drop my pen. He indicated the open journal in my lap.

"Nope," I said, feeling my face flame red as I remembered an earlier entry.

I was surprised by the hurt expression on his face. "Really? I'm not?"

"I mean, obviously you are. As are Zara, Coby, and now Sloan."

"What did you say about me?" he asked, closing the book I'd given him. It was a battered copy of *The Princess Bride*, and I was happy to see how far he'd got into the story already. It was one of my favorites.

"You'll never know," I said, closing the journal.

"Oh, come on," he said, grinning. "It's the end of the world. What you're writing in there could be the last record of human existence. And you won't tell me how you're portraying me?"

He grinned, but my own smile had vanished. "We're not humans, Jake. 'Human' existence is gone, besides the doctor. And I don't want to write about him."

"We're human enough," he said, wrapping an arm around me. I didn't want to shrug it off. Instead I nestled my head against his shoulder, realizing how tired I was after the nearly sleepless night. I listened to his heartbeat and steady breathing. My eyes slipped closed.

"Yeah," I mumbled. "I'm really tired." Between Zara's nightmare and Sloan I hadn't had much sleep.

"Let's take a nap," Jake said. "I doubt we'll get much sleep tonight either."

I nodded and started to get up, but he wrapped his arm tighter around me.

"Stay like this. It's comfortable," he said.

"Alright," I agreed, letting my eyes close.

"Sleep tight, Nadia." There was a smile in his voice, and he changed position so he could wrap his warm hand around mine.

As I drifted toward sleep I didn't think, just basked in how right this felt. If the doctor exterminated us tomorrow, at least we'd had this moment today.

"You're more than human," Jake whispered after he thought I'd fallen asleep. Then he kissed the top of my head. "You're perfect."

11: Far From Here
Nadia

I woke to knocking on the door. It took me a moment to realize where I was and untangle myself from Jake's arms. His face looked peaceful and vulnerable as he slept. Had he really said what I thought I'd heard before I fell asleep? *But he doesn't know the real you. You're far from perfect*, I thought, and my stomach clenched.

There was more pounding on the door, and Zara's worried voice came through, "Nod, is everything okay?"

I walked over, rubbing my eyes, and opened the door a crack. "Yeah, Zara, everything's fine." I said, yawning and rubbing my eyes.

A smirk spread across her face. "Where's Jake? Is he in there?"

"Yes," I said, my face reddening. "We were sleeping—*just* sleeping," I said.

"Why was the door locked?" Zara asked, raising an eyebrow and grinning.

I shot her my best death glare. "We always lock it. Because there's a mad scientist here, remember?"

"Yeah, *we*—you and I—lock it because of that..."

Her grin widened as she tried to peek around me into the room. I glanced at Coby behind her. He was politely pretending that he couldn't hear us, but the corners of his mouth were turned up a little.

"Just come in," I said, opening the door wide and turning on my heel. My face was ablaze, and I went to the bathroom to rinse it with cool water while the other two woke Jake.

When I came back into the room, they were eating apples the doctor had given them from his greenhouse and discussing what they'd learned.

"He wants us to find the other eight?" Jake said.

Zara chewed a bite of apple and nodded. "Yup, that's all he wants. And he said if we don't want to do that, it's fine, but the chances of them surviving on their own are probably getting slimmer by the day."

"Did he have names? Or any idea where they are?" I asked, joining the circle and grabbing an apple. We all sat on the bed, facing each other, and I was glad the subject of me and Jake had been dropped—for now, anyway.

"Yeah, he said he could help us find them," Coby said.

"You mean the way you helped us find *him*? With cryptic clues and anagrams?" I asked.

"Yeah, Coby," Jake said. "Why didn't you tell us the doctor's name when we were looking for him? It would have saved Nadia from the rabid dog."

Coby shrank from Jake's biting tone. Then he looked at me. "I'm so sorry about that, Nadia. I feel so guilty, and if you had… I never would have forgiven myself."

"Then why didn't you give it up? Just tell us to look for Peter Winthrop?" Zara said, setting her apple core upright on the nightstand.

"I didn't know how to explain how I knew the name. And I didn't know that he'd published any books. You have to understand. I barely knew anything outside of this laboratory. I had no idea the names were anagrams, either. I honestly didn't know where to start."

"You couldn't have given up and told us after Nadia almost *died*?" Jake asked, his voice still low and growling.

"It wouldn't have changed what happened. We needed to get her the vaccine; explaining everything then would have been a distraction," Coby said. "I'm sorry, Nadia."

"It's okay," I said, wanting him to stop apologizing. "And Jake, lay off him. We need to focus on tonight."

Jake swallowed a bite of apple and said, "Speaking of which, what about dinner tonight? Don't tell me we're supposed to get all dressed up again."

"Actually, he did want to do another 'formal dinner', as he calls them," Zara said. "But we told him that we weren't up for it, and he was fine with that."

"He's a reasonable person," Coby said. He hadn't eaten his apple yet and tossed it between his hands.

"Did he do these dinners before? Or is it a new thing?" I asked.

"He did them, but not with me." The apple fell into Coby's lap.

There was a beat of silence before I said, "Zara—your dress!"

"What about it?" she asked.

"Remember the slits in the back? They're for *wings*. I bet mine had them, too," I said, getting up and crossing to the closet, where I'd shoved my gown the night before. I pulled it out and examined the back, the velvet soft between my fingers. Then I showed the parallel slits to the others. "He must have used these for dinners with the Sirin. They're real," I breathed, more to myself than to the others.

"You didn't think they were?" Coby asked.

"If the doctor is so reasonable," Jake interrupted, "what's Sloan's deal? Why does he think he's going to get rid of us?"

Coby's face darkened. "Sloan's kind came first; they were a failed experiment. I don't think he's ever forgiven the doctor for that."

I nodded to myself, trying to weigh all the evidence we had and decide who was right about what. But we didn't have enough pieces of the puzzle. We'd have to wait until the "evidence", if it existed, was found tonight.

I hadn't realized I'd zoned out until Zara snapped her fingers in front of my face. "Oh, sorry," I said.

"It's fine," she said. "We were saying we should all get some sleep before ton—"

She was cut off by a knock on the door. My muscles tensed—was it the doctor? I'd gone the whole day without seeing him, which had done wonders for my nerves. But Jake opened the door to reveal Sloan. The memory of his scaled appearance must have softened in my mind, because now that he was in front of me, I was struck again by how strange and otherworldly he looked. He'd be right at home on a *Star Trek* set, but here, in a simply furnished bedroom, he didn't belong. I tried not to stare.

"Oh," he said. "You're all here. Excellent."

"I thought we were waiting until dark," Jake said.

"We were, but the doctor retired early since you aren't having dinner. It'ss besst that we start now. It could be a long night." His slithery S's were messing with me again, and part of me wondered if I was still in an odd dream.

"Okay," Jake said, opening the door wider so Sloan could walk through. "What are we looking for and where do we find it?"

Sloan glanced at Zara and me as we sat on the bed. Coby had moved to the desk chair and was glaring at Sloan with his arms crossed.

"Proof," Sloan said cryptically.

"Of *what?*" I asked, tired of being kept in the dark about everything. I wanted to know the truth, ugly as it may be.

The scales around his mouth rippled as his face moved through several indecipherable expressions. Then he seemed to decide something. "Proof that Doctor Winthrop ended the world."

My jaw dropped, and Zara gasped. Coby stood, his fists clenched. Jake put a hand up to stop him from advancing toward Sloan. He seemed the least fazed by the news, as if he'd suspected something like this all along. Knowing Jake, maybe he had.

"What do you mean by that?" Jake asked.

"I think he created the viruss," Sloan said simply. "And used it to wipe out the whole world so his Sirin could replace humans."

"Do you have any idea how *insane* you sound?" Coby spat.

"I know how it sounds," Sloan said. "That'ss why we're finding evidence before we accuse him."

"What happens if we, as you said, accuse him?" I asked.

Sloan trained his eyes, which were a gentle green, like the sage my mother used to grow in the garden, on me for a moment, then said, "We'll cross that bridge if we get to it."

"Okay," Zara said quietly, standing up from the bed. "Where do we look?"

"I assume there's something in here, since you were in our room last night?" I asked, crossing my arms. I felt on edge around Sloan, but that could have been my fear of snakes kicking in. *He's part lizard, not snake*, I told myself, but that wasn't exactly comforting.

"Yess," Sloan said, kneeling next to a corner of the rug that covered most of the room. "Right here." He pulled back the rug. Beneath it was a trapdoor.

"Holy shit," Zara said. "Is that what I think it is?"

Sloan nodded as we moved closer to examine the door. It was stainless steel, but nearly flat on top and sunk into the floor so it wouldn't be noticed beneath the rug.

"How did you know this was here?" Jake asked.

"I made mysself a blueprint of the laboratory," Sloan said. "There were a few square feet of unaccounted-for space beneath thiss room on all floors."

Coby's eyes were wide, and he reluctantly admitted, "This room was the doctor's bedroom before he had to sleep in the clean room."

"Where does it go?" I asked, kneeling. I wrapped my fingers around the cool, smooth metal of the handle and pulled.

It wouldn't budge.

Jake, who had knelt beside me, moved his hand over the door's surface and stopped over a spot near one end of the handle. He leaned in closer, and I tried to ignore his scent, which made me long to be back in the woods and far, far from here. "There's a keyhole," he said. "It's locked."

"Do you have the key?" I asked Sloan. He shook his head.

Zara, who was next to Sloan on the other side of the door, grinned. "Allow me," she said, slipping a bobby pin from her hair. Sloan watched in awe as she pulled it to a right angle and jiggled it around inside the lock.

"Okay, I think I got it," she said. I pulled on the handle again. The door was heavy, but I managed to pull it open.

"How did you do that?" Sloan asked.

Zara shrugged. "It's come in handy a few times. Even *before* the end of the world."

She winked at him, and I laughed. "Oh Zara, what would we do without you?"

"Have a lot fewer adventures, probably," she said as she looked into the darkness. Jake clicked on his flashlight. All we could see was a metal ladder, which reached a concrete floor thirty feet below us.

"I can't believe this," Coby breathed. Sloan put a hand on his shoulder, but Coby swatted it off.

"Ladies first!" Zara said, her smile wavering for a moment and her fingers twitching at the hem of her mini skirt. Then she sat on the edge of the trapdoor opening, grabbed the first rung, and swung herself onto the ladder. Her journey into the depths of Winthrop Enterprises had begun.

An icy chill ran down my spine. I was no expert, but trapdoors generally didn't hide pleasant things. I swallowed, then shouldered my pack and turned on my flashlight, holding it tightly in my fist and aiming it downward, illuminating the still-descending Zara. I started the climb down, then looked back up at Jake, Sloan and Coby.

"I'll be behind you, after Coby and Sloan," Jake said. There was a crease between his eyebrows. Coby looked stunned and, as usual, I couldn't tell what Sloan was thinking. Was he happy we'd found something?

"I know," I said to Jake, then followed Zara down the ladder. Each time my boots hit a new rung, the metallic sound echoed around the unknown space below us.

12: Children of a Lesser God
Nadia

The ladder was surrounded by four walls until we got to the very bottom. Halfway down, I looked at the square of light on the ground, far below. My chest was tight, making it hard to breathe, and the walls seemed to be closing in around me. *Keep going.* Coby was already descending above me, and Zara called up when she reached the floor. There was no turning back now.

At the bottom of the stairs, I couldn't see much. The shaft of light coming through the trapdoor was partially blocked by Coby and Sloan's descent. Squinting into the light and through the floating dust particles, I could make out Jake's form starting down as well. I turned back into the room to see Zara's flashlight beam moving across its walls. I clicked on mine too.

The space was surprisingly empty. A large desk, centered with the far wall, faced us. A marked-up map hung on the wall over it and an old office chair sat behind it. The wall to our right was made up of a bank of filing cabinets like the ones at the adoption agency. I moved my flashlight to the left wall, which was only concrete blocks, and to the one behind us, accidentally shining it in Coby's eyes. More concrete.

I felt chilled through my thin shirt. The air was damp and the ceiling low. The ladder, which I could see now was attached to the wall opposite the map, must have taken us below Winthrop Enterprises' ground floor. Though the room was large, it was too small to encompass the entire floor plan of the building. I didn't see any doors. Either this was all the basement there was, or you couldn't enter it from the basement's other rooms.

"Is this what you were expecting?" I asked Sloan as he dismounted from the ladder.

Zara searched the wall to our left and flipped on the light switch she found. We all blinked, adjusting to the light as a few dangling bulbs flickered on. They filled the wide space with a dull yellow glow.

"Yess, thiss is what I expected. Doctor Winthrop takess detailed notess on everything he does," Sloan said as he took in the room. "If he did what I susspect, we'll find the evidence here."

I nodded and walked to the back wall. The map was of the world, and he'd drawn arrows spreading out from a few locations. One was on the East Coast of the US, one was in Russia—Moscow or St. Petersburg, maybe—and another started at a coastal city in China. I ran my fingers over the smooth paper and onto the cold concrete bricks of the wall.

I heard Jake's footsteps beside me. "The spread of the virus," he said softly.

"Do you think that's what it is?" I asked. My lungs felt constricted, down in this dank space, and my skin was crawling. If Sloan was right, what would we do?

Zara approached the map. She ran her fingers along one of the arrows, reverently. "I saw a map like this on the news," she whispered. "Right before the second strain."

"This doesn't prove he caused it." Coby's voice was too loud, echoing around the room. "Just that he studied it."

I wanted to believe him, but so far Sloan had been right.

Half-buried amidst stacks of papers and manila folders on the desk, Sloan found a slim laptop and flipped it open.

"Can one of you help me?" Sloan asked. "I'm not great with computers."

"I've got it," Zara said, crossing over to him.

"Try 'Sirin' for the password," Sloan said, but Zara had already got in. "Where did you find thiss girl?" Sloan asked me. I laughed and Zara patted his shoulder.

"I'm a rare breed," she said, then laughed again at the irony of her joke.

The two of them scanned the computer for any damning files. I examined the other objects hanging above the desk next to the map. His diplomas and a few awards were framed, along with a plaque. There was something engraved on it in gold lettering, and I leaned in with my flashlight to read it.

"'It is easier to build strong children than to repair broken men'," I read. "'Frederick Douglass'." A chill bolted down my spine. Is that what he thought we were? 'Strong children' that he built?

"Nadia," Jake said, and I joined him in front of an open filing cabinet drawer. The folders in the drawer were marked with our names and others I recognized from my adoption agency records—Diego and Esperanza Perez, Vivian Freeman, Nysa Nassar...

Then Jake held out a folder to me. "Jacob Atwater" was written on the tab in tiny block letters. Inside were pictures of a newborn Jake, his real birth certificate, a copy of the adoption record I'd seen. He set these aside and handed me other things that made the hairs on my neck stand up. A newspaper clipping of Jake's junior varsity soccer team, his middle school diploma, photos of him laughing in a restaurant with friends. There was a report of his activities over a weekend four years ago, prepared by Hudson Private Investigators.

"Oh my God. He's been keeping tabs on us our whole lives." Rifling through the folders, I pulled out the one marked with my name.

Its contents were similar to Jake's—a birth record and newborn photos, newspaper clippings, a copy of a resume I'd submitted for a part-time job, photos of me and Anna that I'd posted online. My hands trembled and I shoved the folder back into the drawer, trying to breathe steadily despite the tightness in my chest and the heaviness of the underground air.

"Okay," I said, smoothing my hair down and clasping my hands behind my neck. "This proves that he's kept tabs us our whole lives. But that's not unexpected, is it?"

Jake shook his head. "We need to keep looking. At least these files could help us find the others," he said as he thumbed through the folders, counting. "All twelve of us are here, even Coby."

He shut the drawer, and we moved on to the next ones. A few of them were empty, but another had records of Sloan's kind. All besides Sloan's had a red X next to the name, and I shivered when I realized it meant they were deceased. What had Sloan said? They hadn't lived past eight years old? I felt a sudden flare of anger toward this madman.

There were three drawers of files on the Sirin, so Sloan was right. They existed, and the doctor made more of them than he did of us. I counted them as Jake moved on to the next drawers.

"There were 77 of them—of the Sirin," I said, getting the attention of everyone in the room. "Sixty-one still living, if his records are right. Your estimate wasn't too far off, Sloan."

My mind was full of questions. What would we do about the Sirin? Where were they? And why had the doctor created them? Were the answers in these drawers?

"I found it," Jake said, his voice trembling. "I found the evidence." I walked over to him slowly, my legs unsteady. Through the roaring in my ears, I heard Sloan and Zara follow behind me. This dark basement felt like a dream, Jake's comment a figment of my imagination.

"Tests on lab rats," Jake continued, his voice toneless. "Of all three strains. He called it the *finis mundi* virus."

"That'ss 'the end of the world' in Latin," Sloan said.

"You speak Latin?" Zara asked, turning to him.

"Yess. And four other languages," he replied, a little sheepishly.

"Are you sure that's what you're seeing?" I asked, grabbing the handle of one of the drawers for support. "He really developed the virus?"

"It's not possible," Coby said, his eyes wide.

"He engineered the first strain to have a long dormancy period. The first rats infected became immune, but then he

190

exposed new rats to them. Those only had a 52% survival rate," Jake said, dropping each file back into the folder as he read it. "The second strain—18% survival rate. The third, airborne strain—0%. Two hundred rats tested, no survivors."

"Oh my God," I breathed, sitting against the filing cabinets, unsure my knees would support me. One of the drawer handles poked into my back, but I barely felt it. I looked at the map again and realized what it was—his master plan to spread his world-ending disease to everyone on Earth.

Zara's voice cracked when she spoke. "We were getting close to finding something on the computer, too," she said. "Let's make sure we know what we're looking at."

Sloan nodded. His mouth was a firm line, and my heart twisted when I realized he wasn't at all happy he was right. Like Coby—who was now sitting against the wall across from me and staring into space, his knee bouncing as he tapped his foot on the floor—he'd wanted the doctor to be innocent of this.

In a daze, I pulled open the drawer to the right of me and piled files into my lap. I opened them to find depictions of angels. Famous oil paintings, sketches signed by the doctor, and finally, a photo of an actual Sirin. I held the picture in my shaking hands and tried to make myself believe such a creature existed.

The figure was a muscular male, faced away from the photographer, and without clothes. The most striking things, though, were the huge, feathered wings. They were partially outstretched, too large to tuck into their bodies the way birdwings do. The base of each wing sprouted from where the shoulder blades would be on a regular human, then ascended into the air above the subject's head before sweeping down to his ankles, where the tips of each wing brushed the floor. The plumage wasn't white, as I had envisioned it, but various hues of gold and brown.

"Jake," I said softly, and he sat beside me to see.

"Christ," he said. "I wouldn't want to get on the wrong side of one of those."

I put the picture to one side, scanning the doctor's other notes. I found the one where he'd come up with the name "Sirin". They were half-woman, half-bird creatures based on the Greek sirens and found in Russian mythology. He had also scrawled notes about the nephilim.

The offspring of angels and men that were giants of their time and the mighty men of old. I shall begin the world anew with them.

"Oh my God," I said, dropping the folder. Papers and photos spilled across the floor. I turned to Jake. "He thinks he's God—or a god, anyway."

Zara walked over to us, her face ashen. "What did you find?" she asked.

Jake handed her the picture of the male Sirin. "And he's got a god complex. He was trying to start over creation, in a way."

She took the picture, examined it for a moment, and then said, "Sloan and I found something else you should see." We rose to follow her over to the desk. On the way she said, "You too, Coby."

He followed, and we all stood around Zara and Sloan and the computer. They exchanged a look, and then Sloan spoke. "After he releassed the viruss," he said. "He predicted the war."

"No," Coby said firmly. "You can't pin the nuclear attacks on him too."

Sloan frowned as he pulled up the files. Spreadsheets, emails, graphs, and more lab test results like the ones Jake had shown us.

"What are we looking at?" Jake asked.

"He released the weapon strategically," Zara said. "He knew if he released it where he did, each country would be suspicious, think that one of the others had developed the virus as a weapon." Her voice trembled, and she sank into the chair at the desk, covered her face with her hands.

"That'ss how it came to war," Sloan said. "He knew what would happen."

"How could he do this?" I whispered. It hadn't been humanity—we weren't victims of ourselves. It was just him. "Why did he need to wipe out everyone?"

No one had an answer. We stared at the computer for a while longer, all lost in our own thoughts. Mine ranged from disbelief—trying to find a way we could be misinterpreting all this evidence—to confusion over what to do with this information now that we had it.

"What time is it?" Sloan asked. We all shook our heads, and he said, "We should get back. It could be closse to dawn. We can decide what to do when we get back up there."

I slipped the files on the other roach-hybrids and the photo of the Sirin into my pack. Jake handed me the virus test data wordlessly, so I added that too. We all moved toward the shaft of light still coming from above.

Zara climbed the ladder first. She yelped when she reached the top, then stumbled across the bedroom floor. The other four of us scrambled up the ladder to see what happened.

The doctor sat there, on our bed. Between his yellow gloved hands was my journal. *Shit. He knows everything.*

13: Point of No Return
Nadia

While it was happening, I didn't give much thought to the *cause* of the end of the world. My father and I were too busy surviving, trying to get somewhere safe. But after he was gone, I had nowhere to go and no one left. Though I'd mindlessly followed in the direction we'd been heading (southeast) there was no destination, no purpose. I sometimes let my mind wander, then, to what could have caused the apocalypse. I'd always reached the same conclusion: it was us.

I speculated that a group of scientists had accidentally created the virus while trying to cure a disease, that the nuclear attacks had been a result of decades-old tension and miscommunication between countries. Maybe the changes to the climate had mutated an already-existing virus and made it deadlier. When I heard that the disease was supposed to be a weapon, I was surprised, but at the same time it made sense. I'd always thought it had been unintentional, but unavoidable— that a joint act of hubris had led to our downfall. In other words, we, humanity, had brought it upon ourselves.

Never had I considered that The End might have been orchestrated by one man. And now, that one man sat before me, grinning smugly, and I wanted—no, *needed*—him to pay.

I pulled my gun from its hidden holster and pointed it at him. I tried to keep my hands from shaking, but it felt so wrong. My gun safety instructor's voice, from a time and place long gone, entered my thoughts. "Never point your gun at a person. Follow that one rule and everything else is just details."

"Stand up and drop that," I said, my voice surprisingly steely. His hands were on one of the few possessions that still meant something to me.

Jake stepped to my side. "We know the truth now," he said.

194

"Nod, don't—" Zara whispered on the other side of me, her face deathly pale. She turned to the doctor. "Why did you do this?"

"Drop it!" I repeated. "And stand."

As usual, it was impossible to read the doctor's expression through the shiny plastic of his face mask. He lay the journal on the bed beside him and stood.

"Answer Zara," I commanded.

"Why did I do what?"

"We saw the records," Jake said. "The virus... we know what you did."

"Why?" Zara asked again, softer this time.

"Because," the doctor said calmly, "humanity had gone too far. It was past the point of no return, past saving. I created a new race to replace them. My first attempt was most disappointing."

I glanced at Sloan. His nostrils flared, but he didn't otherwise react to what the doctor said. I wondered how many times he'd heard that before.

"I came close," the doctor continued, "with your race. But I left too much human in you."

The mechanical tone the mask lent his voice gave his words more weight. Shivers ran down my body. My arm was growing tired, shaking. I clasped both hands around the gun and waited for the doctor.

"This can't be true," Coby said. He stepped to the doctor's side. "Tell me this isn't true. You weren't going to destroy me."

The doctor reached out to touch Coby's shoulder. "No!" I shouted. "Don't touch him." The *click* as I cocked the gun sounded loud in my ears, but the doctor barely seemed to register it.

"Humanity was broken, Coby," he said, dropping his hand back to his side. "It was easier to begin anew—build it from the ground up—than to repair it."

"But things were getting better," I said, trying to keep the tears from my voice.

195

"No," the doctor said. "They would have continued to worsen until humanity destroyed itself, and the whole world with them. Take the war, for example. Look how easy it was to set the world at each other's throats. How many died before my disease could even reach them? It took nothing. Just a little push."

"You're wrong," I said, shaking my head. "The global population was stabilizing. Things were more democratic and equal than they have been for most of history. Efforts were being made to end climate change."

Everyone glanced between me and the doctor, on edge about whether I would pull the trigger. I didn't know myself. The doctor didn't seem to care. *Or he knows you won't.* He had that file on me, had tracked me my whole life, and now he'd read the journal I'd kept since the beginning of The End. I felt sick; he might know me better than I knew myself.

"Hope wasn't lost," I said through clenched teeth. "*You* gave up. You destroyed everything. Well, almost everything." I glanced at my companions. Sloan's face was unreadable as ever. Jake looked determined, and I knew he was with me. Zara's eyes were wide with fear. Coby's face showed a mixture of fear, anger, and surprise.

I thought of my family, of Anna. Jake's parents and his brother. Zara's mother, and Nick. The bodies decaying outside of this laboratory—the whole world. "Now I'm going to destroy you," I said.

Several things happened at once, and all before I could pull the trigger. Zara grabbed at my arms, Coby stood to shield the doctor from the blow, and Sloan tried to pull Coby away from him.

"We need to disscuss this," Sloan said. "Act rationally, think it through—don't lash out in pain and anger."

He managed to pull Coby away from the doctor, who was surprisingly quiet and nonreactive.

"Please, Nod, can we talk about this?" Zara asked, placing a hand on my shoulder after I'd elbowed her hands away from the gun.

"Fine," I said. "but not in front of him." I gestured at the doctor with my revolver.

"We need to tie him up," Jake said.

"Let's lock him below the trapdoor," Sloan said. "I've extenssively mapped the building. There's no other exit or entrance to it."

"Brilliant," I said. "Get down there." I pointed my revolver from him to the still-open steel door.

"You just saved yourselves from a costly mistake," the doctor said, lowering himself onto the ladder. His suit made rubbery noises as he went down. Jake slammed the door shut once the doctor was clear of it and pulled to make sure it was locked.

"It can't be unlocked from the inside?" he asked Sloan.

"I don't think so," Sloan said. "But let'ss move the bed over it jusst in casse." He and Jake each took a corner of the bed and pulled it on top of the door.

"What did he mean?" I asked, relieved that I could finally put down my arms and re-holster my gun. "What was the mistake?"

"He just doesn't want to die," Coby said, turning his fierce gaze to me. "And I don't want you to kill him."

"He deserves death," I said with finality.

"I agree," Jake said.

"Nod, no, please," Zara said. "I know what he's done is unforgivable, but I also know what it's like to… to kill someone. You don't want to do this."

I turned to Sloan. "I guess you're the tiebreaker. What do we do?"

14: Wicked
Jake

"We need to disscuss thiss," Sloan said. "The matter of taking a life isn't a simple one, and it would be better if we could come to an agreement insstead of acting rashly."

"Okay," Nadia said, folding her arms. "Where do we start?"

"I'll get uss some tea firsst," Sloan said.

"Seriously?" I asked, lifting an eyebrow. "We're going to discuss offing Winthrop over *tea?*"

Sloan shrugged apologetically. "I don't have much experience with humans. It seems appropriate to me."

"We're not humans," Zara said. "Not really."

"But you were raised by them," he replied. "It makess a difference. Now, I'm going to brew some tea. It always calms me, and a calm persson makes better decisions."

He slipped out of the room, shutting the door behind him. Zara and Coby stood on one side of the room, Nadia and I on the other. Divided. The tension hung thick in the air. Nadia twisted a piece of her hair, and Zara bit her lip.

Nadia picked up her bow and quiver, which lay exposed on the floor now that the bed had been moved out from over it. Slinging the quiver strap across her chest, she pulled out an arrow and nocked it. An arrow would be much cleaner at this range than a round from her revolver.

"He could be the last actual human on Earth," Coby said, shattering the silence.

"It doesn't matter if he's the last human," I said. "It's because of him that there aren't any others! He needs to pay for what he's done."

"We could lock him up," Zara said, her voice still trembling. "Keep him here for... for the rest of his life."

198

"I'm not spending the rest of my life tending to that madman's needs," Nadia said. "And I won't let any of you do that, either. He needs to die. It's justice. He tried to kill everyone on Earth—and succeeded, mostly. He wanted his own species to go extinct! Is there any greater betrayal than that?" Her voice edged on hysterical.

"Only blood can pay for blood," I said quietly.

"I've lost people, too!" Zara said, angry. "I know how you feel—my first instinct is violence, too—but we can't do this. We can't become murderers like him."

You mean a murderer like you, shot through my mind.

"Zara. You're thinking of what happened with Nick," Nadia said softly. "But that was different—you'd just lost your mom, and your actions weren't intentional. The doctor's were."

She shook her head. "It doesn't matter," she said. Her eyes were wide, dark. Hollow. "You don't know what taking a person's life does to you. To your *soul*. It's a stain you can never wash off."

"He created us," Coby said. "We owe him our lives. Doesn't that mean anything to you?"

"No," I said. "Not when he destroyed everyone else. And it was an accident that we lived through the virus, so I don't see why that counts."

Sloan came back into the room then, carrying a tray with a steaming teapot and five cups. While he handed one to each of us, Nadia sat beside Coby.

"I know you've known him a lot longer than we have. He raised you. But he's a bad man, Coby. The worst in history—he *ended the world*. We can't let him live," she said.

"You don't know the same man I know," Sloan said. "He was kind to you, but he was not so to me. He is a cruel man, full of hate."

"Clearly he's lost it," Coby said. "Gone insane. People can't commit a crime if they don't know what they're doing is wrong." His eyes were panicked. He knew he was grasping at straws.

Zara sat beside Nadia, placing her hand on her shoulder. "His death won't bring anyone back, Nod," she said quietly. "You know that, right?"

"Of course I know that. But he's killed too many people," she said, shrugging her hand off and pacing the room. "The body count's too high. I don't know what the limit is, but he killed the entire world, Zara. He'd kill us right now if he had the chance. We can't let him get away with that. We owe it to everyone who came before us."

I wondered for a moment if Zara was right, if mercy was the better option. Then I felt the hardened, cold place inside me that was my hatred for the doctor and I set my jaw.

"He dies tonight," I said through gritted teeth.

"We could send him away," Coby said desperately. "Make him leave here."

Nadia shook her head. "He'd die without his clean room. Same result, just slower."

"Then let him stay here," Coby tried. "And we can leave, like you and Jake wanted to."

"We can't leave him here. He's a danger to us and to whoever else might be alive," I said. "What if he has another virus, another plan to wipe out anyone who's left?"

"Do you really believe that?" Coby asked coldly. "That anyone else is left alive?"

"Yes," Nadia said, her voice faint. "Surely there were remote places still untouched by the virus, or people who had natural immunity. Maybe I'll never come across any of them in my lifetime, but I want to believe there are human survivors— or at least others like us. I need to believe that we aren't it."

"He could be the last real human left," Coby said. "If you kill him, *you* would be the one killing off the last of humanity."

The room went quiet then and I felt deathly cold. I shivered, but my mind was set. One way or another, the doctor wouldn't survive the night.

"He has to die," I finally said. "There's no other way to make him pay for what he's done. We won't torture him—we won't make it slow, though he'd deserve it."

"Sloan, we're not getting anywhere," Nadia said, turning to him and sniffling. "No one's minds have changed. What do you suggest?"

"There's no rush," Sloan said. "We can leave him locked there for now—"

"Oh my God," Nadia interrupted. "No, we can't."

I took a step toward her. "What do you mean?"

"We have him locked in there now, right?" There were nods all around. "Why didn't *he* lock *us* down there when he had the chance? He could've let us starve to death, dropped down poisonous gas or something."

"What are you saying?" Zara looked worried now. Not wanting to kill the doctor wasn't the same as trusting him.

"He *wanted* to go down there," Nadia said. "I don't know why, but—"

"He could be escaping," I said, jumping to push the bed off the trapdoor. It made a creaking noise as it scraped the floor.

"That'ss impossible," Sloan hissed. "I thoroughly mapped the building."

"You must have made a mistake," Coby snapped.

"Maybe he needed something down there," Nadia said, lifting the carpet back up and motioning for Zara to unlock the door. After a few moments, she nodded. Nadia took a step forward, pulling her arrow back and training it on the trapdoor. Zara and I pulled the door open and we all waited expectantly, our breaths held.

We couldn't see anything but the ladder and our heads silhouetted in the shaft of light that reached the floor. "Doctor Winthrop?" Coby called. "Are you there?"

15: Fallen Angel
Nadia

The familiar rubbery noises of the doctor's suit floated up to us as he came forward. We let out a collective breath. At least he hadn't escaped.

He stopped at the bottom of the ladder and squinted up at us. The scene was a strange one—a yellow-garbed scientist looking up at his creations, which included a scaled man, a girl with an arrow trained on him, and three other part-cockroach hybrids.

"Yes," the doctor said unnecessarily. "I'm here."

I glanced around at my four companions. None of us knew where to go from here.

"Keep him down there another minute," Jake said before abruptly leaving the room. I hoped he had a plan, because I sure didn't.

"We should put him on trial," Sloan said quietly, so the doctor couldn't hear. "Let him defend himsself—"

Zara nodded, her eyes wide and pleading. "Please, Nod?"

Coby and Sloan were looking at me too, and I wondered when I'd started making the decisions around here. *Right, because I'm the one with an arrow trained on the doctor.* I checked again to make sure the doctor didn't have anything he could use to harm us, then unnocked my arrow. Coby tapped his foot rapidly on the floor and wiped his palms on his jeans.

"So," the doctor said in his too-calm voice. "What are you going to do with me?"

Jake came back to the room with his rifle. I saw Zara flinch, and I could imagine why. The two people who wanted the doctor dead were the two with weapons.

"Sloan wants to have a trial," I told Jake quietly as he stepped to my side.

"Why?" he asked, looking at Sloan. "We already know the verdict: guilty as fu—"

"Please!" Coby cried. "Give him a chance to explain himself—you'll see he isn't right in the head, that he didn't know what he was doing."

I studied Coby, trying to imagine being him. If my father had cobbled me together from cockroach parts, destroyed the whole world, then sent me on a death mission to find his other experiments, would I still want him alive? *No*, I thought, but with a twinge of doubt. Maybe deep down Coby was a better person than the rest of us for standing by the only family he'd ever had, for believing in the doctor. Or he was just an idiot.

"Fine," I said to Coby. "Get up here, Peter!" I barked down the ladder. "It's time for your trial."

He ascended slowly, mechanically. Jake's rifle was trained on him the whole time. I felt he should have been moving faster, like a regular person who fears for their life. Apparently he either didn't believe he was going to die or didn't care. Something about his attitude made me feel sick to my stomach, like this was all part of his grand plan.

When he reached the top of the ladder, Jake motioned with his rifle for him to sit in the desk chair. We all stood around him in an arc, Jake and I on one side of Sloan, Coby and Zara on the other. Though Sloan stood directly in front of him, the doctor's eyes seemed to look through him, as if he wasn't there at all.

"Why did you do it?" I asked, not wanting to waste time or allow him more undeserved breaths than necessary. "Do you have some excuse for what motivated you? What caused such an intense hatred for your own species?"

The doctor turned his head toward me. His cold eyes studied me for a moment before he spoke.

"I see. You want a sob story from me. You want to hear how my parents neglected me, how mercilessly I was bullied as a child, how no one took my vision seriously—" He cut off. It was barely detectable, but his voice had begun to tremble. He cleared his throat and turned to me.

"A girl like *you*, Nadia—a girl who hates herself so much she self-mutilates, who has to cut into her own skin to feel alright, to feel anything—*you* are going to ask me why I hate humanity as a whole? As if I needed a reason."

I knew what he was doing—trying to demonstrate that he and I weren't so different—but his words cut into my core, deeper than I'd ever cut myself. My nails dug into my palms as I willed the tears welling in my eyes to go away. I didn't trust myself to respond.

"Humanity has done wrong," Jake said, "but why did you believe it past saving? What made you believe that?"

The doctor turned his gaze to Jake at his unsettling, slow pace. "Are you asking me why I didn't *save* humanity instead? Why I didn't bring it back to the light, instead of pulling it up by the roots and disposing of every last person?"

Jake inclined his head in a brief nod, barely acknowledging that the doctor had spoken. I felt physically ill, nauseated and dizzy, from the conversation. To Jake's credit he stood, legs planted, and faced the doctor. But then, the doctor hadn't delivered his Jake-specific blow yet.

"Says the boy who couldn't save anyone in his life—least of all his brother." The wicked gleam in the doctor's eyes showed through the mask. "My plague didn't even get to him! His death is on *you*—you couldn't save him from himself. Thanks for helping me out with that one." The doctor's laugh came harsh and metallic and shudder-inducing through his respirator.

But he wasn't done. He turned to Zara now and she shrank away from him. His gaze no longer on me, I relaxed my hands and noticed that my nails had dug deep crescents into my palms.

"Ah, and here we have Team Let the Doctor Live," he said, motioning to Coby and Zara. "How funny that our own little murderer doesn't want any more blood on her hands. Someday you might learn that being *ruthless* is the only way to survive in this world. I can tell you from experience that killing one person and killing seven billion isn't as different as one would think."

Zara swayed for a moment as he spoke, as if one of her knees had buckled. She crossed her arms and closed her eyes tight, as if that would make his words go away. He'd hit her Achilles' heel straight on. Jake looked like a tightened coil, ready to spring at any moment.

Focus. Why was the doctor goading us, as if he wanted us to kill him? *Is he trying to prove we're as bad as him?* With no other foreseeable way out, did he just want to cause us as much pain as he could before he died?

"And Coby," the doctor said. "Of all people, you should want me dead. But you're still in denial, aren't you?"

There was that laugh again. No, the doctor wasn't trying to convince us to let him live. If he was, he would have appealed to our mercy, told us that we would be as bad as he was if we labeled him beyond the point of redemption. This whole thing had been a chess game from the moment we stepped into his laboratory—or earlier, when he sent Coby to find us, or the moment he inserted us with nonhuman DNA. I was tired of being five moves behind him.

"You cling to this idea that I *care* about you, don't you Coby? As if I'm your father." He spat the last word in disgust.

Think, Nadia, think.

"But I'm not your family, Coby. I wanted you dead as soon as I saw how superior the Sirin were. You're nothing to me. You have nothing and no one." His gaze slid to Sloan for a moment. Coby was shaking, but I couldn't tell if it was from anger or if the doctor's words had crushed him.

When I first pointed the gun at him, the doctor hadn't flinched, as if it didn't matter if I killed him. And maybe it didn't. His hate for humanity might not exclude himself, and once the Sirin were ready and he killed us all, he would have done himself in. So why was he stalling?

Then I realized: he was trying to anger us. He had no problem dying; he didn't want to *suffer*. That's why my revolver in his face didn't ruffle him. It would be a quick death.

"Why do you need the suit?" I asked as the thought came to me.

The doctor whirled toward me, surprised. "What do you mean?" There, *that* was the pace of fear, the speed he should have been moving this whole time.

"Why not immunize yourself?" I asked.

"That's not how the disease works," the doctor said quietly. "I had to make you and my other creatures with fundamentally different DNA for you to survive. There is no cure, no preventative measure. I couldn't allow a chance for someone to find it before it was too late."

"So, you're not immune," Jake said, taking a step closer to the him.

"No, I'm not."

For the first time, the doctor looked uncomfortable, maybe even afraid. He tried to regain his assertive calm but couldn't grasp it. Perhaps he knew that none of us wanted to be the one to put a bullet or arrow through him, but now, thanks to him, we had another option. "No one was," he said firmly.

"Are there truly no other humans left? You wiped them all out?" I hated the way my voice sounded, small and childlike and afraid.

The doctor's smile came back. It reached his cold eyes as he said, "Yes. Obliterated."

Before anyone could react, Jake pulled his knife from his pocket and stabbed into the doctor's protective suit, tearing a six-inch gap.

16: His Own Hands
Nadia

"There," Jake said. His eyes looked glasslike, hard and cold, as he set down his rifle and dropped the knife. "Now he'll die at his own hands, not ours."

Possibilities flew through my mind. What if the suit had been an act? What if he had to be within range of an infected person for the virus to kill him? What if it did kill him, but this was the plan he'd had all along?

I soon had an answer to most of my questions. The doctor's breathing slowed, then came out in rasps. The virus affected him quickly—as the third strain always did. His breathing became increasingly labored. He tried to stand but instead fell off the chair. He landed in a half-sitting position against the desk, knocking a teacup onto the floor on his way down. It broke, and the brown liquid spread in a wide pool across the floor, blood-like.

Coby knelt beside the doctor, his face a mask of confusion and pain.

My stomach turned over as his breath came out in bursts, grating and harsh through his mask. I'd heard it before—my father had made that sound when—

I covered my ears and slumped against the wall, sinking to the floor, but I couldn't look away. He didn't say anything, as if he'd already said all he wanted to say to us. I watched his face through the hard plastic of the respirator's face-shield. A part of my mind that seemed detached from what was happening wondered how many people I'd watch die in my lifetime. It also wondered whether taking off the respirator would be merciful—would it make his death come faster or last longer?

He writhed, his body spasming as it struggled to fill his uncooperative lungs with air. The first and second strain killed slowly, and at the end it wasn't like this for their victims. The gasping, the flailing, was a special torture that came with the third strain. I tried again to look away, but my gaze was fixed to the scene. Everything happened so fast that I wasn't sure if I should be happy that our enemy was dead or worried about the way in which it had happened.

It was only twenty minutes before he was motionless, but it felt like days. I slowly released my shaking hands from my ears, battling to keep down the contents of my stomach.

Coby cut away one of the doctor's gloves and checked his pulse, then said, in a choked voice, "He's gone."

"Good riddance," Jake said.

"What happened to all of us deciding together?" Zara croaked.

Then I noticed Coby's face, scrunched and purple, and the murderous glare he was shooting at Jake. He clenched his hands and bent his knees, ready to attack.

I jumped to my feet, but Sloan beat me to it, moving between them before I got the chance. To my surprise, Sloan's eyes seemed as watery as mine or Zara's.

Sloan put his hand up to stop Coby. "Please," he said. "Stop. What'ss done is done, Coby. We need not have more bloodshed here."

I'd never seen Jake the way he looked right now. Cornered, with disbelief in his fearful eyes. He said breathlessly, "He had to die."

Coby took a step forward, and Sloan put a hand against his chest to stop him. I didn't like where this was going. Coby stopped advancing and spat at Jake, "What if he had more to tell us? We still have no idea what the hell is going on, and we'll never know now!"

"Are you kidding me? This guy has thirty years of notes, a catalog of his fall to insanity. We'll get more than we need from them." The words made sense, but the way Jake said them, panicked and rushed, made me doubt him.

They continued to argue, but my gaze moved around the room. I took in Zara, who was still on the bed, staring vacantly into space. Her thumb rubbing her pendant was the only thing to show that she was still with us in the room. My eyes landed on the doctor. He was a yellow lump on the floor, his face turned toward all of us.

It disturbed me. His eyes were still open, looking at us. Accusing? Vacant? Happy? I didn't know.

My heart lurched and I felt compelled to walk to his side. Coby, Jake, and Sloan continued their argument while I knelt beside the doctor. I picked up Jake's knife and cut around the plastic face mask.

I wanted to close his eyes. Isn't that what you did when someone died? As horrible as he was, he was still a person. We needed to remember that if we wanted to keep ourselves from becoming like him.

Vaguely, I heard Coby yell one last thing at Jake, then storm out of the room and slam the door behind him.

My trembling hands unfastened the respirator and lifted the face mask, but I gasped when, for the first time, I saw his face.

"Oh my God, oh my God," I breathed, starting to hyperventilate. I scrambled backward and sat against the wall, the doctor's eyes boring into me.

Jake moved to my side quickly, but I was afraid to look at him. "What is it? Are you okay?"

The tone of his voice steadied me, and I saw that he was back from wherever he'd gone that had made his eyes seem so cold and dead. For good, I hoped.

Zara and Sloan looked at me now too. Sloan's brow was furrowed in concern, but Zara still seemed vacant, a little angry.

I tried to breathe steadily and slowly. "It's… I knew him. Or, I've seen him before. Before The End."

Jake's jaw set firmly and he said in a tight voice, "What do you mean, Nadia?"

"I remember now," I said, trying to control myself. "When I was very young, my dad had this picture on his desk." I hugged myself, envisioning the less-wrinkled, less-grey version of my dad from the photo. "He was on a golf course, and his arm was around another man. I asked him who it was once, and—"

My chest tightened. It was hard enough to think about my family now that they were gone, but if they knew...

"And he said, 'Oh, that's Peter. He's a good friend from college.' He said I'd meet him, when I was older."

I pointed at the pile of flesh and yellow jumpsuit that had previously been Peter Winthrop. "That's the same person I saw in the picture, just older. The photo disappeared from my dad's desk a while after that, and the next time I asked about him my dad claimed he didn't remember the conversation. I figured I'd imagined it; I was so young."

Zara was focused on me now. Jake tucked a strand of my hair behind my ear. "It's okay, Nadia."

I looked back and forth between them. "It all came back to me when I saw his face. Maybe... maybe my dad even told me his full name. It had seemed familiar when I worked out the anagrams."

They exchanged a glance, then Zara nodded slowly. "I think we might have seen that same picture in the doctor's house."

The tears started flowing, and I couldn't stop them. What did this mean? Had my parents known the madman who destroyed the world?

"I wish you'd been with us," Jake said. "I'm sorry you're finding out now, like this."

Sloan cleared his throat, and we glanced up at him. He stood so silently and so still that it was easy to forget he was there, even with the scales and greenish skin.

"Jake," he said. "Why don't you take Nadia somewhere elsse, get her away from this?" He indicated the doctor's lifeless form.

I nodded, and Jake helped me to my feet. I stooped and closed the doctor's eyes, touching his already-cooling flesh as little as necessary, then turned away.

"What about you?" Jake asked Sloan.

"I'm going down the trapdoor again," he said. "He seemed happy when we put him there, and I'd like to find out why."

"I'll go, too," Zara said. She wasn't vacant anymore. She was avoiding looking in the doctor's direction, but seemed stable, as if she'd accepted what had happened.

I was the one dissolved in a pile of tears, who needed Jake's arm around me to keep me standing, and I hated myself for it.

Sloan and Zara descended the ladder, and Jake ushered me down the hall. He took me to his room and wrapped me in a blanket. Then he sat beside me, put both arms around me, and pulled me close, resting his chin on top of my head. He didn't ask questions or make me talk about it, instead letting me cry until his shirt was soaked with tears.

Eventually he asked, "Would you like something to eat?"

I shook my head and said quietly, "No. I'm fine."

"Okay," he said, but something wasn't right about his voice. I turned to look at his face. He hadn't flicked the light on when we got in the room, so it was hard to tell through the darkness, but I thought his eyes were shiny with tears.

I wiped my own cheeks roughly with my hands and sat up. "Jake?" I asked. "What is it? What's wrong?"

He withdrew his arms from around me and looked at his hands. Then he whispered, "I don't know if I did the right thing. I'm a killer."

"You didn't kill him, Jake, the virus did."

"Because of my actions," he said quietly.

"He deserved to die," I said. No matter what happened before The End or in the last hour, that much was true. I clung to it.

"Yeah, but maybe I shouldn't have done what I did."

My tears were drying, my breathing steadying. "If you hadn't done it, I would've put an arrow through him a few minutes later. Same result. He wasn't leaving that room alive."

"I guess so," Jake said. "And if that's true I'm glad I did it. I wouldn't want this to be on you."

I squeezed his hand once. Exhaustion came over me, and I was suddenly grateful not to be alone with my tangled thoughts.

"Nadia?" Jake said after a few minutes.

"Yes?"

"We should get some sleep."

I nodded into his shoulder and we lay back on the bed. I nestled my head onto his chest and he wrapped his arm around me. We'd been up all night and under immense stress. Of course I was confused. I let my eyes close and my breathing slow and pretended we were somewhere else, anywhere else, so I could sleep.

17: Not Okay
Nadia

I woke when the bed shifted and I lost the warmth of Jake's body against my back. I rubbed my eyes and a sliver of light came into focus as the door opened. "Jake?" My voice croaked.

"Sorry," he said softly. "I didn't mean to wake you. Just getting some water."

I nodded and lay back on my pillow, enjoying the return of darkness as he shut the door behind him. But as my mind cleared from sleep, the events of the last night came flooding back—the secrets beneath the trapdoor, the doctor's death, recognizing his face—until I thought I would drown in them.

By the time Jake came back, I was sobbing again and doing everything I could to stop, but to no avail.

He shut the door and rushed over to the bed, wrapping his arms around me. "Shh, it's okay," he said, stroking my hair.

"No, Jake," I said through my sobs. "I'm really not okay."

"Is it... because of me? Winthrop, I mean, what I did—?" Jake asked, his voice tender. He turned the lamp beside his bed on and looked at me.

I shook my head. "No, it's not you. It's—they knew," I got out as another onslaught of tears shook my body.

"Who?" he asked, sitting back on the bed.

"My parents, they knew all along. They knew I was a freak." Saying the words aloud both helped and hurt. The sobs abated, but there was a tightness in my chest, over my heart. *How could they?*

"The doctor prefers the term 'superhuman', remember?"

He expected me to laugh, but instead I said forcefully: "I don't think you should joke about the doctor, Jake. It's too soon after... what happened."

"I know," he said, his voice hoarse. "I'm sorry."

I stared at his boots. His legs were stretched out on the bed and I was wrapped up in a ball next to him. I could hear his heartbeat through his chest.

"How do you know about your parents?" Jake asked gently. He was stroking my arm, just below my shoulder, with his thumb.

I took a deep breath. "I didn't tell any of you, but back at the bookstore, when I found my records, I learned I was born through a surrogate. I'm probably still a DNA match for my parents."

"Alright," Jake said, "but that doesn't mean they knew. Winthrop could have altered your embryo before it got to the surrogate."

"No, they knew. I told you about the picture. My dad was *friends* with him," I said. My voice came out weak and small. "And when my sister Nicole was young, she got really sick for a while. I don't remember what she was sick with; I was pretty young myself. But she needed blood and a kidney transplant. The doctors said I was a blood type match and I told my parents I would do it.

"I didn't understand at the time, but they freaked out. They told me I couldn't do the donation, that I should never give blood or anything like that. I asked why and they said something like 'because we don't know what would happen'.

"Eventually I must have forgot about it, buried the strange memory or half-disbelieved it. But I always felt weird about donating blood, so I never did. I didn't check the organ donor box on my driver's license, though I wanted to. And now I realize—my parents knew all along. They knew the doctor and they let him experiment on me, their own daughter."

Tears slid down my cheeks again, and I felt a surge of gratitude toward Jake. He'd let me tell the whole story without interruption. I wiped my tears away and scrutinized the white lines scarring my forearm. If he wasn't here, I might be adding to them right now.

What if I'd always felt out-of-place because, subconsciously, my parents treated me that way? Because they knew?

"I'm sorry," Jake said. "But if you look at it another way, you survived *because* your parents let the doctor do this to you."

"They let me be a science experiment, Jake. Would you do that to your child?"

"Of course not, Nadia, but I'm glad they did. Otherwise I wouldn't be here with you right now." He held me tighter, and I sniffled until I managed to stop crying.

"From everything else you've told me, it's obvious your parents loved you. I'm sure they did what they thought was best, and that's all that matters, right?"

I nodded into his shoulder.

We sat like that for a while, sharing each other's warmth. My thoughts ran over all the tragedies of our past and the empty future before us.

"Do you think we can be forgiven?" I whispered.

Jake shifted to look at my face but kept his arm around me. "What do you mean?"

"I mean… we were supposed to be a new, improved human race, created by the doctor. And we killed him."

"I killed him," Jake said.

"We didn't exactly stop you."

His voice cracked as he spoke. "I didn't give you time."

"I agree with what you did, so I'm as guilty as you. And I'm not sure if we can ever forgive ourselves."

"He wanted to wipe us all out shortly after he made us."

"Maybe that was his right, since he made us. But instead we killed our Creator. I don't think a sin like that can be forgiven."

Jake sighed. "You're right. I feel guilty now, and I didn't think I would. Maybe Zara was right about… it staining your soul."

"No, Jake, that's not what I mean. I didn't mean that *you're* guilty, but that all of us are, and… never mind me. I'm tired, and I'm not making any sense."

"You're making perfect sense. I killed the doctor, the man who created me and allowed me to live through the end of the world, and there's nothing I can do to change it."

I didn't know what to say, so I buried my face into his neck and put my arm around his chest.

A while later, he said, so softly I wondered if he was talking to himself, "And the doctor was right about what he said, too. I couldn't save Ben. It's on me that he's gone."

"Don't think like that. Surviving the end of the world is a lot to expect of someone; asking that they go through it undamaged,"—I swallowed—"unscarred, is too much. It wasn't your fault."

"It was. And now I've killed the doctor, and Coby and Zara hate me for it. You think I'll never be forgiven and I agree. And… the doctor was right about me."

I sat up and said, louder than I meant to, "No Jake, he wasn't."

He wouldn't look at me. "It would've been better if I'd died in the third strain like everyone else."

I had a sudden urge to shove him, or slap him, or do something to bring back the old Jake. "You're wrong. I need you. Zara and Coby need you too…" I trailed off, watching his expression. It didn't change, and he still wouldn't look at me. *Confession time.*

I took a deep breath. "You've saved my life three times already, Jake," I whispered. "Please don't think that way about yourself."

"What?" he asked. "Three times?"

I bit my lip and stayed silent, unable to look at him.

"When Coby and I found the vaccine?" he asked. I nodded. "Once, then. But the other two times?"

"Once," I said, my voice already cracking, "when you rescued me from those dogs."

216

He shook his head, studying my face, but I couldn't meet his eyes. "That doesn't count. You would've figured a way out of that. Shot those dogs and got back to the hospital in the nick of time."

I shook my head, the lump in my throat not allowing me to voice my disagreement.

More gently, he said, "And the third time?"

"Look, Jake… I'm not who you think I am. I'm seriously messed up and—when I first heard you on the radio I'd made up my mind to… kill myself." My voice sank to a whisper. "I'd already tried once."

He didn't say anything, just wrapped his arms tighter around me.

I brushed a tear away. "You—you think I'm this survivor, you think I'm…" I almost said "perfect", but he didn't know I'd overheard him say that. "Strong," I said instead. "But I'm not. I wanted to give up. I couldn't take it anymore: the guilt, the isolation. I'm not strong, Jake. And if it wasn't for you, I'd be dead."

The final word sent a shiver down my spine. I waited for Jake to respond, but it took him a moment.

"You're stronger than you think," he said as he stroked my hair. "It takes a lot to survive in this world. Not just 'survive' as in stay alive. I mean, to live and to hold on to who you are. And you've done that, Nadia."

My heart lifted at those words, but I couldn't make my mind believe them.

"I should go," I said, and he released me. Though I didn't know where to go. The doctor's corpse was still in my room, and even if I knew where Zara was sleeping, she wouldn't want to see me tonight. Maybe I could put a couple of chairs together in the lobby and sleep there.

Jake held my hand as I stood to go. "Please stay," he said softly. His eyes looked weary; he hadn't slept yet, too guilt-ridden over what he had done.

In that moment I realized something—something I should have realized much earlier. Jake needed me. We needed each other, and he'd been relying on me for support as much as I had relied on him over the past months.

"Okay," I said, sitting beside him again. "I'm here."

We sat there, in each other's arms, not saying anything. Not needing to say anything.

My mind wandered over all the things we'd learned. It was a lot to process. We survived because we had cockroach DNA; there were eight more of us, some possibly still alive; the doctor created types like Sloan and the Sirin, too; later, he destroyed the whole world with his viruses, and even helped stimulate the nuclear attacks. I almost killed him when I found out; Jake *did* kill him; my parents knew the doctor…

The last one still stung, but I shoved it aside. Where did we go from here? Should we find the rest of our kind? What about the Sirin? When they found out about the doctor, would they be angry, or did they feel the same way we did about what he'd done?

As I considered our future options, the one thing they all had in common was Jake. I wanted our whole group together—Coby, Zara, and Sloan too—but it might not be possible after what had happened. The doctor's death may have created a fissure too wide for us to breach. The thought made another tear slip down my cheek.

But not staying with Jake wasn't a viable option. I couldn't imagine my life without him in it. Not anymore. I'd never felt that way about anyone before.

I thought back to the day we met, when I'd played my usual "game". Would I give up my life now—the life so full of Jake, Zara, Coby, Sloan—for one before-the-end day? Never. One day was not enough.

Would I give up knowing Jake for the rest of my life for that normal, easy day? No.

Slowly, the realization sank in: *I love him.*

It didn't matter that Jake had killed the doctor, or, more accurately, let the virus kill him. Maybe it would matter more if I didn't believe he'd done what he thought was right, or if I hadn't wanted to kill the doctor myself. It didn't matter that Jake was moody and stubborn and impossible at times, paranoid and distrusting. I loved him.

He'd always be there for me, and I for him. He believed in me. He gave me butterflies and made me laugh and let me cry when I needed to.

If I ever lost him, I'd be lost too.

My head rested on his chest, and I heard his heart beat faster. Was he having the same thoughts I was?

I turned my head and my lips met his.

He kissed me slowly, gently, his hand cradling the back of my head. I was lost in his scent and in his arms for a few moments, but then I pulled away.

"I—I'm sorry, Jake, I can't do this."

The wounded look on his face made my heart wrench. "Sorry—I—did I do something wrong?" Jake asked.

I shook my head.

He sighed and raked his hand through his hair. Gently, he asked, "Is—was—there someone else?"

The lump in my throat kept words from my tongue. He wouldn't look at me.

"Okay," he said quietly. "There's someone from before. I get it."

"No," I said, "it's... look, before The End, you and I never would have got together. And I'm so messed up, Jake, with the—the cutting and wanting to... end it. You've already saved me, but that's not what I want. I don't want you to save me from myself, because you can't. *I* have to do that."

"I don't care about any of that—" He stopped, sighing and combing his hand through his hair again so it stuck up in messy spikes before falling over haphazardly. "That's not what I mean. I do care."

I waited for him to continue, trying to keep my expression unreadable.

"What I'm trying to say is that I accept you the way you are, the way you've been. Obviously I'd like to help you stop and get better, but it doesn't make me like you any less. Or any more. It's a part of your past, something you struggle with. That's all."

I hadn't known what I wanted him to say until he said it. "Really?" I asked. I could feel a grin tugging at the corner of my mouth.

"Yes, Nadia," Jake said. "Now can we give us a chance?"

I nodded, throwing my arms around him, laughing and crying all at once.

He kissed me again, on my forehead, my cheeks. He pulled back to look me in the eyes, and he looked so happy that it made me smile too. My heart felt light, and for the first time I believed happiness might still be found, even after the end of the world.

Our lips met again, his warm and soft against mine. His hands clasped together at the small of my back as he pulled me closer to him. I ran my fingers through his hair and tried to make myself believe this was happening.

We pulled apart, smiling and breathless, still linked by my hands on his shoulders and his at my sides.

The world felt full of possibilities again, whole.

I said the words I'd thought from before, "I think I'm in love with you," then flushed scarlet.

A smile slowly spread across his face, then he crushed me into another hug and whispered, "I love you too."

◆ ◆ ◆

Later, we agreed we should sleep, but neither of us could at a time like this, so we talked the rest of the night and into the morning.

"I think I've loved you since before we met," Jake said.

I shifted to look at him, my head still against his shoulder. "Really?" I couldn't help but smile.

"Yes," he said as he ran his hand up and down my arm. "Since I first heard your voice, I think."

"Are you sure that wasn't because you thought I was the last other person alive?"

"I'm positive," he said. "Your voice, when I first heard you on the radio, sounded…"

"Scared shitless?" I offered.

He laughed. "That, too. But there was something beneath the fear—the stuff you're really made of."

I picked up one of his hands and played with it. I pressed my palm to his and he curled the tips of his fingers over mine.

"Do you think so?"

"I know so," he said, interlacing our fingers. It seemed they fit together perfectly.

Someone pounded on the door, startling us, and we both sat up. I felt my face flame pink, thinking of the look Zara was going to give me—give us. Then I remembered how she felt about what Jake had done, and my stomach knotted.

We crossed the room and opened the door to reveal Zara and Sloan. Zara didn't send me a knowing look as I had predicted. Instead, she looked terrified.

"The doctor got a message to the Sirin while he was in the bassement," Sloan said breathlessly.

"What does that mean?" I asked, though the unease that had spread from my chest outward, over my whole body, told me it wasn't anything good.

"It means they're coming for us," Zara said with a pointed glance at Jake. "To avenge the doctor's death."

18: Follow the Plan
Nadia

I tried to ask too many questions at once and found my tongue tied. Jake beat me to asking, "When will they be here?"

Sloan shook his head as they stepped into the room. "I'm not sure. We should have at leasst a few days, because mosst of the Sirin are at the Academy."

"How far away is that?" Jake asked.

"It'ss about 1500 miles from here," Sloan replied. "But we should be off as soon as possible."

"How did he get a message to them?" I asked.

Zara spoke up. "He had a satellite phone in the basement. It was hidden under one of the drawers full of Sirin files."

"But how do we know he called them?" Jake asked. His arms were crossed over his chest and he seemed calmer than I felt.

"There was an outgoing call tonight. It was placed when he was down there."

"Are we sure they responded?" I asked. "How do we know they're coming?"

"The call was eleven minutes long," Zara said.

"They're coming," Sloan said. "I know the Sirin. I've... seen what they can do."

Footsteps sounded down the hall, and we all jumped, then listened carefully. *The Sirin can't be here already.* Then I realized Coby wasn't with us.

We watched the doorway, and there was an awkward silence as he entered. He looked much calmer than when he'd stormed out of the room before.

"Can I speak with you, Jake?" he asked as he came in, between Sloan and Zara.

My hand instinctively shifted to the revolver at my hip. "Anything you want to say to him you can say in front of all of us," I said, narrowing my eyes. "No more secrets."

Jake and Coby exchanged a look, and Jake said, "It's fine. Give us a minute."

They left, shutting the door behind them. I hoped Coby was just apologizing.

There wasn't any furniture in Jake's room besides the bed, so Sloan and Zara awkwardly stood in front of me, and we all pretended we weren't trying to overhear Jake and Coby's conversation.

It was no use, though. We couldn't hear anything beyond the closed door. Maybe that was a good thing—it meant nothing violent was happening between them.

"These Sirin—are you sure they'd hurt us?" I asked Sloan, giving up on eavesdropping. "Maybe they feel the same way about what the doctor has done. But I suppose there's no chance he trained them not to harm humans, like Asimov's first rule of robotics?"

"Huh?" Zara asked.

"'A robot may not injure a human being or, through inaction, allow a human being to come to harm'," Sloan quoted verbatim.

"Right. It's from *I, Robot,*" I told Zara. Turning back to Sloan, I asked, "Any chance the doctor gave them similar orders?"

He pursed his lips. "I'm afraid not. Rather the opposite. The doctor has made them believe they are so far superior to humans, and that humans are so vile, that I wouldn't doubt they would kill one on sight."

"Does that include our kind of... mostly-humans?" Zara asked, biting the inside of her cheek.

"Mosst likely," Sloan said. "Keep in mind that they're all sixteen years old. It would be closser to a *Lord of the Flies* scenario."

"You've read it?" I asked Sloan. "What did you think of it? I think it's a pretty pessimistic view of humanity, don't you?"

Sloan smiled at me in his peculiar way—the corners of his lips quirked up and shifted the scales around his mouth outward. "As you can imagine, my view of humanity has been rather... *influenced* by the only one I've known."

"I can see that. But you really think they'll go all savage on us?"

"We'd be Simon—mistaken for an imaginary evil that the doctor has warned them of."

"Shit," I said. Zara looked confused, so I said, "Oh it's this book about a bunch of British schoolboys stranded on an island. They go all primitive and end up killing each other. They think Simon is this beast that doesn't exist and... it doesn't end well."

"Oh," Zara said. "That doesn't sound good."

"You've read a lot of books, haven't you?" I asked Sloan, excited. Bookworm friends were worth their weight in gold.

"There wasn't much elsse with which to entertain mysself here," Sloan said, still smiling. "Are you a bibliophile yoursself?"

"Yes, of course! Tell me, who's your fav—"

Zara groaned. "This is no time for starting a book club. How about we figure out how we're getting the hell out of here first?"

I sighed. "Fine, we can continue this later, Sloan."

"I look forward to it. Now, about esscaping—"

The door opened, and Coby and Jake stepped in. I breathed out in relief to see them both still in one piece. Jake frowned, his arms still crossed over his chest, but Coby seemed almost cheerful.

"Do we have a plan?" Coby asked.

"We were about to disscuss where to go," Sloan said. "I suggest we head south, since the Academy is northwesst of here."

"I *could* use a day at the beach," Zara said.

"What's the best way to keep them from finding us?" Jake asked.

We looked to Sloan. "We should keep to foresstss and wooded lands as much as we can," he said. "They can see well from the air, so it will be besst to travel with some cover."

"Would traveling at night help?" I asked.

Sloan shook his head. "I don't think so. They've been trained with night-vision goggles. We'll be better off during the day, when we can see as well as they can."

"We should head out now," Zara said. "There are a few hours of daylight left."

"No," Coby said. "I think we should gather supplies here first, do anything we need to prepare using the electricity."

"Yes," Jake said. It was the first time I could remember him outright agreeing to anything Coby said. Their talk must have gone well. "And none of us slept much the last two nights. We should sleep here tonight, where it's safe, and leave at dawn tomorrow, with as many supplies as we can fit in the car."

"You're coming with us, aren't you Sloan?" Zara asked. She turned to him, and I thought for a moment that she would grab his hand.

"If you'll have me," he said modestly.

I laughed. "Of course we'll have you. You're the only one who knows anything about the Sirin."

He smiled a little, scales rippling across one cheek.

"Why don't we raid the freezer?" I said. "We should eat anything perishable that we want tonight. It'll be a while before we can have steak or toaster waffles again."

"Sure," Zara said. "I'll help you." She still seemed shaken from last night's events, but Sloan's calming presence had helped.

"Coby and I will..." Jake hesitated. "Clean up. In Zara and Nadia's room. Then we'll load the Mustang with supplies."

"I'll head back to the hidden room again and check the clean room," Sloan said. "To see if I can turn up anything elsse usseful about the doctor or the Sirin."

"Okay," I said. "Let's meet here for dinner around sunset?"

Everyone agreed and we left Jake's room. I headed down the stairs after Zara but paused in the stairwell while she went on to the kitchen.

I felt less anxious now that we had a plan, but I couldn't help pulling the photo of the Sirin from my pack. The powerful muscles, the even more powerful wings. If they really were raised to hate us, to hate humans… I shuddered.

But Sloan thought we could escape them by heading south. *Everything will be fine if we follow the plan.*

19: Fight or Flight
Nadia

"Holy shit," Zara said as we walked into the room off the kitchen. Two rows of four freezers lined each wall, and at the back of the room hung shelves bursting with nonperishable foods.

"How much food do you think is in here?" I asked, lifting the lid of the freezer to my right. Colorful packages of frozen vegetables were piled in it, almost to the top.

"Enough for the rest of his life. That bastard," Zara said as she investigated another freezer. "Ooh, ice cream!" She pulled out a tub of chocolate chip cookie dough, and I couldn't help but smile.

"I never thought I'd have ice cream again," I said.

"I know what we're eating for dinner!" she sang, pulling out a tub of Neapolitan and another of mint chocolate chip. *"Bon appétit!"*

I'd moved on to the next freezer, which was full of meat. I pulled out a vacuum-packed t-bone. "Don't you think we should have something more like this? We're going to need protein if we're spending the rest of our lives running."

Zara's smile faltered. She shook her head, then smiled again, and said, "Of course. We'll eat it all! Steak *and* ice cream and whatever else we can find that looks good."

I laughed. "There's so much here. We could try to find coolers and take some with us."

"It's too bad we can't stay here with a lifetime's supply of food," Zara said. "But, *c'est la vie.*"

She grew quiet as we prepared dinner, a feast of the best things we could find in the freezers—perfectly marbled steak, asparagus that we roasted with garlic and parmesan, croissants, cheesecake, and, of course, ice cream. Zara ran out to the greenhouse and retrieved vegetables for a side salad, too. Neither of us commented on how similar the dinner was to the one we'd shared with the doctor a few nights ago.

I was pensive, performing the tasks in a ritualistic way. Many of them were things I may never be able to do again— cook with an electric stove, spoon ice cream out of a carton, obtain meat by tearing into a plastic bag. Before The End, I hadn't known that I'd done these things I'd taken for granted for the last time. It felt good to acknowledge it now. It was an evening of lasts, and both Zara and I recognized it.

I hadn't realized that a tear had slipped down my cheek until Zara looked at me and asked, in a soft voice, "Are you okay, Nod?"

Sniffling and wiping my tears, I said, "Yeah. We've just been through a lot. And I'm anxious about the Sirin."

Zara nodded and put an arm around my shoulders. "I am, too," she said.

"Do you think we can escape them?" I felt a new wave of panic set in just as I'd been calming myself down.

"Maybe we shouldn't," Zara said, stepping away from me.

"What do you mean?"

She bit her lip and looked away for a moment, then back at me. "You know how adrenaline is part of the fear response?"

I nodded, setting down the knife I'd been using to chop carrots for the salad.

"It gives you two options: fight or flight. And… I think we're choosing the wrong one."

It took me a moment to grasp what she was saying, but then my eyes widened and I took in a sharp breath. "You think we should *fight* them? Zara, there's 61 of them, and only four— or I guess, five—of us!"

"Not *fight* them, exactly, but we could try to face them. If we explain what happened…" She held out her hands in a helpless gesture.

"I don't think that will work," I said slowly. "And we might have to face them anyway if they find us. If we can't run away fast enough, if we can't hide…" I forced myself to breathe slowly, but my hands trembled.

"I know, I know," Zara said. She was looking off into the distance and tracing circles around her pendant with her thumb. "It's just… I don't think I can live like that." She turned to me again, her eyes shining with tears. "I can't spend the rest of my life—however short it will be—running and hiding. Living in fear. I've never lived like that. I can't."

Impulsively, I drew her into a hug. "I know what you mean," I didn't want to run either, but what other option did we have? "I don't think we can face them, though. They'll destroy us. You heard what Sloan said."

She pulled out of the hug, and something besides tears shone in her eyes. "We have to try," she said. "If we wave the white flag and surrender, maybe they'll listen to us, be merciful. Or at least rational."

The oven timer dinged, and I grabbed a potholder to pull out the tray of asparagus. "Okay," I said. "We'll mention it to the others and see what they think."

She nodded. We finished setting out the plates and then she found the guys and brought them to dinner.

Sloan, Jake, and Coby were much more enthusiastic about the feast we'd prepared than about our plan. They praised the steaks, vegetables, and croissants, eating them quickly. Over our dessert course we told them about Zara's idea. They immediately said it wouldn't work.

"But," Zara said, "I don't want to spend the rest of my life running and hiding, in constant fear that the Sirin will come and destroy us. That's not living, and I won't to do it. I'd rather be dead than not able to truly live."

"It'ss possible we could negotiate with them," Sloan said after a pause. "We do have the phone. We could call, explain the situation. It could be worth a try." Coby and Jake exchanged a look.

"That sounds like a good compromise," I said.

"We shouldn't try to reason with them," Coby said. "It won't work. I've seen them once or twice—I know what they're like."

"Any information you have would help," Zara said, stabbing a spoon into her tub of ice cream violently.

"Look," Coby said. "One of the few times that Sloan and I have been out of this building the doctor took us to the Academy for the Sirin."

"He did?" I asked.

Coby nodded.

"Yess," Sloan said. "He wanted to show them off, but since he couldn't reveal them to the population at large, he showed them to uss."

"What was it like there?" Zara asked.

"A boot camp. The Sirin have been trained as an army. Remember the night-vision goggles I mentioned? They have military-grade technology and weapons." Sloan swallowed, rippling the scales on his neck.

I bit my lip. The odds of us living through an encounter with the Sirin were already slim. The five of us, all unskilled and untrained, against an *army* of winged humans? The Sirin were all in peak physical condition, trained in combat, and had weapons they knew how to use. We were screwed.

The foods that had been so appetizing before now made my stomach turn. I pushed my plate of cheesecake away and looked at Jake and Coby, then Sloan.

"So we have no chance against them," I said.

"We have to *try*," Zara insisted.

"What about the satellite phone?" I asked. "If we tell them what happened…"

"It'ss possible they could track uss through it, so we shouldn't bring it when we run. But we could call them on the satellite phone in the morning before we leave," Sloan said. "We'll tell them what happened, what we learned about the doctor, and see if they can be reasoned with." He glanced between the four of us. "Does that seem fair to everyone?"

Jake and Coby exchanged another glance, and I looked at Zara. Her lips were pursed, but at least we were coming to a deal.

"I think that's fair," I said.

Zara finally nodded. Jake inclined his head, and Coby said, "Alright then. I'm going to turn in for the night. We'll have an early morning and a long day tomorrow."

"Okay," Jake said. "I should be getting to bed too."

I found myself wondering if I should join him in his room tonight and looked at him expectantly, but he didn't seem to notice as he turned to leave the room. "Sleep tight," he said on his way out.

"Sweet dreams," I responded, my face flushing. With everything going on I hadn't taken time to process what had happened between us. Maybe it hadn't meant anything: the kiss, the "I love you"s exchanged—but I felt that it had. Our relationship had fundamentally changed and deepened. I hoped Jake just needed rest before tomorrow's journey.

We'd have plenty of time to figure it out. If the Sirin didn't get to us first.

Sloan excused himself, and I cleared the plates from the table. I'd brought them to the sink and started to wash them when I realized what I was doing and laughed—a little hysterically—to myself. We could never come back here, and these plates would never be used again. They'd outlived their usefulness on Earth. I grabbed a plate and slammed it into the garbage. It hit the bottom and shattered.

I became conscious of the satisfied smile they'd elicited from me when Zara walked in the room. "What happened? Did you drop something?" she asked, then took a step back when she saw my grin.

"No," I said. "I smashed the plates."

"Why?"

"Because they were the doctor's plates, and they're not useful to us anymore," I said. "Or to anyone."

"That... doesn't seem like you, Nadia."

I shrugged, then handed her a plate, hoping she'd join me in destroying the doctor's things. "Here, do one yourself."

"That's okay, Nod," Zara said, setting the plate back on the counter. "I'm just going to take a shower and go to bed. You should, too."

"Okay," I said.

"Come on," she said, gently placing a hand on my back to usher me out of the kitchen. She glanced at the plate shards in the trash on our way out.

"Wait," I said, "where are we sleeping?"

"Our room," Zara said.

"But—the doctor."

"Jake and Coby got him out of there. And there's nowhere else that's comfortable to sleep." `

"But someone *died* there."

"Someone *you* wanted dead," Zara shot back. Then, in her normal tone, she said, "It doesn't matter, Nod. Everything I've used since the end of the world was touched by death. And it's only for one night."

"Okay," I said as we reached the stairs. "One more night here." *Then, never again.* Even without the threat of the Sirin, I'd be happy to leave Winthrop Enterprises behind forever.

20: Here I Go
Jake

I slipped my note into the book she'd given me to hold onto back at the bookstore. Christ, that was a long time ago now. I wish we'd been wiser. We could've stayed in Newbury and lived comfortably our whole lives. What was it with humans and that insatiable need to understand, to solve the mysteries around us?

Curiosity kills more humans than cats, I thought. And more almost-humans like us too, probably.

Swallowing back the guilt that was already taking root, I knocked on Nadia's door. She opened it, and I heard Zara singing in the shower. Good. A few last moments alone with Nadia was all I'd hoped for.

She smiled and leaned her head against the door. "What's up?" Her hair wasn't in its usual braid. It fell over her shoulders in golden waves.

"I wanted to give this back to you," I said, handing her the book.

"I forgot about this!" Her eyes lit up when she looked at me, piercing me. "I had no idea you still had it."

"Sorry."

"No, no, I'm glad. That day was a long time ago, wasn't it?" she asked, echoing my thoughts.

"Yeah," I said, "a lifetime ago." I couldn't meet her eyes.

"Are you okay?" Nadia asked, biting her lip.

"Yeah," I lied. "I'm fine. Just tired."

"Okay. Thanks for the book."

"I think you'll like the ending."

"You read it?" Nadia looked up at me, her eyes smiling. She had to make this harder, didn't she?

233

"Yeah," I said. "You were right, it's pretty good." I turned to go, then looked back at her. "Just don't read it tonight."

Her eyebrows drew together. "Why?"

"Because..." *I don't want you to find the note yet.* "Because you'll stay up all night reading if you start now." I managed a half-convincing half-smile. "We all need our rest these days."

Nadia laughed, and the realization that it was the last time I'd hear it was a dagger through my chest. "Okay, I won't read it tonight." She held out her smallest finger for a pinky-swear.

I linked my pinky with hers and then, unable to resist, pulled her into a hug. I breathed in her fresh scent, with hints of vanilla, one last time and stroked her hair.

All I wanted right then was to kiss her, but I couldn't do it. What I was about to do was already unforgivable. A goodbye kiss would make my betrayal that much worse. Instead I squeezed her tightly, then let go and took a step back. "Sleep tight," I said.

Nadia's eyes were clear and blue. They made my breath catch in my throat. She pressed her lips together as she studied me. I feared if I stayed longer she'd see right through me. "Sweet dreams, Jake," she said finally.

I returned to my room, feeling like the world's biggest tool. All because of Coby.

PART THREE

In the midst of winter, I found there was,
within me, an invincible summer.
And that makes me happy.
For it says that no matter
how hard the world pushes against me, within me,
there's something stronger—something better,
pushing right back.
      — Albert Camus

1: A Note
Nadia

The next morning, Jake and Coby were gone.

I'd gotten up at dawn and decided to wake the guys first to give Zara a few more moments of sleep. Her nightmares had been especially bad, and it had been the darkest part of the night before she'd finally stopped thrashing and was able to sleep peacefully.

I knocked on Jake's door and received no answer. When I tried the knob, it was unlocked. Jake wasn't inside, though. Neither was his pack, his gun, any supplies…

I checked Coby's room. Empty.

Be calm. They probably got up early and are packing up the Mustang.

I returned to my room, where Zara was still lightly snoring, and threw on my jacket. I told myself I didn't need to wake her yet—there was no need to panic. The hard knot in the pit of my stomach and the vague nausea I felt told me otherwise.

I ran downstairs and pushed open the door, dreading the putrid scent that would hit me as I stepped out into the morning air. Trying to breathe through my nose, I ran to the Mustang, but couldn't run fast enough, so I ended up gulping lungfuls of the chilly morning air, corpse particles and all. Then I stopped dead in my tracks, still panting.

The Mustang was gone.

I jogged around the blocks surrounding the hospital, a shred of hope remaining. I could've mis-remembered where we'd parked it. But with each step the cold certainty that they'd really gone crept over me.

We were left with only the ownerless cars and corpses strewn about the streets of this godforsaken city.

When my last flame of hope flickered out, I returned to the laboratory. I'd forgotten to unlock the door before I ran out and had to crawl through the window again. I hoped to see Jake and Coby sitting in the lobby, eating breakfast as we had a few days ago. But they were long gone.

I woke Zara, and though it was clear they weren't here anymore, we searched the whole lab again anyway. We found Sloan, sleeping in a room on the second floor, and decided not to wake him yet. A few more minutes of sleep would be his reward for not abandoning us.

We trudged up the stairs to our room, both of us grim.

"Oh my God. What are we going to do?" I pushed my hair back from my face and bit my lip, willing myself not to cry.

"Those assholes," she said, her hands balled into fists.

"How could they leave us like this? They took the car, half our supplies—they didn't even say goodbye."

Zara looked up at me. "Did you talk to Jake last night? I thought I heard your voice while I was in the shower."

"Yeah," I said. "He didn't say anything about leaving. He gave me… *Oh*," I breathed. We entered our room and I stooped to rummage through my pack.

My heart was racing as I pulled the book out, but Zara's gaze steadied me. She gave me a nod as I flipped through the pages, trying to find a farewell from Jake.

Between two pages, close to the middle of the book, was a folded note. *That's why he didn't want me to read it last night.* That bastard.

I swallowed. This was how it ended, whatever was between Jake and me.

Zara plucked the note from the book and handed it to me, a solemn expression on her face. I unfolded it with shaking fingers, and, though I'd never seen his neat, compact handwriting before, I knew it was Jake's.

I read the note aloud, my voice trembling, each sentence further widening the tear in my heart:

Dear Nadia,
Before I say anything else: I'm sorry.

240

What I'm doing is unforgivable, I know, but I have to do it. I hope you can try to understand that. Coby and I are leaving. We're going to meet the Sirin, try to convince them to spare you and the rest of our kind that may still be alive.

Coby doesn't think the doctor told them how many of us, or which of us, arrived at the lab. He said that the doctor didn't tell them much about our kind, since we were so "inferior", and he wanted to do away with us himself, without involving the Sirin. They only knew of Coby's existence before this, and it's possible they still don't know about you and Zara. We hope to keep it that way.

If all else fails, I'll admit that I am the one who killed the doctor and take whatever punishment they give in order to spare the rest of you.

I hope it doesn't come to that. I hope the Sirin can be reasoned with, and we can return to you and Zara, then find the rest of our kind. I hope more than anything that I can see you again.

Don't even think about following us. Coby and I are taking a risk, and there's no need to jeopardize your lives too.

When you leave Winthrop Enterprises, leave us a clue to where you've gone so that, if the impossible happens, we can find you again. If we somehow do survive, I'll spend the rest of my life looking for you.

If I can't find you, it will all have been for nothing. If I make it through this, I wouldn't be able to survive the rest of my life without you, Nadia.

I love you.

Jake

2: Another Option
Nadia

"Those bastards," Zara seethed as I read the last line of the note.

My whole body went cold, and I trembled as if shivering, the note slipping from my fingers and onto the floor.

"We promised each other: no notes," I said quietly.

"What? What are you talking about?" Zara asked. She paced the room, becoming increasingly agitated.

"Back in Newbury. Jake told me about his—" I stopped, some last shred of loyalty keeping me from giving away Jake's secret. *But he's gone*, I thought bitterly. And the doctor had all but spelled it out to the others anyway. "His brother... killed himself before the virus could. And he left Jake a note before... He made me promise I wouldn't do that."

Zara nodded. "And now he's done essentially the same thing to you."

I didn't know what to say, or how to feel. I was numb.

"That 'I love you' was a low blow," Zara said, crossing her arms. "I think he forfeited his chance to confess his undying love by abandoning you."

"It—" I croaked, clearing my throat. "It wasn't the first time he said it."

Zara perked up. "What do you mean?"

"The other night. We... kissed," I whispered, staring at the floor. "And we said we loved each other."

"Oh honey," Zara said, pulling me into a hug. I thought it would send me over the edge, that I'd start crying, but I just stared at the floor, empty, as she hugged me tighter. "We're going to be okay."

"But we won't!" The strangled words came out before I could stop them. "They're gone and the Sirin will kill them and then they'll kill us."

"No, they won't," Zara said, setting her jaw. "We'll find a way to survive." She grasped my shoulders. "We always do."

"This is just like Jake," I said. "Trying to save everyone. I should have seen it coming. Coby, too, I guess. He's more of a hero than we thought."

"How *gallant* of them," Zara sneered.

"They mean well," I said hollowly.

"Are you kidding? This is the stupidest thing they could have done. We could have all survived and now they've signed their dea—" she stopped when the color drained from my face.

"I'm not saying it's not idiotic," I said, unable to look at her. "But I think their hearts were in a good place."

Now that I was calmer, Zara let herself get angry. "If I ever see him again, the first thing I'm going to do is punch Coby in the face. This whole plan reeks of him. But I'll slug Jake, too, for good measure. *Men!*" she said, shaking her head.

The betrayal of it. Hadn't he made me promise him? Hadn't we agreed that notes were no way to end things? True, he wasn't killing himself directly, but the result might be the same.

"What can we do?" I asked, feeling helpless. "Can we go after them?"

"I don't know. Jake was right. It's fight or flight, and they left us with only the flight option. If we go after them, we'll all die."

"So we just run as planned? Without Jake and Coby." I sat on the floor, leaning against the wall. Closing my eyes, I tried to breathe deeply. When I opened them, Sloan was there.

He must have slipped into the room without me noticing, standing eerily silent and still as only he could. Now he blinked and let his arms, which he'd been holding behind his back, fall to his sides. The sullen look on his face showed he knew what had happened.

"Sloan?" I asked softly. "You've seen the Sirin, right?"

"Yess," he said.

"Is there any chance Jake and Coby will… that reasoning with them will work?" I could imagine the desperation in my eyes. Zara looked at him expectantly too.

"I wish I could tell you otherwise," Sloan said. "But the chances are slim. They won't be able to fight them, and reasoning won't work."

"Ugh. We need to rescue those morons?" Zara asked. Her black-painted nails dug into her folded arms.

I shook my head. "They have a head start, and we should be putting miles between us and the Sirin, not going toward them!"

"So we run and leave Jake and Coby to their fates? I don't think their idiocy is a good enough reason to let them get killed," Zara said.

"There may be another option," Sloan said in his steady voice. "Sun Tzu wrote, *'the supreme art of war is to subdue the enemy without fighting'.*"

Zara studied him, her face weary. "What are you saying? What's our third option?"

"To show them what you have is valuable."

"What the hell do we have?" I asked.

"Humanity accomplished great things as well as evil ones," Sloan said, sounding like Yoda. The greenish tinge of his skin solidified the resemblance.

"What exactly are we supposed to do?" I asked. "Make a PowerPoint of all of the great people of the world and the accomplishments of humanity? Mother Theresa, the internet, the Seven Wonders of the World? That'll never work!"

Sloan shook his head. "No. You can save one of the Sirin from himsself."

Zara looked perplexed. "How?"

"You can show the one here that humanity didn't need to be desstroyed. Teach him some of humanity's redeeming ways."

"Hold up," Zara said. "There's a Sirin *here?*"

Sloan nodded, and I grabbed the bed to pull myself back to a standing position.

"And you don't mention that until *now?*" Zara asked.

"I told you the doctor keepss one of each kind here at the laboratory," Sloan said, looking at us like we were total idiots. Maybe we were.

"That must have slipped our minds with everything else going on," I said dryly.

"Where is it?" Zara asked, taking a step closer to Sloan.

"Not 'it', 'him'," Sloan said. "His name is Vicente. And he's in the bassement."

"It's always the basement, isn't it?" Zara muttered.

"Take us to him," I said. If there was a chance to save ourselves—and hopefully Jake and Coby in the process—I was going to take it.

Sloan inclined his head. "Follow me."

3: One of Them
Nadia

The sound of our three pairs of shoes on the steps resonated throughout the stairwell as we descended to the underground level of the building.

"Wait, you were going to let us leave the lab this morning without this... Vicente?" Zara asked as we rounded another railing. "When he could be our best chance for survival?"

"No," Sloan said. "I was going to tell you all thiss morning before we left. I found the key to his room last night. As for him being our best chance for survival... I never said that."

"What do you mean?" I asked.

"You'll undersstand once you've met him."

"Well, why didn't Coby mention him?" Zara asked. We'd reached the bottom of the stairs.

"Oh, that," Sloan said. "Coby didn't know."

He pushed the door open and we stepped into the hallway. The fluorescent lights overhead were off, and when Zara tried the switch nothing happened. I pulled my flashlight from my bag and clicked it on. The hallway looked like the ones on every other floor.

"Why didn't he know?" Zara asked.

"Coby and I," Sloan said carefully. "Were always very different. He took things at face value. Vicente was a secret of the doctor's. I wasn't supposed to know there was a Sirin here either. Thiss way," he said, directing us to the right.

"How did you find out about him?" I asked, starting to shiver. I wasn't sure if it was from the grim anticipation of finally meeting a Sirin or because the basement had a chill the rest of the laboratory was without.

"I used to do a lot of... exploring," Sloan said. "I have terrible inssomnia—I only sleep a few hours a night—and during the resst of those hours I would look around the laboratory. That's how I realized the doctor had hidden something in the basement. I've spent years mapping and recording every inch of thiss place."

"Why didn't you look into it before we came?" Zara asked. "How long had you suspected?"

"I have susspected the doctor was not what he seemed, or what he claimed to be, from a young age. One getss that impression when one is hidden from the public in the bassement of a laboratory." He let out a small snicker and stopped in front of a door.

I had to keep from fidgeting. My emotions were swinging like a pendulum from hopeful excitement to dread.

Sloan continued, "I only realized the disscrepancy in my blueprint of the laboratory a few monthss ago. I've wanted to find the hidden room since then, and I theorized that the entrance was in the room which you two occupied. I didn't have the opportunity, though, until the four of you arrived. The doctor was disstracted, and I was able to slip away from my room and steal the key without his detection."

I nodded. "How long have you known about Vicente?"

"Are you guys like, friends?" Zara asked. Her face looked calm, but she fiddled with her necklace and tapped her foot on the floor.

A strange expression, made stranger by the movement of his scales, flashed across Sloan's face. "Not exactly. Shall we?" he asked, his hand on the door handle. As he pushed it open, I briefly wondered why the door wasn't locked to keep Vicente in. My question was quickly answered.

There was another smaller room within the one we stepped into. Its walls were concrete, broken by a one-way mirror on one side and a steel door on the other. Outside that room sat only an old metal folding chair and a matching table.

Zara and I stepped up to the one-way mirror and peered in, cupping our hands around our eyes to see better. A small, high window lit the jail cell-like room. There was a bed, a desk and chair, and a toilet and sink behind a small privacy wall. These things were hardly notable, however, compared to the occupant of the room.

"Holy shit," Zara said, and the creature perked up. Seeing that the walls weren't soundproof, she whispered to me: "That is the hottest human being I've ever seen in person."

"In person?" I whispered back. "He's the most attractive guy I've seen *period*."

Vicente sat on the bed. He wore jeans but nothing else, and his broad wings were half-outstretched behind him. The feathers on his wings were long and straight, ranging in tone from gold to coffee-colored. His torso and arms were so well-sculpted that I wondered if he'd been the muse for the doctor's angel statue. His skin was an olive tone and his dark hair hung in waves to his shoulders. When he'd heard Zara's exclamation he looked up, right at us, with his piercing eyes. They were light brown, almost amber, in color.

"I understand why the doctor thought we were inferior." Zara said, back to her normal volume. She turned to Sloan. "Do they *all* look like this?"

"More or less," Sloan said. Poor Sloan. After seeing Vicente, he looked less human than ever.

"By thiss point," he continued. "The doctor had access to a wide array of DNA through his on-the-bookss ressearch. He carefully chose the parentss and then edited the genes for each Sirin. They're nearly all intelligent, capable, and attractive. Thankss to the Academy, they're all fearless and in peak physical condition, too."

Vicente, who could clearly hear us, crossed to the door on the other wall of his room. He seemed to be waiting for it to open.

"Did he go to the Academy too then?" Zara asked. She'd returned to the mirror and was looking through it at Vicente.

"Yess," Sloan said. "The doctor never had any Sirin here until shortly before he released the viruss. That'ss probably another reason Coby didn't know—they weren't here long

248

before the doctor sent him away. Since that time, the doctor has had Vicente here. Every few months another would come from the Academy to visit him. There were a few times when he had two or three visitors at once. Then the doctor would have dinner parties with them, much as he did with you the other night."

"That explains our Sirin-dresses," I said. "When are Vicente's next, uh, visitors coming?"

"If my guess is right, another will be coming in a few days. That'ss why I wanted to leave thiss morning." He dropped his voice so Vicente couldn't hear. "If the Sirin don't know or believe that the doctor is gone yet, they will once Vicente or his visitor get word back to them."

Suddenly, Zara threw her arms around Sloan, embracing him. "Thank you for not being an asshole, Sloan."

"What?" he and I asked at the same time.

She drew back from the embrace. "You seem to know everything, or at least a lot more about the doctor and what went on here than we do. We'd be lost if you had gone off with Jake and Coby."

I nodded. "That's true. Thanks, Sloan."

"O-of course," he said, looking uncomfortable. I wondered: had he ever been hugged before?

To change the subject I asked, "Can we talk to him? Is it safe? I mean, the doctor must have him locked up like that for a reason…"

"Better to get the encounter over with," Sloan said. "Have your gun ready, jusst in casse, Nadia."

I nodded as Sloan walked to the cell door. He said something I didn't catch, and through the mirror I saw Vicente nod. Sloan pulled a key from his pocket and unlocked the cell door, swinging it open. Vicente stepped out, blinking as his eyes adjusted from the morning light from his window to the dim outer room.

Once he could see again he stared at Zara and me for several tense moments. Finally, he said to Sloan, "*Ĉu tiuj estas la blatoj?*"

"*Jes,*" Sloan said.

"Um," Zara said. "What the hell did he say?"

"Ah, yess," Sloan said. "I forgot. The Sirin speak Essperanto."

"What? *Why?*" I asked.

"The doctor consssidered it a better language for remaking the world. It'ss a consstructed language, so it doesn't have the irregularities of languages like, say, English or French."

"I take it that Esperanto is one of the five languages you speak?" Zara asked, stepping closer to Sloan.

"Yess," he said modestly.

She lightly punched his shoulder. "See? Didn't I say you were a valuable member of our team?"

Vicente made a scoffing noise at that.

"Wait, does he understand English?" I asked.

"Yess," Sloan said. "But not well. Those who have spent a great deal of time with the doctor know a little, though at the Academy they only speak Essperanto. Vicente may undersstand some of what we're saying, though he would have trouble stringing an English sentence together."

Vicente nodded and said something in Esperanto while looking at us disdainfully.

"He said he wouldn't want to speak English anyway," Sloan said. "Because Essperanto is the language of the doctor's new, better world. There was alsso a bit about uss being inferior creatures, but I won't repeat that in detail."

"The language thing is going to make Coby and Jake's job extra hard," Zara said. "And it might have already been impossible."

I bit my lip. "Sloan?" I asked. "Vicente doesn't know about… you know what yet, does he?"

Sloan shook his head. "We should be prepared for violence when we tell him."

"Would he hurt us?" Zara asked. Vicente stared at her with a less-than-comforting gaze.

"Without a doubt," Sloan said.

"Sloan?" I asked. "What did you mean about... helping 'save him from himself'? How are we—?"

The door to the hall swung wide, interrupting me, and all four of us turned to look. From the hallway came a female Sirin. She was platinum blonde and gorgeous and wore a murderous glare that made my skin feel as if it were burning.

"*Kion vi faris!*" she screamed as she lunged at Zara.

4: Breathless
Nadia

Too many things happened at once. Vicente shouted something at the Sirin, who wrapped her hands around Zara's throat. Sloan and I dove to pull her off Zara.

Zara kneed the Sirin in the stomach but couldn't manage to twist out of her grasp. Her face was going pale and bruises were forming on her neck as I clawed at the Sirin's arms, trying to pull her away from my friend. Finally, I was able to position myself to elbow her in the stomach. She gasped and released Zara, who desperately panted for air and grabbed at her neck.

Far faster than seemed possible, the Sirin recovered and moved her vicious attention to me. She lunged, but I managed to duck out of the way. I put myself between her and Zara, who was still gasping behind me. Out of the corner of my eye, I saw Sloan push Vicente back into his cell and locked the door. Our new Sirin acquaintance seemed undisturbed by the scene going on before him.

While I was distracted, the wild Sirin lunged at me again. I twisted out of the way and she whirled, turning toward Sloan. She shouted something at him in Esperanto and I jumped, grabbing one of her wings with both my hands to hold her back.

She screeched and flapped her wings powerfully, throwing me back against the wall and creating a gust of wind that filled the room. The breath left my lungs and all I could do was stare at the feathers that had come off her wings through black dots in my vision while I gasped for air.

Zara had recovered and, as the Sirin approached, she delivered an uppercut to her chin, knocking the winged creature back a step. She responded by stomping on Zara's foot; Sloan tried to jump into the fight again, but she shoved the heel of her hand into his chest, knocking him over effortlessly.

She turned her attention back to Zara just as I managed to catch my breath and clear the stars from my vision. I lunged at her from behind, aiming for her wings, but too late. She took another swing at Zara and knocked her off balance. Bright red blood flowed from Zara's nose as she landed on the floor.

I grabbed the Sirin, placing one hand on each wing where feathers met human flesh, then dropped like a dead weight. The wings felt surprisingly light and delicate. She shrieked and thrashed around, trying to shake me off, but I dug in my fingernails, feathers falling to the ground around me. She tried to reach me, swat me away with her hands, but couldn't with her wings in the way.

Suddenly, she stopped thrashing. It caught me off guard, and without meaning to, I loosened my grip.

She spun around, quickly and violently, throwing me off her and onto the ground. I landed on my side and the impact sent a shock from my hip through my whole body.

"Nod!" Zara shouted when I didn't get up right away. She crawled toward me, blood dripping from her nose onto the floor.

My hip—my gun. God, I'm an idiot.

With a grunt and a huge effort, I flipped onto my other side as the Sirin shoved Sloan off her again and started back toward me. I pulled my gun out of the holster with my trembling, injured arm.

"I'll shoot," I said. I tried to sound and look like I meant it, but I could barely hold my arm straight and my voice was raspy and breathless.

For the first time I saw something besides rage in the Sirin's eyes. A quick bolt of fear, then a flash. A plan formed, a decision made.

She spun on her heel and was out the door faster than seemed possible.

Zara stood, leaning heavily on the table and holding her nose, trying to stem the bleeding.

"Do we go after her?" I asked Sloan as Zara stumbled toward the door.

Sloan seemed solid and calm, the way he always was, though his hands were shaking. "No," he said as he peeked down the hall. "She'll be long gone."

I nodded and set my gun on the ground. Even that small motion hurt.

Zara collapsed into the folding chair, pressing her thumb and forefinger to her nose.

Sloan unbuttoned his shirt with a pained effort, then slipped off his white undershirt. He had fewer scales on his chest than on his face and hands. He put his blue shirt back on, not bothering to button it, then folded his undershirt and helped Zara use it to stop her bleeding nose.

"Thanks," she said, her voice muffled. "What the hell just happened?"

"Are there more?" I asked. "I know the doctor called them but how did she get here so fast?"

"*They're* not here; it was jusst her," Sloan said. "She musst have been the next to visit the doctor—either I was a few days off in my esstimate or she came early."

"And she just decided to attack us?" Zara asked. Her voice was hoarse and strained, and the finger-marks on her neck were deepening to purple.

"She found out about the doctor," Sloan said, quietly, so Vicente wouldn't hear.

"Is that what Vicente is going to do when he finds out?" I asked in an equally quiet tone. It was awkward sitting on the floor and looking up at Zara and Sloan but I wasn't sure I had the strength to stand.

"Speaking of which, why did he just stand there?" Zara asked. "He didn't help her."

"Or us," I added.

Sloan sighed. "Thiss is what I've been trying to tell you. The Sirin… the doctor took too much humanity out of them."

"Huh?" I asked. I flexed my arms and wiggled my fingers, taking stock of the damage. At least nothing seemed broken.

"They take an every-man-for-himself approach to things," Sloan said. "And they take it too far. Humanity has survived so long because of itss social structures and the way people work together—or that'ss what I believe, anyway."

"We're supposed to teach them how to get along?" I asked. "*How?*"

Sloan sighed again. "I don't know exactly how we'll show them, but I do know that if the Sirin continue to live the way the doctor taught them—with complete apathy toward each other, with none of the good things humanity had—they won't lasst long. We can show them that."

"Then they'll repay us," Zara asked, interrupted by strained coughs, "by not killing us?"

Before Sloan could sigh again, I said, "What other chance do we have? We've got to try *something*. Otherwise Jake and Coby and the rest of us are all dead."

Zara nodded. Her nose had stopped bleeding. She gingerly felt her throat, wincing as her fingers reached the bruises.

"What's he going to do,"—I tilted my head toward Vicente's cell—"when he finds out?"

Sloan stepped over to a cabinet on the wall, pulling out a leather device with metal buckles. "We'll have him put thiss on firsst."

"Um… what is that?" Zara asked.

"It'ss a resstraint the doctor uses," he said. "It holds their wings against their back to keep them from flying, and it alsso limitss their strength a bit. If Sigrath had been wearing one, we might have been able to take her. Maybe."

"Sigrath?" I asked.

"Oh," Sloan said. "That was the Sirin's name. The one who jusst tried to kill uss."

"Badass name for a badass girl," Zara said, standing.

"How do you know her name?" I asked, grabbing the side of the table and pulling myself up. Everything hurt. If that thing didn't work on Vicente we'd be in trouble. I didn't have the energy for another fight.

"Vicente said it when she came in," Sloan said. "He asshed her why she was angry. Luckily we kept her too disstracted to resspond."

"Luckily," I said dryly. "How will we get him to wear it?"

"We'll tell him the doctor wantss uss to put it on him."

"And he'll fall for that?" Zara asked. Her knuckles were bruised purple from hitting Sigrath in the face.

Sloan smirked. "The Sirin do anything the doctor asks."

"He's going to be pissed when he finds out," Zara said, lowering her voice to a whisper as Sloan opened Vicente's cell.

Sloan said something in Esperanto and Vicente nodded, then turned around. He slipped the leather straps over his chest and around his arms. A set of three straps went over the wings, crushing them into his back. It looked uncomfortable, if not outright painful, but Vicente didn't flinch as Sloan carefully fastened the buckles. They were all in the back, making it impossible for Vicente to undo them himself.

"I suggesst we leave as soon as we have tended to our injuries," Sloan said.

"We're not going to tell—" Zara started.

"I agree, Sloan," I said, cutting Zara off and shooting her a look. We didn't know how much English Vicente understood, and maybe Sloan was right not to tell him yet. He'd been right about most things so far.

"I'll tell him to pack anything he needs," Sloan said. "I'm going to say we're taking him to the Academy, that the doctor is there." Then he turned back to Vicente and told him the lies in Esperanto.

"We're not going to tell him?" I asked after Vicente left the room.

"We will eventually," Sloan said.

"Didn't he figure it out?" Zara asked. "I mean, why does he think Sigrath attacked us?"

"He doesn't care why," Sloan said. "That's how the Sirin are."

"He'd let her kill us without batting an eye?" Zara asked. "That's harsh."

"We need to stop Jake and Coby," I said. "They have no idea what they're up against. It was all three of us against one angry Sirin and look at the shape we're in now."

"I agree," Zara said. "We can still catch up and stop them. If we're all going to the Academy… maybe we can get there at the same time. Figure out a plan together."

"I agree as well. The only reason Sigrath didn't desstroy uss is because she couldn't use her wings to her advantage in this small room. Out in the open…" Sloan trailed off, then asked, "Do you have your mapss?"

I nodded and crossed the room to where I'd dropped my bag, limping thanks to my injured hip. I pulled out my road atlas and Sloan flipped to the full map of the United States.

"We're here," he said, placing one of his scaled fingers on the map. "And the Academy is here."

I whistled softly. "That really is fifteen-hundred miles."

"Which route do you think Jake and Coby will take to get there?" Zara asked me.

I stared at the map. Jake was savvier about navigating these roads than Coby was, so he was probably the one picking the route. And I knew Jake. I could figure this out.

"He would take this highway out of here," I said, tracing the route with my finger. "Then he'd move onto this one. He won't take freeways because the towns are usually too picked over to find good supplies. He's been through this part before; the city was bombed, so he'd avoid it. Oh, and then he'd take this one, this road through the National Forest here. There would be good hunting and—look at the river right there— good fishing, too. I think he has that fear—it's like the opposite of claustrophobia? Where you don't like wide open spaces. Plus, staying in the forest would make it harder to be spotted by Sirin."

I pulled out a pen from my pack and traced the route I thought Jake would take.

When I was done, Zara held my gaze steadily. "Are you sure about this?"

I looked at the black line I'd drawn. It snaked halfway across the country. "I'm sure. Are we ready to go?"

"Yes," Zara said. She smiled, but then it faded. "Oh, wait. We don't have a car anymore..."

"There are plenty outside," I said. "Many with keys still in the ignition. But we don't know if they still work and I don't feel like pulling corpses out of them."

"We can use the doctor's," Sloan said. "I'll show you where it is. Though I don't know where he keepss the keys. It'll take a while to search for them."

"Don't worry about that," I said, a smile spreading across my face. I turned to Zara. "I assume you can hotwire a car?"

She broke into a grin, then threw her arm over my sore shoulders. "You know me so well."

5: Keep It Going
Nadia

Loading the car with the food and supplies Jake and Coby left us didn't take long. Everything had already been laid out for the journey all five of us were supposed to have made together.

We also freed all the lab animals except Humphrey. His glowing stripes worried us. They'd make him an easy target for a predator, especially at night. We placed him in the greenhouse instead, where he'd have plenty of spinach and carrot tops to nibble. Zara laid out pans of water, and we hoped we'd survive and make it back to him.

Now Sloan and I stared at the doctor's sleek, black Jaguar while Zara rifled through the wires below the dash, her tongue a tiny pink triangle out the corner of her mouth as she concentrated.

"This thing looks fast," I said, turning to Sloan. "Is it?"

He shrugged. "I've rarely been in a car, and never thiss one."

I bit my nail, and Zara looked at me as if she knew what I would ask before I said it. "Can we catch up to Jake and Coby with it?"

Sloan didn't respond.

"Of course," Zara said. "A Jaguar can catch a Mustang. And eat it. That's just basic biology—the circle of life." She snickered, then looked at Sloan. "Hey, I'm almost done here. You can get Bird Boy now."

"Very well," Sloan said. "Though I don't recommend you call him that to his face," he said over his shoulder as he left the garage.

Zara sat sideways in the seat, her legs dangling out of the car, and squinted at me. "You're not okay," she stated.

259

I'd been twisting and untwisting a strand of hair. Now I dropped it and shook my head. "I'm not."

"We're going to find them," Zara said fiercely. "We'll stop them before it's too late. I know it."

"Yeah?" I said, my voice cracking. "Then what?"

She waved her hand dismissively. "We'll figure that out as we go. We've been good at that so far. *Pretty* good. Murders aside."

"My stomach is in knots. I'm worried, and I can't tell if it's because I love Jake or because I hate him now."

Zara grinned. "It's a fine line sometimes, isn't it?"

I couldn't match her smile. "How long do you think before Vicente figures out what's going on?"

"He won't," Zara said. "We'll keep him from finding out about the doc and get to Jake and Coby before they get to the Sirin."

"And if we don't?"

"Failure's not an option here."

"I know," I said, my eyes stinging. "That's why I think I do hate Jake now. If they would've waited until morning—just a few more hours—or asked Sloan a few more questions…"

"Nod," Zara said, "you've got to keep it together. Sloan and I need you. Jake and Coby need you, even if they are idiots. *Especially* because they're idiots."

I nodded, taking a deep breath and blinking away the oncoming tears.

"Can you open the garage door?" Zara asked. "I'm ready to hear this baby growl." She patted the dash lovingly.

I crossed the small garage that was tucked beneath one side of the laboratory and lifted the door. The strong light of the late morning sun warmed my face and chilled my heart. *How many hours behind Jake and Coby are we? Can we catch them before—?*

The engine roared to life behind me and Zara whooped. "Yeah! Now that's what I'm talking about. Man, it's been a while since I had to do that," she said. She popped her head out of the car. "Ready to go?" she asked.

As my eyes adjusted to the sun, I caught a glimpse of a huddle of white lab coats. "Oh my God, Zara."

"What is it?" she asked, the smile draining from her face as she hopped out of the car and approached me.

The garage door opened to a wide concrete ramp that must have served as a loading dock. There was another garage door to our left, and that part of the ramp was covered by a concrete awning. Huddled beneath it were what was left of the doctor's assistants.

There were six or seven of them, a mix of men and women. All wore lab coats, some had goggles or respirators. A few lay on the ground, the white gleam of bone showing where scavengers had consumed a meal. Rigor mortis had frozen others into sitting positions against the wall.

"He... he must have locked them out when he released the virus," I whispered. "Turned on them."

Without thinking, I stepped toward them. Zara grabbed my arm, pulling me back. "No," she said. "There's nothing we can do for them now."

"Do you think they knew? Did they help with the virus, or just with us?" My voice shook and my eyes were wide, unable to look away from what was left of their faces.

Zara shook her head. "That doesn't matter. We need to focus on getting out of here, finding Jake and Coby."

I nodded, turning away and letting Zara lead me back toward the car. Sloan and Vicente entered the garage then.

"Are you guys ready to go?" I asked, trying to keep from looking like I was about to vomit. Sloan nodded.

Zara had composed herself. She looked between Sloan and Vicente for a moment and then yelled, "Shotgun!"

Vicente narrowed his eyes and peered at her, his spine stiff. Being Zara, this made her laugh. "Explain shotgun to him, Sloan," she said.

Sloan raised his arms in a helpless gesture. "I can't. I assume you don't mean the weapon..."

Zara laughed, too loud. "Sometimes I forget. I forget that this is the end of the world and that all the stuff that used to be normal is gone unless *we* keep it going." And with that she launched into a detailed explanation of the rules of Shotgun, which Sloan struggled to translate to Vicente.

"I never forget," I said to myself as I looked out the door and over the devastated city. I sent up a silent prayer that the path to the Sirin wouldn't be as strewn with bodies as this, the doctor's city, was.

"Okay," Zara said. "Let's go! You drive, I've got shotgun,"—she sent a pointed glance at Sloan and Vicente to remind them that they'd just learned the rules—"and the boys can take up the rear."

"Can you drive?" I asked Zara, turning my gaze out into the wasteland once more. "At least until we're out of the city."

I turned back to Zara and she bit her lip. "Um," she said. "I can't. I never learned."

"What?" I asked, turning abruptly. "You can hotwire a car but you can't drive one?"

She held up her hands. "My mom and I usually lived in cities so there wasn't much use for it. And when Nick—when he and I would go out on our misadventures, I'd hotwire and he'd drive."

A slow realization came over me and I turned to Sloan. "Can you drive?"

"I'm afraid not. I could try, but with thiss being a manual…"

"And we're not letting him drive, even if he could…" I said, shrugging a shoulder at Vicente. "So I get to be chauffeur on this journey none of us want to take." And I got my license right before the world ended. Great.

Zara lightly punched my arm as she got out of the driver's seat to let me in. "Don't be so glum, Nadia. Consider it an adventure."

"An adventure with some pretty big consequences."

"Those are the best kind," Zara said, a gleam in her dark eyes. "I've never done anything where the stakes were this high before. It's terrifying, but exciting. My heart's beating fast, and I feel like we're so *alive* in this moment."

Sloan nodded, agreeing with her. "I spent a great deal of time sneaking around the lab, but thiss will be my firsst 'adventure' worthy of the name." He got into the seat behind the driver's, which I flopped into.

"Tell Vicente to buckle up!" Zara said, and Sloan translated the command into Esperanto for him.

"Can you navigate?" I asked, shoving my maps and compass into Zara's hands.

"Of course, *Capitaine*," she said.

I backed the car up the ramp, careful to keep my eyes away from the huddle of cadavers in lab coats, and we were off. Zara directed me, turning us out of this cursed city. Within half an hour we were free of the suffocating aura of that place—away from the dead, the decaying—and on the open highway. It felt good to drive again, and to drive *fast*. The road was mostly empty of abandoned cars, so I could push the pedal to the floor and let the landscape blur behind us.

Evergreen trees fringed the edges of the road, but the forest was also sprinkled through with the white trunks of birch and the yellowing autumn leaves of elm trees. I rolled down my window and let my hair blow in the breeze, smelling the fresh air of the wilderness for the first time in what seemed like a very long time.

Somehow, I found myself smiling.

6: Save Her
Jake

Miles of road, occasionally interspersed with abandoned cars and bodies, stretched before us, and the sun rose and set. We spoke and stopped as little as necessary. I was plenty occupied with my own thoughts, but it was strange to be with an un-chatty Coby.

Finally, I couldn't take it. I felt my chance, our chance, slipping away.

"We should go back. Zara and—" I found myself unable to say Nadia's name, and my voice was hoarse from a full day without speaking except to tell Coby where to turn. "They might still forgive us."

"They can only forgive us if they're alive," Coby replied, keeping his eyes on the road.

"We could all live." My tone didn't match the hope in the words.

Coby glared at me, his mouth set in an unwavering line. His voice was harsh and restrained. "Jake, you owe me this."

I jerked around in my seat to face him. "What?"

He looked away, out his window at the trees flashing by. Then he said, quietly, "You killed the closest thing I had to a father."

I sat stunned for a moment, then said, "He killed the whole world! And the disease he created to murder everyone else is what killed him."

"As a direct result of *your* actions." Coby's hands clenched the steering wheel.

"You don't think he deserved it?" I stared at him in disbelief.

Coby sighed and his shoulders slumped. "Look, I'm not saying he wasn't guilty. I saw the evidence. I *know* he was."

"Did you know it then? When the whole world was dying, did you know it was his fault?" My voice cut through the tense air between us.

The wounded look that crossed Coby's face gave me my answer. He whispered, "No, I didn't. I had no idea."

I nodded slowly and flexed my hand, the stitches tightening across my not-quite-healed cut from the lab window.

"But," Coby continued. "He was one of the only people I knew for most of my life, Jake."

"Cutting his suit, his death—it was justice," I said, crossing my arms. "It doesn't *begin* to make up for everything he did."

"If he was my father, should I kill you in revenge? Would that also be justice?"

I stiffened. "You and I both know that's different."

For the first time, I started to sweat. I'd only known Coby for a few weeks, and I'd only begun to trust him a few days ago. Was his real plan for us to go off together so he could exact his revenge?

"I know. But you still owe me *something*. The doctor—he wasn't right. Mentally ill. It wasn't right to do what you did."

I swallowed. "I'm sorry, Coby. I am. I didn't know it would hurt you like this. But I don't regret it." I waited for Coby to do something—maybe stop the car or turn a weapon on me.

Instead, he said, "It's fine. I might forgive you someday. For now, you just need to trust me. We're going to save Zara and Nadia."

"What about ourselves?"

Coby didn't respond.

◆◆◆

After hundreds more miles of tense silence between us, Coby pulled over to the side of the road next to an abandoned car. Without a word he set to work siphoning gas from the tank and transferring it to ours.

"Let's make camp," he grunted. "We need rest."

I nodded and went around to the trunk. Coby shouldered the tent, and I filled my pack with food and found my fishing gear. We walked along the road toward the stream we'd seen a quarter mile back.

A suspicion had been growing since Coby first told me his plan back at Winthrop Enterprises. For hours I'd been considering strategic ways to voice it, but in the end I went for a direct question.

"You're going to turn me over to them, aren't you?" I asked, looking straight ahead, my voice steady.

Neither of us stopped walking. The crunch of our boots on the pavement filled the space between us.

"What do you mean?" Coby asked carefully.

His answer made my anger flare. I stopped, grabbing his shoulder and turning him to face me. "I mean, we aren't going there to talk sense into the Sirin. You're going to tell them I acted alone. You're hoping they take me and let the rest of you live. Sacrificing me for the good of the many, so to speak."

Coby swatted my hand off his shoulder, his eyes wild with the look of cornered prey. "I—I don't know," he said. "I don't know yet."

His answer was a punch to the gut. I'd expected him to deny it, and for that denial to be a lie. The truth was worse.

"Okay then," I said. "Let's keep going."

He looked relieved, then confused. I could always read his face like a book. Maybe that's why I was the only one with misgivings about him when we first met. Zara and Nadia must not have noticed.

The thought of Nadia calmed my nerves, which, though I didn't acknowledge it, were shaken by what Coby had said. She was the reason I wasn't going back now, the reason I was headed into the lion's den. I'd turn myself in if it meant I could save her and Zara and Sloan. But mostly her.

7: Nothing Gold Can Stay
Nadia

There was a violent *thwang* and then a clatter as Zara dropped the bow to the ground and cursed. I spun around, quickly realizing what had happened.

A red welt was already appearing on Zara's forearm. She swore again as she surveyed the damage.

"Zara, what did I tell—?"

"I know, I know," she said, holding her hands up innocently. "Don't pull the bow back without an arrow. I learned my lesson." She rubbed her arm and winced.

"Don't dry-fire the bow," I corrected as I picked it up and examined it. There didn't seem to be much damage, just a few scuff marks.

"Maybe a bow's just not my weapon," Zara said, crossing over to another rack in the store. Hours after dusk had descended upon us, we'd taken a break from driving and stopped by an abandoned Wal Mart for the night. We used Coby's generator trick for electricity, and there were futons and roll-up mattresses to sleep on. As Zara had aptly pointed out when I protested, they were mattresses that (probably) no one had died on. I planned to convince them to keep driving afterward, but we at least needed to stop to get Zara a better weapon.

Zara had taken one of the few hunting knives that still hung on the rack and was hefting it in her hand. "This feels good," she said, grinning.

"I still don't get how you made it this far without any weapons," I said, surveying the empty gun racks around the counter. There were a couple of boxes of ammo in uncommon sizes lying around, but no firearms left.

"Sometimes," she said, tapping her forefinger against her temple, "the only weapon you need is up here." She smirked and then negated her statement by tossing the knife in the air, spinning around, and catching it by the handle.

"You're going to hurt yourself."

She grinned. "No, I'm not. Did you see that? I'm a ninja!"

I gave her a stern glare, but she smiled wider.

"It's still in the packaging. No harm, no foul."

I shook my head. "If you say so. But I still think you need more than a knife. Can we try the bow again?"

She shook her head, her black-and-faded-pink hair sweeping over her shoulders. "I'll never be a tenth as good as you. I don't have the patience for it."

I weighed our options. There were only two bows left in the store—a kiddie compound and the recurve that was now lying on the floor. Neither had worked for Zara.

My hand moved to my hip and unbuckled the belt of my holster. I slipped it off and handed it to her. The small gesture took more effort than I expected. That gun had been with me since the beginning of The End, one of the few constants in my life since the world had fallen apart. It had saved me from the dogs. It had spared me on the worst night of my life.

"There are only four rounds left," I said. "But you should take it. It's better than nothing."

"No," Zara said. "I couldn't. It's yours. And like you said, it only has four bullets left. I don't know how to shoot it anyway." She crossed over to the counter and hoisted herself onto the glass. Then she examined her somehow-still-perfectly-painted nails. "You know, before the virus, I never would've shot a gun. I just don't like them. They scare me and I think they cause more problems than they solve, if you know what I mean."

I tried to hide my relief at being able to keep my revolver. "Maybe in the old world," I said.

"Yeah," she said. "Maybe now, too."

I was about to buckle the holster back around my waist when I heard a noise. Spinning toward it, I raised the gun, only to see Sloan at the end of the aisle.

"Oh," I said, lowering the gun quickly. "It's you."

"Yess," he said. "I believe I found some things of usse."

He set the box he was carrying on the counter next to Zara. "Can I open it?" she asked eagerly.

"Please do," Sloan said. "I found these, too." He handed me a set of walkie-talkies and a small pair of binoculars, the kind used for birdwatching.

"Thanks," I said, smiling. "These will be useful. Where's Vicente?"

"Eating," Sloan said. "With their wings the Sirin need a higher caloric intake than you or I. He started on the cereal aisle and I left him to it."

"Is he suspicious yet?" I asked, biting my thumbnail. "I mean, does he have any idea...?"

"It'ss hard to say," Sloan said. "I think as long as he doesn't realize that the doctor—well, you know."

I nodded. "Okay. We should be cautious about mentioning the lab or anything like that."

"Yess," Sloan said. We hadn't discussed anything important around Vicente today, anyway. It was easier to laugh and joke with Zara than to think about the dark possibilities of the future.

Zara finished unwrapping the box and exclaimed, "Oh my gosh, Sloan, this is perfect! Nod, this is just what I need, don't you think?"

Inside the box lay a crossbow and twelve bolts. "That's perfect for you," I said. "Easier to shoot than a bow but you have reusable ammo, unlike a gun."

She took out of the package and loaded a bolt. After walking to the end of the aisle, she aimed it at something on the other end of the store.

"Zara…" I started, but it was too late. She'd already let the bolt loose. She flashed a smile at me as I rushed to survey the damage.

"I could get used to this baby," she said, following me. Her voice was getting hoarse; the finger-marks on her neck had faded from purple to green.

Halfway down the store from us, her bolt had pierced a bean bag chair, which now dangled from an end cap. White stuffing beads flowed from it, forming a mountain on the floor.

"Be careful where you point that thing," I said, but I was glad she'd found something to defend herself with if shit hit the fan. *When* shit hit the fan.

"So, Sloan," Zara said, draping an arm over his shoulders. "Wanna explain what your plan is with Bird Boy?"

Sloan looked startled at the physical contact and stammered when he replied. "I—I think we—you—can show them how you rely on each other. That there's a better way."

"What do you mean?" Zara asked, setting her crossbow gently back in the box and giving her full attention to Sloan.

"The Sirin were raised to be… *independent* of each other."

"You've got that right," I said, thinking of the fight with Sigrath and Vicente's lack of reaction to it. "But you've already told us that. Is there something more to your plan?"

He glanced to the side for a moment and swallowed. "We'll have to figure that out as we go."

There was more he wasn't telling us, but I ignored it for the moment. "Alright. We're loaded up on food and, now, weapons. Let's hit the road."

Zara shook her head. "No, Nod. You've been driving non-stop since this morning, and it's got to be around midnight now. You need sleep—we all do."

"I'm fine," I lied. "We've got to keep going or…" I trailed off, a lump forming in my throat.

"A few hours of sleep won't hurt," Sloan said. "We're making good time."

I was about to protest, but saw I was outnumbered, and I couldn't deny how exhausted I was. "Okay," I said. "But we're leaving at first light."

"Whatever you say, *Capitaine*," Zara said. "I'm headed for the furniture section to catch some Z's. I suggest you both do the same after Sloan makes sure Bird Boy's not up to no good."

"I'll look into that now," Sloan said, inclining his head and heading back toward the grocery side of the store.

"C'mon, Nod," Zara said, pulling on my wrist. "We need our beauty sleep."

◆◆◆

Compartmentalization had been the name of the game since Jake and Coby left. Keeping thoughts of them separate from me was how I kept myself together.

But right before I flopped onto the pillow-and-futon cushion nest that Zara had formed for me, I couldn't help taking everything out of my pack until I found the two books I'd shoved to the bottom.

One was the book Jake had given me: the one with the note. I tossed it aside; I'd already memorized those injurious words and I didn't need a refresher.

The other was the book I'd pressed the leaf from Jake in, that night by the fire. I hadn't checked it since, but I hoped the heavy book and the weight of everything else in my pack had been enough to preserve its colors.

Taking a deep breath, I separated the pages.

The leaf, once vibrant with autumn colors, was now dull brown and crinkled. Everything good about it was gone, the same way everything between Jake and I would be gone if we failed. And what chance did we have? With the whole world dead, we were all living on borrowed time.

As my favorite poet wrote, nothing gold can stay.

I crunched the dead leaf in my hands and threw it on the ground. There was so much dust on the floor that the pieces blended in, as if it had never been there at all.

Something inside me cracked, then. The dam broke, the floodgates opened, and I sobbed into a pillow, desperately hoping it would tire me out enough to sleep.

Zara came back from the bathroom, and I was too upset and tired to hide my tears. She knelt beside me, pushing my tangled hair behind my ears and wiping my face with her pajama sleeve.

"Shh," she said. "It's okay. Tell me what's wrong."

I sniffled and tried to control the sobs that were racking my body, but it took a full minute. When I'd finally calmed down, I didn't know what to say. "The leaf's gone," I croaked out pathetically.

"A leaf?" Zara's eyebrows pulled together. "What leaf?"

She studied me for a moment, and I shrugged helplessly. I didn't know how to explain what it had meant, the metaphor for me and Jake, for the end of the world.

"Oh," Zara said. "I get it. It's about *him*."

I nodded, holding back a fresh round of tears.

"You do what you've gotta do then," Zara said, hugging me and not minding that I soaked her pajama shirt. "Feel better?"

"No," I croaked, wiping the tears from my cheeks with my sleeves. "Not really."

She gave me a bittersweet smile. "It's okay. I get it."

"Let's go to sleep," I said.

She nodded and lay down in the pillow-nest she'd made for herself. "We're going to catch up to them. We will."

I didn't bother voicing my disagreement. I was so exhausted—physically, mentally, emotionally—that I blacked out as soon as my head hit the pillow.

8: Wasteland
Nadia

When I woke my body was so stiff that I couldn't move. The day got worse from there.

The fight with Sigrath had taken its toll, and the hours spent driving had stiffened all my muscles to the point where any attempts at movement were slow and incredibly painful.

Zara must have been having similar issues because I heard her groan and slowly roll out of her "bed". It was dark in the store, though the sun would be rising outside. Sloan must have turned the lights off before bed. Zara stumbled across the store and the lights overhead flickered on, making me squint.

I dug the picture frame out of my pack. I kept my ritual of looking at it every morning, though some days I skipped lighting the candles. Zara had seen me with it, gazing at my loved ones' faces, as I did now. She never commented, just as I'd never mentioned seeing her cross off days in her pocket calendar with a lipstick kiss each morning.

This morning, though, and on other bad days, their faces didn't seem to be smiling at me. Instead they were accusatory. *Why should you live? Out of all of us, why you?*

I quickly shoved the frame back in my bag.

Zara came back, walking laboriously, and I noted the green bruises on her neck and the deep circles under her eyes. She smiled when she saw I was looking at her, but it seemed forced.

"You okay, Zara?" I asked.

Her voice was still hoarse. "Never better." Her smile didn't reach her eyes.

I took a deep breath and pushed past the pain and stiffness to sit up. "We've got to get on the road," I said.

"Hold on there," Zara said. She searched her pack for something and pulled out a few syringes.

I groaned. "I thought I was done with those?"

She shook her head. "No, this is your third dose. I'm going to take out your sutures, too."

"I was supposed to get the third dose a week after the bite. It's too late now for it to do anything."

She squinted at me for a moment. "My count might be off, but it hasn't been much more than a week since you were bitten. And you'll get the last in a week."

"Seriously?" I mulled the idea over. "We've had a busy week," I said dryly.

She laughed—a harsh, grating sound that made her wince. "You could say that."

Zara carefully pulled up my sleeve, and for a moment I was glad there weren't any fresh cuts for her to see. It had been a struggle the night before, but I'd stopped myself. Everything else on my body hurt so much that I barely registered the three pricks of pain as she injected me with the vaccine.

"There," she said. "One more dose, and you'll be out of the woods as far as rabies goes."

I wondered if I'd live to need the last dose. "If we can find more of that stuff we should all vaccinate ourselves," I said, then vaguely wondered if Coby and Jake would be included in that. Would we find them? I cleared my throat. "And boost our tetanus ones too, if we can. It'd be a shame to live this long after The End and die of something stupid like that."

Zara nodded, now working on my stitches with a small pair of scissors and a tweezers. Her movements were slow, cautious, but I couldn't tell if it was because she was in pain or if she was trying to ease mine.

She was cutting through one of the half-moons of sewn-together flesh when Sloan approached us. He moved so silently that Zara and I both jumped when he came up behind us and said, "Good morning."

"Morning, Sloan," I said, trying to relax. "How's Vicente?"

"He's... beginning to assk quesstions," Sloan said carefully.

I nodded. "If I were him, I would've been asking questions yesterday morning." I inhaled sharply as Zara nicked my skin with the scissors.

"Sorry," she murmured, then kept going, the tip of her tongue poking out the side of her mouth as she concentrated. The wound tickled with each stitch she pulled out.

"What have you told him?" I asked Sloan.

"That the doctor will explain all to him when we arrive at the Academy," Sloan said.

"Is he buying that?" I asked.

"For now," Sloan said. "But I don't know for how much longer."

I nodded. "Okay. Keep us posted. Did you find yourself a weapon yet?"

The scales on Sloan's face shifted, his expression changing a few times before he answered. Finally, he said, "Despite my name, I'd prefer not to have one."

I managed to keep myself from rolling my eyes. We were about to take on a fleet of terrifying, otherworldly beings with years of training and of my two companions, one didn't believe in guns, and the other wouldn't use a weapon at all.

Zara pulled out the last stitch. "Your name?" she asked Sloan.

"It'ss a Gaelic name that means 'warrior'," Sloan said. "The doctor gave all my kind names in a similar vein."

"Did the doctor name us, too?" Zara asked.

Sloan nodded; I didn't like where this conversation was going.

Zara bit her lip. "What do ours mean?"

"The doctor had patterns for the names of all his... creations. The Sirin have names that mean things like 'conqueror'. Victoria, Liam, Sigourney, Rahul..."

"That's... telling," I said, feeling sick. I didn't want to know what the doctor had named me or why.

"'Jake' and 'Coby'," Sloan said. "Both stem from a Hebrew word meaning 'supplanter'. The other males of your kind had similar names."

I found myself wondering again whether any of the rest of us were still alive. If we survived this mess could we find them? "'Supplanter'?" I asked.

Sloan half-smiled. "Yes. I think his plans to replace the human race may have originated with your subspecies."

I shivered as a chill ran down my spine.

"And the females?" Zara asked. Her voice was stifled, face ashen.

"He was more poetic with you," Sloan said. "The female names have to do with new beginnings, a new start." Neither of us said a word, but Sloan continued, "'Nadia' is a Slavic word meaning 'hope'."

The irony. The doctor named me hope, but his actions had caused the many hopeless, sleepless nights I'd spent alone after The End.

"'Zara'," Sloan looked down for a moment, then at Zara, who was sitting utterly still beside me. "Has many meanings. It stems from an Arabic word meaning 'to blossom', but can mean 'princess', 'flower', 'the dawn'…"

He looked away, and I didn't blame him. The light had gone out of Zara's face. She swallowed. "It would be a pretty name if it hadn't been from him. I thought it was my mom…" Her posture crumbled.

I wrapped an arm around her. "I know, I know." She cried into my shoulder and tried to catch her breath.

Sloan stood awkwardly for a moment, then reached out his hand as if to stroke her hair. Something stopped him, and he rapidly withdrew his hand.

"I'll… check on Vicente," he said, not looking at either of us.

"We should go soon," I said. "Get Vicente in the car and we'll meet you out there in a minute."

Sloan nodded and turned to go.

"And Sloan?" I said.

"Yess?"

"At least grab a knife or something. Seriously, I don't want you to be defenseless out there."

"As you wish," he said, and was off.

Zara had calmed, and she sat up, wiping her tears. There was a steely look in her eyes.

"Let's change our names," she said.

"What?" I asked, my heart sinking. My name was a connection to the doctor, but it was also one of the few ties I still had to my family, my friends, everyone from before.

"Let's pick new names. What would be a good one for me?" I looked at my friend—her usually perfect hair was matted, her cheeks tearstained, and her hands twitching.

I shrugged. "You just seem like a Zara to me."

"And you're a Nadia," she said, sighing.

"It doesn't matter that the doctor picked our names," I said, though I didn't quite believe it myself. "They're what our family used, what our friends used—they're a part of us."

She nodded, but it seemed her thoughts were elsewhere.

Not knowing what else to say, I went with, "Should we hit the road?"

◆ ◆ ◆

Two hours later, we reached a wasteland.

I stopped the car and killed the engine. We sat in silence for a moment.

"What is this place?" Sloan asked, his voice infused with awed fear.

"This is what the doctor did to my home," Zara said bitterly. "This is what it looked like after the nuclear attack. Everyone—everything—was gone except for me."

We'd been driving through untouched forest when, suddenly, we'd crested a hill and there was nothing but toppled, blackened trees and rubble.

"I'll see if we can go around," I said, getting out of the car. "Don't drink any of the water that we got from the stream back there. It might be irradiated."

"Aren't we immune?" Zara said wryly.

"I'm not going to ingest any of that shit," I said. "And those two aren't immune, as far as we know. We need to get away as soon as possible since they're probably being exposed right now."

I slung my pack over my shoulder and shut the car door on them. I walked back about twenty yards to the nearest intact trees, found the tallest one, and climbed.

I went as high as I thought the tree would allow and tried not to panic. There was no green in the valley below or to either side of us. Carefully, I extracted the binoculars from my pack and looked out as far as I could see in all directions.

To our right was a large body of water. To our left was nothing but more destroyed forest. Behind us, even, there were areas of decimated forest that we hadn't seen as we drove. Destroyed trees blocked our way ahead, but further down the road the rubble changed.

Where there had once been a city, there was now a pile of wreckage: huge, twisted spires of metal, chunks of concrete, a few burned-out shells of cars. That was as much as I could see through the binoculars, but I wasn't itching to see more.

I took a deep breath and climbed down the tree, slowly making my way back to the car.

"Well?" Zara said as I sat. She was still in the passenger seat, rubbing circles around her pendant with her thumb.

"We can't go forward," I said. "Or left, or right."

"Let's look at a map," Zara said, pulling one out of the glovebox. She opened it and laid it across the steering wheel in front of me. "Where would Jake have gone once he saw this? He'd backtrack somewhere…"

My heart sank, and I shook my head. I didn't know. I didn't even know if he'd come this way—I was guessing. I thought I'd known Jake so well, but then why hadn't I seen that he would leave? Why hadn't I stopped them? And why hadn't *he* known what a betrayal it would be to me; how I'd have to follow him?

I think Zara understood. Or she saw the hopelessness in my eyes.

"It's okay if you're not sure," she said gently. "Where do *you* think we should go?" She pointed at the map with a black fingernail.

"I... I don't know."

9: Pain or Panic
Nadia

Zara and Sloan took the map from me and discussed what to do while I sat in the driver's seat, but at the same time, far away. I let my eyes go blurry as I stared out over the destruction. The doctor had won.

It didn't matter what we did, or how we fought. We'd never escape him or what he did to the world or what we did to him. Every breath we'd taken—every moment, before we had breath in our lungs, even our names—had been poisoned by the doctor, and the rest of our lives, however short they may be, would be the same.

"Nod?" Zara's voice came from faraway. "Nod. Nadia!"

"What?" I asked, letting my eyes refocus on the mounds of rubble that had once been people's homes, lives.

"We figured out what to do."

"Good."

"If you look here," Zara said, pointing at the map, "at some point Coby and Jake are going to have to take this road to get to the Academy, so all we have to do is find our way—"

"Okay," I said, cutting her off and starting the car.

Zara folded the map onto her lap as I backed up to turn around. "Nod?"

"What?"

"You okay?"

"Fine. Just tell me where to drive and I'll do it."

Out of the corner of my eye, I saw her purse her lips. I kept driving. I heard Vicente's voice, deep and unexpected, from the backseat, asking Sloan a question. I looked at the pair of them in the rearview mirror and raised my eyebrows.

Sloan said, "He's… getting susspiciouss. He wantss to know why we were unaware of thiss area and need to change our route."

"What are you going to tell him?" Zara asked. She kept her tone carefree and smiled, trying to show Vicente that nothing was wrong. I was too apathetic to pretend anything anymore.

"Tell him he doesn't need to know," I said harshly. "He'll find out soon enough anyway."

"I'll tell him that the doctor will explain—"

"How much longer is he going to buy that, Sloan? He's not an idiot."

Vicente spoke again.

"What's he saying?" Zara asked, still maintaining her facade of calm. "Nod, you're going to turn west in about a mile… exit 60."

"He doesn't believe uss," Sloan said.

"It doesn't matter," I said. "He's stuck with us until we get to the Academy."

"What if he gets violent?" Zara asked slowly.

"Perhapss tonight we can think of a better explanation to give him."

"Now would be a good time for your plan, Sloan. How, exactly, are we supposed to show him how good humans are? A lot of good it ever did us, being almost-human."

I wasn't paying attention and missed the turn. I braked hard and whipped a U-turn in the road so I could head west. Everyone was silent while they were jostled inside the car.

"I didn't know," Sloan said softly. "I still don't. But I always wanted…"

He trailed off, and my heart twisted. I bit my lip. I shouldn't be taking this out on Sloan. He wasn't the one who got us into this mess—Jake was.

Zara sighed. "We should treat him more like one of us. If we talked to him… Sloan, you could teach me some Esperanto."

I glanced in the mirror again and saw Sloan nod, with a hint of a smile. Then his expression hardened again.

"Yess," Sloan said. "Let'ss try that."

I let my companions talk, only vaguely aware of their Esperanto lessons and laughter. My mind wandered over various things, but I quickly realized there were no topics that didn't incite pain or panic. My memories of before The End, surviving with my father, getting to know Jake, the horrifying possibilities that lay before us. I did my best to leave my mind blank and focus on driving.

The road was strewn with debris and at times I had to continue at an unbearably slow pace, worried about popping one of our tires. Skirting the edge of a city like this would normally be a good way to balance scavenging and hunting for food, but anything worth scavenging had been demolished in the attack.

On our second stop of the day to relieve ourselves, I walked along one of the ditches, trying to get rid of the tight feeling over my knees and the stiffness in my neck and shoulders. Zara approached me.

"You alright, Nod?" She spread her legs and arms wide and twisted her shoulders so they were perpendicular to her hips in a yoga pose.

"I told you I was, didn't I?"

She dropped the pose and gave me a look, one eyebrow raised. Then she twisted in the other direction.

"Can any of us really be okay anymore?" I asked.

"Touché," she said. She lifted her arms over her head, then swan dove down to touch her toes. "Hey," she said as she rose back up, "I'm glad we have all of this bottled water and canned food, but can we find some berries while we're stopped? I need something fresh."

I shook my head and pointed to the wildflowers I'd been observing before she approached. White daisies lined the ditch. Some had perfectly round yellow centers, but others looked more like Dalí's melted clocks. Others still looked like two mangled flowers competing to grow out of the same stem.

"Oh," Zara said, kneeling to look closer. "I didn't notice."

"Everything's messed up by the radiation. I don't think we should eat or drink anything around here." I looked up the road and wondered how long this hellscape was going to continue. Near the roadside there were signs of remaining life, like evergreen trees, and new life trying to come back, like the mutant daisies. But off to the east there was nothing left.

"What's Vicente looking at?" Zara asked.

I pulled my gaze away from the wasteland and toward Vicente. He was staring at the sky. "I don't know," I said. "But we should get moving."

I'd just sat in the driver seat, Vicente was already in the back, and Zara and Sloan were making their way toward the car, laughing about something, when Zara shouted, "The sky! Look at the sky!"

"Don't move," Sloan hissed.

My hands shook, and I clenched them around the steering wheel until my knuckles turned white. We sat perfectly still. My lungs strained, too full of air, but I didn't dare exhale, didn't dare look.

After an eternity, the Sirin passed over us, flying southward. Their winged forms grew smaller until they dissolved into the sky.

We let out a collective breath. I turned to look at the backseat and caught Vicente smirking to himself. When he noticed me looking at him he shifted his expression instantaneously back to the neutral, bored one he'd worn the whole trip.

He knows. I squeezed the steering wheel harder and watched my fingers curl together. Maybe he'd known the whole time that we were full of shit. He might even know the doctor was dead.

He couldn't know that I'd noticed. And I couldn't tell the others—not yet. I cleared my throat to say something else—

anything else—but Zara beat me to it. She and Sloan slipped into their respective seats, her in the front and Sloan behind me.

"What was that?" Zara asked, turning to Sloan and glancing at Vicente.

"There were only three," Sloan said. He was trying to keep his voice even so Vicente didn't suspect anything. *Not that it mattered.*

"Is that good?" Zara asked. She had her pendant clasped in the palm of her hand but kept her tone and expression neutral.

"Yess. I can't disscuss now but I'll explain later, the next time we stop. I believe it'ss good news."

I let out a slow breath, trying to calm myself. I grabbed my pack from at Zara's feet and pulled out the binoculars. "Here," I said, trying to keep my voice steady as I pressed them into Zara's hand. "You're on lookout duty."

She nodded and I started the car, trying to keep my hands tight on the steering wheel so they wouldn't shake. I'd glanced at the map before we set off; we were only about halfway to the Academy, if that. How had the Sirin come this far already? Were they the ones the doctor had called to his aid?

The tension in the car lifted as Zara and Sloan went back to talking and joking with Vicente. It seemed disingenuous to me now. I didn't know what his long game was, but Vicente was playing us.

Despite their casual conversation, Zara was on edge. She scanned the sky with the binoculars every few minutes and wouldn't let go of her yin-yang pendant.

Miles later, I was able to drive faster. The road was clearer, and I hoped we were reaching the end of the destruction. I wanted to be back in my element again—surrounded by trees, living off the land.

On our next break, Zara, Sloan, and I went into the woods to discuss what had happened with the Sirin. We went far enough that Vicente was out of earshot, and Zara asked, "Well? What do you think it means?"

"There were only a few of them," Sloan said. "And the timing suggesstss that these are the ones sent to rescue the doctor two days ago, when he called."

"So Sigrath didn't make it back yet," I said. "What happens when they all find out?"

"Sigrath will make it there tomorrow or the next day— she'll be slower since she's injured. I don't know what they'll do then, but at leasst seeing these Sirin means Jake and Coby haven't been found yet."

I nodded. "The road's clearing. We might be back on good land again soon."

"I was noticing that," Zara said. "And I was thinking, have Jake and Coby been through here?"

"What?" I asked, surprised.

"I saw a huge tree branch back there, and you could see the tree it had fallen from, but it was at a weird angle—it couldn't have fallen like that. I think someone moved it."

"Jake and Coby?" I asked. My heartbeat sped up, but I tried to stomp my hopes back down.

"That's my guess," Zara said. "It makes sense, right?"

I couldn't stop myself from smiling. "If they're having to move this much stuff off the road, they can't be moving very fast. I bet we'll catch up to them soon."

Zara squeezed my shoulders. "I can't wait to give them both what-for," she said. "They'll be sorry they left us—sorrier than they already are!"

"I'm going to climb up. Maybe I'll see them," I said. "It's a long shot, but they might be close."

Zara handed me the binoculars, smiling. There were a couple of trees around that were still green and upright. I picked a sturdy-looking one, though it was shorter than the others, and began to climb.

My heart sank as I ascended. We weren't near the end of the destruction. Though there was green along the road and to the west, the east remained shades of grey and brown as far as

I could see. I'd been hoping to see a patch of red—the Mustang—but was disappointed there too.

Movement caught my eye and I turned the binoculars to our car. Vicente had the trunk open, but I couldn't tell what he was doing. It couldn't be good, though—all our supplies were in the trunk.

I scrambled down the tree, trying to make my still-stiff limbs move quickly and gracefully. I fell at the bottom, rolling onto my side to stand. Out of breath, I said to Sloan and Zara, "Get to the car."

"Did you see Coby and Jake?" Zara asked.

I shook my head. "No—Vicente. Just go!"

We ran through the trees. Zara quickly outpaced Sloan and me. I heard her shout, "Vicente!" and then some of her newly learned Esperanto at him.

I'd been afraid he was after Zara's crossbow, but what he'd done was worse. Dented, empty cans lay strewn about the ground. Wrappers of protein bars, dried fruit, and other food blew around his feet in the gentle breeze. He'd even managed to pour out half our water bottles. We'd gone from being supplied for weeks to only a day or two.

He swallowed whatever he'd been chewing and grinned at us. Then he spewed words at us in Esperanto so fast that Sloan could barely keep up to translate.

"He says he knows we've done something horrible— there's no way the doctor told uss to bring him to the Academy. He doesn't know everything we've done but promises we'll be punished," Sloan translated. "He ate our food to slow uss down and ensure we'll be defensseless when the other Sirin come."

I swallowed and glanced at Zara. She was pale, her lips parted. It was a shock for her, after she'd been chatting with Vicente all day, to see him turn on us like this.

"A-and now," Sloan said, "he knows you're angry and he'll... gladly fight you to the death."

"Say what?" Zara said as Vicente jumped at me, muscled arms outstretched.

286

10: Northward
Jake

"Shit," Coby hissed, then unleashed a string of expletives and threw the red-and-yellow gas can on the ground. A pool of liquid poured onto the pavement before I put the can upright.

"What are you doing?" I asked, trying to control my temper.

Coby turned away from me, his hands on his face. He was usually so easygoing that his outburst had me on edge. When he didn't respond, I knelt next to the Jeep we'd been siphoning gas from and grabbed the tube.

He finally turned around. "Don't bother."

"What?" I asked, then froze when I saw his expression: defeat.

"The gas is bad." He punctuated the last word by throwing his car keys to the ground.

"Bad?" I asked stupidly.

"Yeah," he said, looking away from me and off to west, toward the lake. "Gas with ethanol doesn't last forever. This stuff,"—he turned and kicked the gas can back over—"is past its expiration date."

"So... what now?" I asked, watching the liquid pour out and noticing how dark it was, how sour it smelled. "We drive back and get more?"

He shook his head. "We rolled in on fumes. My car won't even start now. And I haven't seen any good gas for the past two days. This area used too much ethanol."

I exhaled. "Why didn't you tell me?"

"What would you have done, Jake?" He sat with his back against the Mustang and looked at me. I was struck again by how beat he looked. "It's over. There's no time to go back and find gas. The Sirin will find us first—they've probably made it to the lab by now, found Doctor Winthrop."

I sat on the road beside him and stared at my scuffed boots. Coby squinted at the sky. I'd asked him what he kept looking for yesterday. "Sirin," was all he'd said.

Looking up, I saw nothing but the bright sun—it was close to high noon. "Maybe..." I started, then stopped myself.

"What?" Coby asked, turning to me. His gaze seemed too intense.

I swallowed and waited a moment, but he didn't look away. "Zara and Nadia might find us."

"How would they do that?" Coby's voice was sharp and got sharper when I didn't respond. "You told them—I knew you'd do that! I warned you. For the plan to work they have to believe we abandoned them!"

He was right, and I winced. "I know, I just... couldn't."

Coby rolled his eyes. "Of course you couldn't. That would be too *cowardly* for you. What did you tell her?"

"I said we were going to find the Sirin and told her not to follow us." I managed to get the words out around the lump in my throat. I sat carefully, ready for Coby to make a move, but he slumped against the car. "I swear, I didn't tell them any details that would help them find us."

I should have, though. Now they might be our only hope.

"You didn't think they'd follow us?" Coby asked. He shook his head. "You don't know Nadia at all."

I tensed and finally looked at him. "What are you saying?"

"She's in love with you, man," Coby said, repositioning his elbows on his folded legs.

I looked down.

"Zara would come after us too, because that's Zara. If they do find us I'm sure she'll gloat over how stupid we were to leave them." He cracked a small smile, then looked back off into the dead forest. Slumping against the Mustang, he said in a low voice, "I shouldn't have gone for such a gas guzzler, I guess.

And this whole plan—going to the Academy, saving them. It was stupid."

The only sound was the wind in the trees that were left. It carried a hint of the dead-leaves smell of autumn. Everything alive but us had left a long time ago.

"Coby, I owe you an apology."

"For what?" he asked, sounding genuinely surprised.

"For a lot of things. Most recently, for telling Nadia what we were doing. But I've been a jackass to you since day one, and you didn't deserve that."

Coby looked back down the road, squinting into the sun again. "Maybe I did."

I gave him a hard look. "No, you didn't."

"I lied to you guys from the beginning," he said. "And with everything Doctor Winthrop did..."

"You said you didn't know."

"I didn't, I swear I didn't," He looked at me, on the edge of tears. "But I should have. Like Sloan. I should've suspected."

"You couldn't have," I said firmly. "Look, Coby, I don't blame you. None of us do. In fact, I respect you."

He didn't need to ask, "You do?" because his face said it for him.

"Like I said, I've been a jackass to you, but I respect you for being able to hold your own out there. It's not easy for any of us, but to survive, and especially to track down the rest of us, when you had no training. You'd never even been out in the real world on your own."

"I guess," Coby said. I was relieved that he seemed back to normal; I wouldn't have known what to do if he'd broken down and cried.

"It wasn't so hard for me," I said, surprising myself at how willing I was to open up to him now. Once you're screwed it doesn't matter. "I had my older brother with me for a long time. He was in the army, so he was trained in all of this survival shit. Even now, after he... now that he's gone I can still ask myself

'What would Ben do?' and it keeps me alive. You? You were on your own."

"Doctor Winthrop made it sound like…" He shook his head, rubbing the back of his neck. "Sorry, never mind."

I took a deep breath. "Made it sound like Ben killed himself?"

Coby met my eyes then, too surprised to respond.

"He did. Winthrop must have read it in Nadia's journal." I looked away, swallowing past the lump in my throat.

"That sucks. Sorry—I know that's a dumb thing to say, but it does. He left you alone?"

I shrugged. "Ben was fighting a battle I'll never fully understand. He would've been gone after the third strain anyway. But if I'd been enough to keep him alive—if I'd had a few more months with him…"

"It wasn't your fault," Coby said. "You can't save everyone, Jake."

As much as I wanted to believe Coby, I didn't think my conscience would ever be completely clear of guilt.

"But I guess we might still have a chance to save Zara and Nadia." He sighed and got to his feet. Brushing his hands off on his jeans, he asked, "Come on, what would Ben do now?"

"He'd keep going," I said, finding myself half-smiling. "He wasn't one to throw in the towel because he ran out of gas." The smile vanished as I remembered his last day. I still didn't know what *had* made him give up, after all we'd been through. I never would.

But I couldn't give in yet, and Coby was made of stronger stuff than that too. I got to my feet, Coby pocketed his keys, and the two of us packed our bags with supplies. We set off on foot, northward.

11: Impossible
Nadia

If anything good came out of being mauled by a rabid dog and attacked by a powerful blonde Sirin, at least I'd finally learned to keep my weapon close. The holster made for uncomfortable driving, but it allowed me to whip out the revolver and stop Vicente cold in his tracks.

"I don't want to shoot you, Vicente," I said, struggling to keep both my hands and voice from trembling. "But I will if I have to."

The tension was thick as Sloan translated. Vicente dropped his arms, but his knees were still bent, ready. He looked confused by what Sloan was saying, and responded in the same angry, rapid Esperanto he'd used before. Sloan started to reply, but—in a flash—Vicente gave up on listening.

He lunged at me again, arms outstretched. I wrapped my other hand around the grip of the revolver, using my right thumb to cock the round into place. He didn't stop and I willed myself to pull the trigger, but—

I can't do it. He's too human, I thought as his hands wrapped around my neck and he knocked me to the ground. There was a sharp pain as he pushed his knee into my stomach.

I kicked and coughed and gasped until I found my muscles no longer obeyed me, my vision blurred, then going white. *The end. This is the end, the end, the end.*

Then suddenly the weight lifted from my neck. My chest and lungs burned as I gasped and took in too much air at once. I coughed and sputtered and got sick on the ground as Zara reached me, gently rolling me onto my side. I heard rapid words—Zara and Vicente arguing and Sloan trying to translate between them—but the sounds were far off, muddled.

My vision cleared, and the grooves in the pavement in front of me seemed vivid. I convulsed, shivers wracking my body and chattering my teeth, and squeaked out, "I'm cold."

Zara stopped yelling at Vicente and knelt beside me. She stroked my hair and whispered, "Shh, it's okay, Nod. Stay with me. You're okay." Louder, to Sloan, she said, "Get a blanket from the trunk!"

The sun seemed too bright, so I shut my eyes and tried to stop shivering. I felt the jagged pavement against my cheek, the itchy wool blanket descending on me after Sloan and Zara shook it out. I heard my breathing, sharp and staccato, and my heart beating too fast. Zara spoke in a low voice, pleading with me, or with some higher power, to stay with her, to be okay…

Then, footsteps. Coming toward me. I opened my eyes and saw Vicente. I twitched, tried to roll away from him, and let out a strangled, "No!"

Zara brandished her hunting knife at him, but he didn't flinch. Instead he knelt, studying me, and said something.

"What did he say?" Zara demanded, turning to Sloan but keeping her knife out toward Vicente.

"He wantss to know why she didn't shoot."

My heart was beating faster now—impossibly fast. "Couldn't," I gasped out.

"She's not a cold-blooded murderer like your kind," Zara said fiercely. "We don't *enjoy* killing."

Sloan translated, but I couldn't tell if Vicente was listening because he kept his gaze focused on me. My teeth clicked together as I shook, and Zara rubbed my arms vigorously, warming me.

Vicente said something else to Sloan, then abruptly stood, finally looking away. I was afraid he would pounce at one of us again, but he was casual, relaxed.

"Wha—" I croaked, and Zara shushed me.

Sloan looked uncomfortable for a moment, then kicked at the ground with his polished shoe and said, "He thinkss the only reason you didn't shoot was because we need him as a hostage."

So this was a test?

"What?" Zara asked. "That's insane! It's not like we're going to trade him for—" She halted when she saw Sloan's sheepish expression. "Oh my God, Sloan!"

He shrugged. "It wasn't my firsst plan, but if the original failed…"

Shocked, I attempted to sit up before Zara gently pushed me back down. "No—" I managed. "We can't."

Zara cleared her throat. "He's not our prisoner."

I looked at Vicente, at the contraption pressing his wings to his back, and had to wonder whether that was true.

"I'll tell him so," Sloan said, then translated. I watched Vicente's expression. He looked skeptical, and I couldn't blame him. My head felt clearer, and I tried to sit up again. This time Zara helped me, putting her arm around my shoulders to stabilize me.

"What I want to know," Zara said quietly, though Vicente probably couldn't understand. "Is why Vicente stopped. Are we getting through to him, do you think?"

But when Sloan asked, Vicente shrugged.

"Is he going to attack one of us again?" Zara re-sheathed her knife but was still glaring daggers at Vicente.

I tried to get my breathing steady while Sloan and Vicente talked. My head still swam, and I hoped I'd be well enough to drive soon. I had to be. I gently ran my fingers over my throat and winced at the tenderness. Vicente saw me doing it, and for an instant he stopped talking and looked… *guilty?*

Then he abruptly turned and got into the backseat of the car.

"He says he won't," Sloan said. "He thinkss we can straighten everything out at the Academy."

Zara helped me stand and rearranged the blanket around my shoulders. "Do you trust him?" she asked.

Sloan held out his hands, palms up. "How can I?"

"No choice," I croaked, and Zara nodded.

"We'll find Jake and Coby soon," she said. "That will help balance out the numbers."

"Keep," I gasped, "going."

"Oh Nod," Zara said, looking at me in a pitying way that I didn't like one bit. "Don't strain yourself like that."

Shrugging her arms off me, I made my way to the driver's side of the car. My throat and gut ached, and it felt as if my upper left arm had been crushed. I wondered how many injuries were from Sigrath and how many were from Vicente.

I sat in the car and examined Vicente in the rearview mirror. He watched the other two talk out the window. I couldn't shake the feeling that he was playing us, that he had some other plan. But there weren't any options. I couldn't kill him, and Zara and Sloan certainly wouldn't either. We couldn't risk letting him go. Maybe he *was* our hostage.

I cleared my thoughts by shaking my head, which hurt more than I expected.

Growing impatient, I honked the horn. Vicente jumped, and Sloan and Zara reluctantly got into the car.

I swallowed and gasped out, "Keep your... weapons... close."

Zara nodded, refusing to look in the backseat, and we set off.

◆◆◆

Near dusk, we found the Mustang.

Coby and Jake weren't with it.

I expected to cry, to break down in tears at the hopelessness of coming this far and not finding them. But instead something changed inside me, shifted, and I was numb. My mind turned cold and clinical, as if my emotions had been shut off. That's what I'd wanted all this time—to not feel anything—but now that it was happening it didn't bring the relief I'd thought it would.

I was slipping away from myself, and I didn't care enough to stop it.

Absently running my fingertips over the scars on my arm, I circled the car. This cold *unfeeling* was worse than anything, and I was afraid a relapse was coming on. Then I saw Sloan and Vicente watching me and hurriedly pulled my sleeve down over my scars.

Zara came around and hugged me, looking both angry and close to tears. "They're not here, Nod. We failed."

I shook my head, pulling away from her. "No sign of struggle," I said, trying out my vocal chords again. After the pain meds Zara had given me it wasn't too bad.

"What about the gas can?" Zara asked, indicating the one that was tipped over and spilled all over the highway.

I shrugged. The doors on the car were closed and I didn't see evidence of a fight, though it was hard to tell on pavement. At least there was no blood. The gas can was next to an abandoned car, and the siphoning tube still stuck out of the tank.

Sloan and Vicente stood back by our car, the doctor's car, silent as they watched us. Zara got into the Mustang's driver's seat and started messing around under the dash.

"It won't start," she said. "Maybe they had to ditch it." Then she looked at the dashboard. "Oh. They're out of gas."

Staring at the gas can, I said, "They were trying… to get more." Vicente hadn't got around to dumping out our reserve gas supplies from the trunk before we'd stopped his rampage, or we would've been in the same boat.

Zara stared at the other car, at the siphon, at the gas can which had bled out on the ground. She looked at me, helpless. "What can we do?"

I tilted my head toward the Jaguar and grunted, "Keep going."

"No," Zara said, and I turned back to her. "Let's camp here. It's almost dark anyway."

Her face was pale and dark shadows had appeared under her eyes. She looked the way I felt: tired of running, of struggling, of fighting. Rest might do us good. I nodded.

She stared out into the woods, her small hand clasped around her necklace. "And that way," Zara said, more to herself than me, "if they're around here, just hunting or something, we'll be here when they come back."

I didn't believe that was possible, but that's not the sort of thing you say to someone so short on hope.

◆◆◆

Later that night, Zara and I talked while Sloan and Vicente slept. I volunteered for the first watch, to make sure Vicente didn't try anything and to watch for Sirin overhead. Zara, unable to sleep, stayed up with me. She took swigs from a bottle of whiskey every now and then, saying it would help her when she finally went to bed.

After taking a long pull, she sighed softly. I asked what she was thinking.

"Thinking… that I don't want to talk about Jake and Coby," Zara said. "Or Sloan or Vicente, or the Sirin, or the doctor."

"Then let's not. What should we talk about?"

I watched her shrug in an uncoordinated way. She'd had too much to drink already. "I don't know," she slurred. "The meaning of life."

As I gazed at the stars I sighed, sending stabbing pains through my bruised throat and chest. Since The End, the night sky always made me feel the solitude. But at the same time, I hoped there was someone else out there, under the same stars.

"I used to think that… life's meaning came from our relationships with other people. How we helped each other, laughed together, grew together, things like that," I said, taking another swig. The biting liquid made it easier for me to talk—

296

maybe it numbed the pain. "Then there weren't any people and I didn't know what to think anymore. I got really messed up."

"I thought life was about finding your passion and pursuing it," Zara said. She drank from the bottle and wiped her mouth with the back of her hand.

I rubbed my cold nose, wishing we could have a fire, but it wouldn't be wise with the Sirin hunting us. The forest sounds—the wind in the trees, an owl hooting somewhere far away—were calming as I waited for Zara to continue. When she didn't, I asked, "What do you think it's about now?"

She paused for a moment, looking into the bottle. "Life was never about anything," she said. "There was never a point to it. It's just more obvious now because there's no one left to philosophize about what it all means."

"Except us," I said softly.

"And we both know it doesn't mean jack shit. Nothing at all," Zara said. She tilted the bottle into her mouth again and emptied it. "I'm going to bed," she said, standing and brushing leaves off her jeans.

"Sweet dreams," I said.

She laughed coldly. "Yeah right."

As she crawled into her tent I wondered if she was right. Was there a point to it all?

I heard movement, like something crawling, to my right. Panicked, I pointed the revolver and clicked on my flashlight in that direction.

It was only Sloan.

"Sorry, sorry," he said, holding one hand in front of him as I holstered the gun and put out the flashlight.

"You should be asleep," I said, feeling foolish for overreacting.

"Inssomnia," he said. "I've already had the sleep I need. Why don't you resst now?"

I started to thank him, getting up, but something in his voice stopped me. "Do you want to talk for a minute first?"

He nodded and sat beside me. The autumn nights were getting colder, and I pulled the soft leather of my jacket around me tighter.

Minutes passed in silence, but not an uncomfortable one. I found myself wondering about Sloan, growing up in the lab but turning out so different than Coby or the Sirin. Was it the lizard DNA? Or because he was the first?

"What's your story, Sloan?" I asked, my voice still hoarse.

"Story?"

"What was it like for you, growing up? Compared to Coby…"

"I suppose you mean, why don't I worship Doctor Winthrop like he and the Sirin do?"

I shrugged. That was at least part of it. "Yeah, I guess."

"Coby has a blindsspot. He understands machines—he was always taking apart our toaster or radio and putting them back together. But people are harder for him. And though one could say the doctor was neglectful, all things considered, Coby wasn't mistreated. Whereas I…" Sloan looked to the side, cleared his throat. "The doctor always made it clear to me that my group of hybrids was botched. I'm the only one left. The others didn't make it passt eight years old."

I thought I'd known what it was like to be alone.

Sloan exhaled and said, "He always said that he kept me around to remind him not to repeat his greatesst misstake."

I winced. "I'm sorry, Sloan. That's awful."

He nodded and said, "I'd like to say I got ussed to it after a while, but the truth is I never did. It always hurt."

He stared off into the distance. After a moment, he said, "Nadia, please don't tell Zara what I told you."

I frowned; I was so over secrets. "Why?"

"Because I don't want her to pity me." It sounded like he wanted to say more but didn't.

"Oh," I said. Then I realized: he wanted something *else* from her. "*Oh*," I repeated.

Sloan wouldn't look at me. "It'ss already impossible, I know."

I was sure my heart would tear in half. I didn't know what to tell him. Zara was awesome, but was she ready for a Beauty-and-the-Beast romance? Sloan had scales, after all. And if she could get over that, there was still Nick. Could she forgive herself for what had happened to him? Could she let someone else love her? But Sloan didn't know about Nick, and it wasn't my secret to tell.

I struggled to come up with something to say. When words failed, I took his hand in mine and pressed it. The scales didn't feel as strange as I expected.

He looked at me again and smiled sadly.

"I've read all the stories of monsters like me—*Frankenstein, The Hunchback of Notre Dame, The Phantom of the Opera.* Thiss won't end well for Sloan of Winthrop Enterprises either."

"What about Beauty and the Beast?"

"That'ss a fairy tale," Sloan said bitterly.

"There's a bit of truth at the core of any story."

He shrugged, and I admired the starlight glinting off his scales. Biologically, he was less human than us, and socially—raised by the doctor—he should have seemed worlds apart. But somehow he understood things better than we did. Zara should've asked him about the meaning of life—he probably knew better than either of us.

"I should be getting to bed," I finally said. "Are you sure you're okay taking the rest of the watch?"

He nodded and smiled. "I don't sleep much, remember?"

"Right," I said as I stood awkwardly before him. "Well, good night."

He inclined his head, closing his eyes for a moment, and I entered the tent, lying next to the lightly-snoring Zara. Sleep was elusive, and instead I found myself repeating a phrase over and over in my head, like a mantra, until I finally drifted off.

Jake and Coby are okay. Jake and Coby are okay. They have to be okay...

12: Loneliness Won't Last
Nadia

The next three days were the longest of my life. We neared the end of the nuclear strike zone, but there was more shrapnel along the road than before and I had to maneuver the car through the debris. We moved along at barely faster than walking pace and saw no signs of Jake and Coby—or any evidence that they were alive—during the whole three days.

Hunger gnawed at us.

Vicente had eaten or destroyed nearly all our food, and we quickly consumed what was left. For the first day and a half, I wouldn't let us eat any fruit or plants because everything still seemed affected by radiation, and there were no sources of meat to be found.

Eventually, on the third day, the landscape started to clear. We weren't going to last much longer on our dwindling supply of bottled water, so we stopped a few hours before dark to hunt and set traps. I hoped to catch something overnight. Unfortunately, the hunting and gathering didn't go as planned.

Sloan and Zara were equally hopeless at anything survival-related that I tried to teach them—tying snares, hunting, gathering food, even building a fire. Vicente, predictably, wouldn't try. Sloan always apologized profusely for his shortcomings, but Zara would laugh and say things like, "Good thing we have you, Nod!" I'm not sure which was worse.

I grew frustrated with the three of them, and with myself for not being able to keep all of us safe and fed. Every day my worries about Jake and Coby and what we'd do if we found them increased. The pressure of keeping all four—all six—of us alive and the mounting worry only agitated my already-fragile state. I couldn't sleep through the night at all while we were on the road.

It was to my great regret, then, that when I found Zara crying, her hands tangled in a hopelessly twisted snare, my first reaction was not to ask what was wrong.

Instead, I said, "Just give it to me. You're never going to get it anyway." I ripped the wire away from her. We were on a bluff overlooking a river. The wind howled around us through the trees, and the ends of my hair whipped against my face. I turned away from Zara, trying to re-fasten my hair into a knot at the nape of my neck. Remembering the loss of my last real hair-tie only added to my formidable mood as I tried to wrangle my hair with a bit of string.

"Let me help you," Zara said meekly.

"You'll mess it up, like you did this snare," I seethed, turning to leave and clutching the ruined snare in my hand.

She burst into tears again, and I felt guilt tug at my heart. I turned back to her. "I'm sorry. I... shouldn't have said that."

"No," Zara sobbed, "you're right. I'm hopeless. I'd never be okay out here on my own like you were. I don't know how you did it." She sat against a tree, her knees tight to her chest. With the last words she looked up at me with wide, almost reverent eyes. I felt like shit.

"No one should have to survive like that," I said, sitting beside her. I picked up a twig and spun it in my fingers. "I barely made it."

"But you did," Zara said. "You're stronger than you think. Me? If I hadn't found Coby I would've been a goner."

"It sucked. Being alone, fearing your next mistake would be deadly and you'd just... die. All alone, possibly the last person on Earth. The end of the line."

Zara nodded. "It messes with your head." She slipped something out of her jacket pocket and handed it to me. It was a shiny metal flask, smooth and heavy in my hands. "Drink up," she said. "It helps."

Not one to turn down any form of calories at that point, I obliged but coughed and sputtered after the first swallow. I didn't recognize the liquor—something flavorless and astringent.

Zara smirked and took a few gulps. "That's better."

The liquor moved through my body and warmed it, but with nothing else in my stomach it made me nauseated. The wind was still strong, but I managed to get my hair braided and tied it with my string. I clasped the end between two fingers and examined it. Zara dyeing it turquoise had been a lifetime ago. Now it was faded to a dull green, barely darker than my natural hair color.

"Long time ago, huh?" Zara said when she saw what I was looking at. Then she took another pull from her flask and wiped her mouth with the back of her hand.

"You know," I said, not really listening. "I'm never going to forgive the Doctor."

"That makes two of us," Zara said, lifting the flask as if in a toast and gulping down the last drops.

"It scares me," I said quietly.

"What does?" Zara asked, screwing the cap back on.

"How much I hate him," I said. "I've changed, Zara. I used to think I was a good person. But now, look at me. I wanted the doctor killed and I might as well have killed him myself. I'm yelling at you. I'm so angry so much of the time. I don't feel like me anymore."

"You didn't shoot Vicente," Zara said. "I would have— even if I didn't mean to, I would've panicked and shot. But you didn't."

I shrugged, staring at the toes of my weathered boots.

"Look," Zara said, her words starting to slur. "The way I see it, in the old world being a 'good person' might have mattered, but now, sometimes… you gotta do what you gotta do to survive, you know? Sometimes being a good person isn't an option."

She looked away, but not before I saw her eyes turn glassy. She meant what had happened with Nick.

"Zara?" I asked as the thought struck me. "How much do you usually drink? I don't think I've seen that flask before…"

She smiled grimly, the tears gone from her eyes. "Ah, you've found my secret."

"What do you mean?"

"Fire-water, some call it," Zara said. "It's been my good friend this past year. It helps me sleep when I'm too afraid of the nightmares to close my eyes. Some days it helps me wake up in the morning, too."

My eyebrows pulled together, and I bit my lip. How had I not noticed?

As if she'd read my mind she said, "Don't beat yourself up, Nod." She clumsily patted my shoulder. "I was sneaky about it—didn't want you to know. And you don't need to fix me. I'm good. No worries."

"Can you stop?"

She closed her eyes and shrugged, slipping the flask back in her pocket.

"Look, I get it. I do. I've had my own demons to fight and it hasn't been easy, but… we both need to be sharp if we're going to face the Sirin. How will we do that?"

She opened her eyes and looked through me. "I don't know," she whispered.

"I don't know either," I said. "But can you try to tone it down? I can help you, hold you accountable. We're going to need everything we've got."

"Okay, Nod," Zara said, nodding repeatedly but not looking at me.

"I'm serious," I said.

"I know. I will. And anyway…" She reopened the cap and turned the flask upside down. "I'm out now. No more 'til civilization."

This was my moment, I suddenly felt. "Wait," I said, unzipping the inner pocket of my pack. I pulled out the blade I'd preferred since The End—wicked sharp and scalpel-like—and released a slow breath.

"If you get rid of that, I'll get rid of this."

Zara's eyes caught the glint of sunlight on the blade in the fading light, and I knew she understood what this was and what I wanted. "Alright then," she said, nodding a few too many times. "Let's do this."

We stepped forward, to the edge of the bluff. A few bushes clung to the side of the cliff, and we could just hear the rapids below over the rush of the wind.

"On three?" I asked, as she held out the flask and I the blade.

"To fighting inner demons," she said. "One."

"Two," I said, my fingers suddenly sparking, tightening on the blade handle. I didn't want to let go.

"Three." Zara let the flask fall.

I watched it for a beat before I found it in me to release the blade. It spun through the air, flashing like the rapids below. Each object made a small splash as it hit the water. First hers, then mine.

"Feel better?" I asked. I was torn. Proud for giving it up, and for having gone so long without. Worried I wouldn't be able to stay that way and knowing there were others out there I could use if I went to that place again. The blade was just a symbol.

She shrugged. "Maybe once I sober up."

"Why don't you head back and sleep it off? I can finish the snares. It'll be dark soon anyway."

"Okay," Zara said, barely keeping her eyes open. I remembered the walkie-talkie and paged Sloan, who had its mate.

"How's Vicente?" I asked. "Over."

There was a pause, then Sloan's voice. "Hungry, not very happy, but mosstly behaving. Over."

"Okay. I'm finishing these snares up here, but Zara's not feeling well. Could you come walk her back to camp? Over."

"On my way," Sloan said, and the walkie-talkie went crackly again. But then, there was a faint sound over the airwaves.

Zara's eyes were wide; she'd heard it too. I held it in the air, trying to tune in to the source of the sound. *Please be Jake*, I thought. *Be alive.* I lost the signal for a moment, but with a turn to the right it came in clearer. But it wasn't Jake or Coby.

"This is Fort O'Brien," a confident male voice said. "Broadcasting on all frequencies. We are an outpost for survivors. Our settlement currently numbers over 200 men, women, and children. We make daily checks for other survivors at the following GPS coordinates…"

I rummaged through my pack for a pen and paper. Failing to find the latter, I scribbled the latitude and longitude on my arm. The broadcast repeated twice, Zara and I hanging on every word, before it ended. We stared at each other, eyes wide, unable to speak.

We weren't alone.

13: On Our Shoulders
Nadia

The night Zara and I heard the radio transmission I cried, for the first time I could remember, tears of joy. Something had constricted my lungs before, never allowing me to breathe easy, but it lifted then. I'd lived with that weight on my chest so long—the pressure of humanity's survival. The pressure had eased when I heard Jake's voice, and then Zara's, but not to this extent. The survival of the human race had always been too much for a few people to bear. Now it no longer rested squarely on our shoulders.

Even if we got ourselves killed trying to rescue Jake and Coby, humanity would live on through the settlement—and if this one existed, others must too. *The doctor hasn't won.* I didn't realize how much I'd wanted humanity to survive, to overcome, until that weight lifted.

Zara and I hugged and wiped our tears and talked joyfully and nonsensically for a few minutes after the broadcast. Then doubt began to set in.

"What if it's the Sirin?" I asked. Then I remembered Sloan. I held up a finger to Zara and paged Sloan on the walkie-talkie. "Sloan? Don't worry about it, I've got Zara. We'll be back soon. Oh, and turn off the walkie-talkie. Over."

I tried to think of an excuse for the question I knew he'd ask.

"Are you sure? What if…?"

"We need to save the batteries," I came up with. "We'll be down soon, I promise. Over."

There was a pause, and I tensed, afraid the transmission from the settlement would come in again and that Vicente would overhear. Finally, Sloan said, "Okay. Turning it off now. Over."

Zara played with her pendant silently while I talked to Sloan. Once he hung up she said, words still slurring a little from her earlier drink, "I don't think it's the Sirin."

I sighed. "But how can we tell? How would we know?"

"I'm the one who's been trying to teach Vicente English and he's nowhere close to speaking like the guy on the transmission did."

"I suppose, but there could be *some* Sirin who speak English well."

Suddenly Zara grinned her contagious smile, and I found myself catching it. "Why are you smiling like that?"

"There's one way to find out."

I raised an eyebrow, and Zara laughed.

"We need to sneak into the settlement, obviously."

"Um…"

"Come on!" Zara said, grabbing my shoulders. "This is the stuff I live for! We *need* to know, don't we?"

"I guess," I said. "But this also sounds like a good way to get killed."

"Nod, have I ever steered you wrong?" she asked in an unusually serious tone.

I considered that, then said, "I guess not."

"I used to do this all the time! Nick—" She swallowed, her smile catching for a moment, but managed to continue. "Nick and I… we liked going places we weren't allowed when we were young. And when we got older it was more about knowing things we shouldn't know."

"Really? Like what?"

"Well…" Zara looked into the distance, a nostalgic smile on her face. "In junior high, we had this 'investigative journalism' column in the school newspaper. I didn't write it— Nick was the one who liked to write. Like you. I'd come up with these ridiculous ideas, sneak into places we shouldn't have been, find out people's secrets. I'd make Nick go on my adventures, but he enjoyed writing about them more than participating."

"Did you ever find anything really shocking?" I asked. I wanted to help Zara hang onto this sudden happiness as long as she could.

"Mostly it was nonsense." Zara said, her smile fading. "But there was one thing—the local paper investigated after we did. We figured out a developer had forged documents to pass an environmental study on some land where he wanted to put condos."

"That's crazy."

She nodded. "Yeah, it was a pretty big deal. Nick was proud of us then. Don't you want to investigate?"

I shrugged. "I guess so. But how about after we find Jake and Coby?"

"For all we know they have Jake and Coby at the fort," Zara said. "We've got to check it out."

"If they have Jake and Coby, they're probably prisoners," I said. "I don't think Jake would go willingly. I always thought he was suited for this end-of-the-world stuff. He doesn't trust anyone, really, and he likes being on his own."

"Not as much as he likes being with *you*," Zara said, playfully swatting my shoulder.

I couldn't bring myself to smile. My hands were starting to shake, thinking about Jake, but I tried to tell myself that it was just because it was getting dark. The nights were getting chillier; we might have the first frost that evening.

"Let's ask Sloan," Zara said.

I nodded, and we walked back down the hill. Sloan had set up our tent for us already. I glanced around for Vicente, panicking for a moment, but he was sprawled out asleep in the backseat of the car.

"We have something to tell you," Zara said, barely concealing her excitement.

"What?" Sloan asked, looking between us for explanation.

Zara grabbed his hand and pulled him out of Vicente's earshot, just in case. We briefly related what we'd heard. As

Zara explained her plan for sneaking in another thought occurred to me.

"What if the Sirin find out about the fort from *us*?" I interrupted with a pointed glance at the sleeping Vicente. "We can go in, see if the settlement is real or not, but then if we go to the Academy, looking for Jake and Coby, and the Sirin catch us… we could put everyone there in danger."

She shook her head. "I don't know, Nod. We could go to this settlement afterward and the Sirin follow us there, or we could go now, and the people at the fort can help us."

I took a deep breath. "Okay, Sloan, help us out here. What are our options?"

"The way I see it," Sloan said slowly. "Sneaking in isn't a good option. There are too many risskss, and it will delay uss catching up to Jake and Coby. So, we have a few optionss. We continue thiss journey as planned. If we survive it, we could bring Coby and Jake to the fort."

I nodded. I liked that plan.

"You could go to thiss settlement now, but there's a chance the Sirin could find it because of you. You'd have to go without me or Vicente, or at leasst we'd have to keep Vicente away so he couldn't tell the Sirin later. You could possibly warn the inhabitantss of the city about the Sirin, or assk for help, though I doubt they'd believe you."

Was that a note of pain in his voice when he mentioned being left behind? Would Sloan ever fit in at a settlement like this? The people left could be hard, desperate, looking for someone or something to blame for The End… His inhuman looks could make him a target.

"Or?" Zara asked.

"You run south, away from both the settlement and the Sirin."

"I'm for option one," I said. "If there's a chance we can save Jake and Coby, I'll take it. Do we tell the city about our existence though, or not?"

"No," Zara said, giving me a sideways glance. "The less we know about them, and they know about us, the better. For now. You'd better wash off those coordinates"—she indicated the scribbles on my arm—"in case the Sirin find them."

"I agree," Sloan said. "We musst be cautiouss."

"Alright," I said. "We continue as planned. No discussing this settlement or our plan in front of Vicente either."

◆◆◆

Later that night, Zara woke me in our shared tent.

"Hm?" I asked, trying to see in the dark.

"We should still go to the settlement," she whispered.

Despite Sloan's warning, I was curious. "When?" I asked. "It's too close to dawn—we can't go tonight."

"I know," Zara said. "And we would have to sneak around Sloan in the few hours he sleeps at night. I vote tomorrow night, if we haven't…"

She didn't finish the sentence. What could she say? "If we haven't found Jake and Coby"? The odds of that were getting slimmer every hour. "If the Sirin haven't caught us?" I didn't want to calculate those odds.

"Yeah," I agreed quietly. "We'll be closer to the coordinates they mentioned tomorrow night. We'll go then."

◆◆◆

We packed up before dawn, as usual, and set off. The mood in the car was lighter than it had been, and I wondered if Vicente noticed the difference. I was excited at the prospect of visiting the settlement, and despite our circumstances, Zara and I were hopeful. If nothing else, at least we weren't the only survivors.

It was still morning, the sun barely risen over the tall pines along the road when I noticed a movement in the ditch ahead. I slowed the car, hoping for something we could eat. But when

I was close enough to make out shapes I gasped. My hands gripped the steering wheel, turning my knuckles white.

"What is it?" Zara asked, peering over the dash. "Holy shit. We found them!"

I stopped the car. They'd heard the engine and stopped walking, turning toward us. We were too far away for me to make out their expressions.

Zara and I got out, slamming our doors. Vicente and Sloan followed suit. My stomach felt light and fluttery, as if we were meeting for the first time. As Coby and Jake walked toward us, I noticed Coby's grimace. Jake's expression was unreadable.

"Well, well, well, it's our knights in shining armor," Zara said, her arms crossed. We stood in formation: Zara and I next to each other, Vicente and Sloan flanking us. Jake and Coby stopped on the road, about ten paces away.

"What are you doing here?" Coby asked, raising his voice so we could hear him.

"Saving your asses," Zara said. Her anger hadn't burnt out yet, even after so many days on the road. She examined her fingernails, feigning nonchalance. "The way you guys tried to save ours. Except more successfully." She raised one eyebrow and glared at them.

Now that the moment had come, I couldn't pretend to be angry. Relief flooded me. They were *alive,* and I wanted to fling my arms around Jake. Instead I stood resolute, imperceptibly shifting my weight from foot to foot and trying to nonverbally support Zara's indignation.

"What is that?" Jake said, nodding his head toward Vicente.

"You mean '*who* is that'," Zara said. "His name's Vicente."

"Is he one of *them*?" Coby asked. "One of the things that are going to kill us all?"

Vicente cleared his throat. "No. Not now."

Zara grinned, proud of his language progress. Coby's eyes were wide and Jake's mouth fell open as they stared at him. His stubble had grown in, and he seemed leaner, older. He turned his attention from Vicente to me, sizing me up too, trying to see if there had been any damage.

"And," Zara said, tossing a hand onto Vicente's shoulder, "he's our key to saving humanity."

"Okay then," Coby said. Jake was through with his inspection of me, and the corners of his mouth pulled up, not quite into a smile. He hadn't been listening to Zara and Coby's conversation.

Suddenly I couldn't stand still anymore. As if by their own accord, my legs sprinted toward Jake, then launched me into his arms. When my brain caught up to my body I backed off and said, "I am really, really,"——I tried not to grin——"pissed at you right now. You're the world's biggest idiot." I tried to look fierce, but Jake couldn't stop smiling at me.

He pulled me back to him and nuzzled my neck. "I know," he whispered. "I was so, so stupid."

"Yes," I said, standing rigidly and trying not to react to him. "Completely moronic." His breath tickled my ear.

"Completely," he said, his smile coming through in his voice. "I'll never leave again, I swear." He held me so tightly I believed him. My body relaxed, and I wrapped my arms around him, my hands soaking in the familiar warmth of his back, the feel of his shoulder blades.

"Would you get off so I can slug him like he deserves?" Zara asked behind me.

Jake smiled at her, refusing to let me go, then gently turned my head away from her and toward him. His lips met mine and we kissed, well, as if we'd done it more than once before.

"Oh, get a room," Zara said, but there was relief in her voice, too. Against all odds, we'd found each other again.

14: Careful Out There
Jake

Too soon, she pulled away.

"We need to talk," she said. My shoulders dropped. I should've known forgiveness wouldn't be so easy. She glanced at Zara, then said, "Alone, please."

I glanced back at the group—I don't know why. For support? Zara's face was hard to read. She was clearly angry at me and Coby, but there was a spark in her eyes. Sloan smiled in a sad way. Vicente eyed me as if he didn't know what to make of me, which mirrored how I looked at him.

Coby gave me a nod, and I turned to follow Nadia into the woods, out of earshot of the others. I tried to rehearse an apology in my head, something that would make her understand, but lost any trace of it as we stopped. I ended up blurting out, "Nadia I mean it—I'm sorry. I don't know how to make it up to you, but let me try." I cleared my throat and added, stupidly, "Please."

"What?" Nadia asked. I'd expected her to be upset or angry, like Zara, but she looked confused. "Oh, about leaving us? It's okay. Well, it isn't," she said, getting flustered. "But I'm not mad. Or maybe I am? But—there's something more important we need to talk about."

I paused, letting that sink in. "This isn't about what Coby and I did? We—I mean, you and me—are okay?"

"I guess so, I just... you need to listen, Jake. Will you *stop* smiling?" She was on the edge of rolling her eyes at me. "This is serious."

"I can't," I said, grinning wider because she was wrinkling her nose in the cute way she did when trying to look fierce.

313

"What we have to talk about is something Vicente doesn't—and can't—know. So I'm telling you and then Zara will figure out how to tell Coby so he doesn't get suspicious."

Sobered now, I asked, "What is it? Tell me."

"Last night, Zara and I heard something on the walkie-talkie. A radio broadcast."

"From the Sirin?"

She shrugged. "It could be. That's what we need to find out—but the man on the broadcast, he said they were from a settlement." I wasn't processing it yet, so she said, "There might be other survivors, Jake."

I realized my jaw was hanging open and shut it quickly. "What?"

"It's called Fort O'Brien. The man on the radio gave coordinates for where to meet them. He said they have about two hundred people."

"I don't like the sound of this," I said, feeling a tightness across my chest.

Now she did roll her eyes. "Of course *you* don't. I'm sure if you were on your own you'd keep on living out in the woods, hermit-style. But Zara and I are excited. Don't you see? The doctor didn't win."

"They might not be survivors," I said. "It could be a trap by the Sirin."

"It could be. That's why we need to check it out. But... I don't think it's them, Jake. I have a good feeling about this."

I sighed. I was half-hoping there *weren't* any survivors. Not that I wanted it to be the Sirin, but the message could have been a recording from months ago, set to automatically play long after everyone was dead. If there were people, it was just as likely they'd be threats as allies, or even burdens if it came time to face the Sirin and we had to protect them, too.

Possibly, Nadia was right and I did have loner tendencies.

"You and I should check it out," she said. "Sloan and Vicente obviously can't go."

"Okay," I agreed. "As long as it's *just* you and me."

She nodded absently, and said, "Yeah, Zara will be disappointed, but she can stay and make sure Coby doesn't do anything stupid again." She narrowed her eyes at me; I hadn't been forgiven yet.

I finally got a good look at her, and what I saw gave me a twinge of guilt. The circles under her eyes were deep, as if she hadn't slept in days. Her braid was looser than usual. Tendrils of her hair had fallen out and curled over her shoulders. There was so much weariness in her face, and it was my fault.

"Nadia," I said, clearing my throat. "I'm sorry."

She looked at me, her sky-blue eyes piercing. "I know," she said, but not in a forgiving way.

I searched for something to say, but all I could think was that I was losing her. Still, the way she'd just run into my arms. There was some hope.

"Let's get back," she said, abruptly striding through the trees. I followed. "We can tell them we're hunting," she said, "which wouldn't be a bad idea, if anything's alive in this area. Vicente ate most of our rations a few days ago. We've been running on fumes."

More guilt. She and Zara hadn't eaten for a few days? I vowed I would make it up to them.

"Coby and I don't have much," I said weakly, "but we'll share."

We rejoined the others. Coby had already taken out the jerky he had left and doled it out to the others. I took off my pack to do the same and caught Nadia's eye. I smiled, but she didn't return it. She was withdrawing from me, and I needed to figure out what to do about it.

◆ ◆ ◆

"We'll hunt on the way back," Nadia said. She was in the lead as we made our way through the woods. "If there *is* a way back."

She held the compass and I had the map. We were only a few miles from the broadcast's coordinates, and every step might move us closer to our last. We had all the weapons on us, save Zara's crossbow, but our odds didn't look good if this *was* a Sirin trick.

Nadia moved stiffly, and at one point she stopped, winced in pain, and stretched.

"What's wrong?" I asked.

She grimaced, stretching her arm up and to the left. "Oh. We didn't tell you. After you left and we found Vicente, another Sirin found us."

I winced. That was what Coby and I had tried to prevent. "What happened?"

"She found the doctor's body, then attacked Zara and me. It was… pretty bad. We're still a little beat up. And Sigrath— that's the Sirin's name—managed to escape, so we were even more worried about you guys."

Damn it. I'd wanted to bury the doctor's body, but Coby wouldn't hear of anything other than laying him out on his bed in the clean room.

I exhaled. "Nadia," I said, but again I couldn't find words to make things right. "I don't know how to fix this, but I will. I'll find a way."

Nadia stopped and I almost ran into her. She turned to look at me, but she was at a loss too.

"If I could change it…"

"You can't, Jake. What's done is done. You left. And you— you left me a note! I thought we agreed we wouldn't give up on each other. No notes." Her eyes were rimmed with tears, and my chest ached.

"I know, I know." I raked my fingers through my hair. "I wanted to at least save you two."

"We didn't need saving."

Her words hung in the air. I wanted to tell her I loved her, but knew it wasn't the time.

A tear slid down her cheek. "You could have been *dead*, Jake," she choked out. "We didn't know, we were so worried. What would I have done without you?"

It hit me, how selfish I'd been. I'd been motivated to leave to avoid the same pain I'd caused—to avoid losing her. To think of her no longer alive... I couldn't. So I'd left with Coby, fooling myself into thinking we were doing the right thing.

When I didn't say anything, she said, "I don't know if I can trust you anymore. I thought you were the one person I could rely on."

"Nadia," I said, without thinking, "I love you. I just... don't know what to do."

"I still love you too," she said. "But I don't know if I can trust you, and that's what hurts."

Without thinking I pulled her into my arms. She was shivering from the cold, and for a moment I thought she'd pull away, but then she hugged me back. "I swear," I said, "whatever happens, I won't leave you again."

She nodded, and I inhaled the sweet scent of her hair. Yesterday I thought I'd never be this close to her again, but now her smell and warmth were very real.

Finally, she pulled away. "I need time, Jake."

I nodded. I couldn't expect any less.

"Wait," she whispered, her spine straightening. "Do you hear something?"

I nodded. Human footsteps. Or Sirin, possibly, but it seemed a good sign to me; why travel by foot if you have wings?

Silently, we narrowed down their direction and ducked behind the outstretched boughs of a pine. Its spicy scent overwhelmed my nose. We peered through the branches until we could make out two forms moving through the woods, about a quarter mile away. One was taller and broader than the other. They wore military fatigues with a camouflage pattern, and both had rifles slung over their backs.

When they were out of sight, we let out our breaths, and Nadia said, "There are other survivors after all."

I grimaced, still unable to feel anything but suspicion. "At least we know what we're up against."

We stalked the pair through the woods, careful to stay barely within sight so when they turned to look behind them, which they did every fifty paces, they wouldn't see us. Nadia had carefully pulled her binoculars from her pack to get a better look.

When I saw them—a tall, boxy woman in her mid-forties, and a boy younger than us—I sighed with relief. But still, they were armed.

Finally, the pair stopped at what must have been the rendezvous point given out in the broadcast. The woman sat on a log, untied her boot and started to re-lace it. The boy stood alert, one hand on his rifle.

Nadia's eyes slid over to me, and she said, "There's no one else. I checked with the binoculars. It's just these two."

"The Sirin aren't far," I said. "If this settlement is for real I'm surprised they made it this long without the Sirin picking up the radio broadcast and taking them out."

Nadia shrugged. "Maybe the Sirin didn't want to take on that many people at once."

"So the settlement puts two people at a time in danger from the Sirin, like this?"

"I don't know," Nadia said. "Let's talk to them."

I nodded and she grabbed my hand, squeezing it once before letting go. Then we approached, our hands placed so they could see we were ready to fire our weapons if necessary.

The woman noticed us first. When she stood the boy turned toward us, too. They were as ready to shoot as we were but didn't look frightened. In fact, the boy smiled.

"Wow," he said. "We haven't seen any new survivors in months! We thought we'd found all of them around here."

Nadia's stance relaxed, but mine didn't.

"We're passing through," she said evenly.

"Name's Jeremy," the boy said, holding out his hand.

Nadia smiled and said, "Elise," using her middle name.

"Ray," I said, taking the hint. I nodded, not wanting to remove my hand from its strategic position. Jeremy seemed to accept that.

"Oh," he said, still smiling and gesturing to his companion. "This is Maud."

She inclined her head to us, and he explained, "She doesn't talk much. Or at all, actually. Not since we found her a few months ago."

"How does it work," I asked, "this settlement of yours?"

Maud stood, and I almost took a step back. She was tall and clearly well-muscled. She nudged Jeremy with her elbow.

"Oh, right," he said, suddenly more businesslike than chatty. "I need you to take off your packs and turn around."

"We're not doing that," I said immediately.

He stopped smiling for the first time. "Oh, I see," he said. "You thought—well, you don't need to worry, we're not going to—"

"Can we do it one at a time?" Nadia asked.

Jeremy relaxed. "Yes, that would be fine."

Nadia met my eyes, then took off her pack and turned. I grasped my rifle, finger hovering over the trigger. After a moment, Jeremy said cheerfully, "Okay, you're fine."

I didn't exhale until Nadia turned back around. I lowered my pack and turned, watching Nadia in my peripheral vision.

"You're good too," Jeremy said, and I quickly turned to face him again.

"What was that for?" Nadia asked. Her hands were on her hips, her right hand still close to her revolver.

Jeremy glanced at Maud, seeming to lose his confidence for the first time. Up close he seemed even younger than before, not older than thirteen.

"Can we sit?" Jeremy asked. Maud sat on her stump and Nadia glanced at me, then shrugged. We both sat with our backs against trees, and Jeremy sat cross-legged next to Maud.

"This is going to sound crazy," Jeremy said. He looked at Maud again, and she nodded, signaling him to continue. "There are these... people, I guess. But they have wings."

"*Wings?*" Nadia asked skeptically, and I was glad she'd remembered to act surprised. I hadn't, so I worked on keeping my expression neutral.

Jeremy nodded solemnly. "At first we thought the people who saw them were crazy, or religious nuts, thinking they were seeing angels. But most of us have seen them now. We've killed a few, and these—whatever they are—they've killed some of our people."

Nadia shivered next to me and I wanted to put my arm around her.

"What else do you know about them?" I asked.

Jeremy shook his head. "Not much. They can fly really fast, and they have weapons—better ones than ours. We have to be careful, make sure anyone new doesn't have wings. That's why we made you turn around. To be safe."

Nadia scratched a mosquito bite on her arm. "Tell us more about your settlement."

"You'll see when you come back with us," Jeremy said, and I bristled. *If* we went with them. "There are about two hundred of us. We have a city inside the fort, and there's food, houses, doctors. It's almost like before."

"That sounds nice," Nadia said.

"It is," Jeremy replied. "We haven't found anyone new in a long time, though—everyone will be so excited! After your quarantine, we'll have the biggest party."

"Quarantine?" Nadia asked, trying to sound friendly, but I caught the note of concern in her voice.

"Oh, yeah, but only for a week," Jeremy said. "Everyone goes through it. We think everyone who's left is immune, but we need to make sure. It's not bad. When you get out, it'll be fun! Mine was so much fun, back in the spring." He smiled to himself at the memory.

"Besides the quarantine," Nadia said, "how does joining Fort O'Brien work?"

"That's all there is to it. You have to agree to live by the rules, of course, and they'll help you figure out what you want to do at the fort—you know, for a job."

"That does sound nice," Nadia said, smiling. "I'm curious though. What would you have done if, when we turned around, we had wings?"

I hadn't thought to ask; Nadia must have been concerned for Sloan. Maybe for Vicente too.

Jeremy's face darkened. "I would have had to shoot one of you, then Maud and I would have to take the other one back for... questioning."

"Really?" Nadia asked, keeping her tone light, as if only mildly interested. "Even if we weren't trying to shoot or anything?"

"Even then. They've killed too many of us. And..." He glanced at Maud before continuing. "Not many people at the settlement know this, but we're figuring out where they're coming from. We're narrowing it down. If we captured one alive for questioning, we'd have it."

"And when you find out?" Nadia asked, her voice on the edge of trembling.

"We'll get rid of them," Jeremy said. "There are crazy theories out there, but everyone agrees: they must have been part of everything, the disease. Everyone's scared, especially after the last attack. They took out four people on a scavenging trip; only one made it back to tell us about it, and he was in rough shape."

Nadia was silent, so I said, "Sounds terrible."

He nodded solemnly. "They don't bother us this close to the settlement, I don't know why. But it's dangerous farther out."

I was ready to return to our companions. Carefully, I said, "You've given us a lot to think about. But we've been on our own for so long, I don't know if we're ready for civilization again."

Nadia smiled and said, "We'll talk it over tonight and meet you here tomorrow?"

I held my breath. This was the part I'd been most worried about. Would Jeremy and Maud let us leave or force us back to the fort with them?

Jeremy was puzzled. "You don't want to check it out with us first? I think you'll like it."

Maud put a hand on his knee and he stopped talking. She looked at him for a moment, then glanced at us. I tensed my leg muscles, ready to run if push came to shove.

"Okay," Jeremy said. "If you want to talk about it, we'll be here at the same time tomorrow."

Nadia smiled, clearly relieved, and we both stood. "We'd like to get some hunting done too," she said. "We haven't eaten for a few days."

"Are you *sure* you don't want to come back with us? There's plenty of food, and it's not safe out there."

"Give us some time," Nadia said. "We're still adjusting to the idea that there are other people alive!" She forced a pleasant laugh.

"Alright," Jeremy said, and Maud put a hand on his shoulder to hold him back. "But,"—he glanced to each side— "be careful out there. I mean it. Those *things* are around."

Didn't we know it.

"We will," Nadia said as we walked away. Maud nodded to us. I did my best not to glance behind me every few steps, but I disliked turning my back to them.

We headed north, not wanting to give away our companions to the west, and were silent until we were sure we were out of sight of Maud and Jeremy. Only then did I feel like I could breathe.

Nadia turned to me, a crease between her eyebrows. "What do we do now?"

15: What I've Become
Nadia

Jake and I took a circuitous route back to camp, in case Maud and Jeremy tried to follow us. We didn't speak along the way, and not in the comfortable way we used to spend time with each other. We made good progress and were able to rejoin the others quickly, arriving at high noon.

Zara and I went for a stroll under the pretense of collecting firewood so I could relay what we'd learned.

"They already know about the Sirin?" she asked. "They've been fighting them?"

I grabbed a few sticks from the ground, adding them to the bundle in my other arm, and nodded. "It seems like great news. We could join them, tell them what we know, and they could keep us safe from the Sirin."

"But…" Zara said, biting her lip.

I sighed and sat against a tree, flopping my legs out in front of me and dropping the bundle at my side. "I know. What about Sloan? Even Vicente. We could let him back to the Sirin I suppose, but…" I ran my fingers over the spruce needles that carpeted the forest floor around me. "I don't feel right about going into an all-out war with them, now that we've got to know him. And all of this is assuming they don't notice we're different during the quarantine process and destroy us." I blew hair out of my face as Zara left the tree she'd been leaning against and began to pace.

"We should run," Zara said. "Let Vicente go, then the rest of us can head south or west. We've evaded the Sirin this long; if we keep going…"

"That's what I've been thinking too. For all we know, the people at the fort will defeat the Sirin at some point and then we'll be free. If this fort exists, there are probably other survivors. Somewhere."

Zara sat on a fallen tree. Her hands were shaking a little; I'd noticed it a few times since she gave up alcohol.

"This is what the end of the world does to you," she said. "You wish and wish for there to be someone else out there, other people left alive. But when you find them it's complicated. I don't want to be jaded and not trust people but look what even Coby and Jake did."

For a moment, neither of us spoke. I vaguely registered a crow cawing in the distance.

"I'm sorry," Zara said. "I shouldn't have mentioned Jake. I can tell you two aren't okay right now."

A lump rose in my throat, and I nodded, not trusting my voice.

"But you will be," Zara said, brightening. "You should draw it out—pay him back for ditching us."

When I couldn't manage a smile, she moved closer and said, "Oh, Nod, come on. It'll work out. You guys are so great together—really good for each other."

"Are we? I'm afraid…" I cleared my throat. Without looking at Zara, I continued. "It's just—maybe we shouldn't be together. For a while we thought we were the last two people on Earth. That messes with your head. Now that we know there are other people… maybe it was circumstances outside our control that made us think we'd work."

I was struck by how immensely fortunate I was to have Zara; I couldn't express these thoughts to anyone else alive. They were hardly clear to me.

"Don't be silly," Zara said. She laughed, and it was so unexpected I jumped. "You two definitely work together. You have magic fairy dust that makes him trust you."

"What?"

"Look, he trusts you when he's suspicious of absolutely everyone else. Everyone we know exists, anyway. And that's not an exaggeration!"

"I guess that's true. But he didn't trust me at first either."

"He got over that quickly enough, especially by comparison. Think about it—he never trusted Coby. I bet he still doesn't, not even after their escapade together. He didn't trust me, even before I told you about—about my past." Her smile faltered for a moment, but she continued, "And look at Sloan. He's done nothing but help us from the start and Jake *still* gives him these ridiculous sideways glances. It drives me crazy!"

The corner of my mouth twitched up involuntarily. "Did you see him around Vicente?"

"Yes! He was squirming in his boots just standing near him! What a drama queen—Vicente's a human hybrid, same as us. He was just... raised differently."

She laughed again, and I found myself laughing too.

"You and Jake will be fine," she said.

"I hope so. He trusts me, I'll give you that. I'm just not sure if I can trust him again."

"Girl, you will. Do what I did to Coby. He was going on about how sorry he was and how much our friendship means to him and how he'd almost ruined it for the second time—you know how he rambles sometimes. In the end I said that of course I forgave him, but that I still wanted to punch him." She grinned. "He let me."

"Ah, yes, I noticed his eye looked a bit purple and assumed it was your doing. I don't feel the need to injure Jake, though."

She finished applying a fresh coat of lipstick and smiled. "Are you sure? Sometimes violence *is* the answer."

Smiling, I shook my head. "I'm sure. That does remind me though—Jake and I didn't get a chance to actually hunt this morning, so I'd like to go now. Can you tell the others I'll be back before dark?"

"Sure," Zara said, standing and extending her hand to help me up. "All Coby and Jake have left is jerky. Something fresh would be great after all these days with nothing."

I handed her the bundle of firewood, grabbed my bow, and shouldered my quiver. "Thanks, Zara. For everything."

"Of course. But hey, are you sure you want to go alone? I can go with, or I can get one of the guys. It doesn't have to be Jake. Sloan, maybe."

"I won't be long. Just need to clear my head."

She nodded. "I get that." She turned to go, then looked back. "And, Nod?"

"Yeah?"

"Happy birthday." Her mouth twisted into a bittersweet grin.

"Is that today?"

"I think so. If I haven't messed up my calendar." She patted her zippered coat pocket. "It's the doctor's real birthday. Sloan told me."

Her words hung in the air as we remembered what birthdays used to mean and what our doctor-assigned birthdays meant now. All I could say was, "Why didn't you tell me this morning?"

She grinned. "Because I would've *had* to tell you my birthday wish—you know me. And then it wouldn't have come true!"

I shook my head, laughing.

"And hey," she said. "We found Jake and Coby this morning, so look how marvelously it worked out!"

"Oh, Zara," I said. "Don't ever change."

"I won't," she said, winking. "But hey, you can use your wish on something else... like hoping certain people don't get their asses kicked by certain other lab creations? Don't tell me though!"

◆ ◆ ◆

It didn't take long for hunting to become frustrating. There were a few animals alive—chickadees flitting among the tree branches and frogs croaking in a nearly dried-up ravine—but nothing big enough to make a decent meal. Fallen leaves covered the ground so the crunching of my boots scared away any rabbits or squirrels well before I saw them. I'd never mastered the technique my father had tried to teach me to move quietly through the forest: lifting each foot with an exaggerated knee bend and softly rolling each step from heel to toe. I could do it, but it forced me to move about one-third of my normal pace.

Thinking of my father sent a pang through my chest. Only a year ago we'd been getting the hang of living in the wild, preparing for winter. If not for the seasons, I'd have guessed a decade had gone by, not twelve months. I felt older, and so many things had happened. Most of them bad.

I *was* older. Today I turned eighteen, which in the before-the-end world would have made me a legal adult. What did it change now? Nothing?

What would my parents, my sisters, everyone who'd known me before, think of what I'd become? Nadia, the quiet, rule-following bookworm now a survivalist who once had to fight off a winged creature straight out of a nightmare—and who very soon may have to fight a whole lot more of them. I took a moment to make my birthday wish as Zara had suggested. It was silly, but it couldn't hurt.

Then I spotted a deer print in a patch of mud and proceeded in the direction it pointed.

The people from my past life might hate me. What else could the dead feel for the living, especially when the living had the unfair advantage of inhuman DNA? But then again, my parents had known all along. I wished I could ask them why they did it, if they were proud of who I'd become because of their choice. Or would they be ashamed of my involvement in the doctor's death? Afraid of me? I'd never know.

The familiar smell of damp earth and fallen leaves—with just a hint of pine—filled my nose, and branches swished against my jacket sleeves as I trekked. My hair got caught in a twig briefly, and I reached back with my free hand to unknot it before continuing.

There—a bit of movement off to my left pulled me from my thoughts. It was a buck, a young one. Each of its antlers had three points. I took a deep breath. My first deer hunt. We certainly had enough people to eat it now, so I couldn't use that excuse. Its peaceful brown eyes and thoughts of Bambi seemed to have no effect on me after days without food. Time to move in.

I wasn't close enough for a clean shot, but it hadn't seen me yet. I made my way through the trees at a glacial pace. When I was close enough to shoot, I carefully pulled an arrow from my quiver and nocked it. Barely daring to breathe, I lifted the bow and wrapped three fingers around the bowstring.

Suddenly, the buck's ears twitched and it lifted its head. I froze. I hadn't made any noise, but it looked in my direction and sprinted away.

I let out an expletive under my breath, re-quivered my arrow, and turned to go back the way I'd come. Then I saw what the deer had seen.

Not twenty yards from me was a wolf, standing with its fangs bared and muscles coiled. There was no way of knowing whether it had first been stalking me or the buck, but now, with the deer gone, I was its target.

Someone like me wouldn't be seen as prey by a healthy wolf unacclimated to our species. But this was not a healthy wolf; it was starving. I could see every one of its ribs, and its skin hung loose on its body. Clumps of hair were missing—evidence of mange.

I read once that the body's fight or flight response was imperfect, not as simple as those two options. I was about to find out what that meant.

I could have lifted my bow, pulled back the arrow, and shot. It would have slowed the wolf, even if I didn't manage to kill it. Then I could have climbed a tree or run back toward camp, or maybe pulled out my revolver to finish the job.

Instead, as all these scenarios ran through my head, my mind flashed back to my encounter with the rabid dog and I was filled with an unrelenting panic. As the wolf advanced, my mind screamed—*shoot, run, get down, fight, do* something—but my body wouldn't obey.

Sometimes you don't fight and you don't run. Sometimes you freeze and can't do anything.

16: Leave No Man Behind
Nadia

Each agonizing step the wolf took was an eternity—an eternity of my mind screaming orders at my disconnected and unresponsive body.

On the fourth step, I found my voice. "Help!" I shouted. Then, relieved that I could do anything at all, I shouted louder, "Help! Jake! Zara! I need you! Help!"

If they could even hear me, it would take them so long to reach me that all they'd be able to do was keep the wolf from completely devouring my corpse. But I had to try. I swallowed and shouted again, trying to force my arms or legs to move.

The wolf didn't like my shouting. He let out a low, deep growl and snapped at the air, his yellowed teeth flashing. But he was frightened, too. He didn't want to do this, to try to take down an armed human with no pack to help him. Desperation drove him to it.

He advanced more quickly, closing the space between us. I let out a scream that echoed through the woods as I finally managed to reanimate my legs, stumbling backward into a tree.

I caught myself, my hand scraping against the rough bark, and stumbled sideways to get around it. If I turned my back on the wolf now, it was over. Even facing him, he was close enough that all it would take was one good leap…

I'd dropped my bow. I fumbled at my holster to free the gun as I took careful steps backward. My hands moved clumsily and the wolf leaned back, coiled to pounce. I prayed death would be quick. Then a fierce wind rushed through the trees. In a moment, I was airborne, watching the wolf shrink below me as I ascended.

A few gusts of wind blew tendrils of my hair loose from its braid before I realized what was happening. Vicente had snatched me away, and his wings created the wind. I looked up, gasping in surprise, and managed to get out, "Thank you."

Vicente studied me, then set his angular jaw and focused his eyes straight ahead.

I barely had time to admire the way his feathers ranged from honey to chestnut to umber in color, the dewy feel of the breeze on my face, and the fresh scent of the air before we descended. He set me gently on my feet near the car, then backed away.

Immediately, Zara's arms were around me, then Jake's too. I heard Jake murmur, "You're safe, you're safe," into my hair as if he didn't quite believe it. I gently pushed them off me so I could face Vicente.

"You saved me. Thank you."

He stood apart from us. His wings were partially outstretched, his arms crossed. Anger flashed in his dark eyes.

"Vicente?" Zara said, stepping forward. "What's wrong?"

Within the blink of an eye, he'd snatched Zara's crossbow and pointed it at her. All our hands went up instinctively.

"Vicente, stop!" I said as Sloan said something in Esperanto and stepped in front of Zara.

He retreated a step and Zara said, over Sloan's shoulder, "Please, Vicente. You don't need to do this."

"Listen," Vicente said in thickly accented English. "I know—the doctor—what you did."

"Vicente," Sloan said in a soothing tone, his voice lingering on the soft C as always. He continued speaking calmly in Esperanto.

A few tense seconds into Sloan's speech, Vicente let out a war cry and leapt into the air. His wings unfurled, and for a moment we all froze at the sight of his massive wingspan, the brown and gold feathers splayed out against the blue sky.

His gaze shifted between the five of us, crossbow swinging wildly. It lingered longest on Zara, then Sloan. Vicente's eyes flashed as if he'd made a decision.

There was a *thwang* as the bolt released from the crossbow, then Vicente shot into the sky. Sloan collapsed and we all came to our senses, rushing to his aid. The bolt had gone through his right shoulder.

"Sloan!" Zara shouted, kneeling beside him.

He was still alive, thank God.

"Can you breathe?" Zara asked frantically. "Did it get your lungs?"

He shook his head once. His skin was taut over his face as he tried not to cry out in pain.

"We need to get it out of him," Jake said. He cut away part of Sloan's shirt with his pocketknife to examine the wound and propped his shoulder on his knee. The bolt had gone all the way through his body and stuck out his back.

"He'll bleed to death," Zara said.

Jake glanced at me, then back to Zara. "We'll have to cauterize it."

Zara shook her head. "No, we need to get help." As she said it her voice broke; there was no one to help us.

"We can't stay here. We'll need to move him before the Sirin come—and to do that we can't have this tearing into him and doing more damage," Jake said.

I turned to Coby. "Can you make a fire?"

"On it."

"I'll get the first aid kit," I said, opening the car door so I could dig through Zara's pack. We'd need all the rubbing alcohol we had left to make this any kind of a sterile procedure.

"Coby, wait," Jake said, handing him his hunting knife. "Once the fire's hot, put my blade in it."

Coby nodded and returned to building a fire. I handed Jake alcohol-soaked gauze and he and Zara carefully wiped the two sides of the wound. Sloan groaned as his face went white. Then his eyes fell shut.

"He passed out," Zara said. "I think—I think he lost too much blood."

"It could be the pain," I said, but the blood that soaked Sloan's shirt, the ground, and the hands of Zara and Jake wasn't reassuring. "He wouldn't want to be awake for this next part anyway."

◆ ◆ ◆

A half hour later the deed was done, and we were able to move Sloan into his tent, which Coby had set up in a dense copse of trees not far from where Vicente had left us. He'd also hidden the car. It wasn't much, but it was the best we could do under the circumstances.

Jake and Zara were in the tent, getting the unconscious Sloan settled while Coby and I camouflaged the outside with brush and earth.

"How was it?" Coby asked me.

"Terrible," I said quietly, not wanting Zara to hear. "I don't blame you for not wanting to watch. I… had to look away myself."

"He didn't wake up, did he?" Coby asked as he caked more mud and a handful of leaves onto the tent.

"No, thank God. I didn't look but there was still the… sound of it. And the smell." I gagged thinking about it, remembering the sizzle, the burning smell of searing flesh as Jake pressed the heated blade against the wound, stopping the flow of blood after they'd removed the bolt. First one side, then the other. I turned away to compose myself.

Coby came up beside me. "You okay?"

I nodded. "I will be. This is my fault. I went off hunting on my own. Why didn't I learn after the dogs?"

"Hey, don't blame yourself. We had no idea Vicente would do this. And we never had much chance of escaping the Sirin."

"If anything happens to Sloan… or any of you." I bit my lip. "I just hope…"

"I know," Coby said. After a pause, he said, "But Sloan will be alright. I'm just glad Zara and Jake's stomachs are stronger than ours."

He smiled. He was trying to make a joke, but I found I couldn't laugh.

"Sorry," he said. "I shouldn't even be here. If I hadn't done what the doctor wanted, you all could have gone on with your lives. None of us would be in this mess."

"Don't blame yourself. Not now. We've got to stick together, okay? We'll get through this." I didn't sound convincing to my own ears.

Coby studied me for a moment, a bitter half-smile on his face. Then he put a hand on my shoulder and squeezed it.

He started to walk away, but I said, "And Coby?"

"Yeah?"

"I really am sorry about the doctor, too. I know he was important to you."

Coby shoved his hands in his pockets and looked down. "Yeah. He and Sloan were the closest thing I had to family, before I met you guys."

"What do you want to do now? I mean, if we survive tonight?"

His mouth pulled up in a half-grin, and he pulled his keys from his pocket, twirling them around a finger. "Now that we know there's a settlement, I'd really like to move to it. I have a lot of ideas about bringing electricity back. Sloan got me a book once—well, he was always getting me books. But the only one I liked was about renewable energy. Using wind, water, the sun to generate electricity. That's what I want to do."

"That's a great dream, Coby. I hope we live to see you do it." It was my turn to tell a joke that fell flat.

He laughed anyway, his keys jingling as he repocketed them. "I hope so, too. I'll keep watch to the north."

He left and I circled the tent once more to make sure no vivid nylon was visible. Then I swallowed and made myself enter.

◆◆◆

When Sloan woke up, only Zara and I were in the tent; Jake had gone to keep watch with Coby.

Sloan regained consciousness slowly, blinking and moving his head. "Sloan!" Zara rushed to his side.

"Water," he croaked, and I pressed my bottle into Zara's hands.

She knelt beside him, gently propping his head onto her knee, then tilted the bottle at his lips. Afterward, he said, "Vicente—the others."

"We know," Zara said. "We'll move out as soon as you're better."

He shook his head. "Go now. Save—"

"Shut. Up." Zara said through gritted teeth. "We're not leaving you behind and I won't hear you say we should."

She looked to me for support, mascara smudged beneath her eyes. "We're not leaving you, Sloan," I said firmly. "Jake and Coby are outside standing guard, and they've hidden the car. The Sirin might not find us."

Too tired to protest, he accepted more water from the bottle. Zara took a piece of gauze from our first aid kit, wet it, and placed it on his forehead. "You're going to be okay," she said softly.

Feeling I'd been watching too long, I slipped off into the woods. Jake stood a hundred yards from where we'd hidden Sloan and I stopped at his side. He squinted at the sky intently, his hand clasped around his rifle.

When he saw me approach, he said, "How's he look?"

I shrugged. "I don't know. The bolt didn't get his heart or lungs, or he'd be dead already. The bleeding has slowed but not stopped. If we were anywhere near a hospital, or people who knew what they were doing—"

"We are."

"What? Oh, the settlement? I don't know… do you think we could get him there without causing more damage?"

"No, but one of us could get a doctor from there to come out to him." He turned his gaze away from me again, looking over the forest and then at the sky in the fading daylight.

"I don't want to bring any of those people out here when the Sirin could attack at any minute. It wouldn't be fair. God, I can't believe Vicente. He knew about the doctor the whole time, and he played us." I scraped at a tree root with my boot.

Jake hesitated a moment, then said, "I wouldn't be too hard on Vicente."

"What?" I said, too loud. Quieter, I hissed, "He tried to kill Sloan!"

"Did he? Sloan's still alive, and I'm guessing if he wanted to Vicente could've taken all of us out. And he saved you. He didn't have to."

"I suppose. What happened with that anyway? How was he able to help me?"

Jake took a deep breath and let it out slowly. It was chilly enough that I could see it in the air. "Vicente heard something the rest of us couldn't. It must have been you."

I nodded. "I was calling for help, though I figured no one would hear."

"What happened?" Jake asked gently.

"It was a wolf," I said, swallowing. "He was sick and starving and he almost… I would've been okay, I think, except I had a flashback to those dogs and I froze." I shuddered, imagining its snapping jaws again.

Jake wrapped an arm around me. "I should have been there," he said, his voice strained.

I shook my head and pulled away. "No, it was my fault for going off on my own. What did Vicente do next?"

"He told Sloan and Zara he could hear you, that you needed help. Said if they took off that thing he wears that holds his wings down he could get to you in time."

"And they believed him?" I raised my eyebrows.

Jake held out his hands. "Zara did. And what choice did we have? If you really were in danger..."

I folded one side of my jacket over the other and ran my hands over my arms for warmth. The leather felt supple, broken-in under my fingers. "He swooped in and grabbed me just in time. But why? Why not just fly off?"

"Beats me," Jake said. "Maybe Zara's right and their 'humanizing' project or whatever was working."

"But then he shot Sloan. Why?"

Jake shrugged. "He wanted to slow us down, keep us here. We should've known we couldn't trust him. But I don't regret that we did. At least you're alive."

"And Sloan?"

"He might make it," Jake said, "We might, too."

The sun had set as we talked, and I could no longer see it through the trees. "Let's hope," I said, then returned to Zara and Sloan.

I threw a few more unnecessary branches on the tent for camouflage before I stepped inside. Sloan was asleep, and Zara sat beside him. She held his hand, stroking the scales on the back with her thumb.

"How is he?" I asked.

"His temperature's elevated, but it's not quite a fever." Her voice was shaking.

"That's good." I sat beside her.

She turned to me and said, "Nadia, I can't—we can't lose him."

"I know," I said. "We won't. We've all lost so many people. But he won't be one of them."

"We haven't known him long," she said, turning back to look at him and smoothing the cool cloth on his forehead.

I hesitated, weighing whether to say anything. In all likelihood the Sirin would capture and kill us tonight, so I went for it. "But he's special to us," I said. "And I think especially to you."

Zara looked at me, her eyes wide, then glanced at Sloan quickly to make sure he was still asleep. "I don't know," she said, turning back to me. "I've started to... feel things... that I haven't felt since—"

She sniffed and wiped a tear from her eye. "But I shouldn't," she said. "Not after what I did... the last time."

"Don't talk like that, Zara," I said. "What you did was a mistake—God knows we all make mistakes. You shouldn't be unhappy forever."

"It may not be forever," she said, smiling bitterly. "Just a few more hours, until the Sirin get here."

I didn't know what to say, so I put an arm around her, squeezed once, and said, "Hang in there. We might make it out of this yet." She turned back to Sloan and I left the tent again, quietly.

First I approached Coby, though I could barely make him out in the starlight. He didn't need anything, so I made my way back to Jake. As I walked I thought about what I'd said to Zara and felt a pang of guilt about my attitude toward Jake. Hadn't he just made a mistake, and a well-intentioned one at that?

"How are they?" Jake asked as I approached.

"Okay for now," I said. "Jake..."

"Yeah?"

I breathed in through my nose to settle myself, then said, "If you still want to—try again. With us, I mean. I want that too."

His grin flashed in the darkness. "You mean that?"

I nodded, then realized he might not be able to tell in the dark. "Yes."

"Are you just saying this because we're about to die?" he said, his tone only half-joking.

I couldn't manage a laugh. "I'm saying it because I mean it."

The hours passed slowly, and I spent them mostly by Jake's side, in comfortable silence, checking on Zara and Sloan at intervals. It was a new moon, and we struggled to see by the light of the stars. I hoped it would make the Sirin struggle as well, but I doubted we'd be that lucky.

I was rejoining Jake after a visit to Sloan's tent when patches of stars went black above us. There was a great rush of wind. I just had time to draw my revolver—feeling naked without my bow—when the Sirin landed, surrounding us. After a moment of silence, they broke into a battle cry.

17: If I Can Help It
Jake

All was confusion while the Sirin yelled to each other and we tried to fight back. I got off a few shots that didn't hit their mark before something heavy was thrown onto me. I tried to shove it off my back, not realizing it was a net until my feet tripped out from under me. One of the Sirin, holding the ends of the net, leapt into the air, and my stomach lurched as my feet were pulled from solid ground.

"Jake!" I heard Nadia cry—another Sirin had done the same to her.

I reached for her, trying to untangle my arms and rifle from the net for a few seconds before it was in my best interest to stop. We were too high, and getting free or shooting Nadia's Sirin would mean a long fall and a grisly splat for one of us.

I made the mistake of looking down and inhaled sharply. I glanced around me, trying to make out shapes in the starlight. Eight sets of Sirin wings and four nets rushing through the night sky. My body tumbled to one side for a moment as my Sirin handed off one side of the net to his partner, a muscular female. I swallowed, trying not to think about my life being held precariously in these two Sirin's hands. *Focus.* Four nets. So they hadn't found Sloan yet. That was something.

Why the nets? Why no weapons? I thought they wanted us dead.

Maybe they still did. But not quickly.

I wriggled around in my net, trying to reach my rifle. If I could get ahold of it, I might have a chance of fighting back when we landed. Its reflective barrel, ensnared in the ropes, poked out near my foot. The Sirin responded to my movements by wrenching on the net, pinching my arm in the nylon and leaving a searing rope burn. I got the message and stopped moving.

I grit my teeth and tried not to become dizzy or disoriented as the starlit treetops sped by below us. If I paid attention to where they were taking us, we could find our supplies again. In the event we managed to escape.

But if they hadn't blindfolded or subdued us, the chances of them letting us live long enough to escape were slim-to-none.

Eventually I made out the others in the darkness. Nadia held my eyes for a moment; she didn't look injured, at least. Zara and Coby were farther away, but they seemed alright as well.

An abrupt, shooting pain went through my thigh and I caught a flash of Sirin wings underneath me. I twisted around to see a device, somewhere between a dart and syringe, sticking out above my knee. *Shit.* My hands fumbled to pull it out but my arms were caught in the net and I couldn't reach it.

The Sirin who'd stabbed me was flying toward Nadia next. "Watch out!" I yelled, but my voice was already slurring and my vision clouding over. The Sirin dipped below Nadia and I saw her knee jerk in pain. Then all was dark.

◆◆◆

When I opened my eyes again, it was still dark. I reached instinctively for my rifle, which always lay beside me as I slept, but my hand hit cool concrete instead. The air felt heavy and stale, as if we were below ground. I blinked, trying to adjust my vision to my new environs.

"Jake?" Coby's voice.

"Yeah," I said, rubbing my eyes. He sounded close. "Where are we? Where are Nadia and Zara?"

"They're here too," Coby said. "But still out."

I clapped my hand against my jacket pocket and was relieved the Sirin hadn't taken my flashlight, though they'd stripped me of my knife and rifle. I shone the light around what turned out to be a square room, concrete on all sides, with a steel door on one wall. Coby sat between Nadia and Zara, who both lay on the ground as if asleep.

"Christ," I said, moving to Nadia's side.

"Don't worry," Coby said. "They're breathing, I checked. I'm glad you still have your flashlight."

I nodded, my mind still clouded. "Whatever sedative they gave us… do you know how long we were out?"

"No idea," Coby said. "I only woke up about ten minutes ago."

"Have you seen anyone? Any Sirin?"

"No. All I did was check that the three of you were breathing. Then I sat over here so I could see if the door opened."

I set my flashlight between us so it illuminated the door and we could watch for the others to wake up. I started by sitting against the wall closest to Nadia. But in a moment, I was up and pacing, too jumpy to stay still. Captured by enemies, half our team unconscious, and weaponless. Things weren't looking good. Coby's face was drawn and tense, his eyes locked on the door.

My mind raced, trying to think of a plan. How would we get out? Fight? But my thoughts were too twisted, tangled like my arms had been in the net. After a moment Nadia made a noise and I knelt beside her.

"Nadia," I said. "I'm here. Wake up."

She moved her head, slowly, then rolled onto her side. "Jake?"

"It's me. Coby and Zara are here, too. We're all still alive."

She propped herself onto an elbow and nodded at me, still groggy. A *tap* made me jump, but it was just Zara's foot kicking the wall. She rolled over and blinked, adjusting to the darkness.

"Where are we?" Nadia asked, sitting up and scratching her scalp.

"Underground, I think," I said. "The Sirin have us prisoner. We were all unconscious when they brought us here."

Zara sat up and moved to sit against the wall between Nadia and Coby. She shuddered at my mention of the Sirin. "Did they—" Zara's voice cracked, and she swallowed. "Did any of you see if they got…?"

She stopped, and I grabbed my flashlight, searching the perimeter of the room to make sure we weren't being listened to or watched.

"No," Nadia said. "I didn't see."

Zara looked at Coby and me. We both shook our heads. I finished my perimeter sweep and said, "I don't think we're bugged. These walls are smooth concrete, that door is steel. If there was a camera or a peephole or something, we'd see it."

"Okay," Nadia said. "I don't think they found him Zara. He was well-hidden and not very close to us."

"When I heard them, I ran out of the tent and they caught me after a few minutes. I don't think they got him… Do you think they're out looking for him now? And that's why we're here?" Zara asked, sniffing.

We didn't respond. None of us knew.

Nadia moved closer to Zara, who rested her head on Nadia's shoulder and said, in a small voice, "I can't go through this again."

"Go through what?" I asked. Zara let out a sob and Nadia shot me a look that was part I'll-tell-you-later with a hint of shut-it.

I held up my hands in mock surrender, then let them drop to my sides. "We need a plan," I said, glancing at Coby, then Nadia.

"Yeah," Coby said, nodding. "They could come back at any minute, and we should be ready."

"Okay," Nadia said. "What do we do?"

"We don't have any weapons," I said. "And they could have anything and everything."

"Why do you think we're still alive?" Zara asked, sitting straight again. "What if they aren't coming back?"

Coby looked stunned for a moment, then said, "You mean, they'd leave us here until…"

Zara shrugged. "I don't know why else they haven't killed us already."

"We killed the doctor," Nadia said. "I don't think they'll want to take care of us quickly."

"Or," Zara said, "they want to hear our side of the story first. We can explain to them what happened. They might not know how guilty the doctor was."

"I don't know," Nadia said, pursing her lips. "You were there when Sigrath found out what happened."

Zara shrugged. "So Sigrath has a temper. I was also there when Vicente saved you—they can feel something for us besides hatred."

Nadia studied Zara for a moment, then said, "Okay. What did you have in mind?"

"What are you talking about?" Coby asked. "We have to fight! They'll never let us go free."

"I agree," I said, getting up and pacing the room again. "The best we can do is attack as soon as they come for us and try to escape. I doubt we'll all make it out alive, but at least we can try to take out a few of them in the process."

Zara stood. "No," she said. "They haven't done us any real harm yet. If we attack them, we'll be proving every horrible thing the doctor probably told them about humans."

"They've been brainwashed!" Coby said. "I should know. I used to think of the doctor as my father. It's still hard for me to believe him capable of a fraction of the things he did."

"We can convince them," Zara said. "They might trust you more because you lived with the doctor so long. Sloan said something about subduing the enemy without fighting. That's what we need to do."

"If we fight," Nadia said, standing, "there will be injuries—deaths, most likely—on both sides. We won't be able to escape, and the four of us will end up dead anyway."

The logic was sound, but how was being weak going to help us?

"I could try to turn myself in," I said. "In exchange for freedom for the rest of you, as I originally set out to do."

"Jake, no," Nadia said. "We're in this together."

"It won't work anyway," Coby pointed out. "They already have us. Clearly they blame us *all* for what happened. You're already a prisoner; you can't use yourself as a bargaining chip."

I grimaced, acknowledging his point. Nadia turned to Zara. "What's your idea?" she repeated.

Zara took a deep breath. "It's not much of an idea, but when they come in here to get us, we don't try to fight. We stand united. We do what they tell us, and if we get a chance, we try to explain ourselves. And maybe we can do more than that."

"What do you mean?" Nadia asked.

"Sloan and I—" Her voice caught, but she continued. "We discussed how ironic it is that the Sirin hate everything humans have done, but they do things just as terrible, if not worse, because they believe humans are evil. But what about us? We're only a little more human than they are. If we show them we don't mean them or anyone else harm, maybe we can convince them not to kill us."

"I don't know," Coby said. He and I were agreeing, for once.

"Or if we can't do that," Zara said, "it'll at least make them think. There are human survivors out there, as we've seen, and they're in as much danger as we are. But if we help the Sirin understand our perspective... I don't know. I'm not good with words. Good thing you are." She winked at Nadia.

"Oh God, not me," Nadia said. "I can't convince them of anything. And we don't speak Esperanto."

"Sloan taught me some," Zara said. "And they might speak some English. Who knows? Vicente might even help us translate."

345

"Maybe," Nadia said, biting her thumbnail. "Did any of you see him with the Sirin that captured us?"

"No," Coby and Zara said together, and I shook my head.

"There was time for him to get back here, so he must have known about the raid," I said. "But we're still alive…" Could he be our ally on the Sirin side?

"Can we agree to Zara's plan?" Nadia asked. "We won't fight; we'll be peaceful. And try to explain ourselves to the Sirin if possible?"

"And if we can't explain?" I asked. "If all chances of that are lost, do we fight?"

"No," Zara said. "If we don't fight—even if we die—at least we'll show that not all humans are out to kill and destroy."

She looked to Coby, who shrugged. "We don't have any weapons, and I'm no good with my hands. Fighting would be pointless anyway."

Nadia looked up, arms crossed, and met Zara's gaze. "I agree. Sometimes I get glimpses of myself that… aren't really me. This person that's capable of things I couldn't have imagined a year ago. I don't want to be that person if this is it. I want to be me, and I'm not going to cause harm to anyone else before I go."

The others were in agreement, and they looked to me. I clenched my jaw.

"And," Nadia added, with a pointed glance at me, "I'm afraid if I fight and the rest of you don't, it'll get you hurt. Or Sloan, if they find him. Like I said: no harm to anyone else if I can help it."

Going down without a fight went against every instinct, against my pride. But—*what would Ben do?* Safety in numbers…

After a moment, I uncrossed my arms. "Fine, you all got me. Peer pressure, whatever. I won't fight, even if they kill me." I didn't promise not to fight if they tried to kill one of the others, I noted with satisfaction.

"Thank you, Jake," Nadia said, smiling at me. "I know this can't be easy for you."

I shrugged, grimacing again, and sat against the wall, staring at the door. Nadia sat beside me and the others joined us.

"I guess now," Zara said, "we wait."

"*If* they're coming for us," Coby said. "If *this* isn't our punishment."

Nadia shook her head. "No, Coby. We can't think like that. They'll come back. Maybe we'll get a fair trial." She laughed, but it fell flat, dampened by the concrete walls.

There was silence among us. I think we were all contemplating our imminent demise. At least, I was.

I looked at Nadia, happy we were on good terms at the end. She met my eyes. Thinking the same thing, I imagined, as I put my arm around her. She settled into my shoulder. I couldn't find any words to say. The feeling was beyond words.

Suddenly, Nadia broke away and stood.

"Do you hear something?" she asked. There was silence for a few moments. The tightening of our muscles and straining of our ears was palpable.

"Yes," I said quietly, standing beside her. "Footsteps."

"How many?" Nadia asked, as Zara and Coby got to their feet.

"At least three or four," I said, picking up my flashlight from its place on the ground. "Maybe more."

We all stood in a row, facing the door. Zara and Nadia were on the inside, Coby and I flanking them. Zara grabbed Nadia and Coby's hands, and Nadia grabbed mine. I held the flashlight in the other. I wasn't facing my fate blind.

Nadia's hand trembled in mine. I squeezed and she squeezed back. The footsteps grew louder, then stopped outside our door. We held our breaths. The door swung open.

18: The Fight
Nadia

Several figures were silhouetted in the doorway, and it took a few blinks to make out how many there were. Six, and the most surprising was the one closest to the door.

"Sigrath!" Zara said before I could, almost letting go of my hand.

She stepped into the room and looked down on us imperiously. I'd forgotten how tall she was. On this second glimpse of her, I noted that her features were not quite flawless. Her nose had a crook, as if it had been broken once or twice, and a white scar slashed through her eyebrow. She barked orders at the two male Sirin behind her and they circled us, pulling our hands apart and cuffing them behind our backs with zip ties. Jake tensed. He wanted to fight; I could feel it. I gave his hand one last squeeze before they pulled us apart. He looked back at me with a conflicted expression.

Once we were all cuffed, one of the Sirin handed Jake's flashlight to Sigrath and she passed the light over us slowly. A grin spread over her striking features as she sized us up. Then she turned and stalked out of the room. A few of the Sirin who had stayed in the hall followed, and the others prodded us along after her.

"Where are you taking us?" Coby asked as we started down a hallway similar in construction to our cell, except for a few hanging light bulbs and the steps at the end of it.

They all stopped abruptly and turned to face Coby. A tall, dark-skinned Sirin raised a hand as if to strike him, and Zara yelped, "No!"

"Bittor, *ne*," Sigrath hissed. He dropped hand reluctantly.

Sigrath barked an order and a slim, dark-haired Sirin turned to us. She said, in heavily-accented English, "Silence. If you want to live." She glared at us with her pale grey eyes until we all nodded.

Then we continued down the corridor, our footsteps echoing lightly against the walls. We ascended the stairs slowly—it was difficult to balance with my hands tied behind me—and came out into the fresh air.

Petrichor and rain greeted us as we stepped into a small clearing in the woods. A Sirin dropped the steel trapdoor shut behind us, throwing pine branches over it as camouflage. The sky, half-covered in grey clouds, pelted us with rain. But the increased light allowed us to size up our captors.

The dark-haired one who'd spoken English addressed Sigrath in a low voice. Then—*Vicente?* I managed to catch myself before saying his name, remembering our warning. He stood toward the back of the group, his expression hard. The four of us exchanged glances, saying with our eyes what we couldn't say out loud. *Why is he here?*

The Sirin who'd raised a hand to strike Coby—Bittor— was one of the two male Sirin who had cuffed us. The other was of medium height and stocky build with a few freckles on his nose. The last Sirin was female. She was of average height and build, with a pretty, angular face and remarkable green eyes. All six were dressed head to toe in black uniforms and heavily armed. Each had an assault rifle strapped to their back and various weapons attached to their belts, from hunting knives to hand grenades. If they wanted us dead, it could be easily managed.

Sigrath gave general orders to the group, then said, "Neziah," turning to the interpreter with the sharp grey eyes. Sigrath said more to her, then nodded, and Neziah took a step closer to us.

"You follow the trail," she said, pointing to a narrow dirt path on the forest floor. It was hard to see through the pouring rain. "Stay with us. No running. No speaking."

She turned around without waiting for our response, and we trudged after our captors into the rain-drenched woods.

Do they really need six Sirin to guard us, with our hands tied behind our backs? Sigrath had nearly taken Zara and me out by herself, and there were only four of us now. My mind caught on that. *Four* of us. I imagined Sloan in the woods, laying on his uninjured side, worried about us, and—hopefully—alive.

My eyes slid to Vicente. He knew he'd shot him, that Sloan had been with us; so why wasn't he here? Had they already killed Sloan? Was it not worth the effort to find him since, severely wounded and alone, his luck had already run out?

As these grim thoughts presented themselves, we moved on through the woods. The rain pounded us and my boots were sucked into the mud with each step. Strands of soaked hair plastered my face. I tried to push them away by rubbing my shoulder against my cheek but gave up after a few fruitless attempts. My shoulders were beginning to ache anyway from the unnatural position in which the zip ties held my arms.

Mercifully, before too long we reached the door of a domed building well-concealed in a copse of pine trees. Jake, Coby, and Zara looked as I felt: irritated, wishing they could speak, and trying to hide their fear with varying degrees of success. The Sirin conferred together in a huddle. They seemed dry and comfortable in their rain-slicking uniforms. Every so often one would shake out its wings, droplets flying off and a few feathers falling to the ground. All six wore the surly expression I'd come to consider a Sirin signature.

Finally, their discussions ended, and Vicente broke away from the huddle to speak to us.

Zara opened her mouth to say something to him but closed it again when Sigrath threw her a sharp look and wrapped her hand tighter around the stock of her gun.

"You," Vicente said, addressing all of us. His voice was hard and controlled, so different than the last time he'd spoken to us. "Together. Close," he said, indicating with his hands. He stared us down until we nodded that we understood.

As we shuffled nearer each other, two of the other Sirin pulled open the doors. We proceeded in formation: Vicente and

Sigrath in front, us four wingless flanked by Neziah and Bittor. The two who held open the doors then closed them and brought up the rear.

In a few seconds, my previous question was answered: there were six Sirin around us because they were protecting us from the *other* fifty-odd Sirin who clearly wanted to rip us apart on the spot.

Our guardians ushered us down an aisle, clearing a path by shoving the Sirin who tried to approach us back and barking sharp commands at them in Esperanto. Between the angry shouting of the crowd and the stern warnings of our Sirin protectors, the whole dome echoed, and my ears rang from the noise. I met Zara's eyes—hers were wide with fear, mirroring my own.

Jake moved closer to me and risked speaking—correctly guessing that our Sirin would be too distracted by the din of the crowd and the work of defending us to notice.

"These ones in the crowd," he said in a low voice. "They don't have weapons."

I glanced over Neziah's shoulder as she kicked an approaching male with buzzed hair in the chest, sending him backward into the mass of uniformed bodies and wings. Jake was right; the crowd was unarmed.

"They don't need weapons to be effective," I said, remembering the encounter with Sigrath. Our group managed a few paces forward.

We could now see what we were moving toward through the crowd. Beneath the apex of the dome was a raised square platform with ropes around the outside, like a boxing ring. Hung above it was a huge banner featuring the doctor's face, his chin up and eyes imperious.

"I don't like the looks of this," Jake said. I nodded and swallowed hard. One of the Sirin overheard Jake, scolding him in Esperanto and elbowing him in the ribs. Jake winced and we both clamped our mouths shut. We were close to the platform now and our Sirin guards herded us as we uncertainly made our

351

way up the steps, struggling a bit without the use of our arms for balance.

On the platform, there was an inner roped-off ring inside the outer one. The six Sirin lined us up outside of the inner ring so we faced the crowd. Suddenly, two males swooped up, spreading their wings wide, and shouted at our protectors.

All six pointed their weapons at the two in the air. Silence fell over the crowd and it was clear they'd done or said something serious. I wondered if the act of flying itself was a violation. It would have been easier for the crowd to attack us if they'd used their wings.

The two Sirin in the air had many of the characteristics I'd come to expect from their kind—good looks, defined muscles, angry expressions, black military uniforms, and beautiful, powerful wings covered in gold and brown feathers. Both had dark hair and one had the beginning of a beard on his square jaw. This detail struck me; he was the first Sirin I'd seen with facial hair. It reminded me that, despite how physically mature they seemed, they were 16-year-old kids. With wings. And assault weapons. And messed-up ideas about how the world should be run.

After several warnings from Sigrath, the pair landed on the raised platform, not far from us, and the tension in the room relaxed. I exhaled in relief when they folded their wings and our Sirin guards lowered their guns.

The bearded one was pale and tall, and the other looked to be of East Asian descent. They both stepped forward, I guessed partially to get a look at us and partially to antagonize Sigrath. The discussion was less heated now, but it continued. Sigrath and Vicente argued with the two rebellious Sirin, and I didn't like the way all of them pointed and looked at us. Their words came out faster and faster, and I knew I'd never pick up anything familiar.

I met Zara's eyes, wondering if she could deduce any meaning after her brief lessons with Sloan and Vicente. She shook her head slightly, and I perked up one corner of my mouth as if to say, "Ah, well."

Suddenly my attention turned to Coby—the bearded Sirin had grabbed him and thrown him into the inner ring. I barely stopped myself from crying out. Coby fell, hitting the ropes as he went down, and struggled to get up with his hands still tied behind him. Sigrath and Vicente moved as though to help but stopped when the other Sirin held up a hand. There was another exchange. Sigrath was upset, and he tried to calm her. Sigrath looked out at the crowd; it was clear from their shouting they were in support of these two. There was something in her expression I didn't like: compromise. Finally, she nodded her head and shook his forearm. An agreement had been struck.

In the meantime, the bearded Sirin had hopped into the ring and cut off Coby's zip tie. Coby got to his feet and looked to us for help, but we didn't know what to do or what was happening. The one who had made the deal with Sigrath jumped into the ring then, and Neziah stepped up.

To Coby, she said, "You fight him. Fight Fenyang."

"W-what?" Coby stammered, his eyes wide as he turned to face the Sirin named Fenyang.

"No!" Zara said as she, Jake, and I all tried to jump to Coby's aid.

Neziah put out an arm to stop us as two of the other Sirin held us back. "Fenyang will not kill him," she said, her voice not at all comforting. "It was agreed." Her clear grey eyes looked coolly at Fenyang, at Coby, then to where Sigrath had been standing. But Sigrath was gone.

"*Batalu!*" Neziah yelled. We didn't need a translation to understand that the fight had begun.

19: Stay With Me
Nadia

Fenyang approached Coby, smiling, then attempted to strike him across the face. Coby blocked the blow with his forearm and backed up. He dodged the next hit, took two steps to the side to avoid a kick from Fenyang, and moved back toward the center of the ring, his fists up.

I kept exchanging quick glances with Zara and Jake, shaking in my wet boots. *He'll be okay, he's doing okay,* I tried to tell myself.

It was loud in the dome, with all the Sirin watching the fight. They cheered when Fenyang did something impressive and jeered every time Coby dodged him.

Coby held his own impressively—Fenyang had only been able to clip him once so far, in the ribs. But he wasn't fighting back—defensive moves only. *What are you doing?* He backed up to avoid another kick and his sneaker, still wet from our trudge through the woods, slipped backward. I gasped as he caught himself, but it was too late.

Fenyang delivered a forceful uppercut to his jaw and Coby was knocked into the air for a moment before he fell back and caught himself on the ropes. He righted himself but was off his game now and couldn't dodge as fast. If only he would *fight back.*

Then I realized why he didn't: our conversation in the cell. We'd all agreed not to fight. He was trying to show them that the only way he could. My eyes misted over at the hopelessness of it all. We were outnumbered, outgunned, and Sigrath, who seemed to be protecting us for some reason of her own, was gone. Vicente was still there, though. He stood at the corner of the ring, his hand on his gun, watching the fight intently. It was hard to tell why—was he still our ally? Was he ever?

354

My attention turned back to the fight. Coby was almost finished. His jaw was puffy and bruised, and blood streamed from his lips. Fenyang had him backed into a corner, and Coby was doing all he could to minimize the damage he could inflict. As Fenyang went in for another kick, Coby managed to crouch and sidestep, putting himself closer to the center of the ring once again. This maneuver elicited angry shouts from the crowd.

"You've got this Coby!" I shouted, breaking the rules.

"Go Coby!" Zara shouted, and he gave a quick smile, returning to the fight with more energy.

"Do not speak," Neziah warned us, but it seemed halfhearted this time.

A minute or two later, the fight was over for Coby. He was out of energy and stiff from his injuries while Fenyang seemed to be just getting started. Coby dodged the wrong way and ran squarely into Fenyang's fist. Then, while he was still off balance, Fenyang executed a spinning kick and Coby was knocked to the ground.

"Coby!" Zara shouted, and Jake tensed beside me.

Fenyang took a few more steps toward Coby, who didn't seem to be breathing. Vicente jumped into the ring, flexing his arm that held the gun and spoke to Fenyang. Fenyang backed up and jumped out of the ring, greeted by excited shouts from the crowd and the bearded Sirin, who was smiling broadly.

Coby sucked in a ragged breath, recovering the wind that had been knocked out of him. Zara managed to jump the ropes with her hands still tied and without Vicente seeing. She knelt beside him. Jake and I moved closer too, but Neziah and the others stopped us.

Though he was breathing, his eyes didn't want to stay open. Blood streamed from his broken nose, and half his face was bulging and red. He looked up at Zara, exhausted.

"Coby," she said. "Stay awake, stay with me."

Vicente approached, and I expected him to throw her out of the ring, but instead he knelt and helped Coby sit against the ropes. "Is okay," I heard him tell her. "He is okay."

Just then, doors on the opposite side of the building opened, and Sigrath flew in with a male Sirin we hadn't seen before. He was large, his wingspan immense. In one graceful movement, he tucked in his wings and landed in the center of the ring, close to Vicente and Coby. Sigrath landed behind him. His effect on the crowd was strange.

Every single Sirin in the dome, from Vicente and Sigrath to Fenyang and his partner, stood at attention, wings tucked back, silent. I involuntarily stood a bit straighter too, and Jake did the same. Despite our matching hands-behind-back posture, we didn't blend in with the Sirin. Beyond our physical shortcomings—our weakness and lack of wings—we were still dripping from the rain and not at all dressed for the occasion. Plus we'd never have their haughty expressions.

The Sirin that Sigrath had brought in exchanged words with her, then with Vicente and Neziah. At his command, Fenyang and the bearded Sirin descended from the platform and merged back into the crowd. Vicente and Zara helped Coby up and out of the ring. Zara stood beside Jake and me, propping Coby up with his arm over her shoulder as we faced this newcomer.

Even for a Sirin, he was impressive. He was tall, with wavy chestnut hair that reached his shoulders, a broad forehead, broader jaw, and eyes that were such a deep blue they were almost black. His uniform was black, like those of the other Sirin, but he had a multitude of silver chevrons along his right arm. Clearly, he was their leader, and I could see why the doctor chose him. He had a biblical look about him. A real-life archangel. Surprisingly, he spoke to us in English.

"You have no more to fear from Wicek or Fenyang," he said, motioning with his head toward the bearded Sirin and Coby's attacker in the crowd. "They had their fun." His voice was deep, soothing.

Seeing the confused expressions on our faces, he introduced himself. "I am Qahir," he said. "General of,"—he swept his arm out over the crowd—"the Sirin army."

None of us knew how we were supposed to react to that, but he stood, patiently waiting until someone spoke.

"My name," Zara said in a small voice, then cleared her throat and spoke louder, "is Zara."

The crowd stirred, but none of them dared to speak or break their pose.

Coby tried to talk, but his jaw was too swollen, so Zara spoke for him. There was a note of hatred in her voice as she said, "*He* is Coby."

Jake looked around the dome, his eyes settling on Qahir for a moment before he said, in a steely voice, "Jake."

"And I'm Nadia," I finished, managing to keep my voice steady.

Qahir nodded. "Now," he said in a deceptively conversational tone, "we can have your trial."

20: On Trial
Nadia

There was too much commotion to register what he'd said at first. The crowd was rowdy and, based on their expressions, many of them were cheering for our deaths. A table was brought up and five chairs placed behind it. Qahir sat in the middle. Someone cut my zip tie and I rubbed my wrists and rolled my aching shoulders. The others were released too, and chairs were placed for us in a line perpendicular to the head table. Sigrath and Vicente handed their weapons to two other Sirin from the crowd, who proceeded to stand at the corners of the platform with two of our original Sirin guards: Bittor and the green-eyed female.

Sigrath and Vicente sat on either side of Qahir, and two other Sirin stepped up to take the last places at the table.

Once everything was arranged Qahir stood, raising a hand in the air. The effect wasn't immediate, but the crowd silenced and, when he called an order, stood at attention.

Qahir turned to us. "You are on trial for the murder of Doctor Winthrop, the kidnapping of Vicente, and the crime of being human."

Zara began to protest, probably thinking the same thing we all were about the last charge, but she thought better of it and shut her mouth, crossing her arms.

Neziah translated the charges for the crowd. A wave of angry jeers rose from them when she mentioned the doctor's murder. I glanced up at the doctor's face on the banner; his expression seemed like a knowing smirk. My mouth went dry.

"If you were full-blooded humans," Qahir said with his Esperanto accent, which sounded vaguely Spanish or Portuguese, "we would not allow you to defend yourselves. But as you are creations of Doctor Winthrop, the Honored Creator, we allow each of you to speak on your behalf."

"And that decides our guilt or innocence?" Jake asked, his tone biting. "Or is this just an opportunity for us to speak our last words?"

Qahir grinned and said something in Esperanto to Sigrath. She nodded, and he said, "Your guilt, and your sentence, will be decided by myself and the members of the council after you have spoken. We will take input from all in attendance."

I went cold. The mob surrounding us seemed assured of our guilt, and of the two members of the council with whom I had previous experience, only one was possibly an ally.

Qahir barked another order in Esperanto and the crowd relaxed. He turned to Coby, who was in the seat closest to the council's table. "You will each speak in your defense," he said. "Neziah will translate. Then the council may have questions for you."

My heart raced. This was what it came to: trying to *talk* our way out of this. There was no way we'd live through the day.

Qahir sat and made an order in Esperanto. One of the Sirin guards shot off her weapon into the air, and we all jumped. Zara's hands shook, and Jake's fists curled.

"The trial begins," Neziah translated for us.

I looked at my friends. We were soaked through from the rain, our old, dirty clothing looking especially ragged beside the clean-cut uniforms of the Sirin. Before The End, when a criminal was put on trial they'd be cleaned up and put in nice clothing to appear more sympathetic, more plausibly innocent, to the jurors. We didn't have that advantage.

Coby stood slowly, to keep from showing how his knees were about to buckle, and scanned the crowd before he started.

"I know," Coby said, his voice shaky as his still-bleeding mouth moved painfully. He swallowed. "I know how all of you feel, how you felt, about the doctor."

359

As Neziah translated his words the room grew quiet, as if everyone was holding their breath. Some glanced up at the doctor's face above us with reverent expressions.

"He raised me," Coby continued. I hoped Neziah could understand him well enough; he mumbled due to his bruised jaw. "I saw him as a father, a genius. When I found out how he created me—all of us—I saw him almost as a god."

A few heads in the crowd nodded as Neziah spoke; they understood him. I tried to stifle the small bit of hope that rose in my chest.

"But while he was my only family…" Coby paused, his eyes welling with tears. "He never saw me as his son."

He cleared his throat and wiped away the blood that trickled from his nose. "After the virus, he sent me away, supposedly on a mission to find the others of my kind." Coby's left hand swept toward us. "I had no idea of his plan to exterminate us. Exterminate *me*."

A few in the crowd let out gasps when they heard this in Esperanto—apparently not all the Sirin had known of the plan either.

Coby swallowed again. "I can't tell you how much that hurt. To know that my father and creator wanted to kill me. To off me for being an 'outdated model'. I couldn't comprehend it." He took a deep breath. "And then I learned that he'd created the virus. Caused the deaths of countless people."

He choked on the last words, and as Neziah quickly translated there was a hiss from the crowd: "*Mensogoj!*" More Sirin began to shout. Others milled about, arguing.

Qahir rose, lifting his palm and commanding them in Esperanto. The crowd reluctantly stilled.

"I know," Coby said, determination now marked strongly across his features. "I didn't want it to be true either. But the evidence was there, hidden in his lab. I couldn't deny it. But even then—even after I knew his plans for us, his horrible crimes—I didn't hate him. I didn't want him to die."

A tear spilled over and the audience grew still and silent again.

"I loved him," Coby choked out. "I loved him, but he didn't deserve it. Not all of you can see it now, as I didn't, but he was evil."

Murmurings in the crowd started again, some angry, some shocked, as Neziah translated.

Coby continued, "And if he had lived long enough to create another, better hybrid, he would have thrown all of you aside. He doesn't deserve your loyalty or vengeance. He—" Coby paused.

"He deserved to die," he finished, his voice clear and strong. I wondered if that was the first time Coby had admitted that to himself. A roar rose from the crowd. At least half the Sirin looked enraged—they didn't want to hear such blasphemy against the doctor.

Qahir shot into the air, his wings beating down on us and creating a breeze throughout the dome. He commanded them in Esperanto, and they all stood to attention.

He turned to us. "The next may speak." Descending back into his chair, he tucked in his wings and spoke a command in Esperanto that made the army stand at ease again.

Coby squeezed Zara's shoulder as she stood and he sat. She clasped her pendant tightly, with quivering hands, her thumbnail turning white. Then she took a deep, steadying breath, and began.

"I don't know what the doctor told you about humans. I'm sure much of it was false, and some of it—maybe the parts that sounded most horrible—was true."

She'd been staring at a spot on the floor, but now she looked out at the Sirin crowd.

"There is good and bad in every human—and in every one of you."

She paused, letting Neziah translate. Furrowed brows, glances exchanged, and other signs of confusion flitted through the crowd.

"Humanity has done terrible things—war, destruction, slavery, violence—but it has also done truly amazing things. We created art, music, architecture. We explored our world, crossing oceans in ships and flying across continents, even visiting the Moon. We created cultures and traditions, languages—including the one you all speak. We searched for knowledge everywhere and filled books with what we learned."

I glanced at the council as they listened to Neziah's translation. Qahir stroked his square jaw. I saw something strange—could it be pride?—on Vicente's face. Sigrath's expression was arrogant and angry, as I was learning was usual, and the other two council members were stoic. I wondered if there was a point to any of this or if we'd all be dead soon, whatever we said. My fingers twitched behind me; I had the urge to bite my thumbnail.

"We have a tremendous capacity to hurt, to harm. As, it seems, do you," Zara said, glancing sideways at the armed Sirin guard nearest her. "But we have even more capacity to love, to share, to help those who are hurting. We get much farther when we work together than when we go it alone.

"The end of the world hasn't been easy for *any* of us. I don't know how many of you have seen battle, have killed—but those who have... you know as I do..." She paused for a moment and finished in a quiet tone. "It splinters your soul. You can't be the same again."

Zara waited for Neziah to finish and watched the reactions of the crowd. I thought a tear glistened on a female Sirin's cheek, but I couldn't be sure.

"There's no taking back things that you've done, no do-overs in life," Zara said. "But I've found peace in helping people. In my friends." She looked at each of us and I felt my eyes prick with tears.

"If I survive today, I want to train as a doctor," Zara said. "I want to help, to heal. Never to harm again. If you want to rebuild, you're going to need human help. You need their knowledge, their experience. Their capacity to create.

"It's tempting to think those different from you are the enemy. We believed you were our enemy, too. But then I got to know Vicente. I wouldn't call us friends yet, but I felt that someday we could be."

She glanced at him, a small smile on her face, but he kept his blank. Depending on the outcome, he might not want to be associated with us. I couldn't blame him.

Zara moved her now-steely gaze out over the crowd as she ended her speech. "Stop fighting humanity. Stop the violence. We are not your enemy. They are not your enemy. Humans could be your greatest ally, could help you create the new world you imagine."

As Neziah finished, Zara waited, then said in Esperanto, *"Ili povas helpi vin krei la novan mondon kiun vi imagas."*

Murmurs spread through the crowd as they heard her speak their native tongue. I studied their faces. None of them were angry, as they were at Coby's declaration. Most were quiet, reflective. Some seemed melancholy, others perhaps hopeful. Maybe not all the Sirin wanted us dead. Maybe some didn't want to fight at all.

It was Jake's turn now, and as he stood my chest tightened. I hoped he wouldn't say anything rash, wouldn't decry the doctor as a madman. They'd reacted poorly enough to Coby's final words.

"If you continue to fight the humans, you will continue to lose numbers," Jake said calmly. "From what I can see, you are a force to be reckoned with, but you don't have them outmatched. Not by a long shot. If there are more that can join the ones at Fort O'Brien, all of you could die."

A few Sirin grew restless at his words as Neziah translated, but none burst into shouts as before. *Are we getting somewhere?*

"You're fighting a war," Jake said. "A war against an enemy you don't know. None of you have lived in the human world. Instead, the doctor took you and trained you as soldiers from childhood. To mindlessly do his bidding—that's messed up. You've never known anything else so you can't see how bad that is, but trust me: he never should have done this to any of you."

More confusion flitted across their faces as the words were translated to Esperanto. Confusion was better than anger, I hoped.

"Don't give up your lives fighting someone else's war. He's dead and gone—there's no reason to finish his terrible work or live the way he wanted. You're free. Go and explore the world. See that the humans left are not so bad."

Jake cleared his throat. "And while we are saving lives here, I want to speak for my companions."

I didn't like where this was going.

"I alone killed Winthrop. The others had no control over what I did. Some of them tried to talk me out of it."

More murmurs in the crowd as they received his message, some angry. I tried to swallow again past the lump in my throat. *Jake...*

"It was self-defense and should not be punished. But if you must, if someone must pay for this crime, let it be me and me alone."

If I'd had time to speak to Jake, I would've told him to stop being stupid and always playing the hero. But instead he sat down, as some in the Sirin crowd shot visual daggers at him, and I realized it was my turn. *Is that an amused look on Qahir's face?* I thought as I stood. Was what Jake tried to do *amusing* to him?

I opened my mouth to speak, but nothing came out. I'd had all three speeches before mine to prepare something good, and I foolishly hadn't thought of anything, too busy listening. What could I say that the others hadn't? How could I get through to someone trained from birth to hate me and my kind?

Attempting to swallow, I found my throat parched. I wondered how long it had been since I'd had water, how long we'd been captive. How much longer we'd live.

A few Sirin in the crowd were smirking, mocking my silence. I had to say something.

"There aren't many of us left," I said, surprising myself.

364

"There aren't many survivors—Sirin, human, or other hybrid. If we have a chance in hell of rebuilding—or building something new, something better—this needs to end here and now, with us."

I waited while Neziah finished speaking my words in their language.

"Isn't that what the doctor wanted?" I asked. Acknowledging this was painful. "In his own sick, twisted way, he wanted to create a different world. A better world. You all share his vision. But you can't do it the way he taught you."

My fists hung at my side, and I unclenched them, trying to appear more relaxed than I felt.

"Some of what he told you is true. Humans have done terrible things. But the doctor is guiltiest of all. He tried to wipe out his whole *species*. No one had heard or dreamed of such a thing before. And when he didn't succeed, he trained all of you to finish the job for him. But in doing so he gave you a chance. You can become just as bad as the humans he told you about, or you can choose to do better."

The faces in the crowd made me nervous, so I stopped looking at them, turning to my companions instead. Zara gave me a half-smile, and Coby nodded for me to continue.

"A wise man once said, 'He who fights monsters should see to it that he himself does not become a monster'."

I paused while Neziah translated, hoping the Nietzsche quote would resonate with them.

"Don't become the same as the monsters he described to you. I promise you, the humans who are left are not monsters. They are survivors and they're strong, but they're also afraid and confused, as you are without the doctor.

"We survivors can choose to be different, to create a better world than those who came before us, so that those who come after will have better chances than we did."

As Neziah finished, I saw most of the Sirin nodding. Some spoke to their neighbors, and they seemed to agree on something. I sat and Qahir stood.

Neziah returned to our side so she could translate his words to us. "The council has questions," she said. "Any or all of you may answer."

Qahir spoke again, and the crowd stirred at his words. Whatever he'd said made them uneasy, and they waited expectantly for our answer. Neziah translated, "Why did you not run? You could have run after Vicente escaped. You did not leave the lizard-man. Why not?"

I raised my eyebrows. *That* was the question the council had for us?

Zara stepped forward. "Sloan?" she asked, her voice strained and desperate. "Where is he? Is he alright? Did he survive?"

Qahir rested against the back of his chair as Neziah translated. His was the tallest, throne-like, featuring elaborate carvings. "Interesting," he said in English, seemingly to himself. "You care whether this inferior being lives or dies? Why?"

"Sloan's not inferior," Zara spat. "He's worth more than all of you put together! Or, he was. Is he...?" Her lower lip trembled.

The Sirin were clearly moved as they heard Zara's words from Neziah's lips. Several turned to whisper to each other. A few wore incredulous expressions.

"Answer the question," Qahir said to us.

I stepped forward in the moment it took for Neziah to translate his words. "We didn't leave him because Sloan is our friend. He has been loyal to us; he helped us get here, helped us find each other. He believed we could work toward peace between our kind, the humans, and yours. We would never leave him to die." I winced. He *was* left in the woods, or worse, had been found by the Sirin. We just hadn't made that choice voluntarily.

The crowd was still quiet as Neziah told them our response. Qahir looked thoughtful. "And you would do the same for any of your companions here? Risk your life to save theirs?"

We glanced around at each other, and Jake spoke. "Yes. We all would. We all have."

Qahir said something to himself in Esperanto, then to us, "No questions more. Bittor and Aubrey will escort you to the holding cell and we will discuss."

"We won't hear your deliberations?" Jake said.

A quick smile flashed on Qahir's face. "No," he said. "That is not allowed. You will hear the verdict when you return."

Jake wanted to argue further, but I met his eyes and shrugged. *We've done what we can.*

Bittor and Aubrey, our green-eyed guard, stepped forward and motioned with their guns for us to proceed in single file. The two other guards helped them clear a path for us through the Sirin crowd. They weren't necessary, though.

The mob of crazed Sirin out for blood had been replaced by ones that looked serious and reflective. They easily parted, watching intently as we walked past. I kept my chin up and fought the instinct to shiver, their gaze heavy on my back as we exited.

21: The Verdict
Nadia

The room Bittor and Aubrey led us to was small and narrow, located beneath the ground floor of the dome. The pair left without saying a word, locking the door behind them. There was a window, but it was high, barred, and too small for any of us to fit through. Folding chairs leaned against one wall. Four pairs of protein bars and olive-colored canteens sat on a table.

"Whatever happens," Zara said after we were alone. "I'm proud of us." She hugged Coby and me, then Jake, who stiffened, but let her.

As she pulled away, she said, "Sloan would be proud of us too. If he could have seen..." Her voice cracked and none of us asked the questions on our minds. Was he alive? Would we ever see him again? Even if the first was true, the latter seemed unlikely for more than one reason.

"He would've been," I agreed. "We did our best to get to know Vicente, to show him a different way to live than the everyone-for-themself Sirin way, like Sloan wanted. And I'm glad we were able to speak for the people who are left." I swallowed. "I saw their expressions. We made some of them think. Not all the Sirin can be bloodthirsty—not all of them can want this."

But seeing Coby's discolored and swollen face and remembering how the crowd cheered for Fenyang, I wondered if that was true.

Coby grabbed a canteen of water from the table and unscrewed the lid, moving slowly with his bruised hand. Jake put a hand out to stop him. "Don't," he said. "We don't know what they've done to it."

"We haven't eaten or had water in ages," Coby said, looking startled. His split lip still bled a little.

Zara raised an eyebrow and looked from Jake to me. "I know we just met this Qahir guy but I don't think he's the poisoning type."

I nodded and grabbed a canteen off the table. "With all those Sirin out there, I don't think he could. If they do decide to execute us"—a shiver ran through my body—"it's going to be public." I poured a little of the liquid into my hand. It was clear. I brought it to my lips and tasted it. "Just water, I think."

Jake shrugged and grabbed his own canteen. Soon it wouldn't matter if the water was poisoned or not anyway.

Zara picked up her canteen and toasted, "To us!"

I cleared my throat and lifted my own canteen. "And to Sloan."

We raised them and drank, letting the water soothe our parched throats. Then Zara grabbed a chair from the wall, unfolded it, and sat. The rest of us followed suit. We opened the protein bars and consumed those, too. They had a flavor, but I was too worked up for my sense of taste to function as I washed it down with the probably-not-poisoned water. My stomach didn't care, though. It was just happy not to be empty.

The light through our window faded. The day had passed quickly with everything that had happened. Would we live to see the sun again?

"It's been a while," Coby said. "That could be a good sign. If they all wanted to kill us I think they'd have a decision by now."

"Unless they're deciding how to do it," Jake said. "Choosing a fitting punishment. Maybe that's what the food and water is for—to keep us alive and healthy long enough for the right kind of revenge."

"We don't have any way of knowing," I said. "Let's think about other things."

"Good luck with that," Jake said.

"I'm glad that, if this is the end, we're together for it," Zara said.

"Me too," Coby said, smiling at her.

"We haven't been together long," Zara said, "but so much has happened. Finding each other, learning our birthdays were the same. Solving the mystery, then finding the doc." She swallowed, then smiled as she said, "Meeting Sloan, finding Vicente. Tracking you guys down. And now this."

"It has been a wild ride," I agreed. "Remember that first night, around the fire?"

"Yes," Jake said. The others nodded.

"We seemed younger then, innocent. We had no idea about the doctor, the Sirin, the true cause of The End... any of this." I gazed into the distance, then refocused my eyes. "If you could do it over again, would you?"

"Yes," Jake said. "Except the part where Coby and I left you. Everything else... I would do the same way."

Coby nodded. "I'm glad to have met you all, to become a part of our little family, even if it ends up not lasting very long. You've all been so good to me. A better family than the doctor ever was. Than I've ever had."

Zara smiled. "Same here. I'd do everything over again with all of you."

I swallowed the lump in my throat. I didn't want our "little family", as Coby called it, to end like this. "Me too," I said softly.

We were silent then, reflecting on our time together. Arbitrary moments came to mind. Jake and I fishing by the waterfall. Listening to music in Coby's Mustang, windows down. Teaching Zara to shoot her crossbow in the abandoned Wal Mart. Sitting with Sloan on a starry night. My life may end up being short, and it was full of heartbreak, but there was also a lot of good. I wished I had my journal so I could write something like that. One last entry.

The darkness deepened, and my eyes grew heavy. Coby nodded off a few times, and Zara kept yawning. "Maybe we should sleep," I mumbled.

"Yeah," Zara said, stretching her arms and repositioning herself in her chair. "If this is my Marie Antoinette moment, I'll need my beauty sleep."

Jake pulled his chair closer to mine so he could put his arm around me. I let him and laid my head on his shoulder. As I fell asleep, I wondered if the note of pine in his scent was the last bit of my beloved forest I would ever experience.

◆◆◆

It was pitch dark in our room when I awoke to voices outside the door. I'd fallen asleep on Jake's shoulder and I shook him awake, then turned to Coby and Zara. Zara, as usual, was the hardest to wake.

"They're here," I whispered, shaking her shoulder again. "It's time."

She blinked, groggy for a moment, then nodded, understanding. We stayed in our chairs, not knowing what else to do, but alert. The metallic taste of fear filled my mouth and I clenched my fists to stop my hands from shaking. *This is it.*

The door swung open and Qahir entered, flanked by Sigrath and Vicente. Aubrey and Bittor still guarded the door. I wondered whether they had ensured that we stayed in or that the other Sirin stayed out. Qahir and the others arranged themselves so they stood on the other side of the table from us. Their wings took up a great deal of space in the room, making it feel cramped. Jake and I moved to stand, but Qahir put up his hand to stop us.

"Please," he said in his Esperanto accent. "Sit. We have much to explain."

My heart jumped. A death sentence couldn't take much time to explain, could it?

"Your fate has been decided," Qahir said. "But there are conditions that depend on you."

The four of us exchanged glances. "What was the verdict?" Jake asked. "Our sentence?"

"Not death," Qahir said. "Banishment."

"Banishment?" Zara asked, blinking in surprise. "From where?"

"Please," Qahir said, holding up his palm again. "I will explain."

He waited for us to be silent and still before speaking. He spoke with authority and knew how to command a room. I could see why the doctor had chosen him as the general for his army.

"The council decided that you acted mainly in self-defense in the killing of the doctor, and that, though misguided, your kidnapping of Vicente and treatment of him was not inexcusable," Qahir said. Vicente, beside him, gave us a small nod. "Neither of these offenses warrant death. There are those of us who are starting to believe being human does not warrant it either."

"Really?" I asked, that spark of hope flickering again.

"Yes," Qahir said. "Especially the council. We have seen some of what you mentioned in your defenses. Our numbers have dwindled from altercations with humans, and many of us believe it would be better to arrange a truce for the good of our own race."

We exchanged wide-eyed looks. This was better than we'd dared hope.

"A few of us—Vicente, Sigrath, myself, and others—have long asked if the doctor should be believed without question. Though there are many Sirin who believe he transcended his species, he was still human. Those Sirin I assigned to visit Vicente over the last few months were selected from among that group of skeptics, and Vicente fed them information on the doctor and his doings, which was then passed back to me."

Zara raised an eyebrow. "Vicente was a spy?"

Vicente shrugged, and Qahir said, "One could call him that."

"Sigrath," Qahir continued, and she flexed her wings briefly, "told us about her fight with you, that you had a chance to kill her. We were perplexed. But the strongest evidence in your favor was how you responded to Vicente's tests."

"Tests?" I asked, stupidly.

Qahir inclined his head. "First, he destroyed your supplies. He wanted to see if you would still work together, or if you would turn on each other when your resources were gone."

My eyes shifted to Zara, guilty. I *had* lost my temper with her due to the added stress Vicente's rampage had caused.

"Then, he attacked Nadia, but she did not shoot him."

Vicente nodded and said something to Qahir in Esperanto. He translated, "But this test was not enough. He was unsure if she spared him only because he was their hostage."

I stared at Vicente with wide eyes. He'd said as much to Sloan at the time, and I'd suspected he was playing us, but I'd never dreamed he'd had this much up his sleeve.

"He waited for an opportunity and took it when Nadia was in danger from the wolf. He knew enough about your camaraderie by then to convince you to free him from the restraint. The final test was whether you would leave Sloan— the weakest of your squad—when he was injured, and Vicente had returned to alert us to your location."

Jake met my eyes, cocking one eyebrow in an "I told you so". He'd been right: Vicente hadn't meant to kill Sloan.

"We do not understand your ways, but we may need them, to understand humans, and to ensure our race survives. That solution is in the future, but what we do tonight could be the first step toward it."

Sigrath nudged Qahir, and he continued, "However, there are some who are of the old way of thinking… who want vengeance. We, the council, have a solution that will benefit all parties."

Qahir paused a moment to let that sink in. Then he asked, "Which of you is your sergeant? The leader?"

"We're pretty democratic," I said, glancing at the others for support.

"That may be," Qahir said, "but I need a single leader for this to work."

"It isn't me," Coby said.

"Nod is the one who got us all back together again," Zara said, giving me a small smile. "She's the one who keeps us together."

"I agree," Jake said. "But why do you need a leader? If any harm will come to her, take me instead."

"I wouldn't say 'harm'," Qahir said. "We need her to be the face of the group for a ceremony."

"Okay," I said. "If they all agree, then I'll do this... ceremony. What does it entail?"

"You and I, as the two leaders of our people, will make an oath to each other. We will vow that none of you will harm a Sirin, and none of us will harm one of you, for any reason, again. The council wants peace between our people."

"For any reason?" Jake asked.

"Yes," Qahir said.

"'Our people'. Does that include all humans?" I asked.

Qahir shook his head. "No, only the four of you. Someday I want to form a similar pact with the humans in the area, but we are not there yet."

Jake scowled. "If we leave here and meet up with some humans, you'll be allowed to pick *them* off, just not us?"

Vicente started to speak but Qahir stopped him with a gesture. "Some of us had the same concern," he said. "The agreement is that none of your group or any companions will be harmed, as long as no one in your party harms a Sirin."

"That seems fair," I said, still disbelieving that we might live.

"What about Sloan?" Zara said, crossing her arms. "Do you have him?"

"I will come to that," Qahir said calmly. "Assume he would be included as a 'companion' to your party for the purposes of our agreement."

"As for the banishment," he continued, "you are not allowed within a ten-degree latitude and longitude radius of the Academy without prior permission and a Sirin escort."

I raised my eyebrows. Why would we want to stick around here?

"Why?" Coby asked.

"Some feel... uncomfortable with you."

"Yeah, and us them," Jake said. I shot him a look. We had a chance to live and here he was being snarky. He got my message, but asked, "What do you have here that you don't want us to see?"

"Nothing," Qahir said, in such a sure way I almost believed him. "It is not about what you might see, but what you might do. Though we will have the other part of the agreement—about you not harming the Sirin—some are still... nervous."

"Nervous?" I asked. "About us?"

"Yes," he said. "You brought down the doctor. You survived an attack by Sigrath, one of our greatest warriors,"—Sigrath's chin raised at that—"and your behavior is unpredictable. Vicente tells me that he and Nadia had chances to kill each other twice, yet they both still live."

"*Twice?*" Jake asked, getting angry, and I winced. I hadn't mentioned the time Vicente had lunged at me, choking me, and I'd been unable to shoot him.

"Long story," I said, glancing at Vicente. His face softened; he looked almost apologetic. "But it's in the past."

"We have spoken of the first two conditions," Qahir said, taking control of the conversation again. "You make an oath not to harm any of our kind, and agree to avoid the Academy and surrounding areas unless you have prior permission and a Sirin guide. There are two more."

I nodded. So far so good.

"The third is that you agree to tell no one of us, the Academy, the doctor, or the virus—anything you know about what you call 'the end'. This may be for your benefit as much as our own."

He had a point. If anyone heard the whole story, they may not believe we were against the doctor, that we didn't know what his plan had been. They might even suspect we'd participated in it.

"We're going to leave humanity in the dark about who's responsible?" Jake asked. "Preserve the doctor's 'good name'?"

"No," Qahir said. "Eventually I want to reveal the truth, but we cannot do so until we have established peace with the humans. If it is revealed before then… I am afraid for my people. The humans will not understand, will not believe we did not know he created the virus. Many of my people still do not believe it."

"I think," Jake said, glancing at the rest of us. "We can agree to that, but we should preserve evidence of what the doctor did from his lab and make copies. We could keep one copy and you another."

"The council can agree to that," Qahir said.

"And the fourth condition?" I asked.

Vicente and Sigrath exchanged a look, and Qahir said, "This part is my own. The other councilmembers don't know the full plan yet. I want one of you to work with us, as an ambassador to the humans. As I said, I want to work toward peace with them, but it is difficult to accomplish this alone."

I remembered how Maud and Jeremy had checked for wings before speaking to us as I examined the three Sirin in the room. All were large and muscular, intelligent, with wings that swept into breathtaking arcs behind them. There was no way one of them could walk—or fly—in and be taken as anything other than a threat.

"We want Coby to do it," Qahir added, looking to him. "He might understand us and our way of thinking—Doctor Winthrop's way of thinking—better."

"You're saying we'd have to leave Coby, alone, with you?" Jake said, taking a step forward. "That's not happening."

"Only at times," Qahir said. "We would take him back and forth to you."

"So you'd always know where we are?" Jake said, crossing his arms.

"Not all the time. We will contact you via satellite phone and you will be able to contact us in the same way." When he saw we weren't convinced, Qahir added, "It seems the only way. You will always know where he is as well."

"I don't know if we can agree to that," I said.

"No," Coby said to me. "I want to do it. If I can help them make peace with the people here—if I can at least try—I want to."

Zara put a hand on his shoulder and held his gaze. "Are you sure about this, Coby?"

He nodded. "I am. I trust Qahir. And we'll still have the agreement, the first condition."

"Correct," Qahir said. "I give my word no harm will come to him while he is with us, from us or anyone else."

"That's it, then?" I asked. "We agree to these four conditions, I swear an oath in front of all the Sirin, and we're free to go? What about Sloan?"

Qahir's brows pulled together, the first movement on his smooth, calm facade since he'd come into the room. "We are fascinated by your interest in him. He is alive,"—Zara let out a small gasp—"and you can see him after you make the oath."

"Why after?" Jake asked, crossing his arms again.

Qahir grimaced, then said, "With his... *unusual* appearance and what we have heard of his kind from Doctor Winthrop, it would be best he is not seen here at the Academy. I could not guarantee his safety. But I give my word you will see him after we let you go."

Jake was suspicious, and I was too, but we didn't have any cards to play here. We were getting off easier than expected, and if Sloan was alive too, I was happy.

"Are we ready for the ceremony?" Qahir asked, looking at each one of us.

"Right now?" I asked, glancing out the window. It was still pitch-black outside.

"Yes," Qahir said. "The others are waiting."

Sigrath and Vicente pushed us toward the door. "Wait," I said. "What do I need to do for the ceremony?"

"I will explain as it happens," Qahir said as we left the room. "It is a blood oath."

22: Blood Oath
Nadia

Jake whirled on the two Sirin guards and they drew their guns on him. "A *what?*" he asked, eyes narrowed.

Qahir, whose face was still calm, made a motion with his hand and the guns lowered. "Is human culture without this ritual?"

Jake was about to respond, but I stopped him. "No," I said, trying to ignore the chill that ran down my spine when I heard the word 'blood' from Qahir's mouth. "But can you explain how you do it?"

A flicker of impatience crossed Qahir's placid face, but he relented. "I take a dagger. You and I," he said, pulling a dagger from his belt and laying the flat side of it against the heel of his hand. "Cut our hands"—he demonstrated—"then place them together. Your blood, my blood, after the same."

"She's not doing that," Jake said.

"It is the only way," Qahir replied with a shrug.

I swallowed. "No," I said. "I can—I will."

"Are you sure, Nod?" Zara asked, and Jake studied my face.

It won't be the first time, I wanted to say, but didn't want to explain that statement to the five Sirin listening. "I can handle this," I said instead, trying to give Jake and Zara a meaningful look.

Jake stared me down a moment longer, then nodded. Zara squeezed my hand, and we proceeded down the hallway, Qahir leading the way.

As we entered the dome again, shouts rose up. The Sirin, for all their military training, were not a quiet bunch. Qahir called them to attention, as he'd done before, and a hush fell on the room. No starlight showed through the glass hexagons of the dome; instead, flaming torches encircled the crowd. One stood at each corner of the inner ring to light the ceremony. The Sirin had been up all night waiting for this moment, too.

We ascended the platform, where a small table had been set up in place of the large, long one where the council had sat. The new table was covered in a black cloth, and on it rested a gleaming blade.

Qahir pointed each of us to the place we were to stand, with me closest to the table. He stood on the other side and turned to the Sirin crowd, saying whatever their term for "at ease" was.

Vicente and Sigrath took two corners of the platform, Bittor and Aubrey posting themselves at the others again. The golden light from the torches danced across their features, and I caught a whiff of the burning oil.

Most of the Sirin crowd waited expectantly, although several—including Wicek, the bearded Sirin from before—wore scowls. Neziah stepped onto the platform and I felt a wave of relief. At least we'd have some idea what Qahir was saying. Not that we had any way to know whether her translation was accurate. *What I wouldn't give*, I thought, not for the first time, *to have Sloan here.*

Qahir's booming, confident tones rang out and the ceremony began. Neziah translated, using a low voice that only we could hear.

"My brothers and sisters," she said. "I have reached an agreement with these"—Neziah stumbled over the translation—"cockroach-children."

"Not the worst thing I've been called," Jake quipped, and I had to stop myself from rolling my eyes at him and force myself to focus on the crowd. Gasps and whispers rose up, and a few angry shouts, but most nodded. The treaty was expected.

Qahir detailed the first three of the requirements to them, receiving similar reactions. He'd said the plan for the fourth requirement wasn't fully formed or approved by the council yet, so he didn't mention it. He ended by explaining the blood oath.

"This treaty," Neziah translated, "will be signed in blood. From this moment, until all present have passed, these four and their companions shall be our brethren. No harm shall come to them as long as the treaty is kept."

Qahir turned to me when Neziah finished. It was time. I stepped toward the table, my muscles tense as I tried not to jump at the flash of silver when Qahir took the knife in his hand. What was to stop them from getting rid of us, here and now?

He slowly ran the knife over the heel of his hand, creating a thin, straight line. A drop of his blood—deep red like ours—beaded up as he passed me the knife.

I took it, releasing the breath I'd been holding, and stared at my palm, pink and scar-less. *You can do this,* I thought, pushing my regret aside. *You have done this. It's only one more scar.* But could I feel the blade cut my skin without relapsing? I'd managed to go so long now...

Then, as I took the oath with Qahir, with the Sirin, I made an oath to myself as well.

This will be the last time you ever cut into your own skin.

It scared me, but before I could back out I swiped the knife.

Qahir met my eyes and said, "Your blood and my blood will be one."

Then he said, louder and in Esperanto, "*Via sango kaj mia sango fariĝos unu.*" We put our palms together, our mingled blood dripping onto the black cloth on the table.

Slowly, the Sirin began to applaud. Qahir smiled and withdrew his hand from mine. A female Sirin from the crowd with a white cross on her sleeve stepped up with two white bandages and bound first Qahir's wound, then mine. The applause grew, then excited shouts came from the crowd.

I exchanged smiles with Jake, Zara, and Coby, and felt my heart swell. We'd done it. We would live and be free.

At that moment, a shot rang out in the dome.

I whipped around to see which guard had turned on us but was shoved to the ground by Vicente. I landed on my arm, which was not quite healed from the last time he'd attacked me, and pain shot from my elbow throughout my body.

I kicked out, trying to break free, but he shoved me back down with an exasperated look and stood over me again. It took another moment to realize he was *protecting*, not attacking, me.

The other three guards stood over Jake, Zara, and Coby, their weapons drawn and eyes on a Sirin flying above them. There was a commotion in the crowd, and I rolled to try to see what was happening. The shot must have ricocheted and hit one of the Sirin. A male was down, and a circle of Sirin formed around him. Blood flowed from the wound in one of his wings.

I shifted my attention back to the guards and saw that the Sirin in the air was Fenyang. He'd returned with a pair of pistols and a couple of spare weapons. Wicek, who'd orchestrated Fenyang's earlier fight with Coby, flew up to join him. He grabbed a black, mean-looking gun and turned it on us. I recoiled as, next to me, the girl who'd bandaged my hand shot into the air and grabbed a crossbow from Fenyang.

Wicek shouted something, but didn't get many words out before Qahir, who'd been giving instructions to our guards, flew into the air and gave orders to the crowd. About half of them seemed to listen; a good number of the others were in confusion. But a few had the same fire in their eye that Wicek had.

Our guards handed their spare weapons—daggers and pistols—off to four trusted Sirin Qahir had pulled from the crowd. Vicente and Sigrath vaulted into the air, followed closely by Bittor and Aubrey, to join Qahir in the fight. Our new guards took their places.

The fight was a thing to behold.

The eight Sirin in the air fought fiercely, their wings spread wide against the black ceiling of the dome. I had no words for the attacks and defensive moves; they must use their own brand of martial arts, specially adapted to take place in the air.

Sigrath flew at Wicek, sending her legs into his chest and he rolled through the air until he caught himself and got straight again. Sigrath attempted to grab the weapon and he shot again, the bullet hitting the dome and launching back again, barely missing a female Sirin crouched on the ground.

The female rebel struggled to load her crossbow in the air, then gave up on it and took a dive at Qahir. Only minutes ago, she'd bandaged the cut on his hand, had seemed loyal to him. He pitched to the side and flew up, soaring over her, then drove down and pinned her to the ground. He barked orders to Bittor, who landed and pulled a zip tie out of a pocket of his uniform to cuff her. One down.

Fenyang gave Vicente and Aubrey a run for their money. He managed to spin out of the way of every blow and made several impressive plummets, tightening his wings to his body and then spreading them again at the last second, just above the awestruck Sirin crowd. He took a few more shots with his pistols. None hit Vicente or Aubrey, but one clipped the shoulder and wing of a Sirin in the crowd.

My attention was pulled back to Sigrath as she let out a battle cry. She rushed at Wicek, pushing him upward until his back and outstretched wings hit the dome, pinning him there and making a crunching noise. Broken bones? Sigrath whooped and Qahir joined her, helping her pull the rebel to the ground and cuff him.

Bittor had run off at some point and came back holding three leather objects. As he slipped one over the girl's head, I realized what it was: the same wing-restraint device we'd made Vicente wear.

In the air, Fenyang put up a good fight against Vicente and Aubrey, though Aubrey managed to kick both pistols out of his hands. One had gone flying into the crowd and hit a female Sirin. When Vicente and Sigrath took to the air again, defeat flashed across Fenyang's face. He rolled and pitched, kicking and hitting at them from all angles, but it wasn't a fair fight with four Sirin warriors pulling him to the ground. Eventually Sigrath got behind him, pushing down on the spot where his wings met his back, and the others helped her restrain him.

Bittor had attempted to wrestle Wicek into the wing restraint while he tried desperately to get away. Vicente delivered a spinning kick to him from the air and Aubrey helped Bittor force the device over Wicek while he was dazed. Now all three rebels were cuffed and restrained in the middle of the ring. The crowd was silent, expectant.

Qahir turned to face us as our guards let us stand again. Sweat glistened on his face as he caught his breath. "The treaty is upheld," Qahir said to us.

After seeing the looks on our faces, his brows pulled together, and he asked quietly, "Did you doubt me?"

I cleared my throat. "We don't now."

He nodded once at us. Then he turned toward the Sirin crowd. The three wounded Sirin were gone; some of the others must have taken them to be stitched up.

Qahir gave a long speech in his commanding voice, gesturing to the three restrained Sirin at his feet. Neziah wasn't translating—she'd been lost in the crowd—but it was clear he was warning the other Sirin that such mutinous actions wouldn't be tolerated a second time. I had to wonder how many of them wished they'd joined the fight.

At the end, he dismissed them and they filtered out. Through the doors I saw several leap up and let their wings catch them as they exited.

Bittor and Aubrey exited last, the three restrained Sirin in tow. I wondered if they were destined for the same cell we'd inhabited not twenty-four hours before.

Finally, it was just Qahir, Sigrath, Vicente, and the four of us.

"Now what?" Zara asked, stepping up to Qahir.

"Now," he said, and the weariness he'd been hiding a moment before came over his face, aging him beyond his years, "you go."

◆◆◆

Qahir explained that with some of the Sirin still unsupportive of his cooperation with us, it would be best to leave right away. He'd do his best to keep his side of the oath, but it would be easier for him if we were gone. A large part of me wanted to get the hell out of there, but a small part was curious to see the rest of the Academy and how the Sirin lived. When I told Qahir that, he said he'd let us know when all the excitement had died down so we could visit again.

They took us to a room off the side of the dome. Our packs and supplies were laid out for us, though our weapons were missing. There was also a black uniform for each of us, identical to the ones the Sirin wore. I picked mine up, running my thumb over the rough fabric, and flipped it over to see two sets of crude stitches. Someone had closed the holes where wings should go.

"These are for us?" Zara asked.

Sigrath said something in Esperanto, and an unexpected look came over Qahir's face. Embarrassment? He paused, then said, "We want you to have them since your clothing is worn and… dirty."

Zara laughed. "Thank you," she said, addressing Sigrath more than Qahir.

"Where are our weapons?" Jake asked as he stuffed the Sirin uniform into his pack and hoisted it onto his shoulders.

"With Sloan," Qahir said. He let us grab our belongings, and said, "Come."

The seven of us took a winding path through the woods for a half mile. The sky was lightening to the east, illuminating the frost that laced the leaves and branches. The air held an autumn chill, and I zipped my jacket, crossing my arms.

We reached a clearing. Before I knew what was happening, Zara let out a shriek and bolted to the other side. I panicked, feeling the empty places on my body where my revolver, bow and quiver should have been.

But as I stepped into the light and saw what she'd seen I took off running, too, Jake and Coby at my heels.

Zara threw her arms around him, almost knocking him over with her embrace. A smile crept over his face, rippling the scales on his cheeks.

"Sloan!" I shouted, joining the hug.

"Hello," Sloan said, in his formal manner. "I'm glad to see you all alive and well."

I took a step back as Jake and Coby approached. Zara had already recovered and was examining the wound where the crossbow bolt had gone through his shoulder. He winced as she pulled his shirt back and ran her fingers over the bandaging gently. His arm was in a sling and he looked much healthier than when I'd last seen him.

Qahir had taken to the skies as we set off running, making several unnecessary rounds in the air—stretching his wings, I imagined, after a long night and a strenuous battle. Now he landed.

"Thank you for taking care of him," I said, tears pricking my eyes.

"Yes," Zara said. "Thank you!"

Qahir shook out his wings, a few feathers tumbling to the ground, and shrugged. "I would not have done it myself, but Vicente convinced us he was important to you, and therefore useful in negotiations."

Vicente and Sigrath caught up then. They'd walked instead of flying, and I realized that while their wings gave them an incredible advantage in the air, they were a hindrance on the ground.

"*Dankon*, Vicente," Zara said, beaming at him. A smile tugged at the edge of his lips.

"This is where Sigrath and I leave you," Qahir said. "Vicente will take you to the vehicle we have provided. There is also food and fuel, and you will find your weapons."

We exchanged incredulous glances. Sloan said, "It's true. I was just there."

"Qahir," I asked, "why are you helping us? We didn't expect to live, but now—giving us supplies?"

The sun was rising now, painting the sky in hues of pink and orange and the wispy clouds in purple. Qahir gazed skyward for a moment, then said, "Helping the wounded Sirin, that is the most united my people have ever been. We were not trained to behave so. It was a difficult decision, but I see now that the survival of my people depends on living more as you do—caring for each other. Even after a short time of witnessing your friendships, they wanted to help one another more than before."

He looked back the way we'd come and said, almost to himself, "There are more humans left than the doctor predicted. If we are to survive, we'll need to cooperate."

"We survivors have to stick together, right?" Zara asked, smiling.

"Yes," Qahir said, his face still serious. "We do."

"Goodbye then," Jake said. He stepped forward and held out his hand to Qahir. He grasped Jake's forearm and shook it, then did the same to Coby.

He turned to me next. "Strength to you, Nadia, and to your people."

"To yours, too," I said as I shook his arm. And I meant it.

Zara stepped forward and embraced him. Sigrath stood a distance away, and though she didn't shake our hands she nodded at the group of us and said something in Esperanto.

"She spoke the Sirin farewell," Sloan said. "'I wish you strength; may you be unafraid'."

"*Dankon,*" Zara said. "Thank you."

The two of them, Qahir and Sigrath, leapt into the air, letting their wings catch them and soaring in a loop over us once before flying back toward the Academy.

We'll see them again. I actually looked forward to it.

Vicente said, "Come," and motioned for us to follow him down a path through the woods. We crossed a brook and descended through a copse of strong-smelling pines before we reached a road—perhaps the same road on which the Mustang had been left stranded. We weren't out of the perimeter yet, and Vicente served as our Sirin escort.

Vicente stopped and pointed as we crested a hill, and we stepped up to look. The Sirin had left us a large SUV, painted in forest camouflage. Our weapons were laid beside it on the road, even my bow; Vicente must have gone back to the site of the wolf encounter and retrieved it for me.

We ran to check it out, finding the back of the vehicle loaded with protein bars and MRE's, a supply of water, and two full gas cans. We were well supplied. We could go anywhere.

"*Ĝis la revido, miaj amikoj*," Vicente said as he strolled down to meet us at the vehicle. In his stilted English he said, "Goodbye, my friends."

"*Ĝis*, Vicente," Zara said, smiling and hugging him. "You keep up with those English lessons!"

He nodded, then shook Jake's and Coby's hands the Sirin way, forearm to forearm.

I stepped forward and embraced him. "We've had some rough times, but we'll see each other again." I pulled away. "And when we do, I'll be glad."

Sloan translated for him, and Vicente replied, almost smiling. "I, too."

Vicente took one last look at each of us, then leapt into the air, as the others had done, circling several times. I hoped it was so he could remember this image of us, together and resupplied, smiling up at him. Then he flew higher into the air and swooped down, back toward the Academy.

Zara laughed first, giddy, and the rest of us joined in, embracing each other. "We're free," I said. "We're free."

A few white flakes fell from the sky, slowly, and drifted to the still-frosty ground.

"It's too perfect!" Zara said, as more descended on us, clinging to her curls. "It's beautiful."

I didn't share her sentiment.

Jake pulled his road atlas from his bag. "Where to next?"

"South," I said. "Definitely south."

"Oh, alright," Zara said, smiling. "You lead the way."

Epilogue 1: The Truth About the Past
Jake

The lab burned for hours.

The seven of us hadn't planned on staying to watch the blaze. It wasn't the best strategic move, either. The plume of smoke gave away our position for miles during the day, and now that night had fallen the flames would do the same. But we'd stayed, wordless, eyes transfixed as the glass panels shattered and fell.

As the front door fell in, I thought of the night when I'd packed up to leave the lab. Burning it was a much more satisfying way to leave it behind forever. The urge I'd felt that night—to abandon the group in favor of self-preservation—seemed foreign to me now. I was part of something here.

When a large supporting beam broke, sending much of the internal structure tumbling in on itself, Nadia jumped. I put my arm around her and she moved closer to me. Waves of heat peeled off the ruined laboratory, warming us.

Watching the symbol of Winthrop's life's work destroyed gave me a satisfied feeling of justice, but there was also a twinge of doubt.

We'd saved enough information to explain parts of our creation—Sloan's, the Sirin's, and ours. Enough to show that Winthrop had created the virus, if examined closely. We all had copies, and the records of the others like us would enable us to track them down. We could reveal the truth of the end to the people we met, if we chose.

But humanity would never know the full story or have proof. That was gone to ash with the lab. The main thing was ensuring that no one could create the virus again or have a blueprint for how to end the world if, centuries from now, it got back to normal.

It was better if no one knew the full story. We didn't want to be studied, or used for the abilities we had, or fearfully suspected of playing a role in Winthrop's handiwork.

A sideways glance at Qahir revealed he was not as satisfied as I felt. His arm was in a sling from another altercation with the Sirin rebels and his face wore a grim expression. In addition to our reasons for destroying the lab, he also didn't want the rebel Sirin to have the information they'd need to continue the doctor's vision of a human-free world. Wicek and his followers would treat the lab as a shrine to the doctor and his nearly accomplished plan. We couldn't allow that.

I had to wonder, though, if covering up the past was a good idea. Did humanity deserve to know who'd almost been its downfall?

Nadia leaned her head on my shoulder, her hair tickling my neck. The flames took me back to last night, when we'd lit candles to honor our families.

The idea was Zara's, at first. Most of our family members never got funerals. The virus moved too fast, and then we were too busy surviving to properly mourn them.

We were nearing the end of October, and Nadia suggested we celebrate Day of the Dead. When I told the others that I remembered a few details about the tradition from a visit to my grandmother when I was five or six, they were enthusiastic about recreating it.

Zara tracked down enough silk marigolds to decorate dozens of altars. Coby helped Sloan create detailed sugar skulls and colorful strands of punched paper. Though Sloan had never met any of the other hybrids of his kind, he made an altar or *ofrenda* to honor them, using pictures from Winthrop's files. They'd died so young.

Nadia made *ofrendas* to her parents, sisters, and best friend. After I told her that the custom is to add their favorite things so they'd be comfortable for their visit, hers became heaped with clothing, food, books, and other trinkets. She'd said it was even better than her morning ritual of lighting candles to them, and that we should celebrate every year.

We set up on the beach of a lake. Zara sent floating lanterns onto the water. Dozens more candles lined the sand, making the masses of marigolds and path of orange petals glow.

It seemed silly to pour a glass of wine for my mom and a beer for my dad, and I felt like a complete idiot laying a Snickers bar and a stack of video games beside Ben's military cap.

But as we sat with our altars, remembering our loved ones, I stopped feeling foolish. The lapping of the water on the shore calmed me, and a breeze rustled through the paper flags Sloan and Coby had strung overhead, as if the spirits of our families really were returning to us.

Candles flickered on the family photo I'd placed as the center of my altar. I found myself reaching for it, bringing it close to examine their faces in the darkness. Especially Ben's.

Why did you do it? I wanted to ask him. *Why couldn't I save you?*

Then, for the first time, I allowed tears to fall for him. This wasn't right. The tradition was to share happy memories, to imagine a night spent with them, but I didn't care. My shoulders shook as I let myself be sad and angry and hurt by his loss.

Nadia noticed and silently came to my side. She put an arm around me, then gently laid my head against her shoulder. A sense of calm washed over me, and I lifted my head to take in the others.

Coby and Sloan knelt in front of the pictures of the hybrids who hadn't made it. We'd told Coby we would understand if he wanted to make one for Winthrop, but he'd wanted to help with Sloan's instead.

Zara removed her necklace, kissed it, and laid it in front of the *ofrenda* she'd created for her mom and Nick. The floating lanterns bobbed on the lake as the wind pushed the waves toward us. I caught the scent of the bowl of rabbit stew Nadia had made and set out for her dad.

Then I heard something—whether it was a trick of the wind, my imagination, or truly a message from beyond, I don't know. But I heard a voice that sounded like Ben's say the same thing that Coby had once told me, that Nadia had told me many times.

It wasn't your fault.

My heart stopped. I sat for a while longer, feeling my brother's presence. If he were there in the flesh, he'd be telling me to keep going, to live on for him. I rubbed the goosebumps from my arms as a new feeling settled over me. I was at peace.

With one last glance, I placed the photo at the center of my family's *ofrenda* again.

I will, Ben, I told him. *Rest in peace.*

I was pulled back to the present by a shower of sparks and the echoing sound as the last interior wall of Winthrop Enterprises crumpled and fell.

The fire was going out, with so little fuel left to burn. The full truth was now destroyed. Sigrath had been pacing to my left, next to Qahir, and now the pair approached us.

"It is done," Qahir said. He threw the shoulder strap of his bag over his head and patted its contents—his copies of the records we'd saved.

"We go," Sigrath said. Her disregard for grammar was purposeful; she'd been learning English, but begrudgingly.

"We'll see you in six months," Nadia said. "When Vicente comes for Coby."

Coby nodded and shook Qahir's arm. "I look forward to it."

"Yes," Qahir said. "The rebels should be managed by then."

"Goodbye," I said, grasping his forearm in the Sirin handshake. "And good luck."

Zara and Sloan wished them farewell and the pair of Sirin took off into the sky, their silhouettes blocking the light of fewer and fewer stars as they ascended.

"We have the records," Nadia said. "We can find the hybrids who are left. Camp here and then set off at first light?"

"No," Zara said, glancing at the others. "Let's go now."

"Jake, you have the route to the closest one mapped already, don't you?" Coby asked.

I nodded and moved my bag to one shoulder to pull out my road atlas.

"Alright," Zara said, a grin spreading across her face. "Let's hit the road. We've got brothers and sisters to find!"

That's what she'd been calling them——the others like us. My vote was for sticking with Neziah's "cockroach-children", but it hadn't caught on.

"Yess," Sloan said. "Let uss leave the passt here and look to the future."

"Well said," Nadia replied as she slid into the passenger seat of the SUV.

I moved to the driver's side and the other three piled into the back, Zara in the middle. I handed Nadia the atlas and she opened it carefully, fingers curved over the cover and hands smoothing out the pages, the way she always opened her books when starting a new chapter. I couldn't help smiling.

Impulsively, I interlaced my fingers with hers and brought her hand to my lips, kissing it once. She looked up in surprise, then blushed and smiled.

"Alright, love birds," Zara said, laughing. "Let's get this show on the road!"

I put the car in gear and maneuvered us back onto the highway.

"Adventure awaits," Nadia said as we drove into the night.

Epilogue 2: Life After the End
Nadia

Lately I keep remembering something Jake asked me, back when we first talked on our radios. It seems so long ago—before the Sirin, before the lab, before Zara and Coby. Back when I didn't even know whether Jake was real. At the time it seemed more likely I'd lost it, that my mind had conjured a companion in a last-ditch attempt to appease my loneliness and desperation.

Anyway, what Jake asked was whether I remembered driving at night away from the city. On a dark night, he'd said, you could only see a small circle of the road ahead—just what the headlights illuminated. It was shortly after I'd got my license that the world fell apart, but I remembered that feeling. The sense of the unknown, the solitude under the dim stars.

"That's what our lives feel like now," Jake said. "Dark and empty, with only one path ahead that we can see, and we can't see very far down it. Do I have enough food for today? Where will I go tomorrow?"

I think I'm remembering that conversation so often now because our lives no longer feel that way. We have options; we can make plans. Not just "tomorrow" plans but "someday" ones. I suppose the fact that we are all traveling together (road tripping in our school bus-turned-mobile home) helps too. We're no longer alone.

I closed my journal and stuck my pen behind my ear. I sat at the edge of the canyon, dangling my legs. A mile below me, the river bent, carving its slow path through the rock. The cloudless blue sky contrasted with the fiery hues of the canyon walls. Before the virus, I felt sure I'd visit the Grand Canyon eventually, but it was one of the many dreams I'd given up after The End.

Now I was reclaiming a few of them.

Running my hand over the embossed leather of my journal, I thought how freeing it was to wear short sleeves and let my scars show. I was proud that I hadn't added to them in the months since I made the blood oath. I felt so at home with my companions, who were all so supportive, that I had nothing to hide. Besides, all the survivors of The End had scars, visible or not.

I enjoyed the silence as I took a slow, deep breath of fresh air. It was unusual, with seven of us now, not to hear someone speaking at any given time. Usually Coby or Zara. I smiled at the thought.

Zara was to my right, at the next overlook with Sloan. She held the Polaroid camera she'd been using to document our journey as she gave Sloan directions on how to pose. He was smiling, his hands cupped around Humphrey Bogart. She'd wanted to find the pig and track down all the other animals we'd freed, but luckily Jake convinced her they would be happier out in the wild than road tripping across the country looking for hybrids.

Behind me, Coby changed the oil on the bus while Jake and Seamus, the first other hybrid we found, discussed our route, Jake's road atlas open between them. Seamus was quite an outdoorsman before The End, from what I could tell, so it wasn't surprising that he and Jake were slowly becoming friends.

To my left Nysa, the other hybrid who'd joined us, sat pretzel-legged a few yards back from the edge of the canyon. The girl with the skin and unruly hair was silent when we first found her, but she was opening up now. I wanted to give her all the time she needed, but Zara's continuous efforts to have her socialize were helping.

She glanced up from her sketchbook and noticed me looking at her. I smiled and gave her a small wave. She blushed and looked down, a few black curls falling over her face, then shyly turned her sketchbook toward me. Nysa had sketched me, sitting on the edge of the canyon. It was a great likeness, and I was surprised at how happy I looked in it. I smiled, giving her a thumbs up. She looked away, smiling shyly, and turned to the next blank page.

It was easier to feel happy after I'd learned the truth about my parents. Jake had realized we'd be traveling near my hometown and asked if I wanted to visit. I'd hesitated, feeling so different from the person I'd been the last time I'd been there, but finally decided to see it. One last time.

Zara had wept with me in the backyard, where the three wooden crosses for my mother and sisters stood beneath the swaying branches of our willow tree. Then Jake had accompanied me to my room. It was untouched. A shelf overstuffed with books stood across from my desk, which was piled with notebooks. Vintage travel posters still hung on the wall where my bed's headboard should be. I stood in it like a stranger.

Then Jake spotted an envelope on the desk. My name was written on it in my dad's handwriting, and I shoved it back to Jake with trembling hands, asking him to read it first.

When he'd finished, I asked, "Do I want to know?"

"Yes," he'd said, his tone sure.

The sheet of notebook paper, folded neatly in quarters, now resides in my journal. It reads:

My dear Nadia,

I hope I get the chance to explain everything to you when we arrive where we are headed. But these are uncertain times, so I leave this letter, for you to find if you someday make it home and I do not.

You know that your mother and I were married for many years before we had you. We desperately wanted a child but had no luck. Eventually I remembered a college friend of mine who had become a fertility specialist. His name is Peter Winthrop. He got us in touch with a surrogate and we were blessed to have you, our firstborn.

But after your birth Peter told us something shocking—he hadn't just helped us with the surrogacy; he experimented on your DNA. We were appalled and cut off all contact with him. We prayed our daughter would live despite what he'd done.

And you did live—even as your mother and sisters, God rest their souls, did not. Despite all the sorrow I feel for their loss, I try to be grateful I still have you, Nadia.

This may seem strange, but it is Peter Winthrop we are setting off to find. A few years ago, he reached out to me again. Perhaps my heart had softened toward him after you'd grown into the beautiful, healthy young lady you are now, because I agreed to meet him.

Some of the ideas he shared then were bizarre, horrifying. Now I fear he may know more about this virus than anyone should. As much as I recoil at the thought of seeing him again, I must go. Partially for answers and partially because he may be the only person who knows how to keep you safe.

I love you, Nadia. If you are reading this, I'm sure I did not survive the journey. But I am so, so glad you did.

Stay strong, my dear.

Your loving father, Brad

The anxiety that had lifted when I read the letter brought tears to my eyes. *They didn't know.* My parents had had no idea the doctor would experiment on my DNA. My memories of them were no longer blighted by association with him.

Every new group of surviving humans we found also felt like a victory against the doctor, and made our hope grow. We'd mapped them in Jake's road atlas and decided to move to one once we found all the other hybrids. Our nomadic lifestyle couldn't last forever—good gasoline was harder and harder to find—but we were enjoying it while we could.

We'd found two other hybrids, too. Eva and Vivian were living happily in one of the settlements we passed through on the way here. The community was set up on a group of hobby farms and was one of the most pleasant we'd encountered. Everyone helped with the gardening, artisan trades, and caring for the animals. No one went hungry. Whether to tell them they were hybrids, or about the Doctor or the Sirin, was a long debate among our group.

In the end we compromised: we'd invite them to join us and if they agreed we'd tell them, but if they wanted to stay they could remain blissfully ignorant. They chose the latter.

Jake walked up behind me, interrupting my thoughts.

"Are you sure you should be doing that?"

"Doing what?" I asked, twisting to look up at him.

"Sitting on the edge... like that." He swallowed, and I remembered his fear of heights.

I grinned. "Why shouldn't I?"

"Because you could fall, and do you know what that would do to us all? To me?" There was a note of seriousness beneath his words.

"Don't you remember, Jake? We're superhuman."

"How could I forget?" He held out his hand and I took it, letting him help me up off the edge. He wrapped his arms around me and squeezed, kissing the top of my head.

"Someone's feeling romantic today," I said, unable to help smiling.

"It's the landscape," he said. The sun was setting, making the layers of the canyon glow.

"Hey," I said, pulling away and feigning a stern expression. "We need to talk."

Jake groaned. "No, I haven't got a tuxedo yet. And I'm not going to."

"I don't care for my sake," I said. "But think how disappointed Zara will be when you show up in your raggedy jacket for the picture-perfect prom she's planning."

"It'll be months before it happens—we have four others to find first."

"I have faith Zara can convince you in that time," I said, grinning. "She can be quite... persuasive."

"And *I* can be quite stubborn," Jake said. The corners of his eyes crinkled as he took a step closer to me.

"She already convinced her date. And *they're* just going as friends."

"Are you sure about that?" he asked, raising an eyebrow and smirking. "Like I said, the prom is months away."

I smiled to myself. "Either way, the point stands. Sloan found a tuxedo—with tails, even."

Jake rolled his eyes. "He loves that stuff. Sloan would wear a top hat and monocle to this thing if Zara asked."

"Ooh, good idea!" I teased. I glanced over at Sloan and Zara. They sat next to each other now, watching the sunset. Jake had a point; even from here I could see the shine of Sloan's leather wingtips, and his white Oxford shirt was somehow unstained and unwrinkled.

"Don't you dare," Jake said, pulling me close to him.

I wrapped my arms around him, placing one hand against the muscles of his back and the other in his hair. His hands warmed the small of my back. This close to him, I could see the sprinkling of freckles on his nose. He leaned in, our lips met, and the scenery, breathtaking as it was, melted away.

That night, as we all sat under the stars in this beautiful place, long after Seamus had set down his guitar, I finished my journal entry by the fading embers of our campfire.

I used to think often about my last entry in this journal. Would it be a normal daily log, that became the last because I'd frozen or drowned or otherwise been defeated by nature? Would I plan it out and take my own life? Would it be the ravings of a girl pushed to madness by solitude?

Now I've reached the last page, and this journal is full of the ups and downs of life after The End, with many adventures. Some no one would believe if they hadn't lived them. Tomorrow I'll begin another journal, and I'm looking forward to it. Everything has changed now. We have purpose. I have a family again, and hope.

"The End" wasn't the end at all.

We survivors have a future, and I can't wait to see where it takes us.

Acknowledgements

They say it takes a village to raise a child, and if anyone says the same about creating books, they'd be right! I'd like to take a minute to thank my "village", without whom this book would not be in your hands.

First, I'd like to thank my family, especially my parents, for encouraging any and all of my interests over the years. I know I can rely on them for support no matter what I attempt.

I'm also grateful for my husband, Ryan, who quickly forgave my secretiveness about my writing to become both an invaluable beta reader and the support I needed during the editing and publishing process.

We Survivors had a fantastic team of beta readers. I want to thank them all for their fantastic suggestions that helped me bring this novel to its current, much-improved state. Thanks to Dextyr Adams, Clinton Barrett, Rebecca Froehlich, Ben Green, Arianna Lister, Hester Steel, Angela Vartanian, and Kim Wilch.

I'd also like to thank the members of the Rochester, MN Writing Group who gave me feedback on the first few chapters and answered my questions related to the intimidating process that is self-publishing.

Writing about the end of the world as we know it is a challenge, and I'd like to thank Catherine J Pearce, MA EMHS, for offering her services as a consultant. Her answers to my questions and additional advice enhanced the realism of the story.

Though I've always been fascinated by Esperanto, a constructed language created by L.L. Zamenhoff in the late 1800s, I don't speak it myself. I'd like to thank Simon Varwell for his translations and detailed advice. He greatly improved the accuracy of the lines of Esperanto used in the novel.

Non-writer friends are also important. I'd especially like to thank my friends Carrie and Paul, for all their encouragement and the lunch dates in which they probably learned much more than they ever wanted to know about writing and publishing.

Two of the most crucial aspects of a published novel are quality editing and an attractive cover. I'd like to thank Vicky Brewster, my editor, for helping me polish the final manuscript before publication, and Mallory Rock, my designer, for creating the beautiful, eye-catching cover.

Last, but certainly not least, I'd like to thank my Wattpad readers. I started posting the (very rough) first draft of the story nearly four years ago, and it's safe to say I never would have completed it without the support of my readers on that platform. Thank you all.

About the Author

L.J. Thomas is a writer of speculative fiction. A native of South Dakota, she now lives in Minnesota with her husband and beagle-mix dog Tink. She works as an engineer by day and writes by night. In her free time, she enjoys the great outdoors, traveling, reading, and daydreaming about other worlds. *We Survivors* is her first novel.

Author's Note

Reviews are vital to the success of new authors. If you enjoyed this novel (or even if you didn't), please consider leaving an honest review on Amazon, Goodreads, or your favorite book review website.

Connect!

ljthomasbooks.com

Twitter: ljthomasbooks

Instagram: ljthomasbooks

Wattpad: ljthomas

Made in United States
North Haven, CT
31 August 2023

40989713R00253